Praise for *Ty*

'*The Last September* meets *Downton Abbey*. Part emotional, part historical, it is all consuming – we urge you not to read it in one go' – *Woman's Way*

'Dark and densely plotted, this is *The Thorn Birds* with a dash of Du Maurier's *Rebecca* – brilliant' – *Irish Daily Mail*

'*Tyringham Park* is an exciting read with character stories that leave you in suspense till the end' – *Bord Gais Energy Book Club*

'An Irish period saga with bite. Its vindictive edginess is reminiscent of the novels of Molly Keane' – *Irish Examiner*

'McLoughlin spins a good yarn and the central mystery of what happened to Victoria kept me reading till the end' – *Sunday Independent*

'An entertaining story with great drama' – *Irish Country Living*

'It's great, full of villains, full of intrigue' – Monica McInerney, – *The John Murray Show, RTE Radio 1*

'A fantastic yet melancholic story and well worth a read' – Emma Hannigan, *author*

'McLoughlin marshals the gothic suspense of Daphne Du Maurier, and the good and bad behaviour of Molly Keane's country squires and heartless mothers' – *Irish Independent*

'An engrossing read; you'll burn the dinner while you're reading this' – *LMFM*

TYRINGHAM PARK

ROSEMARY McLOUGHLIN

POOLBEG

This novel is entirely a work of fiction. The names,
characters and incidents portrayed in it are the work of the
author's imagination. Any resemblance to actual persons,
living or dead, events or localities is entirely coincidental.

Published 2012
by Poolbeg Press Ltd
123 Grange Hill, Baldoyle
Dublin 13, Ireland
E-mail: poolbeg@poolbeg.com
www.poolbeg.com

© Rosemary McLoughlin 2012

Copyright for typesetting, layout, design, ebook
© Poolbeg Press Ltd

The moral right of the author has been asserted.

1

A catalogue record for this book is available from the British Library.

ISBN 978-1-84223-520-1

Typeset by Patricia Hope in Sabon
Printed and bound by CPI Group (UK) Ltd, Croydon, CR0 4YY

www.poolbeg.com

ABOUT THE AUTHOR

Rosemary McLoughlin, born and reared as Rosie Fahey in Australia, has lived in Ireland for forty years and isn't sick of it yet. She lives in Rathmines in Dublin with her husband Kevin, and has two adult children, Cian and Orla.

To Kevin, Cian, Eavan,
Orla and Daire

Acknowledgements

Grateful thanks go to my original family: Eric Fahey and Marie Dawson (peerless parents), John Fahey, Marie Blowes, Patricia Eastick, Barry Fahey, Brian Fahey, Kevin Fahey, Anne Herden, Jo Doyle, Jim Fahey, Bill Fahey and Mick Fahey; and to their spouses and partners, past and present: Barbara, Doug, Robert, Val, Beth, Di, Gail, Adrian, Gary, Judy, Ita and Judy.

To those who have helped me in various ways: Clive ('Bricky') Barnes, Frances Berry, Gabrielle Bowe, Marie Bowe, Catherine Brophy, Linda Byrne, Andrew Clancy, Treasa Cody, Ronan Colgan, Audrey Cremin, Ben Fahey, Simon Fahey, Peggy Farrell, Bryde Glynn, Helen Halley, Jennifer Kingston, Davy Lamb, Geraldine Gardiner, Eavan Meagher, John Meagher, Sheila Morris, Dr Donal O'Brien, Bid O'Connor, Dr Mary O'Connor, Daire O'Flaherty, Síne Quinn, Rocke Ritchie, Gayle Roberts, Lorraine Smith.

To the teachers and pupils of Glenferneigh Public School, St Mary's College, Grafton, and Wyong, Gilgandra and Young High Schools, NSW.

To everyone at Poolbeg, especially Paula Campbell and Gaye Shortland, who have been such a delight to work with.

Most importantly, to my present family: Kevin, Cian and Orla McLoughlin, my heroes.

PART 1

THE COUNTRY

1

Tyringham Park
1917

The mother wasn't seen to lose her composure and the father didn't return from London when Victoria Blackshaw, the pretty one, went missing at the age of twenty-two months.

The first person to notice that the baby carriage was empty was the mother, Edwina Blackshaw, and the second was Manus, the horse-trainer.

Edwina, disbelieving, snatched up the tartan quilt and the feather mattress, shook them, and let them drop from her hand to the ground. She felt around the dark interior of the carriage for Victoria's red-headed doll or anything that might provide a clue to the child's absence, but the only things her hands touched were a crumbling biscuit and a teething ring.

Manus noted with relief that all the stalls and the gate leading into the paddock were closed, but was sickened to see that one of the double doors of the stables entrance was unsecured and standing slightly open. He wrenched the door fully open and raced to check the avenue in front of the stables, and the banks of the flooded river behind it, then the weir and the bridge with its view downstream, before running around the perimeters of the outbuildings, expecting to see a little figure in white every time he turned a corner.

Edwina tested the latches of the seven occupied stalls first, rattling the lower half-doors to see if they were fastened and not merely closed over. The instinct of a horse, no matter how docile, to lash out if grabbed by the back leg without warning was what she feared; a little body smashed up against a wall was what she dreaded to find.

In a state of heightened expectation Manus ran back into the courtyard in the hope that Edwina had found Victoria in his absence, a hope so strong he thought for one second he saw the child's outline, but the image quickly dissolved. With uncharacteristic roughness he pulled Mandrake out from his stall and, despite the gelding's sidestepping in reaction to the panic in the atmosphere, had him bridled and saddled in a minute.

"I'll follow the river in case she went in," he said, mounting.

"Get help first in the hope that she didn't." Edwina was standing in the middle of the yard, swaying slightly. "We need to widen the search immediately."

By now he presumed the child had fallen into the river and been carried away but he didn't want to take away her hope by disobeying her order. Silently cursing the minutes he would lose by riding up to the house, he did as she commanded.

Edwina found herself turning in circles as one indecision followed another. She knew so little about her daughter. Was she two yet? Having falsified the date of birth on official records, she could never remember which was Victoria's real birth date and which was her registered one. Surely the child must be two by now? Were two-year-olds capable of clambering out of carriages unaided, or would someone have to lift them? Could Victoria climb? Walk a distance? Make her way back to the house?

If Edwina knew the answers to these questions and if she had any idea how long the child had been missing she might have had some inkling of what to do next.

Later she explained to the policemen that she had positioned the baby carriage on the shady side of the courtyard, confident that Victoria would sleep for an hour (information supplied by the nanny, though she didn't mention that to them) while she helped Manus change the dressings on the shin of a nervous filly. The wound exposed the bone and a flap of skin and flesh was dangling, she elaborated to add realism to her account. Manus couldn't have managed on his own without causing distress to the animal. Of course he could have waited until the stable lads returned but, seeing she was there, it would have been foolish not to make use of her expertise. So Victoria was unattended for about twenty minutes (it was actually forty but Edwina affected vagueness so she wouldn't have to admit to that) and the child could have disappeared any time during that period.

When they asked her if she had felt the mattress before lifting it out, to see if it was still warm, she had to admit that in her distracted state she hadn't thought of it, and when they asked if the double doors had been open or closed at the time she went to attend to the filly, she said that they certainly were closed – she would have shut them behind her out of habit after she'd wheeled Victoria into the courtyard.

And what was Victoria's date of birth? The inspector turned the page of his notebook and, pen poised, waited for the answer.

Edwina's mind went blank.

"Excuse me a moment," she said, rising from her chair and leaving the room, feeling no obligation to give any reason for her departure to the two policemen.

The housekeeper Miss East never forgot how Manus appeared on horseback like a messenger from the Apocalypse to bring the bad news up the hill to the house.

His shouting brought her flying out through the front door.

"Victoria has gone missing. Round up everyone!" he called across to her, making no attempt to prevent the swerving, stamping Mandrake from damaging the lawn with deep gouges and hoofprints.

Despite her fear of horseflesh Miss East ran onto the grass right in front of the animal to find out more details. Mandrake high-stepped backwards at her approach and Manus didn't check him.

"I'm searching the river. I fear she's drowned," were his only responses to her outpouring of questions. He turned with a snap of the reins and Mandrake, reacting, accelerated with such speed that Manus barely had time to shout over his shoulder, "The stables!" before he was gone, leaving Miss East's person splattered with clods of earth.

Fired by an awful dread, she rushed around the house to the walled garden adjoining the kitchens. With relief she saw quite a number of the servants in the enclosure, all making the most of the sun: some sleeping, some talking or playing cards and one poking at a line of ants with a stick.

"Listen! Everyone listen!" she thought she shouted, and then clapped her hands when no one moved. She called out in a stronger voice. "Victoria is missing! Come quickly!" This time they heard and stumbled upright, dazed and sluggish from the sun, exclaiming and cursing. "Stables," she pointed, then flapped her hands as if herding geese. "Immediately. Go quickly. Run!"

They were already moving off.

She followed them through the garden gate, and called to the youngest boy, "Ned! Your legs are younger than mine," and had to pause to catch her breath before adding, "Run as fast as you can. Tell Sid and then the steward. Tell them to go to the stables. There's a good lad."

The boy looked pleased to be singled out. He promptly changed direction and headed for the coachman's little cottage behind the rowan trees, some distance from the house.

Miss East felt her agitation quieten a little. The servants would be able to cover a lot of ground in a short time, and the steward and Sid would take charge and know what to do.

I wouldn't want to be in Nurse Dixon's shoes, she thought to herself, not for all the tea in China. With all her faults, and God knows she has plenty of them, she's never managed to lose a child before now.

As she ran after the others, two maids, mindful of the limitations of middle age, turned back to check that she was all right but she waved them on, saying she was fine, she would only hold them back, and to keep going. When they rounded the corner of the house her legs weakened and she sank to the ground on her knees. Dear God, she prayed, let the precious little one already be found. Please, Lord, have pity and don't let her come to any harm.

2

With her back to the window and a hand mirror held to reflect light on her face, Nurse Dixon searched for laughter lines around her eyes and was relieved to see there weren't any. Look at her friend Teresa Kelly, run out of options, gone with her wrinkly old face to the other side of the earth at the age of forty to marry a sixty-year-old stranger because she was desperate to have a child and a home of her own before it was too late.

There's no way I'd let that happen to me, Nurse Dixon told herself with feeling. Not that it ever could, not with my youth and looks, and the divine Manus about to propose at any moment.

Tilting the cheval mirror, she noted her waist and ankles were still slender, and, angling the hand mirror, checked her back and side views – good posture, good tilt of the head. She must remember that pose – it was particularly flattering. She would try it out next time she saw Manus.

The clock on the nursery wall chimed three. Teresa Kelly would be leaving Ballybrian about now, Lady Blackshaw would be bringing Victoria back soon, and then the long dreary evening would begin.

With the once-placid Victoria, the pretty one, beginning to show signs of alarming wilfulness, Dixon was glad that someone else would be wasting years of effort trying to straighten her out, only in the end to find her turning out like Charlotte, the plain one. How wonderful to leave the Park and marry Manus at last, escaping the bone-aching tedium of rearing two rich brats. Her own children when she had them would be hard-working and sensible and a credit to her. And, of course, bonny. How could they escape being bonny with herself and Manus as parents?

She sat down to rub lemon juice into her hands, and let her mind turn, as it often did, to the injustices in life. If fate had been more kind to her and less kind to Lady Blackshaw, they could be sisters: both light-brown-haired and attractive, both tall and strong, both young. She wouldn't mind the gulf between them so much if Her Ladyship made the most of her position by indulging in a life of luxury and fashion, but she went around all day with her untidy hair piled on the top of her head with a single comb that couldn't cope with the straggly bits, and worse, wore men's riding breeches stained with saddle oil and horse sweat and didn't even dress for dinner while the master was away, which was most of the time. Dixon remembered the day she saw Lady Blackshaw in the full riding habit – top hat, veil, fitted jacket, silk stock, tailored skirt and fine leather gloves and boots – and how she had almost swooned at the elegance of it, and how she couldn't believe it when she heard it was the last time her mistress would dress like that as she intended to switch from the side-saddle to riding astride, as she had done as a girl, so that she could fulfil her ambition of riding like a man. "If it was good enough for Joan of Arc and Marie Antoinette to ride like that, it's good enough for me," she was reported to have told a conservative old neighbour who admonished her for adopting such an immodest and unladylike style. "And look what happened to them," the old woman responded with relish. "And served them right."

As the wait for the servants to arrive lengthened, Edwina, after retracing the route around the stables that Manus had already followed, took the steps up to check the first-storey quarters where the stable lads lived. If Victoria could climb, the steps up to it might have caught her eye. Only one door was open – it revealed a small kitchen – and it took only a moment to see that there was no one in it. The three men had gone to a shebeen in the village as they did every Friday afternoon. She already knew of their routine and hadn't expected to find anyone in their quarters.

Standing on the balcony, looking down on the enclosed courtyard, she sensed that the baby carriage and tartan quilt were accusing her from the opposite wall.

She would not allow herself to think of the child and the river and the open door in a single image.

What Manus had told her earlier came back to puzzle her like a half-forgotten refrain. Teresa Kelly, he'd said, was so devoted to Victoria he couldn't believe she would let herself be parted from her, and right up to the last minute he had thought she would change her mind and, for the sake of the child, not leave the Park. But he'd been mistaken. She had left. She was already gone.

It was the word 'gone' that resonated with Edwina and the fact that Manus, a man not given to idle conversation, had thought the woman's leaving worth mentioning in the first place.

Twenty minutes after he'd told her about Teresa Kelly, Victoria was gone as well.

She wished he hadn't ridden off so abruptly before she'd had time to question him further. It was a seven-mile stretch of river from the Park to the sea. If he had to ride the full distance it would be hours before she saw him again.

It was only when the gravel dug into the soles of her feet that Miss East realised she was wearing her indoor shoes, now wet and looking two sizes larger with all the mud clinging to them. Under ordinary circumstances Lady Blackshaw would be cross if she saw her housekeeper inappropriately shod, with soil stuck to her usually spotless clothing, but at a time like this she would surely hardly notice such things. Was that Sid driving off in a pony and trap along the avenue towards the gate lodge? How had he harnessed up so quickly? Had she miscalculated the time she'd spent in that blackout of anguish after the servants had left her?

Ignoring her tears and her status, she ran the rest of the way to the stables.

3

Edwina's absent husband, Lord Waldron Blackshaw, at present working in the War Office in London, was one of the most hated men in Ireland, though he wasn't aware of it. Nor were most of the inhabitants of Tyringham Park, cocooned as they were in a self-contained kingdom, physically distanced from the local community by the estate's vast stretches of farms, tillage, parkland, gardens and woodlands, and socialising only with their peers in similar Big Houses across the country.

Only three people on the estate knew the reason for the particular hatred: Manus, horse-breaker and trainer, and Teresa Kelly, seamstress – the only two employees from the locality – and the steward, a Tyrone man, who oversaw all the operations of the estate and collected the rents from the tenant farmers on Lord Waldron's behalf.

For more than a year, the steward had been expecting some kind of retaliation for what Waldron had done, so when the young boy burst into his office with the news about Victoria, his first thought was that the time for it had come. But when the boy added, "Manus fears that she is drownded and is searching the river," he allowed himself to hope that the disaster he would be dealing with was domestic rather than political.

When the steward came into the stable yard to find Lady Blackshaw he thought that, with her hair hanging loose about her face, she looked like the twenty-year-old innocent she had been when she first arrived from England as a bride nine years earlier.

"Good man," she said. "You take over here. I need to talk to Miss East and Nurse Dixon."

She turned and strode out the stable's' doors, almost colliding with Miss East who was hurrying in.

"There you are, Miss East. What kept you?"

She took the housekeeper by the elbow, turned her around to face back towards the house and walked ahead, now full of purpose, forcing the older, smaller woman to do half-running and skipping steps to keep up.

"You're just the person I want to see. Tell me which servants weren't in the walled garden this afternoon and everything you know about Teresa Kelly. And stop that snivelling."

Sid Cooper, the coachman, had been sent by Lady Blackshaw to look along the avenue in case the child had wandered in that direction. Rounding each tree-obscured bend, he expected to see Victoria, either on her own or in the care of a solicitous servant who had chanced upon her, but there was no one at all in view. Instead of returning to report, he used his initiative and carried on past the empty gate lodge and the stone pillars to the main road, turned left and continued a quarter mile to the village of Ballybrian. Best ask there. When he arrived in the main square his urgency and the pace of his over-excited pony prompted some villagers to call out to him, to ask if there was anything the matter. The youngest child from the Park was missing and had anyone seen her or anything suspicious? They would ask around immediately – and would they be of any help in a search? They would, and it would be much appreciated, he said, taking it upon himself to issue the invitation – now was not the time to be worrying about formalities. Would they have a look around the village first?

Sid's last place to check was the train station. With the part-time stationmaster not on duty, he looked into all the unlocked rooms himself and found them deserted.

By the time he turned for home, the villagers were already on the move, some spread out along the main road but most already on the mile-long drive up to the house, some of the older youths cycling ahead and the younger boys running alongside, jostling and shoving one another. The sombre cathedral-like atmosphere created by the two-hundred-year-old beeches arching over the length of the avenue had the effect of heightening their spirits rather than dampening them.

Nurse Dixon looked down through the front windows of the nursery and saw the beautiful Lady Blackshaw and the old witch Miss East walking quickly along the gravel drive towards the front entrance. No sign of Victoria. Just as she predicted. Fobbed off on to one of the maids, no doubt, after waking and needing attention. She knew that Lady Blackshaw, with her lack of interest in anything that happened in the nursery, wouldn't know what to do with a child that wasn't asleep.

Crossing to the back windows, she saw that, unusually at this hour, no one was making use of the walled garden. Now that her only friend Teresa Kelly was gone, would she ever have the courage to go there to join the others of an afternoon? Probably not. Hardly worth worrying about, really, seeing as she would be leaving soon. No one liked her. Never had. All down to the old witch Lily East, the very one who should have smoothed her path or 'let her in' to the established circle, seeing they came from the same parish in Huddersfield in England, but Lily had done the opposite. To be reared on tales of Miss East's success and arrive in awe of her and then find herself pushed out in the cold was an upset she didn't intend to forget.

She had slept fitfully the previous night, what with her sadness at Teresa's departure and the disruptions of Victoria's restlessness and Charlotte's talking in her sleep. I need a catnap before Victoria is brought back, she concluded, fetching an eiderdown from her room. If Charlotte comes in, she'll know better than to wake me – she's been warned often enough.

The steward's plan was to search the estate so thoroughly that when Lord Waldron returned from London at the end of the war, there would be no miscalculations or oversights for him to pinpoint and criticise.

Tyringham Park estate, the most impressive in County Cork, consisted of a fifty-two-roomed stone mansion, splendid enough with its single turreted tower to be referred to as a castle, and 19,000 acres of land. It wouldn't be easy to organise a comprehensive search. He would concentrate for the present on everything inside its boundary walls, seeing that was his responsibility, with only a cursory survey of the village and its surroundings.

The only crowd the steward thought he would ever see at the Park in his lifetime would be a hostile one, so he was doubly grateful for the scores of villagers who immediately came to help, and for the hundreds more people who, as the word spread, arrived later in the day from neighbouring Big Houses and from outlying villages.

Lady Blackshaw, in a fit of pique years previously, had decided not to employ anyone to live in the lodge to open and close the gates and check the movements of people entering and leaving the estate. "Why bother when no one visits?" she had said, intimating that it was Lord Waldron's fault, because of his long absences, that there was never any social activity at the Park. Why have someone sitting there doing nothing? she had argued. Let them plant barley on the land instead and make themselves useful.

She must regret that directive now.

Like Manus, the steward had concluded early on that Victoria had drowned, but felt it was his duty to issue instructions to exhaust all other alternatives in the hope the child was still alive.

When Edwina was forced to ask about Teresa Kelly, she left Miss East standing and sat far enough away so she wouldn't have to tilt her head to look up at her. To hear her husband Waldron constantly praise the housekeeper, one would think she was perfection personified, and to hear her speak and observe her attitude, one would think she considered herself the mistress of the house rather than the mere servant that she was, so Edwina didn't like to lose an opportunity, even in circumstances such as these, to put her in her place.

After a quick check on the servants who had been in the garden, Edwina said, "Tell me all you know about Teresa Kelly." She didn't mention Manus's remark about Teresa's attachment to Victoria and

11

his belief that she would never leave the Park because of it. "And pull yourself together. Your blubbering is most unseemly."

Miss East was finding it difficult to concentrate when all she could think of was a lost and frightened Victoria, but she forced herself to speak.

Teresa Kelly was a woman from the village who had run into trouble at home with a difficult sister-in-law. Miss East, who had been friends with her for years, gave her a live-in position after Victoria was born, with instructions to divide her time between sewing and assisting Nurse Dixon in the nursery.

"Two grown women to look after two children?" Edwina interrupted. "Verging on the excessive, one would think." She couldn't very well say 'Why didn't you consult me?' seeing she'd made it clear from the beginning that she wanted nothing to do with domestic matters, and Waldron had instructed Miss East accordingly, but she was still peeved that Miss East was able to exercise such authority. She also disliked the fact that Waldron insisted the woman be addressed as Miss East, rather than just East, which, to Edwina's way of thinking, would have been more in keeping with tradition.

"The local parish priest arranged for Teresa to travel to New South Wales," Miss East continued, "to marry a farmer and look after his aged mother. She has a friend living out there."

"Did she have a special attachment to Victoria?"

"She was very fond of both girls. She was an affectionate, big-hearted person."

Lady Blackshaw raised her eyebrows as she said, "How very admirable."

"Yes, she was admirable," Miss East agreed, pretending not to notice the sarcasm. "She made such an impression in the time she was here it was as if she had been here all her life."

"How charming. Most enlightening. Thank you, Miss East. That will be all. Now find Dixon and send her to me and make sure you clean yourself up and change your shoes by the time I catch sight of you again."

Away from the judgemental gaze of Miss East, she would ask Dixon about Teresa Kelly, who had lived in the Park for nearly two years and, for all Edwina knew about her, might as well have been invisible.

On her way to the third floor, Miss East heard a raised voice as she passed in front of an open window on the ground floor of the west wing. She looked out to see eight-year-old Charlotte, in muddied dress and shoes, kneeling on the ground beside a small bridge she had constructed over pooled water that was blocked by mouldy leaves from entering the gully.

She held a stone in her right hand and her face was turned up to Nurse Dixon who was looming over her hissing, "Well? Well? Say something. Go on, say something." When Charlotte didn't answer, Nurse Dixon drew her own hand back high over her head. Charlotte closed her eyes and scrunched up her face in readiness for a blow which, when it came, made her head swivel.

Nurse Dixon then grabbed Charlotte's arm and yanked her to her feet.

"It's a pity the gypsies didn't steal you instead of sweet little Victoria," she said. "No one would miss your ugly puss around the place."

Miss East found herself running in an undignified fashion along the corridor, out a side door, across flower-beds and a cobbled courtyard until she appeared, breathless, as if by chance, in front of the entangled pair.

Nurse Dixon turned red, but promptly affected a defiant look. "What do you want?" she demanded, holding Charlotte tightly by the upper arm.

Charlotte's face was devoid of colour. She looked as if she was about to faint.

"Lady Blackshaw wants to see you without delay."

"You're the third person to tell me that." She loosened her grip and Charlotte fell to the ground. "I don't know what she wants to see me for when it was her who lost Victoria, not me. I bet you thought it was me."

"I didn't think. I'll look after Charlotte while you're gone."

Miss East held out her hand. "No, you don't, *Lily*." Dixon made the name sound like a swear word. "Charlotte comes with me. Come on, Charlotte, get up. I haven't got all day."

13

Charlotte didn't move.

"Get up, I tell you, or I'll send word to the policeman. You know what that means."

Charlotte stood up slowly and gave her hand to Nurse Dixon, who looked triumphantly at Miss East.

"Come on, then." As she passed the older woman, she deliberately bumped into her, causing her to lose her balance for a moment. "Sorry," Dixon said with a smirk.

4

It was young Constable Declan Doyle who had been on duty when the message from Lady Blackshaw arrived at the barracks in Bandon, the nearest sizeable town, informing them about the missing child, instructing that officers be dispatched to the Park and asking for the family history of Teresa Kelly and details of her final days in Ballybrian. As a young 'blow-in' he didn't realise how important Lady Blackshaw was perceived to be in the district, and had never heard of Teresa Kelly. His older colleague Inspector Christy Barry, who was a native of Ballybrian, had to fill him in on the background of both women.

Charlotte was sketching in a listless fashion. She hadn't spoken since Dixon told her of Victoria's disappearance. No one had noticed. At this time of day she would normally be taking Mandrake over the jumps.

"Go outside and play. You're getting on my nerves with all that scribbling."

Charlotte didn't move.

"Go on. Build another one of those bridges you're so fond of, but stay out of the mud."

Charlotte looked at her sadly.

15

"You was happy enough doing that with Teresa, Miss Street-Angel-House-Devil, wasn't you?"

Charlotte stayed silent.

"You would try the patience of a saint. The world doesn't revolve around you, you know. How many times do I have to tell you?" Dixon strode over to the table, snatched up the five pages of horse drawings, crumpled them and threw them into the fire, then grabbed Charlotte by the arm and dragged her, a dead weight, to the open door and pushed her onto the landing, adding through habit, "And stay away from them banisters."

Dixon needed to think, and couldn't with that sullen face looking at her.

The last twenty months, since Teresa Kelly had come bounding up the stairs on her first day, had been the happiest of her life. The two of them had made a connection right from the start, despite their different backgrounds, religion, accents and age. Dixon felt as if she had climbed out of a damp dungeon into a summer garden by allowing herself to believe she had found a real friend for the first time in her life.

Teresa, unwelcome in her family home in the village since the death of her father and the arrival of a hostile sister-in-law, spent her spare hours, even her monthly day off, in the nursery with Dixon. "Where else would I be going?" she used to say. "My brother's wife would be glad never to see my face again, and him, too, seeing he takes her part – and I love being here." She didn't appear to be bitter even though she had wasted, to Dixon's way of thinking, the fifteen best years of her life caring for her senile father, with nothing to show for it at the end. The brother had inherited everything.

When Teresa left in the evenings to join the other servants for dinner in the downstairs dining hall, leaving Dixon to eat from a tray with only Charlotte and Victoria for company, she thought she might die of jealousy and loneliness. When she saw Teresa and Miss East setting out for the village for their weekly night of cards, she suffered an extra torture. What if Miss East transmitted her dislike of Dixon to Teresa, dripping poison into her ear during the long walk there and back? She watched each week for any sign of a negative change in Teresa's attitude towards her but found none. In fact, if she didn't think she was imagining it, she would swear Teresa's kindness was increasing, if that were possible.

Each morning, Dixon would wait to hear Teresa's footsteps on the stairs, and when she did the day took on a brighter aspect. Even the doleful Charlotte would give a screech of joy and rush to wrap her arms around Teresa, and Victoria, as she grew older, would wriggle free from Dixon's arms and follow her sister's example. Dixon didn't approve of the excessive show of emotion from the girls but let it go unpunished for her friend's sake as she seemed to like it and, besides, there were plenty of other excuses she could use for chastising them.

It was clear to anyone who had eyes to see that Teresa tried her best to treat the two girls equally but wasn't able to disguise the fact that Victoria was her favourite.

If only all interviews could be as pleasurable as this one, Constable Declan Doyle thought when the striking young woman settled herself down to be questioned – back straight, feet together, hands clasped, eyes so downcast they looked closed.

"Tell me in your own words what happened here today, Nurse Dixon," he said in a gentle voice. "Take as much time as you need." May she take all evening, he thought.

Nurse Dixon spoke with little hesitation, not once looking at either Declan Doyle or Inspector Christy Barry.

"After the rain stopped, I thought I'd take little Victoria out for some fresh air as we was cooped up for two days with all that rain. She were in no humour for walking, even though she learnt to walk early and is a good little walker. She couldn't hardly keep her eyes open because she woke early and had missed her morning nap, so I put her in the baby carriage even though she were too big for it. Had to turn her sideways and bend up her legs so she would fit. At least she'll get the fresh air, even if she don't get the exercise, I said to myself. Charlotte went off on her own – indoors she draws and paints non-stop and outdoors, when she isn't riding, she builds things with bricks and stones and wood – she likes to do things that make a mess. I ran into Lady Blackshaw who stopped to admire Victoria, who were already asleep. After I told her Victoria would sleep for more than an hour, she said she would take her for a walk and bring her back after that. I were that surprised you could have knocked me over with a feather. Her Ladyship has never done nothing like that before, certainly not with Charlotte in all her eight years, and it made

17

me feel right peculiar handing over the baby carriage, but then I asked myself what could go wrong, with Her Ladyship the child's mother after all."

She paused to allow the men time to take in the dramatic implication of those words.

"What time was this?" asked the constable, who was concentrating so much on the movement of Nurse Dixon's mouth he was neglecting to write in his notebook.

"About two o'clock."

"What do you personally think of the idea that Teresa Kelly took the little girl with her when she left?"

Dixon blinked three times before answering. "Absolute rubbish. She weren't even at the Park today. She said her goodbyes yesterday, and besides she would never do a thing like –"

"My sentiments exactly," the inspector interrupted with satisfaction. "And who better to know that than you, her best friend? Good girl. Now tell me, what do you say to the idea that the little one drowned?"

"More rubbish. The girls was never allowed near the river. They was warned often enough. I never stopped telling them about them children drowned in the deep Dark Waterhole fifty years ago and the man who went in to save them and was drowned with them. That gave Charlotte a proper fright. Even Victoria had it drummed into her and she were old enough to understand what I were saying."

"As the one who knew her best, what do you think happened to her?"

"I think she wandered off and will still be found. She's a great little walker for her age."

The constable took his chance to study Dixon while Christy Barry was questioning her. He had been expecting a grim matron with iron hair and a starched nurse's hat and apron, so when this fine-looking, mysterious young woman the same age as himself came through the door he'd been nonplussed, and smitten in an instant.

"May I ask for the sake of our official report . . ." and for my sake, he added in his thoughts, "what is your Christian name?"

"I don't have one that I know of. Not a real one. I were a foundling. They called me 'Baby'" – it was really 'Cry Baby' but she saw no reason to disclose that – "until I were old enough to look

18

after the new babies brought into the orphanage, and then they called me 'Nursie' and then 'Nurse'."

The young man's face was suffused with sympathy.

Teresa Kelly's brother, Séamus, even though he didn't work on the estate, presented himself to the policemen to be questioned by order of Lady Blackshaw. According to him, Teresa asked as a special favour if she could stay in her old room for her last night for old time's sake. He had no objection, of course. At eight o'clock in the morning the wife, checking to make sure Teresa hadn't stolen anything, though he didn't say that, found Teresa's bed empty and a farewell note left on the pillow. He hadn't laid eyes on her for the rest of the day and, as far as he knew, nor had their neighbours. He had no idea what mode of transport she was taking. Things hadn't been good between them, as everyone well knew. The only thing he could tell them was that her bicycle was missing – his wife wasn't too pleased about that as she'd had her eye on it, though he didn't mention that either – and that he was upset the way things had turned out so unfriendly seeing he and she used to be so close. He didn't know anything about her life at the Park or anything about the child that was missing.

The constable's gift for getting people to spill their life secrets in minutes was being wasted, and the inspector's own method of questioning which consisted of finishing sentences and cutting long stories short – he'd been in the business longer and had become impatient – had produced no better results, simply because the servants had nothing to say. They hadn't seen anything because they weren't in a position to. The Park's custom of giving everyone the same afternoon off, taken for granted by the staff as they were used to it, seemed unusual to the policemen, who had expected a rota system to be in place. At the time the child went missing, the majority of servants were in the garden with its enclosing eight-foot-high walls, while others were in the village, the shebeen or their own quarters. No wonder no one had seen or heard anything out of the ordinary. The demesne, to all intents and purposes, was unstaffed.

A timid little chambermaid, with the odd name of Peachy, third last on a list of twenty-eight, scuttled in, her eyes wide with apprehension. The inspector thought the constable would have his work cut out to get her to speak at all, but the young man's spaniel eyes, and the patience he exercised to allow long periods of silence to elapse, finally had her saying that she had seen Teresa Kelly at the Park around the same time as the baby had disappeared.

The inspector jerked upright. "Are you sure of that?"

The chambermaid's eyes widened. "She won't get into trouble, will she?"

"Of course not. Why would she?"

A stubborn look came into her face. "Teresa didn't take little Victoria," she said. "Lady Blackshaw thinks she did – I know that because someone heard her and Dixon talking about Teresa."

"I didn't think for one minute she did," said Christy Barry. "I know her personally and I know she would never do a thing like that."

The maid breathed out with relief. "That's exactly what I thought."

"But are you positive it was today you saw her?" Christy continued. "I thought she left the Park yesterday."

"Yes, I'm sure it were today." She screwed up her face in concentration, trying to remember exactly. It hadn't seemed important then. She was dying to join the others in the walled garden but had been delayed, as she had dropped and smashed a jar of Lady Blackshaw's hand cream and it had taken ages to clean up the mess with all those bits of broken glass. Then, on her way to the walled garden she had seen Teresa wheeling her bicycle in a great hurry away from the servants' door at the back of the house. Teresa had called over to her that she couldn't stop, that she was late.

"I thought she had left something in her room or had a message for Nurse Dixon. She's a friend of Dixon's. I called back 'Good luck!' and kept going, and that's all I seen."

"Do you know what time that was?"

"No, but it were only a little while later Miss East came to tell us the bad news and told us all to run off and start looking straight away, and we did."

"Have you told anyone else about seeing Teresa?"

"No."

"Why didn't you say anything?"

"I was the only one who seen her here today. I didn't want to get her into trouble."

"There's no fear of that," said the inspector. "Even if we suspected her of any wrongdoing, which we don't, we wouldn't know where to find her. Tell me, do you remember if she had any of her belongings with her?"

"She did. One of those canvas bags with a drawstring that sailors use. You couldn't miss it, strapped to the back of the bike."

"So she was on her way." Christy thought for a minute before standing up and ushering the young woman to the door. "Many thanks. You've been a great help. Now off you go and don't give it another thought, there's a good girl."

That evening, the villagers, making their way home exhausted and heartsick, met Manus riding up the avenue. In the dying light they couldn't see his face clearly and had to ask if he had found the child, and when he answered that he hadn't even though he had followed the river all the way to the sea, there were moans of sorrow followed by whispered expressions of hope that she might not have gone anywhere near the river after all and might still be found alive.

At the stables Manus handed Mandrake over to Archie, the eldest stable lad, who, glad of the opportunity to hide his brimming eyes, bent to examine the scratches on Mandrake's chest and legs and look for stones in his hooves.

Manus couldn't bring himself to go up to the Big House, let alone cross its threshold, so, citing his wet and muddy clothes as an excuse for not reporting back personally to Lady Blackshaw, sent the second stable lad up instead to relay the message.

5

One of Inspector Christy Barry's fishermen friends reckoned that with a body as small as Victoria's, and the river as high as it was, she had in all probability been washed out to sea and her body would never be recovered. Despite believing him to be right, Christy elected to go through the usual police procedures for the sake of Lady Blackshaw.

By the time he and his young colleague arrived back at the Park at nine the next morning to continue their questioning, the estate was even more crowded with searchers than it had been the previous day. The steward was gratified. With their help they would be able to do in two days what would take weeks if the Park residents alone were the only personnel available.

Around mid-morning, still waiting for a meeting with Lady Blackshaw, the constable suggested they question Charlotte. "Children are so observant," he said. "They see things an adult would never notice."

"Imagine a young bachelor like you knowing that," Christy smiled. "Why don't we send for Nurse Dixon to escort her here?"

The constable reddened and tried to look indifferent. "Yes, that's a good idea."

Fifteen minutes later, Nurse Dixon was holding Charlotte's hand

22

and speaking to her in a soft, coaxing tone of voice. "Come on, Charlotte dear, answer the nice policeman. When did you last see Teresa?"

Charlotte continued to stare at the two men with frightened eyes and didn't attempt to open her mouth.

"You've nothing to be afraid of, Miss Charlotte. We're not bogeymen, you know. I have four children of my own, a lot older than you, of course, and this young fellow here has a crowd of brothers and sisters."

Charlotte wouldn't be drawn.

Nurse Dixon looked straight at the constable for the first time and visibly reacted to his admiring expression. It was as if she had been running at speed at the end of a rope and was snapped up short when she reached the end of it.

"Excuse me a minute," she said, standing up in a hurry and leading Charlotte out of the room and down to the end of the corridor where no one could hear her.

"Just listen to me, young lady. And look at me while I'm talking to you." She gripped the child's chin and tilted up her head. Charlotte's eyes swivelled, trying to look anywhere except at Nurse Dixon. "Them policemen in there aren't the ones who punish naughty children. They're different ones, do you understand? Good, kind ones." Dixon squeezed Charlotte's chin with every word she emphasised. "So will you answer their questions when you're asked and stop making a show of yourself? Do you understand?"

Charlotte's eyes were smarting from the effort of avoiding Dixon's stare.

"Do you?"

Charlotte nodded and Dixon released her grip.

Returning to the room, Dixon placed herself directly opposite the young policeman, rather than at an angle as she had been earlier, with Charlotte on a chair close to her.

"Now, Miss Charlotte, do you mind if we ask you again? Did you see Teresa Kelly yesterday? Or any strangers?"

With pleading eyes, Charlotte looked up at the nanny and then at the two men.

"Now, Charlotte, dear," said Nurse Dixon, putting an arm around her and tucking her hair behind her ear and stroking it, "I'm with you, so you don't have to be afraid of anything. Just tell these nice gentlemen what you seen yesterday and the day before."

Charlotte slumped, stared straight ahead and didn't speak, even when the silence lengthened and the ticking of the clock on the wall became intrusive.

Nurse Dixon let her hand slip from Charlotte's shoulders, drew the child's left arm behind her back, held it in a vice-like grip and dug in her nails. Charlotte's face registered distress but she didn't cry out.

A servant entered without knocking to tell the policemen Her Ladyship would receive them now, this minute.

Dixon dropped Charlotte's arm and the child jumped up and ran out of the room. Nurse Dixon made eye contact with Declan Doyle ('Look what I have to put up with'), smiled angelically, and left slowly with a slight sway of her hips.

Lady Blackshaw, all in the space of two minutes, exploded with temper at the policemen for not telling her earlier what Peachy the chambermaid had said. She ordered them to circulate Teresa's description to all police and army barracks in the country, and personally contacted her nearest neighbours to drive to Queenstown in their new motor car to see if the seamstress had set off from there.

"We've lost over twelve hours," she raged. "I should have called in the army in the first place."

"It's not too late, ma'am," said Declan with a feigned mildness in his tone. He had taken a dislike to her and resented being treated as her private investigating agent. Her accent grated on his ear and he found her reaction to the loss of her daughter, whose birth date he suspected she didn't know, cold and unnatural. If a prize colt had been spirited away, she would have been much more upset than she was now, he believed. Above all that, he couldn't forget the initial outrage he felt when he saw the magnificent castle with its tower overlooking acres of prime fertile land stretching in all directions as far as the eye could see, and realising that it all belonged to one man, and that man a coloniser. He had read about such places in his history books, but had never seen one at first hand before now, as they were always surrounded by walls and trees and set too far back from public roads to be viewed by ordinary people.

The inspector made placatory noises. As far as he was concerned,

Lady Blackshaw's role as a bereaved mother excused her from all ordinary rules of good behaviour. She could rant and bully as much as she liked – that was her prerogative – and he wouldn't bat an eye.

"Why do you think she latched on to blaming Teresa Kelly so quickly?" the constable asked the inspector later, before proceeding to answer his own question. "Because she can't bear the thought of being ridiculed for mislaying her own child the only time she gets to take her out, that's why. Think of the rank stupidity of leaving the little one unattended beside a flooded river with the door wide open – though of course she didn't admit that she was responsible for that. If she didn't have Teresa Kelly to point the finger at she'd come up with some other poor unfortunate to deflect the blame away from herself."

"Perhaps you're right," said Christy.

Nurse Dixon closed the nursery door behind her and Charlotte backed away.

"Are you happy now? Are you? Making a complete fool of me in front of those nice men?"

Charlotte continued to move backwards until she came up against the end of her iron bedstead and couldn't move any further.

"Speak. Say something." Nurse Dixon raised her arm. "Go on. You know you're just putting it on. You always had plenty to say to Teresa when she were here, didn't you, so what's stopping you now? Eh?"

Charlotte cowered against the bed.

"I'm giving you one last chance. If you don't speak by the time I count to three you're going to cop it."

Charlotte braced herself.

"*One! Two! Three!*"

Dixon placed her hands on Charlotte's shoulders and shoved with such force that Charlotte's body arched backwards over the bed and the iron rail dug into her back. When Dixon let go Charlotte slid to the floor.

"Let that be a lesson to you," she said. "Just because you was born with a silver spoon in your mouth don't give you the right to treat other people like rubbish. Don't you ever make a fool of me again in front of other people. Is that clear?"

Breathing heavily, she removed herself to her adjoining room without looking back, slamming the door behind her. From her bedside locker she took out a yellow-haired porcelain doll dressed in sapphire-blue satin. Charlotte's expensive, beautiful doll. She felt like tearing out its yellow hair and smashing its face against the brass bed-knob and watching its marble eyes roll along the floor – serve Charlotte right, refusing to obey her in front of the policemen, making her look incompetent. She would have destroyed the doll, no question about it, if it hadn't been a gift from the girls' maternal grandparents. There was the fear that Lady Blackshaw could enquire about it at any time, especially if she wanted to show what Victoria's matching red-headed one looked like. So far her ladyship hadn't mentioned it – perhaps she had forgotten that Charlotte had ever owned one – but she would need to hold on to it, just in case.

It was over a year since it had been confiscated as a punishment for not handing it over when she had been told. Dixon had been forced to wrestle it out of the incorrigible child's arms. It hadn't helped her temper when she saw a shocked housemaid in the distance looking on at the distraught Charlotte screaming "Give it back! It's mine!" and then at the top of her voice "It's not fair!" After Dixon had bundled the child indoors to silence her unobserved and to give her a lesson in fairness, she pronounced that Charlotte would never see the doll again after a display like that, and if she made so much as a whimper the doll would be smashed into a hundred pieces, and if she so much as touched Victoria's matching one, there would be hell to pay.

Now Dixon stood on a chair and shoved the doll to the back of the top shelf of her wardrobe where the sly Charlotte wouldn't be able to reach if she happened to sneak in to search when there was no one about.

Charlotte was never going to get the better of her. All that fuss over a doll when the house was stuffed with antique toys, while poor orphan children never had anything to call their own, not even a clothes-peg doll with wool for hair.

6

At the end of the second day, the inspector told the constable to go home and leave the written report to him. The young man was too hot-headed and inexperienced to know what to put in and what to leave out, so it was less complicated to do it himself – the last thing he wanted was a big chief from Dublin being drafted in, on account of Lord Waldron's importance and notoriety, to take over the investigation, waking up sleeping dogs at the same time.

No mention was made in his report of his friend's son, Manus. Best not bring that name to the attention of Dublin Castle, whose British administration was eager to discredit any suspected member of the Irish Republican Brotherhood. Like many of his fellow countrymen, Christy worked for the Crown – he wished it were otherwise but he had to live and feed his family. However, he prided himself on acting as honourably as was possible to his own people under the weight of colonial rule. If he were ever questioned about the omission he would say, seeing as Manus and Lady Blackshaw were together when the child disappeared, there seemed little point in replicating her evidence.

Much against the grain, he had to include the little chambermaid's sighting of Teresa Kelly on the day in question seeing as Lady Blackshaw was making no secret of putting a sinister construction on it. He had to keep reminding himself that Her Ladyship was so overcome with grief (though to look at her dry eyes no one would guess, so well did she disguise her feelings – all those centuries of breeding) she needed to clutch at straws. Or save face, the memory of the voice of the unimpressed young constable chimed in. One small consolation: Teresa, on the other side of the world, need never know her name had been blackened. She hadn't left an address with her brother or anyone else as far as he knew, so if she chose to stay out of touch, which he suspected she would, there would be no way anyone could get word to her, thank God.

After he had transcribed Lady Blackshaw's initial account of her daughter's disappearance, dated it the day before – 7th July 1917 – and signed and stamped the report, he re-read all the interview notes and felt proud, as a fellow villager and neighbour, of the high regard in which Teresa was held.

No one had had a bad word to say about her. Considering the short time she had been employed at the Park, she had left a good impression. What particularly interested him, and what he didn't include in his report, was how each servant said more or less the same thing: the only person who would really, deeply miss Victoria was Teresa Kelly. Not Lady Blackshaw, who hardly ever saw her daughter, certainly not the absent Lord Waldron who had seen her briefly only once, and not Nurse Dixon who, according to quite a few servants, wasn't very nice to the girls when she thought no one was looking.

This last observation was disbelieved by the young constable, who immediately spoke up in the nanny's defence. The remarks were inspired by jealousy of the nanny's good looks, he argued. When Nurse Dixon was being interviewed, she had shown so much patience with the uncooperative Charlotte, and had been so kind to her, that he was sure she was genuine – no one could put on an act as convincing as that if they were pretending – and the inspector wrote a note to that effect on the report.

Edwina's neighbours reported back from Queenstown. Only one passenger boat had departed from there during the last four days, and none was due to depart for the next week. The number of sailings was reduced because of the war. When they asked about passenger lists, they were told the authorities weren't at liberty to disclose any information about them. And no, they hadn't seen a middle-aged lady with a child or a middle-aged lady on her own anywhere near the port on or after the 7th of July.

The search continued. Families spent their Sundays after Mass walking along the banks of the river or beside the harbour walls on the south coast, staring into the Atlantic. Bathers sifted the sand along the shore. Fishermen scrutinised their nets. Sid concentrated on the outbuildings on the estate. Manus continued to search the seven miles of river, now returned to its normal depth, in the early morning and late evenings, tending to the horses in between times.

Nothing was found – not a fragment of flesh, bone, hair or white linen fabric, nor any part of a porcelain doll with red hair or any shred of its emerald-green dress.

Those who knew Teresa Kelly well were outraged by Edwina's kidnapping theory, though as time passed many came to entertain it, more from hope than conviction.

Edwina had written to her husband three days after the disappearance. Waldron wrote back from London to say how frightfully sorry he was, but at such a critical time there was no question of his taking leave from the War Office, even for a short period. She must, as a member of a military family with a long and proud history, appreciate the fact that the loss of one small girl, no matter how significant to one personally, was of little consequence compared to the welfare of a million soldiers, all under his jurisdiction.

Edwina had expected exactly that response.

Alone, she continued to puzzle over the anomalies in the Teresa Kelly story.

Every day she contacted the inspector to see if there had been any response to the circulated description, to be told each time with regret there was none.

This brought up another quandary for Edwina. Could she trust the police, port authorities, villagers or even Manus to relay information about Teresa, one of their own, to her, an interloper? Her friend and neighbour, Lady Beatrice, a woman in her sixties, had laughed at the astonishment on Edwina's face when she told her that the Blackshaw family might have lived in Tyringham Park for over four hundred years but they would never be considered the rightful owners. Those who had to labour out of economic necessity as tenants on the Big House estates around the country regarded the land they worked on as their own – it had belonged to their forebears, and one day they would drive out the imperialists and reclaim it.

"It is something you should be aware of, especially with Waldron's position in these troubled times," Lady Beatrice had warned.

Edwina presumed she meant his position in the British army.

She came to the conclusion that concern for the missing child was as genuine as the dearth of information about Teresa's whereabouts was deliberate, and if she wanted results, she would have to obtain them herself.

The steward accompanied her and a maid to Dublin to question the port officials there but, as in Queenstown, passenger lists for sailings were classified and no amount of argument produced them. The clerks were sympathetic, but they had to be especially vigilant after the Easter Rising of the previous year. A trip to Belfast produced the same negative response, and she returned to Cork frustrated and downhearted.

The search was officially called off.

7

Miss East kept her eye out for Charlotte. Normally you could set your clock by her. Five past two, on the dot, she would pass by the window on the way to the stables, sometimes on her own, often accompanied by Nurse Dixon, who didn't need to take her but wanted the excuse to make eyes at Manus – eight years on, she didn't seem to have made any headway in that department and, with her blatant flirting, had turned herself into a bit of a joke among the other servants.

There had been no sign of either of them for two weeks now. Miss East became agitated – not only had Charlotte lost a sister, but an adult she loved and trusted in the person of Teresa Kelly. With a preoccupied mother and only Nurse Dixon for company, there was no one to see how she was faring. Miss East checked with Cook who told her meals were being delivered as usual to the landing outside the nursery by a maid, and taken in personally by Nurse Dixon, who later put the empty trays back on the landing to be collected by the same maid. There was never any leftover food on either tray, Cook said proudly. There never had been in all the years she had been cooking.

Miss East became even more uneasy when she discovered that the chambermaid who was supposed to clean and dust the nursery once a week had been told by Dixon to stay away until further notice as she was doing the cleaning herself.

"Why didn't you report that to me?" Miss East asked her.

"I didn't see the need," answered the maid. "Dixon said Miss Charlotte needed peace and quiet and she would get me back as soon as she was feeling better."

Miss East took it upon herself to go to the nursery, even though that wing of the house was not under her jurisdiction, a rule made specifically by Lady Blackshaw, she knew, to try to undermine and humble her. There would be no point in approaching Lady Blackshaw to ask permission to visit Charlotte over Nurse Dixon's head – she would be refused.

"What are you doing here?" Nurse Dixon asked, opening the door a few inches and glaring when she saw who was standing there.

"I'd like to see Charlotte." Miss East tried to keep her voice confident and steady. Dixon's aggressive attitude unnerved her. She could only imagine what effect it had on the children in her care.

"What for?"

"Just to see how she is. I haven't seen her around lately."

"She's asleep. You don't have to check on how she is. That's what I'm here for, Lily, as if you didn't know."

"Under the circumstances . . ." Miss East gave the door a push, and before Nurse Dixon could make a grab for it to pull it closed behind her, Miss East had glimpsed a white, thin face staring at her from the bed.

The two women were now facing each other on the landing. Miss East took a step back.

"What is wrong with her?" she asked.

"Did Lady Blackshaw send you?"

"No, she didn't."

"Then you've no business snooping around this wing, asking questions. You know I'm in charge here, not you. Why don't you take yourself off and stop poking your nose in where it isn't wanted?" She turned as if to dismiss the older woman.

"Charlotte doesn't look at all well," Miss East persisted, even though she was beginning to feel weak. "Would you like me to call the doctor?"

"She don't need a doctor. And I'd be the one calling him if she did. Go on, get off with you. Shoo!"

Miss East descended the first set of stairs.

"Just tell her I was asking for her," she called up.

"*Just tell her I was asking for her,*" mimicked Dixon in a taunting manner, and then said loudly as she re-entered the room, "The old witch thinks you're ill. Shows how little she knows. Now get yourself off that bed this instant and tidy up those crayons." A pause. "Did you hear what I said?"

Miss East covered her ears and hurried on down the stairs.

The next day Lady Blackshaw informed Miss East that she needed to go to London to see her husband on urgent business and was entrusting the running of the house to her. She would be away for a month.

"Don't contact me unless there's news of Victoria, in which case send a telegram to Lord Waldron's office. Otherwise, deal with everything yourself."

"Everything?"

"Yes, everything. The business of the Park isn't exactly high on my list of priorities at the moment."

Minutes after Lady Blackshaw was driven to the train, Miss East rang Dr John Finn and asked him to come up to the nursery to see Charlotte. She then walked to the steward's house and told him Nurse Dixon would be leaving the employment of the Park that day and could he sort out any wages due to her, and payment in lieu of notice, if that applied.

"Bad business, that," he said sympathetically.

Miss East didn't answer, letting him presume the nanny was leaving because of the heartbreak over Victoria.

"I'll sort that out for you straight away, Miss East, and have it sent up to you. Lady Blackshaw get away all right?"

Miss East sent a maid to inform Nurse Dixon that Dr Finn would be calling shortly. When Dixon began to object, the maid said "Lady Blackshaw's orders," as she had been instructed to do.

While Miss East waited for Dr Finn, she couldn't settle to any occupation. The day she had looked forward to for eight years had come at last.

8

The doctor dreaded seeing Victoria's cot, empty now for seventeen days. He paused on the landing to prepare himself and to catch his breath after running up the three flights of stairs. He considered himself fit for a man of sixty, but the stairs were steeper than he remembered and he should have had the sense to take them at a slower pace.

After the darkness of the stairwell, the bright light in the room blinded him when he entered. He reached sideways automatically and it was the cot that steadied him until his eyes adjusted to the glare. He kept his head facing to the front while he regained his vision, but then found his eyes drawn to the contents of the cot: a rumpled red blanket, and a white linen sheet that was smooth at the outer edges and wrinkled towards the centre.

From the opposite side of the vast room the young child in the bed stared at him.

"I was told to leave it exactly as it was. Not to touch a thing, I was told," said the nanny, standing beside the child's bed.

"You did well, Nurse Dixon." Dr Finn smiled in the direction of the young woman he'd always thought of as "nervy" even though she stood straight and still with her hands clasped in front of her; a picture of calm. Maybe it was the hurried way she spoke or the constant blinking that hinted at an uneasiness beneath the surface.

He wondered if it was the police or the mother who had given the order to leave the cot exactly as it was. Whoever it was had neglected to ensure young Charlotte was moved to another room where she wouldn't have to look, on a daily basis, at the emptiness behind the bars of the cot.

The girl in the bed kept her dull eyes on the doctor and didn't smile or speak as he crossed the room. He hoped that the concern he felt on seeing her looking so ill didn't show on his face.

"Well, how is my favourite girl?" he asked her, before shaking hands and exchanging pleasantries with the nanny, who immediately reverted to standing straight with her eyes cast down and her hands clasped in front of her. "Now let me have a look at you, Miss Charlotte, and we'll see what the problem is." He sat down on the edge of the bed. "Tell your old friend what the trouble is."

"She isn't talking, Doctor," said the nanny. "Not one word since the baby disappeared. And not eating neither. I keep saying if you don't eat you'll lose your strength. I keep telling her that." Her eyes closed as if for emphasis.

"Thank you, Nurse," he said. "How long has she been in bed?"

"Four days, but she were poorly before that. Ever since . . . well, you know. Gets out to use the commode then crawls right back in again. Won't let me help her neither."

He checked Charlotte's pulse, temperature, throat, eyes, heartbeat and abdomen, all the while calling her his pet and his brave girl. "Now your lungs," he said as he helped her into a sitting position, noting how much weight she had lost since he last saw her.

"Take a deep breath and hold it, there's a good girl." He lifted her nightdress and saw the large fading bruises in a line across her back.

"Oh dear, that looks nasty. I thought that you'd given up falling off horses."

The nanny's head bobbed down. "It weren't the horses – it were horseplay on the bed, more like. Gets overexcited and don't know when to stop."

"Will you ever forget your broken arm last year when you couldn't ride for ten weeks? Now that wasn't much fun, was it?"

Charlotte looked at the doctor, then the nanny, and then finally, as she slid back onto the pillows, the ceiling.

The doctor noticed that the nanny cast her eyes down when he spoke to her, but watched him when she thought he wasn't looking. With his peripheral vision, the doctor noted the bobbing head and the blinking eyes.

"Will I ask Manus to find you a quieter pony?" asked the doctor and was pleased to see Charlotte smile as she shook her head. "I saw him on the way up riding your Mandrake. What a big horse for a little girl of eight. He'd frighten the life out of me." The smile grew wider. "Manus told me months ago you're well able to handle Mandrake. He says you've got a special talent and you're nothing short of a champion. Actually, if I told you all the good things he said about you, you'd get a big swelled head."

Charlotte continued to look pleased but, as the doctor began to pack his black bag, a look of disquiet replaced the smile on her face.

"And what's this I'm told? That you're not eating? Would I be right in saying that?" The doctor noticed out of the corner of his eye the nanny lifting her head. Charlotte glanced at her before looking back at the doctor and nodding.

"We'll have to do something about that or Cook won't be too happy, will she? And what about sleeping? Are you getting plenty of sleep?"

Charlotte shook her head.

"She's awake half of the night and when she is asleep she's tossing and turning around and opening her mouth all weird like," said the nanny.

"We can't have that," said the doctor. "Exhausting for both of you. Is it nightmares you're having, Miss Charlotte? Is that the trouble?"

Nod.

The doctor sat for a long period before asking softly, "Are you dreaming about little Victoria?"

He noticed her lip trembling as she nodded.

"I think we're all having bad dreams about her," he said, taking her hand. "It's only natural. It's hard to think of anything else. Of course your dreams are disturbed. How could they not be?" His other hand patted her arm. "Who knows, she might still be found. We can only hope and pray." He turned to Nurse Dixon. "It's important that Charlotte isn't left alone at night even for a minute."

"There's no need to tell me that, Doctor."

"Of course, Nurse. I wasn't suggesting you needed telling, I was thinking of your isolation up here – no one even in earshot. So high up and so far away from the rest of the house. Perhaps you should ask another member of the staff to stay."

"I wouldn't trust no one else, especially not now. I can manage, Doctor."

"I'm sure you can, but I'd hate to see you wearing yourself out with all that broken sleep and no time off. It must be lonely for you at all events. And you must be missing Teresa Kelly." He looked over his half-glasses. "Have you heard from her yet?"

"No, she's only been gone three weeks. She won't have arrived yet."

"Well, I hope when she gets there she'll do well in her new life. She's a great girl and deserves to."

The doctor stood and crossed the room to look out one of the windows which was fitted with iron bars high enough to prevent a child falling out accidentally. "Spectacular view," he said, admiring the green fields disappearing into the oak and beech forest in the distance. "Pity to see you missing this sunshine, ladies. God knows we get little enough of it." He turned. "We'll have to see how soon we can get you out of this bed, Charlotte, and then back into the fresh air with the both of you. I'll have a chat with Miss East and we'll see what we can do." He smiled down at Charlotte. "It's a pity that I can't take you home with me. Mrs Finn would love a dotey little girl like you to fuss over. But we couldn't take you away from Nurse Dixon, could we?" He looked up at the nanny. "You'd be lost without her, wouldn't you, Nurse?"

Charlotte grabbed his hand before he heard a reply and he saw she was weeping and mouthing, but there was no sound.

"What is it, my dear?" he said as he sat down again. He tried to lip-read but she ceased her efforts before he had time to make out a single word.

"Can you write it down?" asked the doctor, taking his pen and a notebook out of his pocket.

"She can't write," said the nanny. "She's had no governess yet."

"Try to slow down, pet," he said, "and I'll see if I can understand."

Charlotte looked over his shoulder at the nanny, then shook her head, sighed, closed her eyes and lay still.

37

The doctor stayed and talked of Manus, Mandrake, Lady Blackshaw in London visiting Lord Waldron and surely planning to bring her back a wonderful gift, the cook's sponge cakes, his new grandchild, until he thought he was annoying rather than comforting her and that it might be time to leave.

"Now try not to fret," he said. "I'll report to Miss East on the way out and I'll be back to see you first thing tomorrow. You are not to upset yourself. We'll have you back on your feet in no time." He bent over her. "You do trust your old doctor friend, don't you?"

Charlotte kept her eyes closed and turned her face to the wall. Her expression was so desolate the doctor wished he could say the one thing that would bring life back into her face – that Victoria had been found safe and well and would soon be reunited with her family – but he couldn't say it, and wondered if it would ever be said.

"You and your father saved my life all those years ago, Dr John. Now I'm asking you to help me save Charlotte's."

If Dr Finn didn't hold her in the high regard that he did, and if he hadn't been so disturbed by what he'd just seen in the nursery, he would have had to accuse Miss East of being overly dramatic.

"What's going on, Lily?" he asked simply, handing over his hat, coat and Gladstone bag and accepting a measure of whiskey before sitting in the chair to the left of the turf fire. "You tell me. That little girl up there looks as if she's dying of a broken heart."

"It might be a broken heart and it might be something else, something to do with Nurse Dixon."

We are all put on this earth to do one great thing, Miss East's mother used often say, and Miss East, believing it, felt the enormity of her responsibility as she prepared to do the 'one great thing' that would justify her existence.

Dr Finn's grim expression continued to darken as Miss East argued for the dismissal of Nurse Dixon and the handing over of Charlotte's care to herself.

It wasn't what she and the servants had seen and heard, though they had seen and heard troubling things, but Charlotte's demeanour that had convinced her that Nurse Dixon wasn't a fit person to be in charge of children.

"I'm sure you can see in your professional capacity that she's no more a nurse than the cat. She gave herself that title, you know."

"That I couldn't comment on," said the doctor. "I've never seen her do anything except stand still with her hands clasped in front of her. I think I make her nervous as she keeps blinking all the time."

"She has a lot to be nervous about," Miss East continued, and then proceeded to tell him everything she'd seen, and everything she suspected.

Dr Finn already knew of Miss East's antipathy to Nurse Dixon, but not the strength and depth of it.

"She has Lady Blackshaw completely hoodwinked, which wouldn't be difficult seeing Her Ladyship takes no interest in the child, but she doesn't fool me."

Charlotte always looked dispirited and morose in the company of Nurse Dixon, signs of a child in despair. Miss East recognised the signs because she had once been like that, and all Nurse Dixon's smiles, concern and ministration while in public, especially for the benefit of Manus and Lady Blackshaw, not only didn't fool her, but filled her with even more misgiving.

Miss East needed the doctor's co-operation, not only for his physical presence to intimidate the tall, strong, young Dixon, but also for his gravitas and reputation, to give authority to what she was about to do.

Dr Finn felt sorry for Nurse Dixon who at her age should be out dancing and courting rather than leading a dreary, isolated life, and he didn't like to interfere in the workings of the estate, but when Miss East said, "We can't chance a second tragedy on our hands, especially while the mistress is away," he felt the truth of it and agreed to support her.

9

"I thought you wasn't coming back till tomorrow," said Nurse Dixon, standing at the half-opened nursery door. Her eyes flicked from one to the other and the cocksure look that she adopted in the presence of Miss East wavered for a second when she saw the intent on their faces. "What's she doing here?" she asked the doctor, while glaring at the housekeeper. "She's not supposed to come here."

"I thought she could look after Charlotte while we have a chat. May we come in?"

"I'm not prepared," she said, indicating with a movement of her hand her stockinged feet.

"That's not important. I'd just like a few words about Charlotte."

The doctor took a step forward, Dixon gave way, and Miss East followed the doctor into the room. "Could we go somewhere else to talk while Miss East stays here?"

Dixon snorted with bitterness. "No. I'll stay right here where I'm supposed to be, thank you very much."

The doctor and housekeeper exchanged a glance that wasn't lost on Nurse Dixon.

"Would you at least step out onto the landing?" said the doctor.

"I'm not moving. Can't see why I should."

"Very well, in that case I'll say what I've come to say. It is my medical opinion that your charge should be moved from this room straight away because of its associations," he said, nodding towards the cot and presuming Charlotte didn't know what "associations" meant.

"Is that all? I don't need no doctor to tell me that. I can see that for myself. We could have moved next door any time if only Her Ladyship had said."

"I wasn't thinking of next door. I was thinking of downstairs in the main part of the house and putting her in the care of Miss East."

Lily felt as if she was about to faint with fright.

There was a movement in the bed.

Dixon's mouth fell open and she let out a yelp. "You snake!" she shouted at Lily East. "You can't get any lower than this. Showing your true colours at last." Outrage showed on her face as she turned to Dr Finn. "She's been plotting this for years. Everyone knows she suffers from child hunger. She begged Lord Waldron for my job but he told her she was too old and she never got over it. Trust me. All she's ever wanted is to get her hands on the girls." Spittle was frothing at the corners of her mouth. "Dried-up old cow – that's all she is!"

"You should mind your tongue, young lady," said Dr Finn.

There was a shudder under the bedclothes.

"Why should I? Why should I take any notice of what you say? You don't even belong here. Lady Blackshaw wouldn't have sent for you – that's my job. Funny you should call on the very day she leaves, isn't it? I wonder whose idea that were?"

"I don't think we should discuss this further in front of Charlotte. I'll take her down to my room now and we can finish talking later." Miss East made a move towards the bed.

"No, you don't," said Dixon, shoving her aside and sitting down heavily on the bed, leaning back against Charlotte.

Miss East stayed where she had ended up after the shove, a few yards from the bed.

"I've looked after Charlotte for eight years and there's been no complaints," Dixon said with fervour to the doctor. "It's not my fault she's sick now. It's the shock of Victoria's disappearance that's done her in. Nothing to do with me. I'll move rooms all right but she stays with me. Do you think you're the only ones worried about the state she's in?"

Charlotte tried to shift her position as Dixon was leaning too heavily on her. Dixon leaned harder until the child kept still.

"I can't say any more at the moment, Nurse Dixon," said the doctor, "but I must insist that Charlotte is removed today. Immediately, in fact."

Dixon turned turkey red and seemed to expand in size. The air around her crackled.

"What's this got to do with you?" she asked, emphasising every syllable. "You can't say who goes here and who goes there. Why should I take any notice of you?"

"Because I'm a doctor. I'm not giving you my personal opinion, but my medical one, and you can't argue with that."

Dixon opened her mouth, shut it, and opened it again after a few seconds' thought. "She did put you up to it, didn't she?" She narrowed her eyes. "She's fooled you just as she's fooled everyone with her posh accent and her books and her grand ways." She turned to face Miss East. "You've come a long way, haven't you, you jumped-up skivvy? All high and mighty. Your old neighbours might mistake you for a lady if they weren't all dead from old age, you old crone!" She concluded with a forced laugh and a look of satisfaction on her face.

"I've only one answer to that." Miss East handed her an envelope.

"What's this?" Dixon took it before she realised what she was doing.

"Your notice. I'm dismissing you."

"You're what?" A look of panic crossed Dixon's face and she turned back to the doctor. "I'm *telling* you that shrivelled-up old maid would do *anything* to get her hands on the girls! That's what this is all about. It's so obvious I don't know how you can't see it. What more proof do you need? Ever since I got here she's been jealous of my looks and me having the girls. You've *got* to believe me!"

Dixon concentrated on the doctor's face.

He stood unmoved.

She threw the envelope at Miss East, hitting her forehead, then jumped from the bed and towered over her, showering spittle as she cursed her.

Dr Finn was at the bedside in a second. He threw back the blankets and picked up Charlotte who clung to him with her legs

42

wrapped around his waist and her head buried in his shoulder. He then made to move between the two women. Dixon turned and saw Charlotte in the doctor's arms. She tried to pull her out of them, but the doctor turned his back and, even though Dixon prised off the legs, Charlotte clung on with her arms, and when she lifted the arms, the legs were back, pressed more tightly.

Dixon was aware she was being made to look foolish. She ran to the door, locked it, and put the large brass key in her skirt pocket. "Now we'll see who's in charge. I'm not finished yet! And I've a lot more to say, and it will do Charlotte good to hear it. The sooner she finds out what's going on in the big, bad world the better. As if she didn't know too much already." Her narrowed eyes and twisted mouth were horrible to see.

Charlotte's head burrowed deeper into the hollow of the doctor's neck and shoulder.

"For the love of God, Nurse Dixon," said Dr Finn, "let's get Charlotte out of here – leave her with Cook – and then you can take as long as you like to say whatever you like."

"You told, you little bitch, didn't you? I'm *talking* to you, Charlotte. Didn't you?" Charlotte shook her head violently, still keeping her face hidden.

"And you know what's going to happen now that you've told, don't you?" She positioned herself at the doctor's back and twisted Charlotte's ear. "I'll put a curse on Mandrake and he'll die –"

"No!" cried Miss East.

"And I'm putting a curse on you and you'll soon know what it is when it happens to you."

"No, Charlotte! Don't listen to her!" said Miss East.

"Oh, go away, you wasp! Go on, go *away*!" Dixon needed little effort to knock over Miss East and didn't even turn her face towards her as she did it.

The doctor whispered to Charlotte, who quivered and shook her head. He continued to whisper. She slackened her hold on him. He walked over to Miss East to help her up and when she was upright transferred Charlotte into her arms.

Dixon gave a howl when she saw what had happened and tried to snatch the child back from Miss East. The only part of Charlotte she could grasp was her hair and she pulled so hard it looked as if the slender neck might snap. The child's face contorted in agony and her mouth opened in a soundless scream. When Miss East turned, Dixon held on and turned with her. The doctor grabbed Dixon's left arm and squeezed it so hard for so long that she was forced to let go of the hair. He then twisted the arm behind her back and kicked her legs out from under her. She landed on her front with the doctor's knee on her back, her arm twisted behind her and her legs flapping to no purpose.

"Charlotte might like to know how Miss East's stepfather protected young girls, I reckon," spat Dixon. "You didn't think I knew about all that, did you?"

Dr Finn, who had been searching with his free hand for the key, now put that hand across her mouth and received such a strong bite he couldn't get it back. He moved his position so that he straddled the nurse, keeping her left arm pinioned by his weight, and freed himself by pushing down hard on her lower jaw with his other hand. "If you don't shut up I'll be forced to do something drastic, so help me God, I will." He turned her head and pushed it into the floorboards so she couldn't speak, and searched quickly and roughly for the key until he found it and handed it to the trembling Miss East, who lost no time in opening the door and fleeing.

Such was her heightened fear, Miss East was able, despite her small physique and her forty-eight-year old legs, to carry Charlotte saying, "You're safe. You'll never see Nurse Dixon ever again," and then, "I'm not a witch, I'm your fairy godmother," over and over, down the three flights of stairs and along lengths of corridors before arriving at the kitchen and thrusting the child into the arms of the startled cook.

"Look after her for a minute," said the breathless Miss East. "Something to do."

She hurried into the back kitchen and told the young kitchen porter to run up to the nursery as fast as his legs could carry him to check that Dr Finn, who might be in a bit of trouble, was all right. She had to give him directions as he had never been to that wing before.

"Lordy, isn't it lovely to see little Charlotte again?" Cook said to Miss East on her return to the kitchen. "It's lovely to see you at last, Charlotte. We were all wondering when you were going to come down to visit us again."

Charlotte loosened her hold on Cook and ran to put her arms around Miss East's waist. Her eyes fixed on a loaf of soda bread upended on the cooling rack and she pointed at it.

"She's hungry, poor thing," said Cook, following the pointing finger. She went over to cut a wedge from the loaf, covered it with butter and blackberry jam and halved it.

Charlotte grabbed it and stuffed so much into her mouth she found it hard to chew.

The two women exchanged glances and Cook mouthed 'Starving' over the child's head.

Charlotte pointed again at the bread to show that she wanted more but Miss East said, "We'll wait a little longer until your tummy settles down after that piece."

"Will you come back to me, Charlotte?" said Cook. "I've been missing our cuddles for such a long time."

Charlotte moved over to the heavily padded sanctuary of Cook's lap and both women were surprised to see her fall asleep within a few minutes.

Miss East couldn't help sharing her good news. "I'll be looking after Charlotte until Lady Blackshaw returns. Now, I'm just going to see Dr Finn to see what he has to say and then I'll explain everything."

She decided to wait at the bottom of the nursery stairs for Dr Finn, standing well back in case Dixon or the kitchen porter came down first.

It's done, she exulted, speaking to her mother in her mind. Rejoice with me. The one great thing is done. Eight years too late, but done at last. Dixon is dismissed. Thank God I lived to see the day.

10

One person would be awake, Nurse Dixon knew, and that would be Manus, and he was the only person she wanted to see. At first light she left her bed and made her way to the stables where he was saddling Mandrake, impatient to be off for the eighteenth day in a row on his daily dawn search for Victoria. As soon as he saw Dixon's tearful face, he guided her into the tack room on the southern side where they could talk without fear of disturbing the lads asleep in the room above the stable on the northern side.

She told him that Miss East, full of jealousy, was getting rid of her while Her Ladyship's back was turned. Dixon would have to wait around for a month until Lady Blackshaw returned to give her back her position, which she would do, as she thought so highly of her. Meanwhile Miss East had removed Charlotte from the nursery the night before, and was no doubt making up nasty, untrue stories which she would later spread to justify her action and everyone would believe them because she was the housekeeper.

"I can't stay at the Park to be pointed at and whispered about."

"No one will be pointing at you and whispering." Manus showed relief that the news wasn't worse. He took Dixon's hand, saying that she must have misunderstood Lily East, who was kindness itself, and if Dixon liked he would speak to Lily and sort out the mistake.

"No, don't talk to her. That's the last thing I want you to do. Believe me, there were no mistake. You don't know her like I do. She suffers from child hunger and would do anything to get her hands on the girls. Girl. And this were her chance. She said Her Ladyship gave her the authority."

"I can't credit this sudden turn of events. And you so good with the girls. Lily must have got the wrong end of the stick. I wonder what got into her." He shook his head in disbelief. "You must let me talk to her."

"No."

"There must be something to be done."

"There is something. I was hoping you would mention it." Dixon paused to make sure she was selecting the correct phrase. "I thought that, seeing that . . ." She took a deep breath. "Can I come and stay with you?"

"Stay with me?" Manus was taken aback. "You mean until Lady Blackshaw returns?"

"No, I didn't mean that. I mean to come and live with you permanently."

"I don't think that would be proper. Even with my father there."

"I mean as your wife."

"Wife?" Manus made an explosive sound of disbelief that sounded to Dixon like a jeering laugh.

Dixon blushed all over her face and neck into her hair-line and hung her head. "I thought you liked me."

"I'm sorry. I didn't mean to react like that. You took me by surprise. I do like you," he said, removing his hand. "Very much. But not in that way."

"Do you have a sweetheart in the village?"

"No, I don't."

"What is it then?"

"I'm sorry. I'll help you any way I can with Miss East and Lady Blackshaw, but I can't marry you."

He reached out to take her hand again.

She snatched it back, kept her eyes averted, and stumbled from the room.

Now dry-eyed and purposeful, Dixon went back to the house and made her way along quiet corridors, up staircases and along further corridors to Lady Blackshaw's bedroom in the south wing. All was quiet. It would be an hour before the first servant began early-morning duty.

She thought back to one day recently when she and the girls had followed Teresa into Edwina's room to collect a worn coverlet that needed to be mended. While they were there Teresa pointed to an open ordinary-looking box on the dressing table containing necklaces of diamonds, rubies and emeralds tangled around matching rings and bracelets. Dixon couldn't believe beautiful things like that were jumbled together in such a careless fashion and felt a desire to lift out all the pieces, untangle them, and sort them out. Before she'd had time to touch a single jewel Teresa said with authority it was time to leave and, scooping up the coverlet, led the way out.

Dixon remembered being miffed that Teresa knew all about the jewels and was at home in Edwina's bedroom whereas she, senior in service if not in age, had never seen the jewels or been in the bedroom before.

This morning the wooden box was in its previous position. The pieces of jewellery were on view in the same state they'd been in when she last saw them. With care she extricated a diamond necklace and its matching ring, along with a sapphire bracelet and its matching ring. She slipped them into her pocket, left the room and went back to the nursery to relive the shock of the previous night.

After Miss East and Charlotte escaped, she'd lost control, howling and raging in a fury that she felt was strong enough to kill her, and at the time she wished it had. A young kitchen porter, obviously sent up by Miss East, had almost fallen backwards with fright when he saw her, but waited around long enough for Dr Finn to reassure him that everything was under control and he could leave with a clear conscience.

Dixon relived all the humiliations at the orphanage where she wasn't deemed worthy of an education, good enough only for minding infants, but they were as nothing compared to being publicly declared unfit to do even that by a woman who came from the same part of the world and same stock as herself. Dr Finn, whose kind perceptive gaze unnerved her as she felt he had an ability to see through her mask and read her thoughts and still think well of her, stayed for over an hour to reassure himself she was calm enough to be left alone and there was no fear she would do anything rash. He apologised for treating her roughly and offered to fetch someone to stay with her, but she said she didn't need his help as she would be leaving the Park first thing in the morning and had no intention of returning. In fact, only for it being dark she would leave this very minute.

And now, all those collective humiliations at the orphanage and in the nursery the previous night were as nothing compared to being laughed at by Manus when she offered herself to him as a wife. She felt a stab in her chest when she thought of it, and she thought of it every few seconds.

To distract herself, she picked up the envelope she had earlier thrown at Lily East and opened it. Inside was a letter, written on Blackshaw notepaper like the one Teresa Kelly received before she left. The Blackshaw family crest and address were at the top of the page and it was signed by the steward on behalf of Lord Waldron at the bottom. "It's a reference," Teresa had explained about her own one. "Worth a fortune for the likes of us." She had read out words like 'honest', 'trustworthy', 'hardworking'. She was particularly pleased because, even though she had worked at the Park for only twenty months, the steward had included the long years of devotion to her father to explain the missing years. "What a thoughtful man," she'd said.

Dixon would have to wait until she found someone to read hers to her, but judging by the generous amount of money the steward had enclosed, he was being thoughtful once again.

Marrying Manus had always been her ambition. She wouldn't have wasted eight of the best years of her life in this morgue if she hadn't thought she would overcome Manus's awe of her and claim him in the end. That look of pleasure, intensified during the last two years, that showed on his delighted face every time he saw her and the girls approaching had sustained her hopes and quietened her impatience during all those dreary months.

She couldn't have misread the signs of love.

It was the timing that had wrecked her plans. He felt so guilty about being unaware that Victoria had disappeared when he was so close by, and was so worn out from searching all hours, that he was not his usual self. What had happened that terrible day had knocked all the stuffing out of him. He didn't seem to know what she was talking about, looking at her as if she were making a joke when she proposed marriage to him.

And now time had run out. Betrayed by Charlotte, outsmarted and outmanoeuvred by Miss East. Who would have thought a young girl and an old woman would defeat her in the end?

Soon the Park would be awake and news of her dismissal would spread. Would anyone take her part? Not likely, not with the hold Miss East had over them all. Would Manus keep to himself what had passed between them?

There was little enough to pack. She secured the jewels and money in the lining of her coat, then stamped on the uniforms she had tossed on the floor as a final gesture.

One last look around the large room, then down the three flights of stairs. The dawn chorus accompanied her along the back of the house, passing Miss East's door, then around the house and down the avenue past the stables where she looked straight ahead for fear she might see Manus.

No one saw her as she made her way through Ballybrian to the station and sat waiting for the first train to Dublin. When it came she felt a stirring of relief that it would take her away from here, the backdrop to her embarrassing miscalculations.

Would the young Constable Declan Doyle, who had taken such an obvious shine to her, be sorry for his missed chance when he heard that she was gone?

More to the point, would Manus regret letting her go when he came back to himself and realised how much he had loved her?

Her mind began racing through scenes of returning in triumph to avenge herself on those who had wronged her, but for the moment she must control it and try to concentrate. A young woman travelling on her own needed a protector. What she must do was keep her wits about her and find a gentleman, a companion or a family to attach herself to as soon as possible.

One other thing she needed was a new name. She had already chosen 'Elizabeth'. No more 'Cry Baby' or 'Baby' or 'Nursie' or 'Nurse'. Because of the name on the reference, 'Dixon' couldn't be changed, but she didn't mind that – at least it was a real name. 'Elizabeth' had a ring to it, a seriousness that would match the new image she intended to invent for herself.

Elizabeth Dixon. Not Eliza, or Betty, or Lizzie or Beth Dixon. Elizabeth Dixon. That would do nicely. No one else had bothered to give her a proper name, so, while she was giving herself one, she might as well make it a royally impressive one.

By the time the train to Dublin pulled in an hour later, Elizabeth Dixon was still imagining returning to Tyringham Park, not in her present form as a disgraced nanny, but as something else entirely. What exactly she didn't know yet, but it would be something worthy of her new name. Something to make Manus and Lily East sit up and take notice, and something to send shivers down the spine of that rich brat Charlotte who by then would be older and wouldn't have Lily East's authority and protection to hide behind.

11

London
1917

Arriving in London, Edwina left her maid and luggage at the Officers' Quarters while she met her husband for an allotted ten minutes before he had to dash back to the War Office.

Her chair was too low. Glad of the space between her husband and herself, she concentrated on the brass buttons and medals on his uniform to avoid looking directly at his face.

"Too bad you had to make the trip over, old thing. No way could I be spared. You know that. You received my letter?" Waldron put his pipe on the ashtray and looked at it while he was talking. He made vague circular hand movements.

"Yes. I realised before I received it that you couldn't leave the Office."

"Quite. Well, what brings you here? Has something new come up?" He picked up a pen, checked the ink, and started doodling.

"Nothing, unfortunately." Edwina managed to control the urge to reach over and knock the pen from his hand. "I need your help."

"My help?" He almost looked at her but raised his eyes only as far as her neck. "I didn't think there was anything I could do from a distance. Otherwise I would have done it, of course."

Edwina's face tightened with the effort of holding back a sarcastic rejoinder. To give herself time to collect herself, she took off her coat and turned to drape it on the back of her chair, all the while telling herself she mustn't fall at the first fence.

"I'm sure you would," she said finally, settling back. She waited.

He was concentrating on making short, repetitive movements with his pen and was unaware of her, so she continued to wait.

"Oh, sorry," he said at last. "Where were we?" He stilled his hands. "You wanted my help. What specifically can I do?"

"I want you to find Teresa Kelly for me."

"Can't say I can put a face to the name. Who is she?"

"One of the servants. A girl from the village . . ."

"You know we never employ local people. Those Papists are likely to shoot one in one's bed with the least hint of an uprising. I thought I told you –"

"I know you did, but you can't blame me. If you must blame someone, make it Miss East. She installed Teresa Kelly when I was in Dublin giving birth to Victoria, and I wasn't informed."

"Oh, dear." Waldron poised his pen and adopted an unblinking attentive expression to avoid having to comment on that piece of information. The effort made his eyes smart. "Why do you want to find this particular servant?"

"I think she stole Victoria."

He made a sound as if to speak, but she talked over him.

"As a matter of fact I'm sure she did. I've no evidence but I just know. Call it a mother's instinct."

Waldron made a sound like a snort that turned into a cough. He tapped his chest and took up his pipe for a puff. The coughing stopped. "Works every time," he said as he wiped his mouth.

Earlier, Edwina had noticed the pipe falling sideways, allowing a revolting brown slime to trickle from the mouthpiece. Now that she'd seen him take a mouthful of it, she was glad she hadn't warned him about it.

"What do the police think?" Waldron pulled a face, drank from the glass beside him and made some throat-clearing noises.

"They think Victoria fell into the river and was washed out to sea. They discounted my theory as a mother's wishful thinking." Her voice had a flat quality to it. "But no one knows anything for sure. No one saw anything and nothing was –"

"Quite. I get your point. Why then do you suspect the servant you

53

mentioned?" His hand had found the pen again. He was making such tiny strokes he must have thought he wouldn't be noticed.

"Te-re-sa Ke-lly," she said, drawing out the syllables of the name as if she were talking to someone with limited understanding, "was seen leaving on the same afternoon Victoria disappeared. That's enough in itself to point to her."

"Could be pure coincidence."

"Too much of a coincidence. What are the chances of those two things happening together?"

"That's what a coincidence is." His pen looked as if it was making flourishes.

Edwina took two deep breaths and continued with what she'd rehearsed on the way over: Teresa was forty, had given up hope of having children of her own, was besotted with Victoria and had begun indoor employment at the Park at the same time Victoria was born.

"Another coincidence?" He was colouring with a red pencil, licking the point after each stroke, and making sure he stayed inside the lines. "What does Miss East think? Sound woman. She always knows what's what."

"No point in asking her. She's completely one-eyed. Blames Dixon for everything and thought the sun shone out of Teresa Kelly. Of course they had a lot in common, both old maids who played cards and hankered after children."

"Wouldn't dismiss her opinion out of hand. A rock of sense, that woman." He was now stretching his arm to reach the top right-hand corner of his drawing while trying not to lean over.

"You always favoured –"

"Come in," he ordered, reacting to a tap on the door.

Edwina started – she was fully occupied with her thoughts and hadn't heard the knock. Waldron sat up straight, patted the long strands of hair across his bald patch to make sure they were in position, smoothed his handlebar moustache, and draped one arm over the back of his chair.

A young soldier entered, saluted, handed Waldron an envelope, saluted, turned, looked intently at Edwina for a second and left the room without speaking.

"Nice-looking boy," said Edwina absent-mindedly. "He looks about fourteen."

"He does, doesn't he? Thatcher. Name, not trade. Talented chap. Lucky to have him. Asthmatic – not eligible for active service. More man than boy, actually. He's twenty-five." Waldron made a surreptitious move to choose a green pencil and lick it. "Allergic to horses, unfortunately. Imagine never being able to ride."

"Why are we wasting our time talking about him?" she asked.

Waldron bridled. "Just making conversation. You brought it up." He was stabbing the paper with the pencil. "So what is it you think I can do that you haven't already done?"

"I want you to use your contacts in the army and fisheries and Civil Service –" Waldron's chest expanded and the medals rose two inches.

"– to force them to show you shipping and ferry records. I want you to find out if a middle-aged woman and a young child left Irish shores on the 7th of July or thereabouts. If they went over to the mainland or wherever else."

"That's quite a list."

"I'm sure a man as powerful and influential as you will have no trouble dealing with it."

Waldron was pleased with the compliment. "I'll certainly pull out all the stops. Everything else over there still the same?"

"More or less. We're quiet enough but there have been rumblings since that uprising in Dublin last year. Did you hear much about that over here?"

For the first time since they'd sat down he looked straight at her and smiled. "Hear much about it, did you say? Hear much about it?" He turned to an imaginary audience, both arms raised as if acknowledging applause, then back to her, pausing for greater impact. "The papers were full of it for weeks, but my name wasn't mentioned which was jolly annoying as I had a pivotal part to play." He paused again to make sure she was listening. "I was one of the advisors who recommended the ringleaders be shot."

Edwina sat stony-faced and was not applauding.

He leaned back in his chair. "I haven't given my life to the service of the Empire for nothing. Troublemakers like that have to be shown who's boss early on in the piece. And they were shown. In no uncertain terms." He emphasised his words with three sharp stabs of his pencil, breaking the lead. "A lesson to the rest. Never fails."

Edwina stood up, dropping her handbag on the floor. "Does anyone in Ireland know you were involved?"

"Can't say, actually." Waldron stood, straightened his jacket and came round to the other side of the desk to pick up the handbag and help her with her coat. "But don't see why not. Never made any secret of it. Proud of it, in fact."

She moved away from him on the pretext of looking at the large piece of paper on his desktop and was surprised to see on it, not doodles, but a fully realised drawing of a battle scene featuring horses with stylised twirls for manes and tails, soldiers on horseback complete with helmets, chin-straps, red coats, black boots and spurs, canons and mountains in the distance, and a tangle of bodies on the ground.

"What's this?"

"The Crimean War. My favourite subject."

"May I have it?"

"Of course. Always giving them away." He smiled as he signed it on the bottom right-hand corner. "Getting quite a name for myself." He rolled up the sheet and gave it to her. "About your Teresa Whatshername. I'll set the wheels in motion straight away even though I'm up to my eyes. Pity you didn't tell me earlier." He opened the door for her.

Thatcher, standing to attention outside the door, saluted.

"Thatcher will see you back to my quarters, old thing," said Waldron.

As he escorted them out, Edwina half-turned her head to say something to her husband but stopped when she saw a look pass between him and the young soldier. Could she be mistaken, or had she seen Waldron actually wink at him?

12

Edwina suspected that Waldron made no effort to trace Teresa Kelly. She could picture him, whiskey in hand, one elbow anchored on a mantelpiece in the mess, holding forth to his subordinates about the insignificant concerns that filled the pretty little heads of women, and wasn't it fortunate that men ruled the world, ensuring that wars would be properly fought?

But the visit had not been a complete failure. Edwina had managed to steel herself sufficiently to be able to fulfil her wifely obligations twice.

As her maid helped her settle herself in a railway carriage for the first part of their trip back to Cork, she felt a heaviness lift from her mind, knowing that from this time on she would never, ever have to submit to Waldron's marital ministrations again. That part of her life with him was over. To celebrate she tore up his drawing of the Crimean War and flung the small pieces out the window.

After the month with him, seeing him brought home drunk at least four nights a week between two slightly less inebriated young soldiers, one of whom was always young Thatcher, she asked herself, not for the first time, what had possessed her to marry him in the first place.

She presumed it was a commonly held belief that she had married her husband for his title, money and status, but it wasn't true. She had married him in good faith. It was he who had acted in bad faith – two months after the wedding, deserting her for India. Edwina had presumed he would take her to that country with him, or accept a local posting or retire from the army altogether after his marriage, but he said he didn't know where she'd got that idea from. He'd always intended to go back. It was a pity it was no place for a woman who was not used to a hot climate, but that's where his life's work was, not on the estate, and certainly not in a local regiment that would bore him with its provincial outlook.

Contrary to her expectations, her lot turned out to be a life of solitude, with only servants for company, witnessing the rituals of a large country estate dying out through lack of attention from the absentee landlord.

What would it have been like if she'd married Dirk? She often tormented herself with the question and re-ran the old scenes to look for clues. As the years passed the answer became clearer.

At the age of nineteen Edwina had suspected that she was different from other girls. Her public failure to snare a husband three years in a row when all her set had secured one with ease confirmed her suspicion.

It wasn't as if she wasn't admired. On the contrary, many suitors were drawn to her beauty and social standing, but every approach filled her with anxiety, knowing that each new admirer would soon sense the emptiness and joylessness that had been her companions for as long as she could remember, and turn away to seek a more congenial partner.

For her part, if she found herself initially attracted to one of the young men her own age, the feeling didn't last. She soon found fault with his accent, tone of voice, hair line, gestures, hands, clothes, shape of ears, nose, chin, back of the head, length of neck, posture, height, teeth, laugh, skin, conversation or demeanour, and sometimes all of them if she gave herself time to list them, and he, sensing the depth of her disapproval, would turn away.

When Edwina returned home from her third unsuccessful London season her father Algernon was in an unusually buoyant mood, and didn't even comment that he now had two daughters who had passed unsold through the market despite the generous dowry he had settled on them.

"Come and see this," he said to his wife and daughter before they had time to divest themselves of their hats and coats.

He led them to the schoolroom, which had been turned into a studio during their absence. Two large portraits, one of Edwina's older sister Verity, and one of her father, mesmerised them as soon as they came through the door. Neither woman had time to say she knew nothing about art, to excuse herself in advance if she said the wrong thing, before the power of the images silenced them both.

"Caught my character, wouldn't you say?" beamed Algernon, enjoying the effect the portrait was having on the two women. "And look how the eyes follow you around the room. Go over there and check."

"More than that," said Prudence, his wife. "It has a glow to it."

"How did he get that effect? Look at the shine on the medals and the gold braid. The paint is so thick in parts," Edwina said, leaning forward.

"Don't touch it," her father yelped as her hand reached out. "It's still wet."

"I can see that." But she had been about to touch it. She withdrew her hand and determined to sneak back later when there was no one else around.

"And look at Verity's likeness. Who would have believed it? Well, my dear," he took his wife's hands in his, "you can begin your sitting tomorrow if you're not too exhausted after all your chaperoning responsibilities. It's surprisingly hard work, sitting. And we have to stop Verity from distracting the young genius. I think she's fallen for him. Keeps following him around with her mouth open. Quite amusing, really." He put his arms around the two women, something out of character, but indicative of his exultant mood. "We're frightfully fortunate to procure his services before he becomes too sought after," he laughed, "or too expensive." He gave the women a final squeeze. "You'll meet him tonight."

"He's not dining with us, is he?" Edwina asked. The thought of making conversation with one more male stranger after three seasons of wasted effort filled her with dismay.

"Of course. He's almost one of the family by now. Don't worry, you'll like him. He's well-travelled and well-educated with wide interests and lots of stories to tell. Came highly recommended by the Earl of Hereford, no less."

Edwina groaned inwardly at the prospect of having to suffer a tiresome know-all impressing her father during the interminable mealtimes.

"Artists don't live in the same world as we do," said her father when the clock showed five minutes past eight and the painter's chair across from her stood unoccupied.

How does he know? Edwina sourly asked herself. He's only ever met one.

"The old Earl could tell you stories that would make your hair stand on end. Not about our young man, I hasten to add. Other artists. Older ones. He collects them."

Her back was to the door. She saw her father lift his head and look towards it, and saw his face take on the expression of a man leading his horse into the winner's enclosure on Derby Day. "Ah, there you are."

Mistake Number One, thought Edwina. Being late for dinner.

Verity looked as if her focus had shifted from the mortal to the celestial.

"Lord Byron," said Prudence, following the gaze of her husband, who was by now standing up. She was never one to lower her voice.

"Dirk Armstrong," Algernon announced, ready to introduce his wife and younger daughter.

"Is that his real name?" Edwina whispered to Verity, knowing he was close beside her and would hear what she was saying. She was weary with exasperation and didn't care if she appeared rude.

Dirk thanked the manservant for holding out his chair for him and directed a humorous remark in his direction.

Mistake Number Two. Addressing a servant at the dinner table in another person's house. Edwina looked meaningfully across at Verity, but her sister chose to ignore her glance. Wrong-footing guests was a game they played, the main rule being the guest was to remain unaware of his gaffe while the girls exchanged sly smirks.

Dirk acknowledged the introductions and sat down.

"Yes, it is my real name," he smiled across at Edwina. "Why do you ask?"

"Well, you know . . . Dirk . . . a dagger . . . strong arm . . ."

"What's this?" asked Algernon who hadn't heard Edwina's question. "Nothing important, Father."

Not to be detected playing it, especially by her father whose disapproval she feared, was another rule of the game.

During the meal, Prudence's dread of choking and difficulty with her ill-fitting new false teeth prevented her from speaking while eating, Verity's nearness to Dirk struck her dumb and Edwina's despondency sapped her spirit, so Algernon monopolised his guest with talk of dams, hydro-electric schemes, motor cars and the first heavier-than-air flight that had taken place a few years earlier.

What had happened to the stories of hunting? All her life, until tonight, they had provided the sole topic of conversation at the table.

At one point, Dirk turned to Prudence and asked if she could see herself taking a spin in a motor car.

Mistake Number Three. Directly addressing the lady of the house without first being addressed. Edwina exaggerated a horrified expression, but once again Verity refused to reciprocate.

Mistake Number Four. Not speaking to her. Only once had he looked at her, giving her the kind of indulgent smile one would give an infant or a grandmother.

She left the table feeling strangely disturbed and lonely.

By the time her mother's portrait was completed four weeks later, Edwina noticed that the apathy that had sucked the colour from her life until now was gone, and she hadn't been aware of its passing.

On the due morning when her turn had come she felt sick and asked her father if she could postpone the sittings.

"Under no circumstances," stormed her father. "His reputation is spreading like wildfire, according to the Earl, and if we let him go now we might miss out altogether. Now, no more of your nonsense. If necessary, I'll get a bed brought down for you to lie on."

She bowed as usual to the strong will of her father. "That won't be necessary, Father. I'm feeling a little better already."

With help from her maid, Edwina put on her debutante's gown, fixed her hair in an intricate sculpture, and made her way to the schoolroom where she sank with relief into the gilt high-backed chair that had been chosen by Dirk for its contours and comfort.

When she heard the door open, the air in the room appeared to lighten and brighten.

Dirk scrutinised her for a full ten minutes after their initial greeting, then in silence moved around to view her from different angles. He stood on a ladder, looking down at her, then sat on a low stool, looking up. Closed one curtain, then two. Opened them again. Half closed one. Asked her to stand while he changed the angle of the chair, holding her upper arm. Three times, three different angles. Moved the chair on to the rostrum. Held her hand to guide her. Stood back.

His scrutiny may have been routine to him, but to her it was alarmingly intimate. She had never been unchaperoned in the presence of a young man before.

He came in close – she could smell the honey on his breath – and, guiding her chin, moved her head a little to the left, then realigned her arms and, taking the fingers of her right hand one by one, positioned them on her thigh with a gap between her index and middle fingers. After each adjustment he stepped back to gauge the effect.

When he was satisfied he began to sketch. His gaze remained impersonal.

After a week, at the beginning of each sitting, Edwina tilted her head or placed her right hand slightly off the angle Dirk had shown her on the first day so that he would have to correct them. He didn't hold her chin or her fingers for a second longer than was necessary. Once, while adjusting her gown, his fingers brushed along the top of her breasts but didn't linger. She didn't know if what he had done was appropriate or not, and looked for clues when he returned to the easel. His expression as usual was abstracted and absorbed so she concluded it must be all right. As her father had said, 'Artists are different'.

So as not to bring attention to her ploy, she waited for three days before deliberately pulling down the left neckline so that it sat lower than the right. When he didn't appear to notice the change she felt a sting of disappointment.

"You can close your eyes if you wish until I'm ready to do them," he often said, and she was sorry that the excuse to look at him looking at her was denied her for any period of time.

After each session he would talk to her in a friendly manner. Sometimes, unaware of time passing, they were both late for dinner.

When she could tell from the angle of his gaze that he was painting her lips, and later the shape of her breasts through the silk, she became uneasy and confused and wondered what was happening to her.

After the third week he made fewer brushstrokes, but the thinking and assessing took longer. He wasn't in such a hurry to begin in the mornings. The offer of tea was at last accepted and the two of them shared the ritual, where finally he encouraged her to talk about hunting, and for the first time she put her enthusiasm into words.

She had been sitting for five weeks, a week longer than the others, and was beginning to dread his departure, which must be imminent.

"I'm doing the finishing touches. No need to keep the pose. Relax, but stay in the chair. Could you ever imagine your life without hunting?"

The question surprised her. "I've never thought about it," was her answer, though a more truthful one would have been 'No'.

"Could you ever see yourself throwing in your lot with a poor itinerant artist?"

He was standing motionless, holding his breath, his brush poised in the air.

"What do you mean?"

"I can't in conscience spin out this portrait much longer just to make sure I see you ever day. I need to have some indication of your feelings." Did he mean what she thought he meant? "You must have some idea how I feel about you."

She didn't.

"Sorry, I should have given you warning. While you recover, do you want to see yourself in your finished state?"

He put his hand over her eyes and guided her to the front of the easel. He watched her, knowing she wouldn't be able to disguise her reaction on first view. She burst into tears. He laughed, took her in his arms and held her reassuringly.

"It's not that bad, is it?"

He smelt of linseed oil, turpentine, soap and himself, and she wanted to climb inside his shirt.

"Come on, you have me worried now."

She was loath to lift her face. His chin was resting on top of her head, his arms increasing their pressure and she thought she might faint with desire.

"It's beautiful," she said at last. "You flattered me."

"What you see is what I saw. Don't tell me you don't know you're beautiful?"

Later, Dirk turned the easel around to face the window and swore when he noticed the left hand was slightly out of proportion, looking smaller than the one on the right. Cursing loudly, he took up a palette knife and scraped off the hand in one stroke, exposing the canvas with its burnt sienna underpainting. "Too busy looking at your face," he said to Edwina, and didn't apologise for his outburst.

That means he has to stay on longer, Edwina thought with relief, and she could postpone the frightening prospect of speaking to her father who expected her to marry an earl.

The following day a telegram addressed to him was delivered. His mother was ill and his presence was needed at home.

"Leave your things here and come back to collect them when your mother recovers," she pleaded, inwardly raging at the bad timing.

He thought it more sensible to take everything.

"Can't you wait to speak to my father first?"

He looked at her oddly, told her to say goodbye to the family for him, kissed her long and deep, manoeuvred one heavy bag onto his back and another over his shoulder and, refusing any offer of a lift, walked to the train station in the village two miles away. When he was gone she wished she had at least accompanied him to the end of the avenue. Everything had happened too quickly.

13

That odd look Dirk gave her on his day of departure haunted her for years. Had he spoken to her father the previous night and had the difference between a favoured artist and an aspiring son-in-law been pointed out to him? Her father could cut and wound more deeply than anyone else she knew and she was horrified to think Dirk might have been on the receiving end of an unrestrained mauling. Or had he taken her lack of an immediate enthusiastic response as a 'No', not appreciating the complexity of marriage traditions among the gentry?

Eleven telegrams had come for Dirk during his stay and they were all to do with commissioning work – she knew because she'd read them. Those he dropped carelessly on the table beside the easel, but the last one he had folded and put in his jacket pocket. Was his mother really ill, or had he invented the story to give credibility to his reason for leaving?

At the end of a fortnight she didn't think she would appear too forward if she wrote to him at his home address – after all, if she had said a straight 'Yes' to his proposal, they would be engaged by now. It was a friendly letter – she had her pride and didn't mention love or the future, making sure to ask at length after his mother's health.

She haunted the front hall waiting for an answer, but none came.

Her father didn't mention the scraped-off hand. Did that mean Dirk had arranged with him to return at some time to repaint it? She didn't ask. Her portrait remained propped against the wall after the other three were hung.

She spent long stretches of time in her room crying, or riding her horse too fast and too hard.

Dirk had either lost interest in her, she concluded, or been sensitive to her father's disapproval and for her sake had withdrawn. Or had he taken justifiable offence and decided it wasn't worth the trouble? It's not as if he'd be short of admirers, and why go where he wasn't wanted? Worse than all that, though she couldn't believe it, was the possibility that she was nothing more than a diversion he had made use of while he was in the house. Did he make advances to all his young female sitters? He seemed too genuine for that, but how could she be sure when she knew so little about men of her own class, let alone those of another?

Nothing that happened in the year that followed could raise her spirits. She went over and over in her mind what had been said during the sittings, trying to understand things from Dirk's point of view and castigating herself for her own behaviour. Should she have said or done this or that, or not said or done this or that? Should she do something now?

"I've just the man for you," Algernon said from behind his newspaper the following autumn, a week after she'd turned twenty. "He's ideal. He has 19,000 acres, a mansion, a string of horses, a title and he's your cousin. He's my second cousin, so that would make him your second cousin once removed."

The words 'horses' and 'cousin' made a small ripple in the dark pool of gloom in her mind.

"He called by yesterday when you were out riding and fell in love with you or, to be more precise, your portrait."

He went on to say Major General Lord Waldron Blackshaw had recently inherited his father's title and land, so the onus was on him to find a wife to supply an heir. Before his father's death he had been stationed in India, and was so career-orientated he hadn't felt the need to find a bride. By rights Verity, being the elder, should have been the chosen one, but Waldron wouldn't be deflected from Edwina after he had seen her likeness in the painting. He wasn't even worried that the missing hand might be true to life.

"I've invited him to stay for a month beginning next week, so he and I can talk about old times in India and you can have a good look at him and see what you think. It's only fair to warn you that he thinks there are two things you might find unacceptable, though personally I don't see why you should – both minor compared to all he has to offer. So unimportant they're hardly worth mentioning, but I thought I'd get them out of the way before you meet him."

He's probably an ugly bore, Edwina thought. "What are they?" she asked aloud.

"You might think he's a bit on the old side."

Worse than being an ugly bore, thought Edwina, remembering Dirk's delicious youth. "How old is he?"

"Around my age."

Disgusting. "What's the other thing?"

"His estate is in Ireland."

"*Ireland?*"

"Yes, Ireland. Don't look so shocked. It's only next door. They do speak English over there, you know – well, most of them do by now."

Was this an arranged marriage he was talking about? "Do I have to marry him?" she asked in a small voice.

Her father lowered his newspaper for the first time during the interview and looked directly at her. "Of course not. Just a hope that you two might get on. The best way to keep a fortune in the family is through marriage. And here's your chance – you're both Blackshaws so you won't even have to change your name. My father lost out as a second son, so it would be nice for the wheel to turn full circle. You share a great-great grandfather but, even though you have the same name and come from the same family, his side got the lion's share of the wealth."

The idea had its tempting aspects. A cousin would be more tolerant of her deficiencies as he probably shared them. She would please her father. And then there were the horses . . .

But the only man she wanted was Dirk.

Before her cousin arrived in his role of suitor, she felt she must finally find out if something had happened to Dirk to prevent him from answering her letters. Perhaps, after all, his continuing silence hadn't indicated a loss of interest in her but something else entirely, something perfectly innocent and understandable that would be cleared up as soon as they met face to face, giving her the strength to stand against her father and dismiss her cousin out of hand.

She travelled by train to Dirk's village of Burnstaple and, trying to hide any outward show of nerves, went into a teashop across the street from Armstrong & Son Emporium, the large shop to which she had addressed her letters.

"Just passing through," she said to the friendly middle-aged woman serving her, and went on to ask after Dirk in as casual a manner as she could affect. Wasn't this where a friend of her brother's lived and had the woman by any chance heard of him or his family? The Armstrongs?

The woman smiled. "You mean the good-looking one? The artist? Father owns the shop over there?"

"Oh, I hadn't noticed it. Yes, that's the one I mean."

"I have the pleasure. He was knee-high to a grasshopper when my late husband and I bought this place, and I watched him grow up. Know his mother well. A real lady. Often brings her sisters in here. Had a bad turn last year –"

So it was true.

"– but back in the pink now and very proud of having an artist in the family once they got over the shock of him wanting no part of the shop and him doing so well."

"So he has done well?" Edwina pulled out the chair beside her. "I would be pleased if you would join me."

Impressed by the authority of Edwina's accent if not her years, the woman said, "Don't mind if I do." She fetched herself a pot of tea and sat opposite. "Lovely to take the weight off my feet before the afternoon-tea rush. I've just sent the waitress to collect the clean linen. Now, where were we? Your brother's friend, you said. Is Dirk doing well, you ask? I can tell you this, he would be doing a lot better if people did the decent thing and didn't refuse to pay him . . ."

"Pay him?"

The woman leaned in close and lowered her voice. "Well, his mother doesn't know all the facts and Dirk doesn't like talking about his clients, but his father got it out of him. Well, it was obvious when he returned after six months with little money and he's not a gambler or a drunk or anything and it appears that one old general refused to pay a penny because he said his nose couldn't be that large and purple – but he kept the painting, mind – and then some spoilt daughter or another had a hand missing. Not in real life, mind, but in the painting and the father didn't pay for the whole family as he said the contract wasn't honoured and hadn't Dirk been living off the fat of the land for five months at his expense? Which just goes to prove that people like that know how to keep what they have."

Edwina spilt her tea over her hand.

The woman rushed off to fetch a cloth and a glass of water.

"There, dear," she said, dabbing the red patch with the wet cloth. "That hot tea can give you a nasty scald."

Two ladies came in and she went off to serve them. After she had taken their order and brought them their tea and cream cakes she returned to Edwina and examined the hand.

"That's not too bad. No permanent damage by the look of it. You were lucky the tea had cooled off or you might have been scarred for life." She leaned in again. "To finish my story. Dirk had intended to return to finish painting the hand but after he got the letter he was so disgusted he cut his losses rather than go back there. He had his pride. You were lucky you didn't meet him as he'd spoil you for anyone else and you're too young for that and it wasn't as if he was just handsome but he was good to his family and a man's man into the bargain. He got a girl into trouble –"

Edwina's throat contracted.

"– and I'm not telling secrets out of school as everybody knew. They were married and they're over in Ireland at the moment and he's painting the Duke of some Irish name or other I can't spell or remember and his family, and I hope he has better luck this time now he has responsibilities and will you leave your name and I'll tell his mother your brother was asking after him?"

"Of course." Edwina was finally able to gulp down the tea she had been holding in her mouth. "No need to do that. My brother will be contacting him. As I said, I was just passing through and thought I'd ask. My aunt wanted to commission a portrait, but it looks as if she'll have to wait. It was nice talking to you."

"You too. Mind how you go, and I hope you'll call in again some time."

Was there a knowing look in her eyes? Does she suspect I'm another girl who got into trouble? Edwina, flustered, left with as much dignity as she could command.

Later she wished she'd asked the owner of the teashop the date the wedding had taken place. Could her unanswered letters mean Dirk was already committed to someone else at the time she wrote the first one? Did he take up with his future wife so quickly after leaving her because he thought she didn't love him? Was the lucky woman waiting in the wings, ready to have an 'accident' as soon as possible? Was he wooing the two of them simultaneously?

Had her father's refusal to pay any bearing on the decisions Dirk made after he returned to Burnstaple?

If Waldron were in any way presentable she would marry him. He wouldn't intimidate her, being a cousin, and her father would be proud to welcome him into the family as a son-in-law. As a bonus she might even run into Dirk in Ireland, its being such a small place, and from her secure position as a married aristocrat, find out the details of why he had forsaken her.

Waldron was dignified, mature, interested, quiet and respectful when she first met him. Her mother and father acted as if they had discovered a unique work of art.

"This will amuse you. Your cousin is quite a wit," her father said after the betrothal had been finalised. "When he first saw your portrait he said he hoped he wouldn't ask for the wrong hand in marriage. Isn't that a good one?"

Edwina laughed, gratified that she was responsible for her father's satisfaction in seeing his daughter transformed, by virtue of one decision, from an odd spinster to a woman of significance.

If only she had known then what she knew now. Nine years later she reinterpreted those qualities that had first impressed her, and saw Waldron as nothing better than an arrogant, drunken narcissist. Had she been a bad judge of character back then or had he been a good actor? For the sake of her self-respect, she clung to her belief that he had deliberately misrepresented himself for as long as it took to win her acceptance.

14

Tyringham Park
1917

The long journey was at an end. As Edwina alighted from the train, she focused her mind on the task ahead. In a short while she would be confronting Nurse Dixon, and this time she wouldn't let her out of her sight until she had elicited Teresa Kelly's address from her. She was now convinced Dixon possessed the information but was keeping it a secret out of loyalty to her friend.

Sid was waiting for them at the station. Edwina composed herself so that she wouldn't show too overtly how relieved she was to be on the last stretch for home.

After her month away Edwina was shocked to see the change in Manus. He had lost weight, which he could ill afford to lose, and looked older than his thirty-three years. When he saw her from a distance he raised a hand in greeting but didn't smile.

"The man's heartbroken," said Sid, driving on past the stables. "I don't think he'll ever give up looking for the child. It's killing him."

He'll never leave Tyringham Park now, Edwina thought, and gained comfort in the conviction. Lord Prothero, a County Tipperary breeder aspiring to win the Derby, impressed by Manus's methods of schooling, had been trying to entice him away from the Park for years. Manus had stayed on in his position, despite Waldron's

71

resentment of his reputation and Edwina's attempts to change his mind about methods of training, but there had always been the fear that one day he might tire of them or receive an offer impossible to refuse. Not any more. He and she were forever bound together in guilt. They would always be searching, always regretting.

She remembered how they had looked at one another in dread and then resignation after the initial search had proved fruitless, both thinking it was all over. And then his ride along the banks and no sighting of a little body, and the hope that the infant might be still alive and standing on the bridge together the next day watching the brown water carrying branches with such speed there was no swirling movement in the middle of the river, only a clear, fast run, knowing there would be no hope for a child caught in it.

That was seven weeks ago and they were no wiser now than they had been then.

At the front door Sid took out the luggage.

"Take those to my room, there's a good chap, and then go up to the nursery and send Dixon down to me."

Sid hesitated. "Won't you be resting first, milady?"

"No, I'll be in the library. I've too much on my mind to relax at the moment. And I won't be able to settle until I've seen Dixon."

Whatever threats or bribery were needed, no matter how extreme, she would use to wrest Teresa Kelly's address from her, now that all other options were closed. She wouldn't be as tentative with her as she had been earlier.

Sid seemed to be standing on one foot and continued to hesitate.

"Is there something the matter?" she said finally, turning to face him, but he was gone.

Miss East waited for the summons. She had seen Lady Blackshaw and her maid arriving, and Sid, whom she'd warned to say nothing, carrying in the luggage. If there was to be any unpleasantness she wanted it over as soon as possible. She would welcome a reprimand or a demotion or a fine: anything, as long as Charlotte wasn't taken from her.

Looking after the child had been difficult and tiring, but she hadn't expected it to be easy. For the first two weeks in her care, Charlotte had woken many times during the night, clutching her throat and gasping as if she couldn't catch her breath. A couple of times she jumped from her single bed to Miss East's double as if she were being pursued. If the light in the room had gone she would shake Miss East until she woke to relight the lamp.

To take her mind off her fears, Miss East would repeat in a sing-song voice all they had to do in the morning: checking and supervising the household servants who dusted, polished, laundered, mended, stitched, knitted, scoured, mopped, cleaned and hauled, and the kitchen staff who sliced, baked, steamed, kneaded, preserved, roasted and pickled under the supervision of Cook. By the time the litany was completed, Charlotte was usually calm and fading into sleep.

From the beginning there had been no difficulty with food – stopping her from eating too much was more of a problem. She had to conclude Dixon was starving the child, but to what end? To make her speak or to keep her silent? To what lengths would she have gone if Charlotte hadn't been removed from her care?

The knock came just as she was thinking Lady Blackshaw was delaying the interview until the morning.

"It's not you she's after, it's Nurse Dixon," said Sid. "I done all I could to delay, but she says she's got to talk to Dixon this afternoon."

"You didn't say anything?"

"Not a word."

"Thank you, Sid. I knew I could rely on you." They smiled at one another. There was still an underlying spark between them even though Sid was a happily married man with six sons. "What kind of mood is she in?"

"Pretty good, considering."

"I hate to be the one to ruin it but it has to be done." She took a deep breath. "Wish me luck."

Edwina was standing in the library flicking through *Horse and Hound*. She often boasted that she'd never read a book in her life.

"I thought I told Sid to send in Nurse Dixon, not you," she said when Miss East entered the room.

"So he told me, ma'am. I've come to inform you that Dixon won't be coming in because she's gone, ma'am." Get it over with quickly.

"Gone? Where?"

"I don't know. She refused to tell anyone where she was going."
Not that anyone asked.

Edwina sat down slowly. "What happened?"

"I told her to leave."

"You what? Who gave you the right to do that?"

"You did, ma'am. Putting me in charge before you left."

"I can't believe this. Are you actually telling me you dismissed
Dixon? That she's not here at the Park at this moment?"

"Yes, ma'am, that's what I'm saying. She has left the estate."

"You have managed to surpass yourself. I meant for you to run
the house as you normally do and take messages for me, not exercise
an authority you don't have. When did she leave?"

"The day after you left for London."

"A whole month ago? She could be halfway to Australia by now
to join Teresa Kelly and Victoria and here are we left with no address
and no clues. We wouldn't even know where to start looking for
them. Do you realise what a catastrophe this is? Do you?"

Miss East made no response.

"All the time I was in London, especially when my husband came
up with nothing, I kept saying to myself that at least Dixon knows
Teresa Kelly's address and I'll get it out of her one way or another.
But what's to be done now? She was the last link and now I'll never
be able to find Victoria." Edwina sprang to her feet. "I should never
have left you in charge, you stupid, stupid woman! Have you *any*
idea what you've done? Why didn't you wait for me? What was so
urgent that couldn't wait a month?"

"Charlotte wasn't eating and seemed to be fading away. I thought
Nurse Dixon was withholding food as a punishment."

Edwina snorted. "Is that all? You dismissed her for that?"

"Yes, ma'am."

"And you didn't presume that Dixon had her reasons, and that
Charlotte could do with the loss of a half stone or more? You'll have
to come up with a better explanation than that."

"I judged the situation to be serious and did what I thought was
best."

"Did you indeed? Best for whom?" A nasty look came into
Edwina's eyes. "Dixon always said you wanted to take the children
away from her. She said you suffered from 'child hunger'. The way

she spoke about it one would think it was a medical condition. It looks as if you managed to get your hands on one of them at last by waiting until my back was turned."

"I was thinking only of the child's welfare. Dr Finn agreed with me that there was something seriously wrong with Charlotte and he was anxious on her account."

"Of course you were. Of course he was," Edwina sneered. "What a pair of experts deciding the fate of my child and interfering in the running of the estate! An ignorant country doctor and a frustrated old maid. Of course the quack would back you up after he was fed malicious tales by you. You don't seem to realise what a terrible blow you two ignoramuses have dealt me." A gleam of hatred came into Edwina's eyes. "And while we're on the subject of your superior ways, where did you pick up that affected way of speaking? Anyone would think you were the mistress of the Park rather than one of its lackeys."

Miss East took a step back as if pushed by the force of the malice in Edwina's tone.

"I think I should leave," she said in as mild a tone as she could manage.

"Stay where you are. I'm the one who tells you when you may leave, in case you'd forgotten in my absence."

There was a sound behind Miss East. Charlotte flew through the door, momentarily freezing at the sight of her mother before edging towards Miss East and putting her arm around the housekeeper, burying her face in the folds of the woman's apron.

Edwina looked on with distaste.

Miss East bent down to whisper to Charlotte, who shook her head and clung tighter.

"Stop acting like a baby and come here and shake your mother's hand like a civilised human being," said Edwina.

No one moved. Miss East bent down again and whispered to Charlotte who shook her head more emphatically.

"She's shy," said Miss East to fill the vibrating silence.

"She's what?" Edwina's response was low and clipped, with the 't' on the end of 'what' sounding like a spit. "Shy of her own mother? Miss East, if ever I want an opinion on *my own child*, I'll ask for it, but until then I'd be obliged if you would keep your mouth firmly closed. You've done enough damage with that mouth of yours to last

75

you a lifetime." She advanced on Charlotte and missed catching an arm as the child dodged behind Miss East. "This kind of conduct is not acceptable," she said, retreating. "Dixon would never have allowed her to get away with such wilful behaviour." Edwina's mouth twisted into an ugly shape.

"No, ma'am."

Edwina stared at the pair, considering.

"Very well," she said at last. "Seeing as you two are getting on so well together it would seem a shame to split you up." Her smile was not friendly. "Here it is nearly September and with all the upheaval," (Victoria's disappearance an 'upheaval'? thought Miss East) "I forgot to hire a governess or enrol Charlotte in a prep school for the year. So you can continue to look after her for twelve months, Miss East, on top of all your other duties, and I advise you both to keep well out of my sight for the year."

The reference he gave Nurse Dixon was so glowing it could secure her a position with the Royal family, the steward told Edwina when she asked him about his part in the nanny's dismissal. It was the only practical way he was able to help the poor woman suffering the loss of her charge, and since he had never heard anything negative about her, and since that rock of sense Miss East had been so sympathetic towards her, he thought he had done the right thing in her ladyship's absence, and did she approve? Of course she did, but what she wanted to know was had Dixon left a forwarding address or given any indication where she was going? He had to confess he hadn't seen her personally before she departed, and that all details had been handled by Miss East.

As expected, said Edwina bitterly, and did he have any idea what Dixon's Christian name was? No, he'd never heard it and there was no mention of it in his records. He had used the title 'Nurse' and hoped it would be acceptable to prospective employers.

Reasoning that Dixon, experienced in only one field, would be forced to seek a similar position to the one she'd filled at the Park, Edwina, at considerable expense, placed personal advertisements in *The Irish Times* and the English *Times* and the various periodicals featuring 'Hunting' in the title seeking news of Nurse Dixon's whereabouts.

She questioned a few selected servants, who said they had no idea why Dixon upped and left. One day she was there and the next she was gone without so much as a by-your-leave or word of goodbye, odd behaviour even from her who was so stand-offish. What they did know was that she would have gone to Australia with her only friend Teresa Kelly if she hadn't been in love with Manus, staying on waiting for him to declare himself. Teresa Kelly had told them that personally so it must be true. They didn't know what had happened between Dixon and Manus, though they could see with their own eyes that he wasn't especially interested in her.

Knowing glances passed among them. One bold one dared look up at Edwina's face to see how she was taking this information but saw no change in her expression.

In the end, the servants said, Dixon had left only three weeks after Teresa, so it was all a bit of a waste of time.

A visit to the parish priest proved fruitless. Father O'Flaherty said he had written out the address of the old farmer for Teresa Kelly to give to her but hadn't kept a copy for his records as there didn't seem any point. He couldn't bring the address to mind as it consisted of a few long aboriginal words that didn't lodge in his memory as they were so unfamiliar to him. Teresa Kelly knew where to contact him if she needed further help, which he presumed she wouldn't as she was so happy with the arrangement, so he was sorry but it didn't look as if he would be able to help Her Ladyship. He didn't offer to supply Edwina with Teresa Kelly's address if Teresa did happen to make contact.

There were no replies to the advertisements in the newspapers and periodicals.

Soon after that Edwina wrote to the Australian Embassy in London, outlining all the facts about the abduction, and asked what course of action she should take to secure the return of her daughter.

Dear Lady Blackshaw, came the reply a month later, *we have read your letter with great interest and concern, and have discussed it from all angles. Our conclusions are as follows: whether you treat the case as a felony or as a missing persons case, whether you offer a reward or threaten imprisonment, you are left with an almost insurmountable problem.*

*Presuming the abductors will have adopted false identities,
identification would depend on the circulation of photographs
(which you say you can supply) through the medium of
newspapers and posters. In a vast country such as ours, such
circulation would be patchy and uncertain. Added to this, we
can be equally sure that the abductors will have made every
effort to change their appearance, rendering such identification
tenuous at best. And who is there to identify them if they are
located? If there is no identification, there can be no arrest.*

*Speaking informally and as an Australian, I can only warn
you that if someone in Australia doesn't want to be found, they
won't be found. Even if their entry into the country is
recorded, which may not be the case with all the confusion
created by the war, they could soon lose themselves and assume
false identities, as I said, in a city or the huge expanses of the
outback, and here something else comes into play. The
Australians have a great regard for the underdog and the
underprivileged, and would surround lone women and
children with a protective ring, asking no questions, and never
think of 'dobbing them in', as the saying goes, for either a
reward or a feeling of righteousness.*

*My advice is that you or someone sent by you would have
to travel to Australia and personally initiate a police or a
private search and be on hand to identify the culprits if they are
found, a highly unlikely event, if you want my personal
opinion.*

No, I don't want your personal opinion thank you very much,
Edwina said aloud, not bothering to finish reading the letter. I'll go
to Australia myself. Beatrice will come with me. We'll find them.
Wait and see. Just as soon as the baby is born and I have recovered
sufficiently to show the county what I'm capable of on Sandstorm.
Then I'll go.

15

Tyringham Park
1883

Waldron's mother, who was called a dowager because of her hump rather than her situation, had been in need of a new personal maid at the time Waldron was a young man of twenty-six. Following the Park's tradition of not employing local people, she contacted her clergyman cousin in Yorkshire, as she usually did, to have one sent over from there. Over the years he had supplied staff, mostly orphans, on a regular basis to Tyringham Park, and all had been deemed most satisfactory. The most recent arrival, young Sid Cooper, had proved to be a real godsend.

Her preference for orphans, as well as reflecting well on her philanthropic reputation, suited her because they had no one to speak up for them if their wages were too low or the hours too long. Added to that, there would be no disruption by parental illnesses, where the servant would be summoned home to nurse the afflicted one and then stay on to look after the remaining one.

As luck would have it, according to the Dowager who never tired of exclaiming over the "gratuitous sense of timing" whenever Miss East's name was mentioned in later years, fourteen-year-old Lily East's mother had just died and left her an orphan in need of a position. True, on the day of the funeral Lily East was so poorly she looked as if she would be joining her mother in the grave shortly: she

79

was gaunt and pale, and her hand trembled when she handed the clergyman cousin a cup of tea. He took in the bitten nails, sparse hair, blotchy skin, convulsive tic and her inability to stand for very long. He also noticed the hovering stepfather who kept preventing Lily from speaking to anyone for more than a minute.

When she arrived at Tyringham Park three days later she was in an even worse state. The Dowager, on seeing her, exclaimed in her penetrating voice to the housekeeper "Perfect!" She even clapped her hands. "She'll do very nicely. My blank canvas."

Miss Timmins, the housekeeper, failed to catch Lily as she fell in a dead faint on the Turkish carpet under the Waterford crystal chandelier.

"I thought I'd specified 'healthy'," said the Dowager, lifting her skirts and heading for the door, making a semi-circular movement to avoid the collapsed figure. "Deal with it, Miss Timmins." She left, revising her ideas about employing an English orphan who had no family to come to collect her and look after her, and who might not be well enough for a long time to make the journey back across the water.

Miss Timmins was grateful the Dowager was not in the room when she bent to minister to Lily East and found her skirt and the carpet drenched in blood. Using the end of the girl's black shawl she hurriedly soaked up most of the blood from the dark red carpet, then rang the bell pull and told the maid to get Sid to bring the pony and trap around to the servants' entrance – the new girl was very ill. She lifted her – she was hardly any weight at all, a little wisp of a thing – carried her to her room, wrapped her tightly in a dark blanket, and rushed to the back door of the Park where Sid was already waiting.

"That was quick, God bless you," she said.

"Here, give her to me," said Sid. "What a tiny little thing!" He peered into her face and loved what he saw. "Are you sure she's not dead already?"

"Stop that kind of talk!" Miss Timmins admonished as she seated herself beside Sid. "She might be able to hear you. Hand her over to me now. Straight to the doctor's house, and hope as you've never hoped before that he is at home."

"What's she got?" asked Sid.

"Anaemia."

"I never seen anyone that pale."

"Try to avoid the potholes – she looks as if she could snap in two."

Sid was only sixteen but he handled the pony and trap with accuracy and confidence.

A young man met them at the door and took a minute to convince them he really was Dr Finn, the son of the older version they were expecting. Sid wanted to stay on, but Miss Timmins sent him back.

Five minutes later old Dr Niall Finn arrived out of breath and joined his son in the surgery attached to the house.

They were in there a long time.

The older doctor explained to Miss Timmins later that it had been touch and go but it looked as if the young girl would pull through. Could she notify the parents?

"She has none."

"She's obviously underage, so who is her guardian?"

"The Dowager, I suppose. She employed her as the new maid."

"Well, in that case I'll talk to you instead so we can spare the Dowager. Is that all right by you?"

"I feel responsible for her anyway. It's my job as housekeeper to look after all the indoor staff, and I'd take particular care of one so young and ill."

Lily had had a miscarriage, as Miss Timmins had already guessed, and lost a lot of blood. It would be better not to move her to a Cork or Dublin hospital, as she was too weak to travel. Young Dr John Finn's new wife, who was a nurse, would look after her until she was well enough to go back to the Park. Lily had an infection and would almost definitely be infertile – he would spare her the details. Lily would be told of this when she regained her strength, but there was no need for anyone else ever to know.

"I've already said anaemia."

"That will do as well as anything."

Six weeks later Miss Timmins stood on the Turkish carpet (which she had personally and secretly managed to clean before anyone noticed) and re-introduced Lily, whom the Dowager found difficult to equate with the sickly waif she had met previously, such was the improvement in the orphan's health and appearance. Rather than sending her back to the Park after the initial danger was over, the doctor's wife had insisted on keeping her until she was fully recovered, captivated as much by her personality as moved by her circumstances.

Most people avoided the Dowager because of her constant talking – it was a mystery how she picked up so much gossip when she didn't pause long enough to let anyone break into her flow. She could clear a large space around her with, "Did I ever tell you about the time Lady Crombie met me by chance in Sackville Street?" or "Just listen to this. This will amuse you. I was in London and passing by St Paul's Cathedral when . . ." Even her growing stock of misused words, examples of which were treasured and quoted by those who noticed, were not enough to prevent the silent withdrawal of guests. But since the arrival of her new maid, the Dowager noticed a change. When everyone else had left, Lily was still there, not missing a word. An audience of one, and a maid at that. The Dowager couldn't believe how the young girl's admiration gratified her need for attention. There was something about Lily that appealed to her – her company was agreeable and comforting, and as the years went by, indispensable.

All the chattering was a joy to Lily who had come from a house that, for the last four years with the arrival of her stepfather, had been filled with hostile silence, some of it bought at the cost of tape across her mouth. To the amusement of the staff, she absorbed the vocabulary and cadences of speech of her mistress from hours of captive listening.

Miss Timmins made sure Lily took time off to have meals in the staff kitchen and often came up to collect her. If one waited for the Dowager to pause in her monologues, one could starve to death. Young Sid always looked forward to her arrival and made sure she didn't sit in a draught.

Lily was allowed to borrow books from the library when it was discovered she could read – her father had taught her – and chose Wilkie Collins and Arthur Conan Doyle, as well as accounts of real-life murders, so that she could share them with Miss Timmins. Because Lily had spent four years fantasising how she could dispose of her stepfather, she felt she had something in common with those who had actually done the deed.

Her dearest wish was that Waldron, who was twelve years her

senior, would marry and father some children, and that she would be appointed as nanny to them, but from what the Dowager said he was in love with the army and, besides, had no opportunity to meet suitable young girls in India.

Lily East, four inches taller and a stone heavier, was twenty-four when the Dowager, who had never actually become a dowager as her husband remained alive and her sons unmarried so she was mistress to the end, died of a heart attack, not from jaw fatigue as her neighbours had predicted. His Lordship personally thanked Lily for being so good to his wife and promoted her to be Miss Timmins's apprentice, as the dear old housekeeper was getting on in years and wasn't really up to the job. Both women were more than pleased with the arrangement, though every now and then there was a dip in efficiency as they became too absorbed in discussing a hand of cards or the latest Sherlock Holmes mystery.

When Lily was thirty, just before the beginning of the twentieth century, Miss Timmins died and Lily became head housekeeper. The indoor staff were pleased that no one had been imported for the position – they were used to Miss East, as she was now addressed, and liked working for her.

Years earlier Sid had wanted to marry her but she refused, saying she preferred to stay free and single. She didn't tell him it was because she couldn't have children – he was such a good man he would have married her in spite of it, but she didn't want the sacrifice weighing on her conscience. He eventually married Kate, one of the younger maids, and they moved to a cottage on the estate. Miss East was asked to stand as godmother to their first child, and when her eyes caught Sid's across the baptismal font and she saw his proud expression, she knew she had done the right thing to refuse him.

Waldron was fifty when his father died and he inherited the title and the estate. Within a year he had brought back to the Park his twenty-year-old cousin, Lady Blackshaw, as a bride. Miss East looked forward to the life of the Park continuing – hunts, balls, weekend guests, tennis and shooting parties, but to everyone's unhappy surprise, Waldron abandoned his young pregnant wife, saying she would be in good hands with Miss East as housekeeper, and went back to India, talking about duty to the Empire.

16

Tyringham Park
1917

"Will she come back?" Charlotte asked, standing shivering beside Miss East's bed in the middle of the night. Miss East, too sleepy at first to register that Charlotte was speaking for the first time since Victoria's disappearance, lifted up the bedclothes, allowing the child to jump in and snuggle up to her.

"Did you have a bad dream?"

Charlotte nodded, her wide eyes shining in the near darkness.

"Did you dream she came back?"

Charlotte nodded.

"Will you tell me about it?"

Charlotte shook her head.

"I don't think we'll ever see her again," Miss East said after a while when Charlotte kept her silence. "Which is just as well. The nerve of her, saying you told tales about her when I know for a fact you didn't. And pulling your hair the way she did. That was dreadful. There's just a tiny chance she might come back to see your mother, but she won't come anywhere near you, I can promise you that. She will never, ever, ever be in the same room with you ever again. Now close your eyes and think of Mandrake asleep in his stall."

Charlotte's body relaxed and minutes later her breathing became slow and regular. Miss East waited for a few minutes before extricating her arm and moving away from Charlotte so that the little girl wouldn't become overheated and wake up again.

"Your father would be delighted to see this drawing," Miss East said the next day as she picked up Charlotte's latest discarded sketch of a horse. "It's the sort of thing he does himself. He'll be pleased to know you've taken after him. We must go up to the nursery and collect all the ones you did there so we can send them to him."

"There's none there. Nurse Dixon burnt them all."

"Oh, dear. That's a pity."

Charlotte shrugged her shoulders to show she didn't care. "I can do plenty more," she said, picking up a fresh page.

Miss East sat at the table working out the next month's roster while Charlotte stood beside her, filling the page with studies of horses viewed from different angles. Every now and then the two would look up from their work and smile at one another.

When Charlotte had asked one day if she could stay with Miss East forever, and become her daughter, the childless woman was given a glimpse of the joy that had been denied her. She cursed her stepfather. If the Lord wanted to forgive, let Him, but she never would.

"You know there are no such things as witches," said Miss East that night after she finished telling a story in which Charlotte featured as the heroine who outsmarted a nasty witch, a theme repeated each night with slight variations. "Despite what Nurse Dixon used to say. They are made up to frighten children into doing what they're told and to make stories more interesting."

Charlotte thought for a while and asked in a small voice, "What about curses?"

Miss East was immediately alert. She had been preparing to bring up this topic for some time.

"No one can put a curse on you because it's not possible," she said, choosing her words carefully. "Mind what I say. Nurse Dixon can't make anything bad happen to Mandrake just by saying it. It's not possible because she doesn't have any special powers. Nothing bad is going to happen to me, and nothing bad is going to happen to you, so you must put Dixon's curse out of your mind and not worry about it again. What she was doing was trying to scare you into keeping a secret."

The trusting look on Charlotte's face changed quickly to one of suspicion, and she moved away from Miss East's side.

"What you have to concentrate on instead," Miss East said as if she hadn't noticed the reaction, "is the one great thing you were put on this earth to do, and knowing you, it will be something wonderful and remarkable."

Later, when Charlotte was sleeping, an unsettling thought came into Lily East's mind. When Charlotte had asked, the night before, "Will she be coming back?" could it have been Victoria she was referring to and not Nurse Dixon?

17

Passage to Australia
1917

On the ferry Elizabeth Dixon had targeted a clergyman who, within a fortnight, put her under the patronage of a benefactor who was travelling to Australia. As soon as Dixon heard the word 'Australia' she felt that destiny had stepped in and was being kind to her for once. Here was her chance to be reunited with her only friend, Teresa Kelly.

Mrs Sinclair, recently widowed, was emigrating to live with her daughter Norma, whom she hadn't seen for eleven years, and Norma's husband Jim – "He's loaded with money, so my daughter tells me. I'll soon be able to see for myself."

Although Dixon had vowed never again to take on the role of carer, she made an exception for Mrs Sinclair because of her rich son-in-law and her level of fitness and health. There was little likelihood she would become a burden during the two-month voyage. The fact that the old lady would organise her travel documents and pay her fare as part of the arrangement (courtesy of the rich son-in-law) made Dixon think her luck really was turning at last.

"It's not as if I need a companion," Mrs Sinclair continued, "but it was either get one or have Norma come over to collect me. The way my daughter's carrying on, you'd think I was in my dotage. I'm a long way from that, I can tell you, but she insisted, so I gave in for peace's sake. I think she's afraid I might get lost and she'll never see me again. But look at you. A beautiful young woman like you should have a lot more interesting offers than mine. If my daughter could snare herself a rich husband there's no reason why you shouldn't be able to." What a tactless thing to say, she thought, as soon as she'd said it, knowing that Elizabeth Dixon could be one of the millions of women facing a manless future because of the war.

What would she think of me if she knew I couldn't even snare myself a poor one? Dixon wondered. She put her hand wearing the diamond ring up to her forehead in a gesture of grief. "My fiancé died in the trenches," she said, squeezing out a genuine tear by thinking of Manus. "His family didn't think I were good enough for him," she added, sensing that the jewellery and her new good-quality clothes were at odds with her accent and limited use of words, "so they shoved me out on the street as soon as they heard and I never seen them again after that."

"Oh, dear," said Mrs Sinclair, commenting on Dixon's grammar as much as the pathos inherent in her explanation.

"So it's lucky I can start a new life and be able to visit a friend of mine at the same time."

"And lucky for me that you came along when you did. Where did your friend settle?"

"Putharra. It's in the outback. Don't know where exactly."

"We'll find out as soon as we get there." Handing back the reference the steward had written on Tyringham Park stationery, Mrs Sinclair asked, "Was it the son of the Park who was killed?"

Dixon nodded, looking too overcome to speak.

Two days into the voyage Mrs Sinclair asked Dixon to read to her, as she needed to give her eyes a rest from the glare reflecting off the sea. She took out a slender volume from inside the pages of a thick book and handed it over with a grin, turning the thick book over on her lap with the title showing.

"It's not that I'm ashamed of reading penny dreadfuls," she whispered in a conspiratorial tone, "it's just that I like people to think I'm reading *War and Peace*."

"I can't read to you," said Dixon. "I can't read at all."

There, she'd said it. It was the first time she had admitted to anyone she couldn't read before they had a chance to find out for themselves. She didn't feel she had the energy to make up two months of excuses as to why she couldn't read at a particular moment.

"Oh. Well, never mind. We'll have a game of cards to pass the time."

She couldn't play cards either.

Mrs Sinclair laughed and the volume of her laughter increased when Dixon confessed, on being questioned, that she couldn't draw, sing, knit, sew, embroider, ride, swim, dance or play chess or a musical instrument.

"Some companion you've turned out to be," the old lady convulsed as the list lengthened. "You must be the most unaccomplished young woman I've ever met."

Dixon looked as if she didn't appreciate being the object of ridicule.

"Sorry about that," Mrs Sinclair said at last, wiping the tears from her cheeks. "At least you're easy on the eye and know how to dress. That's much more important." She looked along the deck. "Especially to those men who have picked this spot to walk up and down all day. It can't be me or *War and Peace* they're interested in."

"They're disgusting," Dixon shuddered. "They've all got bits missing. I wish they'd go and drag themselves around somewhere else."

Mrs Sinclair was taken aback at Dixon's comments but reasoned that Dixon had every right to be bitter and didn't chide her for her lack of sympathy. At least these men were going home, whereas she, poor girl, would never see her beloved's face again.

Oblivious to Mrs Sinclair's reaction, Dixon surveyed the deck. There were other cases being wheeled around by nurses. Fortunately they had rugs covering up their mutilations. It was whispered there were even worse cases, the sight of which would make women faint, too hideous to be seen in public, being cared for in the privacy of their cabins. Dixon was aware that if she had wanted to travel to Australia under her own steam, and if she hadn't had the good fortune to meet Mrs Sinclair, she would be reduced to changing dressings and spoon-feeding cripples such as these to pay for her passage. My luck has definitely turned, she thought as she watched the shuffling soldiers trying not to look as if they were staring at her as they limped by. Even securing a berth at all had been lucky. On the ship's return trip there would be no room for civilians, she had heard. All the berths would be taken by a fresh batch of volunteers, newly turned eighteen, and veterans patched up sufficiently to be judged fit enough to fight again.

Next morning Mrs Sinclair announced to the subdued Dixon that she would personally teach her to read, write, add, subtract, multiply and divide.

Dixon looked stunned. "Why would you do that for me?"

"To honour your brave fiancé who gave his life for our country. I consider it my patriotic duty."

"You're too kind," said Dixon, using one of Lady Blackshaw's phrases, but meaning it.

"Not a bit of it. If he had lived you wouldn't be cast adrift as you are now, forced to earn your own living with so little preparation. You'd be living in the lap of luxury. Besides, I'll enjoy the challenge. It will shorten the journey. I just know you'll catch on in no time. I'm going to do a Pygmalion on you, and for your first lesson I'll explain what that means."

By the time the eight-week voyage was coming to an end, Dixon was devouring the romantic novels faster than the admiring Mrs Sinclair could supply them.

She thrilled to the story of the mousy heroine with the good heart and shabby furniture who thought the stern, hawk-eyed hero – tall, rich, masterful, pursued by a beautiful fair-haired heiress with social connections – didn't think much of her (as she confided to the friendly, adoring boy next door) only to discover he had seen her true worth right from the beginning, noting the shabby furniture as a sign of integrity and sound values.

She thought of Teresa when she read about the city girl travelling to Africa where the square-jawed, rich farmer was contemptuous of her city ways until he saw her true worth when, cut off by flood-waters, she had to nurse him after he broke a leg.

There was something unsettling in all the stories, but she couldn't work out what it was. She kept reading.

It didn't take Norma and Jim Rossiter long to persuade Elizabeth Dixon to stay on with them as Mrs Sinclair's companion. Her reading was coming along at such a thrilling pace she didn't want to stop now. Meeting up with Teresa Kelly could wait a few months.

"You know Putharra's at the back of Bourke," said Jim. "The crows fly backwards out there."

Norma didn't wait for him to explain that tired expression. "More to the point," she said, keen not to have her life's routine interrupted by her mother, much as she loved her, "you don't look like the type who'd want to shrivel up in that heat. You'd be wasting your sweetness on the desert air, as the poem says. Besides, you'll never make it that far with no direct train line and the tough petrol restrictions, isn't that right, Jim?"

Jim agreed that it was.

"Why don't you write to her and tell her you are being well looked after and that you hope she can visit you. She's probably dying for an excuse to make a trip to the city. Who wouldn't, living out there in the middle of nowhere with nothing but dust and flies? Does that sound like a good idea to you?"

It sounded perfect to Dixon.

"There's only one problem. Jim and I work long hours and eat most of our meals out, either at the hotel or at social functions. We have to go to every dogfight in the city to make contacts. Can you cook?"

"No, I never learnt," said Dixon.

Mrs Sinclair erupted in laughter. "Forgot to ask you that one, Elizabeth."

"What's the joke?" asked Norma.

"Nothing important," said Mrs Sinclair, giving Dixon the hint of a wink. "Let's think about things for a bit. We'll come up with something."

She had the answer before the day was out. Along with some prime real estate on the north shore of Sydney, Jim had inherited two large city-centre hotels and had just acquired a third, the Waratah. It was run down and further out of town than the other two, but near a train stop. Mrs Sinclair offered to work there, doing the accounts – she would die of boredom playing ladies in an empty house – and training Dixon at the same time. All her married life she had done her husband's books and knew she had a facility with numbers.

"I'm not ready to be put out to pasture yet. I might be sixty-two but I feel like a spring chicken."

Jim and Norma liked the idea. They could continue their hectic lives exactly as before and Mrs Sinclair, rather than being the liability they expected, had turned herself into an asset.

"One small proviso," said Jim. "I'd like Elizabeth to sit at the front desk and act as receptionist. A lot of commercial travellers use the place."

Mrs Sinclair took Dixon with her to the bank. Funds sent from England had arrived, she was glad to discover. It gave her a feeling of independence to have her own money. When the proceeds from the sale of her house came through she would consider herself comfortably off, so that if things didn't work out with Norma and Jim, she would be able to look after herself. While they were there she opened an account for Dixon.

"We'll start with a guinea, just to impress the teller. My gift to you for giving me so many good laughs."

Not intentionally, Dixon thought sourly, but smiled to pretend she didn't mind.

She signed her new full name, Elizabeth Dixon, and felt a positive shift in the way she thought about herself.

"Every week, put some of your wages in that account," Mrs Sinclair instructed. "It's called a 'running away from home' fund, but seeing you've already run away, you can call it a 'running back home' account."

"Good idea," said Dixon. "I'll do that." A 'being reunited with Manus and getting my own back on my enemies' account would be a more accurate name for it, Dixon thought, tucking the bank slip into her bag.

Mrs Sinclair's first impression of the Waratah Hotel was that the men's bar with its tin chairs and tiled walls and floor was no proper place for a woman so, with Jim's approval, she had the large space beside the office fitted out with a carpet and comfortable armchairs.

Mrs Sinclair fussed over any woman who came to stay, especially those on their first trip, afraid of the pickpockets and confidence tricksters they had been told populated the city. She gave them so much help and information they felt confident setting out to find their way around. Wives of businessmen, Royal Easter Show spectators, women on their own, and those who came to see medical specialists, were all treated as if they were personal friends.

Dixon watched, listened and learned.

In the Ladies' Parlour, women put up their aching feet, drank tea or sherry, discussed the specialists' diagnoses, showed off their purchases, read, exchanged addresses, forged friendships, and wondered about the private lives of the friendly Englishwoman and her good-looking assistant who wore a diamond engagement ring. They returned to their homes full of praise for the Waratah and the city where they hadn't met one pickpocket or confidence trickster.

"One more thing," said Mrs Sinclair, guiding Dixon into a bookshop. In the classics section she took out *Middlemarch* and *Great Expectations* and measured them for size. "This one will do nicely," she said, choosing *Middlemarch* and taking it and a dozen penny dreadfuls to the cashier and paying for them.

Outside the door she tore the middle 200 pages out of *Middlemarch* and inserted one of the romances into the space. It fitted exactly.

"No one will ever know," she grinned. "And it will do your image a power of good, not that it really needs it. Now we should have time to read one of these each . . ." She looked at *Devil Lover* and *Turbulent Heart* before choosing one and handing Dixon the other, "before we have to face those boring old numbers again. And don't show me up by finishing before I do." She smiled fondly at Dixon. "Are you sure you weren't able to read all along?"

Dixon's writing hadn't kept pace with her reading, so after two months Mrs Sinclair helped her write a letter to Teresa Kelly at the remembered address. There was no mention of Tyringham Park – she would stay quiet about what had happened there to give herself time to censor the parts she didn't want Teresa to hear about, especially Miss East's dismissal of her and Manus's rejection of her marriage proposal. After a week she watched for the mail each morning, curious to know how surprised Teresa had been to hear from her, how she was coping with her old husband and older mother-in-law, and if there was a baby on the way.

The reply, when it came, was not what Dixon expected. Written across the top of the envelope was '*Return to sender. Never at this address.*' The word '*Never*' was underlined three times with strokes of the pen so firm that they had torn the paper. The place where the word 'Mrs' had been was scratched out, leaving a hole and messy blots.

"There's a story there," said Mrs Sinclair when she saw it, "and I don't think it has a happy ending for your friend. This was done by a very angry hand. Was your friend especially ugly?"

"Not at all. What gave you that idea? She was attractive for her age with fine skin that made her look ten years younger. Any old farmer would be lucky to get her."

"Well, this one wasn't, for whatever reason," Mrs Sinclair said, examining the envelope in more detail as if it would yield an explanation.

How would one set about tracing someone with no known address in a country as vast as Australia? Dixon berated herself for not thinking to memorise the address of Teresa's friend here as a back-up, but at the time they didn't think there would be any need of one, so keen were both parties on the original plan.

"Perhaps she changed her mind after she left you, and stayed in Ireland," Mrs Sinclair said. "Sometimes the simplest explanations are the correct ones."

18

Tyringham Park
1918

When their youngest boy was twelve, Sid's wife Kate died at the age of forty-four giving birth to their seventh child and first daughter. There had been a lot of joking about the lengths people would go to have a seventh son, especially as Sid was a seventh son, and how they wouldn't be able to control the crowds finding their way to the Park when the time came for the young one to practise his gifts of healing and prophecy.

Kate had been alone when the baby arrived four weeks early. Sid was in the workshop, realigning a coach wheel that had hit a rock and buckled. The older boys no longer lived at home: two had emigrated to America, one was away at the war and two in Dublin worked as apprentices, leaving only Keith, the youngest, who was in the back fields shooting rabbits at the time.

Sid arrived home to find his Kate without any signs of life, lying on the kitchen floor. In her arms was the longed-for daughter, wrapped in a blanket, crying but warm and unharmed. Typical of her to attend to the baby even though she must have been in a dreadful state. Kate had left it too late to look for help. A dinted copper pot and bent ladle were found beside the open back door. No one had responded to the banging. Sid tormented himself remembering how he thought he'd heard a faint echo when he was straightening out the

95

wheel with a sledgehammer and how he'd dismissed the idea as fanciful. It broke his heart to think he could have been alerted to the significance of that sound if he'd stopped to listen for even a minute.

One of the women from the village who had a week-old son took the child, called Catherine after her mother, and cared for her in her own home.

Lily East visited Sid to offer her condolences, and attended the funeral in the small church in the grounds, as did everyone on the estate and so many villagers that a large number had to remain outside in the churchyard during the service.

When Sid returned to work, Lily visited him often for the morning tea break in his workshop but not his cottage as she didn't want to create a scandal.

"That's a laugh," said Sid when she explained why she didn't go near the cottage. "Who'd be looking at two old ones like us?"

"You can't be too careful. I don't want to dishonour the memory of dear Kate." She wondered if anyone remembered that she and Sid had had a five-year romance after she'd arrived at the Park. Probably not. Back then, she and Sid had been the youngest employees, and now they were the oldest.

"It's good of you to take the time. I like to talk about Kate and you're a good listener. You're so peaceful."

Lily let out a burst of laughter. "Not always. I can get riled at times."

"True enough. Like the time last year you gave Nurse Dixon her marching orders the minute Her Ladyship's back were turned."

"Oh dear. Did it look as obvious as that?"

"Only to me and I never talked about it. I seen the way she give Charlotte a hard time so I were glad you done it. My Kate used to worry about Charlotte having that unhappy little face all the time. She's a new girl since you took her on."

"I'm glad to hear you say that. I think she's blossoming nicely. Though slowly."

"It do take time." Sid's voice faltered, and Miss East took the cup out of his hand as the tea was sloshing into the saucer.

"You never said a truer thing," she said.

Six months after Kate's death, Lily asked Sid to her rooms for afternoon tea, and he wondered what was serious enough for her to want to talk about that she would issue such an unusual invitation, so aware was she of propriety at all times.

Instead of the expected tea, Lily gave him a whiskey and poured herself a sherry.

Sid glanced around the room. "You keep it nice," he said. "Real homey."

"If the offer is still open, Sid, I accept," said Lily.

Sid looked bewildered. "What offer's that then, Lily?"

"Marriage, of course. You haven't made me any other offers."

"That were a long time ago, and I were greatly upset when you refused me then."

"Me, too. But things turned out for the best, didn't they?"

"Not for you, I don't think, with no husband or child to call your own."

"I've had employment and peace of mind and friendship. Can't complain about that. That's more than a lot of people have. No need to ask about you."

"Kate were the best wife a man could have, and the boys are a credit to their mother."

"And their father."

"Their mother mostly. I were working all hours. I see so little of Catherine I can't believe she's mine. And every time I look at her I see her mother." He took a long sip. "That's not true, neither. With only Keith in the cottage now I sometimes wonder did it all happen. Everything is fading, like a dream. Sometimes I think I'm going off me head." He took a longer gulp. "I would love to marry you, Lily. I loved you from the first time I seen you, when I carried you into the doctor's and was afraid you was dead. And you was only fourteen years of age. But why would you marry me now when you wouldn't marry me then? Do you feel sorry for me?" He looked up. "Is it Catherine? Everyone knows you love children and always wanted to be a nanny."

"No, it's not Catherine, though I'm aware if we marry you can have her back living with you. And it's not pity. I dearly wanted to marry you back then."

"But you said you'd never marry anyone."

"And I didn't."

"Then why . . . ?"

"Because I knew early on I could never have children because of some early illness, and I didn't want you to be without because of me."

"You should have said. I would have married you anyway."

"I knew that. That's why I didn't tell you. And I'm glad. Look at you now with six fine sons and a daughter and you wouldn't be without them."

He nodded slowly. "I wouldn't. And much as I loved you then, I wouldn't be without those years with Kate."

"Then I did make the right decision."

"Who knows about these things? I put you out of my mind for all them years, but I liked the fact you was around. I wonder did I love the two of you at the same time?"

It was agreed they'd wait for the year out of respect for Kate's memory.

"What about Charlotte? She'll miss you something awful if you leave her now."

"I've thought long and hard about her, but really she'll be leaving me, not the other way around. She's off to boarding school next month when she turns ten and they only come home as visitors after that. And during holidays she'll be staying in the Dublin house or with friends from school. If she needed me, I'd never desert her, but my responsibilities are nearly over. And it's not as if I'll be leaving the estate – she can still come and visit me in your cottage, Sid, now that I know the offer's still open."

"As if there were ever any doubt about that, Lily," said Sid, "though I think you're doing this for the sake of little Catherine."

"Believe me, Sid. I'm doing this just for you and me," said Lily, and when he looked into her face, he knew it to be true.

19

Lady Beatrice had disliked Waldron all through the years they were growing up on neighbouring estates, and often said she would pity the poor girl who was unfortunate enough to marry the drunken popinjay. After he introduced his young English bride to the Park, Beatrice determined to befriend Edwina, and when he returned to India she made a special point of keeping a motherly eye on the deserted stranger.

At the time Victoria went missing, Beatrice and her husband Bertie had been in England searching the military hospitals for one of their sons. They had not been officially informed, but rumour had reached them that someone recognised the young man on the boat bringing back the wounded from France and that he was suffering from memory loss. They hadn't found him. One of their other sons had been killed in action and the third was still on active duty. They had come back to see if they could find any additional information on their side of the water before returning to England to resume their search.

As soon as Beatrice heard about Victoria's disappearance, she put her own sorrows to the side and went to the Park to spend as much time as she could with Edwina to make up for not being available when she was needed. Their friendship was now consolidated by their shared experience of living in the shadow of their missing children.

Edwina welcomed Beatrice's restful company, and didn't want to talk to anyone else. She asked Beatrice to deal with people who called in to enquire after her health, while she went into an adjacent room, sometimes moving away and sometimes listening in.

The day Lady Wentworth called was one of the days she decided to eavesdrop so she left the door between the two rooms slightly ajar.

"She doesn't intend to leave the house until after the confinement. Won't drive past the stables or go anywhere near the river."

Beatrice spoke in what she thought was a whisper, but her imperious tone carried beyond the room. Lady Wentworth's voice, in contrast, was inaudible beyond three feet, and she was facing away from the door, so the conversation Edwina heard was one-sided.

"Quite understandable," Beatrice continued, her voice saturated with sympathy. "Yes, under the circumstances . . . Quite low . . . Poor little Victoria, of course . . . Perhaps she'll have a boy this time . . . Life goes on . . . Yes, yes . . . Exactly. Wonderful rider . . . *wonderful* . . . Yes, Bertie thinks so, too. Perfect hands, perfect seat . . . Couldn't agree with you more. We're privileged to have her in our county. One doesn't often see excellence like that."

Edwina flushed with pleasure to hear herself so described by people whose opinion she respected. A wonderful rider. That was the pinnacle of her life's ambition, to be regarded as such. Did Beatrice and her husband Bertie belong to the school of thought that eschewed praise as detrimental to character building? A pity, as it would have meant so much to hear it from them directly. It gave her goose bumps to think she would have missed hearing it if she hadn't made the effort to hover near the door.

"I'll see you on Thursday to give you more details," Beatrice concluded. "Yes, I'll pass them on to her. Thank you for calling. I'm sure Edwina will be in contact with you when she's feeling better . . . Yes, I'll make sure to tell her. Goodbye, dear."

Edwina moved to a third room so Beatrice wouldn't realise she had been listening.

"She sends you her best wishes. Will drop you a note," Beatrice said when she located her, before gathering her hat and gloves – she hadn't taken off her coat because of the cold in the room. "Bertie will be wondering what's keeping me. Now if there's anything you want . . . ?"

"You've done more than enough," Edwina said with feeling.

Beatrice's departure left Edwina more deflated than she had been earlier, something she didn't think possible. After the initial delight in hearing the compliment about her riding excellence, her despondency resurfaced at the thought that it would be a whole year before she would be able to dazzle the county with a demonstration of it, and how on earth was she to fill in the long days between now and then?

20

Edwina wandered from room to room, not looking at anything in particular, filling in time. Seven more hours until she could retire – any earlier and she would wake long before dawn, unable to control the maelstrom of regret that during daylight hours she was able to repress.

Without her daily stint at the stables she was left with what was, ironically, considering the state she was in, a feeling of hollowness. Whoever first named this section of a woman's life 'confinement' couldn't have chosen a more accurate word.

She found herself facing the corridor leading to the billiard room, a male domain she had seen once during her initial tour of the house after she'd arrived as a bride. She hadn't had the inclination since to view it again. She moved down the corridor. Along the inner wall were oil paintings featuring lots of fruit, especially grapes with the bloom still on them, arranged around silver goblets, joints of meat and dead creatures. They looked so real she felt as if she could taste the grapes, and touch the skin, fur, feathers and scales of the foxes, rabbits, pheasants and fish. She hadn't noticed them before and wished she hadn't now, as the sight of all that food exacerbated her morning sickness.

Twenty yards short of the billiard room was an ornately carved oak door, which was the entrance to the tower she had visited once during that introductory tour and hadn't seen since. At the time she thought it was the defining thing, apart from the horses, that assured her she had made a superior match, but because the marriage had soured so early on, it had lost its appeal. Now, to fill in a few minutes of this endless day, she decided to visit it for a second time. The thickness of the door, the grating noise of the hinges, the cobwebs, dull light and narrowness of the stairs reminded her of a fairy-story illustration that, as a child, promised magic and secrets. She felt a slight lift of spirits as she ascended the stairs.

The room at the top was bare except for a pile of books, a broken table, chewed-up paper, a tea chest and a telescope on a sailor's chair, all covered in dust except for the last two items which had only a light film over them.

She looked through the narrow window. To her left she could see the avenue emerge from the beech trees and curve up towards the house and in the distance she could see the stables. In the practice yard at the back of the stables a small group was assembled. Mandrake and Manus could be identified from their outlines, but she couldn't make out who the other two figures were.

She picked up the telescope. Was it Waldron who had left it there, she wondered? He wasn't a bird watcher, as far as she knew, and she couldn't think of anything else he'd be interested in that would necessitate its use. She tore some pages from one of the leather-bound books on the floor to wipe the dust from the chair seat before settling, leaning her elbows on the window ledge to keep her arms steady, and focused on the group in the yard for a long time.

"I can't believe this," she said aloud at last. "When did she become so accomplished?"

Charlotte on Mandrake was showing a skill Edwina didn't know she possessed. Manus was supervising, and Miss East was watching, clapping at intervals.

Edwina's heart rate increased as she studied the dynamics of the little group.

She had expressly ordered Manus to let one of the lads tutor Charlotte, and not waste his time doing it himself. Had he been instructing her all those years for her daily hour while Edwina was having lunch? Had he expanded that hour? What was Miss East doing down there neglecting her duties? When she had put Charlotte in the housekeeper's care in a moment of fury she didn't mean for her to actually look after her; she expected Charlotte to drag around behind her all day whining and whingeing until Miss East could stand it no longer.

The next day, rather than taking the usual two hours to summon up the energy to move, Edwina rose immediately on waking and was at her station in the tower within thirty minutes.

At around ten Manus appeared in the exercise yard on Sandstorm. The oldest stable lad, Archie, built up all the jumps to a higher level and Manus eased Sandstorm over them, smoothly and calmly. She had expressly told Manus that Sandstorm was not to be tamed while she was housebound, only exercised and fed, and she had instructed Les, the middle lad, to do it, not Manus, as she knew Manus would ignore her wishes and do whatever he was going to do in the first place, and here was proof of it before her eyes.

It was all right for Beatrice to want a Manus-trained hunter – at her age she needed a foolproof mount – but Edwina was half Beatrice's age and what she wanted was wildness and unpredictability.

She and Manus could never agree on training methods, but this flagrant disobeying of her orders was beyond endurance. Fear was the best teacher, she was convinced. "Break a horse's will and it will obey one for life!" she had shouted at Manus one day after she'd lost patience with him. Manus had turned his face away from her after she'd said that, sadly shaking his head.

She had a good mind to march down to the stables this minute and set him straight with commands that he couldn't deliberately misinterpret or ignore.

She often had a good mind to do something with Manus, like putting him in his place. But what was his place? Or showing him who was boss. But who was boss once the threshold of the stables was crossed?

The first time she saw him, such was his air of quiet authority, she took him for Waldron's younger brother Charles until he spoke and she heard the soft musical Cork accent for the first time. He had come upon her beating a mare between the ears with a whip to stop it rearing its head.

"There'll be no more of that now, ma'am," he had said, reaching up and relieving her of her whip as if she were just an ordinary person, and not the new mistress of the Park, and such was his confidence she had obeyed him. At the time, she was only twenty years old to his twenty-five and had no idea how to assert her authority.

Movement in the yard. Charlotte on Mandrake. Manus talking to her, using his hands to demonstrate a point. The two of them laughing (*laughing*?), then becoming serious as she started the course. Manus watching, concentrating.

The excellence of the riding gave Edwina a pain in the region of her chest. She couldn't take her eyes off her daughter, transformed, despite her burgeoning plumpness, into a figure of grace. Only nine years of age (Was she nine yet? Or was she ten?), riding with faultless judgement and timing.

To think her own introduction to riding had been so different – at the age of four being led under the branch of a tree by an older pupil to be scraped off, and hitting the ground, hearing the pupil and her friends chanting "*Get back on! Get back on!*" and when she ran away, "Scaredy cat! Scaredy cat! Eating mother's bread and fat!"

But she had shown them eventually. She was now acknowledged as the most fearless horsewoman on the hunting scene. "She rides like a man," was finally said about her, and she treasured that compliment above all others, even above "wonderful rider", the words Beatrice had used to describe her. Soon, if Manus didn't ruin Sandstorm in the meantime, she would show them that she could ride not just as well, but better than any man. What she lacked in masculine strength she would make up for in training, guile and daring.

Charlotte was still jumping the course – she seemed to spend all her time down there these days now that Dixon wasn't around to make sure she returned to the nursery after only an hour at the stables – and there were Beatrice and Bertie, leaning on the rails, watching her.

At the end of the demonstration Manus lifted Charlotte out of the saddle, even though she was well able to dismount, and Edwina stared at his beautiful, sun-browned hands and face (she knew the ladies of the county referred to him as 'the divine Manus' – Beatrice had told her) and Charlotte's round animated face as he hugged her, twirled her around and placed her on the ground, then patted her on the shoulder as she led Mandrake back to the stable.

Three years into her marriage that had turned out to be no marriage at all, she had watched Manus handling a newly weaned colt, seducing it with the music of his voice, making sounds that might be Gaelic or might be words without sense, turned half away in an unthreatening stance, all the while soothing and stroking with those beautiful hands of his. The colt leaned in towards him, nudging his arm, while Edwina stood transfixed beside him, unnoticed, burning and grieving at the same time. Without premeditation, she caught his hand in mid-stroke and placed it on the side of her face and held it there. Manus turned towards her and his eyes refocused, reading her intent. When he registered her distress, he put his other hand on her back. "There, there," he said. "There, there. Don't upset yourself, ma'am. There, there. It will be all right," and she let herself lean into him, and she remembered how the foal pushed his head in between the two of them and tried to butt her out of the way, and how she managed to ignore it.

Best not to think of those times.

Beatrice was full of apologies about being late when she finally arrived. She and Bertie had lost track of time while watching Charlotte, who showed the most amazing promise for a girl of her age or any age. Edwina must be proud, but then she and Waldron must take some credit, as the apple doesn't fall far from the tree. "Bertie and I both think she is a wonderful rider. *Wonderful.* Perfect seat, perfect hands."

Edwina knew those words by heart, having repeated them often in her mind to give her spirits a boost. She now turned her burning face away from her friend to hide her mortification.

Fool! Fool! Not only had Beatrice, speaking to Lady Wentworth, been praising Charlotte and not her, as she'd thought, but had placed her at the same level of skill as Waldron. How could she bear the double ignominy?

21

Bertie continued to accompany Beatrice to the Park so that he could watch the interaction between Manus, Mandrake and Charlotte, leaving the two women to have their little chats in private.

"He's trying to discover the formula," Beatrice laughed. "Wouldn't we all? Lord Prothero isn't the only one who wants to poach Manus from you. Have you seen – of course you have – the way he gets the foals to leave their dams and follow him? Bertie says it's contrary to nature and he's never seen it done before. He'd love to know how . . ."

So would Edwina, though she would die rather than ask him. In her nine years at the Park, Manus had never once acknowledged her superior horsemanship or asked her advice on anything.

". . . but Manus himself doesn't know, apparently. Or at least he can't put it into words."

It was a cold, bright autumn day. The friends sat on either side of a wood fire and leaned back in the armchairs. Edwina, with her feet tucked under her despite Beatrice's offer of a footstool and warnings that it would cut off her circulation, wondered peevishly why anyone would want to know his main trade secret anyway. Fear impairs judgement, Manus believed. An animal couldn't concentrate on the matter in hand if it expected a punishment to fall at any minute. Its nervousness would make it unreliable. So wrong to her way of thinking, and if Manus would leave Sandstorm alone, she would prove it within the next two years. Because of the fear she had instilled in him, Sandstorm galloped faster and jumped higher than any of Manus's softly reared charges.

"I think Manus is given too much credit," Edwina said aloud. "After all, I'm the better judge of horseflesh and I'm the one who studies the bloodlines and decides which mares to buy in, and which ones will be covered by which stallions, and then he comes along with a few training tricks and ends up with all the recognition, which hardly seems fair."

"I see your point, dear," said Beatrice quickly to mollify her. "The trouble is we take your expertise for granted. Your memory is a wonder of the age and your judgement faultless."

"Thank you for that," said Edwina, trying not to show how much she relished her friend's praise. "All this talk brings me to something I've been meaning to ask you for ages."

Beatrice was immediately alert.

"Tell me, Bea. Is Manus an illegitimate son of the Park?"

Beatrice hesitated before answering in a half-shocked, half-amused tone, "I wasn't expecting *that*."

"It's been known to happen. It's not unusual."

"In what way do you mean a son of the Park?"

"I've worked it out. He could have been sired by Waldron's father, or Waldron or Charles, take your pick. At thirty-four, his age fits all of them."

Beatrice kept shaking her head. "Whatever made you come up with such a notion?"

"The way he's such a law unto himself. His confidence. Being given so much authority so young. It all adds up."

"No, dear. I think you'll find the answer much more mundane. Waldron's father took a shine to Manus, a boy at the time, at the local horse fair. He was impressed by the way he was handling livestock and he liked the look of him. Persuaded him to come and work at the Park. It wasn't easy. Manus's father is a strong republican who said he himself would rather starve to death than work on an estate, but he gave in for the sake of the boy, only fourteen at the time, because of his passion for horses. He realised that working here was the only way Manus would get access to them. Nothing more than that, I'm afraid. Sorry to disappoint you if you were looking for a bit of juicy scandal."

"Do you remember if his mother ever worked here?"

"I can be fairly sure she didn't, knowing the Park's policy on not employing local villagers. Except for Manus himself, of course, who's an exception."

Wasn't that the whole point of the conversation? Edwina wanted to ask but decided instead to change the topic, as it was obvious that even if Beatrice did know anything, she wasn't about to reveal it. "Too much time on my hands, that's my problem, thinking up fanciful notions like that." She stretched. "Not long to go now."

Beatrice didn't need more prompting to talk about preparations for the baby, but she soon returned to the excitement of the moment.

"Charlotte's very pleased," she said as she leaned over to stir the ashes with a poker, releasing a burst of heat and sparks. "I love doing that. Hope you don't mind. Manus has told her she's good enough to ride with the adults in the next hunt that leaves from the Park. That will be a thrill for you. And us. It's always a treat to be there when an exciting new rider makes her first appearance. Bertie can't stop talking about her and is forecasting –"

"No one likes a show-off," Edwina interrupted. "She's going to find it difficult enough to snare a husband with her plainness and ill nature without adding showing-off to her disadvantages."

"Are we talking about the same girl?" Beatrice was taken aback, but responded with spirit. "I think Charlotte looks quite attractive when she smiles, and I've never noticed any evidence of ill nature. She's always most pleasant and agreeable when I see her."

"I think I'd be the better judge of my daughter than you, Beatrice, with due respect. Add being two-faced to that list. You only see her when she's toadying to Manus so that he'll continue to spoil her shamelessly and let her stay at the stables all day."

Beatrice's face became flushed. "I think it's a bit harsh calling Charlotte a show-off, Edwina dear. She was lucky to be born with a natural talent but doesn't seem to be aware of how exceptional she is. To see her take instructions from Manus and so conscientiously put them into practice, always keen to learn more, it's obvious she has no inflated notions about herself." Despite the cold reception her observations were receiving, Beatrice added, "Isn't it a bit early to write Charlotte off as plain when she's only nine? She has plenty of time to turn into a swan."

"That will never happen if she continues to take after her father. I see her as a female version of him. She'll need more than the Dowager's fortune to entice anyone to marry her with a face like that."

"You'll see a big change for the better when she loses her puppy fat, Edwina dear. She has a good bone structure underneath all that."

Edwina was losing her patience. "I'm glad you're such an expert on my daughter," she said with sarcasm. "Would it be too much to ask you to change the subject and talk about something interesting before I expire from boredom?"

22

So many changes occurred in the Blackshaw household during the last year of the war that memories of the missing Victoria were superseded by less momentous but more immediate concerns.

Six weeks before her due date Edwina travelled to the fully staffed Blackshaw townhouse in Dublin to await the birth of her child, explaining her early departure by saying she was taking no chances after what had happened to Sid's wife, Kate. Beatrice would like to have accompanied her but she and Bertie were heading back to England to continue the search for their missing son.

Edwina gave birth to a boy and called him Harcourt, the surname of her paternal grandmother, officially registering the name before Waldron wrote to direct that, in line with five hundred years of tradition, the boy would be named after him. The postal deliveries could be erratic during wartime, she informed him later.

She remained in Dublin for three months.

To replace Nurse Dixon, Beatrice's niece, who knew everyone and everything, recommended Holly Stoddard, a properly trained nanny from a good family, not a stray, untrained orphan like Dixon. Anyone who met her, according to the niece, would warm to her on sight with her soft round smiling face, her erect posture and her white-blonde hair hanging in a single plait down her back. Edwina said she couldn't care less what she looked like as long as she was competent and could take over the care of the baby from the day it was born.

The following September, with the war over, Charlotte was sent to her mother's old school in England to make suitable friends, to separate her from Miss East and Manus who were indulging her, and to rid her of the Huddersfield accent she had picked up from Dixon. The fact that she would be riding on her first hunt during the Christmas break sustained her during her lonely first term. A pony was supplied at the school, as Mandrake was considered too valuable to travel.

Miss East hadn't told Charlotte about her forthcoming marriage to Sid, planned for the following August, a year and a month since the death of Kate. By that time Charlotte, with three terms completed and surrounded by friends, would be able to accept the separation with composure, so she persuaded herself.

Waldron stayed on in London to tie up all the loose ends in the War Office. He sent word he would be home in time to host the hunt from the Park on New Year's Day. A hero's return, Edwina commented to Verity when she read the letter. Waldron's long-running absences were an affront to her, but were preferable to his brief appearances, which caused her nothing but irritation. She wondered if he was considering retiring from the army now that he was sixty-two years of age.

In October she reclaimed Sandstorm who, as she had predicted, had lost his fire. She and Les, the middle stable lad, put in many hours of secret training in a field out of sight of Manus's suspicious eye. The New Year's hunt would be her first since her confinement, Waldron's first since the War, and Charlotte's first ever. Edwina could feel a build-up of vitality on the estate.

The servants were glad to have the Park come back to life, and began to prepare months in advance. Fires had to be set in the twenty-five bedrooms, and every room was aired, swept, polished and dusted. Miss East supervised the transformation.

Waldron was in full uniform when he returned at midday three days before Christmas with the young soldier, Thatcher, walking two paces behind him. The staff lined up in front of the house to cheer him home.

Edwina received him in the hall.

"The first thing I want to see is my son and heir," he beamed after they greeted each other with a kiss on the cheek. "Get him brought down at once. And the second thing: I've decided to have our portraits painted in the New Year by that fellow who did yours when you were younger, only this time," he laughed in Edwina's direction, "I'll make sure there aren't any missing hands, so you can show off the family heirlooms."

23

Tyringham Park
1919

It was New Year's Day, the day Edwina had looked forward to for eighteen months. To mark her return to normal life after Victoria's disappearance and Harcourt's birth, she told her maid to prepare her black taffeta dress and the diamonds to go with it. She intended to shine at the evening entertainment while receiving compliments about her riding during the hunt. 'Better than a man' was what she expected to hear this year. Sandstorm was well prepared and so was she. After today, she expected Beatrice and Bertie to be more effusive in their praise of her than they had ever been in their raptures over Charlotte.

The maid returned to say the dress was ready but the diamond necklace and ring were not in the box.

"That's ridiculous. Did you double check?"

"Yes, ma'am."

"Tell Miss East to go to my room immediately and I'll meet her there."

Edwina checked the box herself and saw that a sapphire set was also missing. After being summoned, Miss East affirmed what Edwina had already guessed. Teresa Kelly used to have access to her room – she had been sent up on many occasions to gather up articles that needed altering or mending. Miss East remembered specifically

114

sending her there shortly before she left the Park to collect an antique coverlet that was fraying around the stitching.

"And I suppose you're going to say Nurse Dixon had access as well." Edwina spoke through closed teeth and did not look in the direction of the servant.

"No, I can't say that," said Miss East. "She had no reason ever to come to this part of the house."

"That will be all."

After Edwina turned her back and Miss East left, Edwina cursed the untrustworthy Teresa Kelly who had not only stolen a child, but jewellery as well. For once Waldron was right. The only way to deal with such people, if one only knew where to find them, was with force.

The day before the hunt, Charlotte chose a riding jacket from the equestrian room. To ensure it would fasten at the waist she was limited to one that was two sizes larger than her previous one. She hoped no one would notice the overlong arms or the four moth-eaten holes along the left side near the waist.

The courtyard was packed with visiting grooms when she arrived early to saddle up. To the disappointment of the visitors and guests, Manus stayed away. Those who came from a distance for the first time since the war knew him only by reputation and wanted to see this legend for themselves.

Les was walking Sandstorm to warm him up for Lady Blackshaw.

Although it was nearly midday, the breaths of horses, hounds and riders were still visible in the frosty air.

"It's not a race and it's not a competition," were Manus's final encouraging words to Charlotte the previous day. "Take it easy. Mandrake won't make a mistake and neither will you. I'm sorry I won't be here in the morning, but I'll try to look in during the afternoon to see how you got on. I know you'll be grand so don't worry. You're a champion, so you've nothing to worry about."

It didn't occur to her to ask why Manus never took part in the hunt despite his outstanding horsemanship.

Edwina made her entrance when most of the riders were already assembled at the front of the Park where Waldron was presiding over the pre-hunt rituals. Lady Beatrice, too short-sighted to see her friend's stormy expression, called to her that the occasion was positively splendid. Edwina acknowledged the comment with a nod, and after a quick glance at Lucifer – Beatrice had got her Manus-trained mount at last – felt sorry she'd agreed to part with him.

Charlotte continued to walk Mandrake quietly in circles, ignoring the activity around her.

Archie the stable lad, all smiles, entered the courtyard to tell her a lot of those assembled at the front of the house wanted to have a look at this young "pro–prod–prodgidy", and when was she going to show herself?

While passing, Edwina heard the compliment and, looking up at Charlotte, was struck by how much she already looked like a female version of Waldron, right down to the plain face with its smug expression and superior air. She *is* a show-off, she thought.

"Get off," she heard herself say.

Charlotte looked down at her in bewilderment.

"Come on, get off and change horses with me," said Edwina more sharply. "You heard me. *Get off*. I'm not going to tell you again." Even as she was saying this she wished she wasn't giving such an unthinkable order, but there was no backing down now that she'd said those words and couldn't see her way to retract them.

"No. No." Charlotte's confidence gave way to panic in a second. "Mandrake's the only one I'm used to. Manus said –"

"Manus said! Manus said! That's all I ever hear around here!" Edwina grabbed the near rein. "I'm in charge here, not Manus, in case you didn't know, and I'm ordering you to get off now. Do as I tell you."

She grabbed Charlotte's boot.

Charlotte instinctively wheeled Mandrake to the right, pulling Edwina off balance for a number of steps, stoking her anger.

"Everyone's looking at you," hissed Edwina, trying to keep her voice down. "You're making a spectacle of yourself."

Five visiting grooms, along with the three from the Park, were the only ones there, leaning against the stalls, arms folded, silently watching. Les stopped walking Sandstorm and stayed in the middle of the yard. It crossed Edwina's mind that she could ask one of them for help, but what if Les didn't move and the others, as visitors, took their cue from him? How ridiculous would she look then?

"I said *get off*." This time she made no mistake. Taking a firm hold, she wrenched Charlotte's left foot out of its stirrup and pulled, using all her weight, until Charlotte slid from the saddle into her arms, her right foot still in its stirrup and her hands holding the reins. Edwina, thanking Manus silently for his good schooling as Mandrake stood still throughout, held Charlotte tightly, and twisted the reins from her fingers. Les, who could contain himself no longer, ran over to remove Charlotte's right foot from its stirrup – her leg had gone right through it – then took her full weight from Edwina and placed her on the ground.

Edwina stayed beside Mandrake. "Ride Sandstorm," she said, not looking Les in the eye while instructing him to change saddles, which he did with an attitude that frightened Charlotte.

"I don't like Sandstorm, I'm not used to him," sobbed Charlotte, wishing Manus was there to tell her what to do.

"Then stay at home. It's your choice," Edwina, now mounted on Mandrake, called back over her shoulder. "Come on if you're coming. We're late."

Les put his arm around Charlotte, unsure of what to do next. If only Manus was here, he thought.

For Charlotte, to stay was out of the question and to ride Sandstorm seemed an impossibility.

"Perhaps you'd better not risk it, Miss," said Les at last. "There'll be plenty more hunts."

"But I'll be away at school," she managed to say between sobs. "And it's this one I want to ride in, not any others. I'll have to wait a whole year if I miss out now."

Les didn't say that wouldn't be the end of the world even though he wanted to, sensing that for Charlotte it would be. "I don't know if I should let you go," he said finally.

"Mother said I could, so that means I can. I'll ride just a little way and stay at the back."

"That sounds fair enough," he heard himself say. "Come on, then, give us your foot. Then you'd better hurry." He gave her a leg up, checked the length of the stirrups and the tightness of the girth strap and handed her back the reins. Her face was stiff with cold or fear. "Good luck, Miss. You'll be fine, don't worry," he said to her receding back as Sandstorm, ears pricked, moved off before being given a signal.

24

The clattering of the hooves of over a hundred horses and the swirling of the hounds as they left the front of the house encouraged Sandstorm to surge forward. Charlotte tightened the reins to slow him down, as she wanted to stay behind everyone else, but he took no notice. She pulled the left rein to make him change direction and he ignored that as well.

There were clusters of people – servants plus members of the gentry who were too young or too old to take part – milling around and drinking, after seeing off the main bunch.

"Is *that* her?" said a penetrating young voice. "I thought she'd look like a princess. She looks nothing like a princess, she looks . . ."

Before the owner of the voice was silenced, the group, who were beginning to move off, stopped and stared at Charlotte.

One whispered comment, "At least she has a good seat," reached her before she was pulled forward by the headstrong Sandstorm. "That's something to be thankful for."

Giving up hope of control, not looking to the left or right, Charlotte concentrated on holding on and keeping her eye out for obstacles so that she wouldn't be taken unawares.

The first jump sent her slightly off balance as Sandstorm's timing was different from Mandrake's – he jumped from further back – but he was sure-footed and that reassured her a little.

The ice on the west side of the walls and hedges had not yet melted, even though it was now afternoon. The sun hung low and its light was weak.

As they cantered along and fanned out across the fields Charlotte didn't know where her mother was in the group and didn't look for her. She knew of Edwina's reputation from conversations overheard in the stables. The grooms were always discussing the standards of horsemanship of themselves and their employers, and comparing them to the expertise of those from other estates. "No one messes with Lady Blackshaw," was a much-heard remark. "She's tough." Edwina deliberately shoved other chasers if she was caught in the middle of a bunch, and usually emerged the leader. "Her mounts are trying to get away from her – that's why they're so fast," Les observed once when he didn't know Charlotte was listening. "They're trying to shake her off. And all that sawing of the bit she does – ruins the animal's mouth for good." Charlotte had noticed her mother's faulty timing, rising from the saddle or sitting back too soon or too late, and the rough snapping of the bit. It offended her sensibilities to watch.

After twenty minutes Sandstorm had jumped a number of fences, ditches and hedges so faultlessly that Charlotte began to think she would last the distance after all. To her relief, he stayed in a group near the back. At one stage, he bumped against a rider who was knocked slightly off balance and who let out a string of curses after he righted himself. Charlotte wished she could turn to apologise but she couldn't afford to take her eyes off her course for a second.

A little later, Lord Crombie overtook her, shouting, "That's the girl, Charlotte, keep it up!" He was known for choosing speed over endurance, according to Les, and Charlotte expected to overtake him later if the hunt went on for any length of time. A loose bay passed her on the left – she didn't recognise it and wondered who had been unseated. Still no sign of her mother.

Children on ponies rode along the paths or through breaks in the hedges and walls. Most of them were older than she was, and none of them had spoken to her at the start – perhaps they would have if Sandstorm hadn't surged past them like an unmannerly host.

The rhythm of Sandstorm's stride was soothing Charlotte's consciousness and she was beginning to understand her mother's often-stated wish that she would hunt every day of the week if she had the chance.

Waldron sounded the horn to indicate that the dogs had picked up the scent of their quarry, a bagged fox released at the right time in the right place. Sandstorm shot forward, almost unseating Charlotte who feared she was on a bolting horse until she saw that those around her had changed from a slow canter to a fast gallop as well. For safety's sake she wanted to pull back but was forced to accept she had no choice but to let Sandstorm have his head along the full length of Langan field.

Galloping at full speed, feeling the power of the animal beneath her and hearing the drumming of hooves on the vibrating earth all around her, she felt an urge to drop the reins, whoop with joy to the heavens, lean back in the saddle with her arms outstretched to embrace the world flying past and give herself up to the ecstasy of the chase, not just for this moment but forever and ever.

"*Move over!*" she heard her mother shout, and Charlotte, jolted back to reality, wondered if Edwina had been behind her all along, rather than in front as she had presumed.

Another loose horse, this time a grey, appeared on Sandstorm's left, just as Mandrake drew abreast on the right.

The gap in the hawthorn hedge about a hundred yards ahead was too narrow for the three to jump at the same time.

Charlotte tried frantically to change direction.

"*Get back!*" her mother screeched, nearer and more urgently.

The flapping stirrup on the saddle of the loose grey hit Sandstorm in the flank, causing him to leap in the air in a movement that was a cross between a shy and a buck, right across the path of Mandrake, who didn't have time to stop and whose front legs were clipped by the passing Sandstorm.

Sandstorm took the jump at such an acute angle that when he landed he was facing in the opposite direction to the other hunters who had veered sharply away after passing through one of the other three gaps in the hawthorn hedge further along to the left. He continued to the right and then followed the high hedges around almost three sides of the field, before picking up the trail of the others who were by now way in the distance.

Charlotte looked out for Mandrake and the grey, but there was no sign of them.

She pulled with all her weight on the left rein to try to turn Sandstorm but the stallion wouldn't deviate from his headstrong flight. She was crying and shouting but no one could hear her. Where were the stragglers? There must be some slow ones bringing up the rear. Even the children on their ponies weren't to be seen. Had they turned back after the first hour or so?

Perhaps Edwina had had a simple fall and, disgusted with herself, decided to retrace her steps rather than be seen, not just splattered with mud like the rest of them but caked with it, a sure sign of a fall. The teasing would be friendly – it could happen to anyone – but for Edwina it would be unendurable, such was her pride in her ability. Yes, that's what she'd do, thought Charlotte. Ride home and then tell everyone later Mandrake had developed a limp.

Or perhaps that didn't happen at all, and Mandrake and her mother were both dead, or badly injured, lying there without help, and *it was all her fault.*

Charlotte was filled with a terrible foreboding. She had never told anyone how Nurse Dixon had hurt Victoria, but Nurse Dixon thought she had snitched so it was the same as if she had as far as activating a curse was concerned, and here was the result of it. Mandrake dead, just as Dixon said he would be.

Charlotte wished that she herself were dead. Anything rather than having to face her mother – if she was still alive – when she returned to the house. 'And you call yourself a horsewoman?' she could hear her saying with deadly rancour. 'You can only ride Mandrake because he's so well trained – a beginner could do just as well. Put you on another and look what happens. Toadying up to Manus all day long, that's all you're good for. You're nothing but a show-off, just like your father.'

Charlotte was jolted by her own thoughts. Had she ever heard her mother speak like that, or were Nurse Dixon's phrases coming back to her, or had she made them up herself?

She didn't have any more time to think as she was now approaching the end of the hunt, where the riders were grouped in a circle. Sandstorm slowed down of his own accord. Charlotte's weeping intensified, but now it was silent.

Waldron turned his back on his daughter when he saw her wiping her nose on the dangling sleeve of her ill-fitting jacket, but not before she had seen the look of disgust on his face.

Lady Beatrice, sitting side-saddle on Lucifer, detached herself from the group watching the hounds tearing at the fox, to move beside Charlotte. "What is it, dear?" she asked, thinking the girl's distress was too extreme to be the result of seeing her first fox kill. "And why are you riding your mother's hunter?"

Waldron turned around again when he heard that, and saw it was Sandstorm standing quietly at the edge of the group with Charlotte snivelling in the saddle. Funny how he hadn't noticed earlier as he usually saw the horse before the rider.

"You're honoured," he said, speaking slowly and deliberately in an attempt to disguise his inebriation. "Not everyone would get that privilege. Where is she anyway?"

Charlotte opened her mouth to answer but there was no sound.

"Not this bloody circus again!" said Waldron, and then to Beatrice. "One of her little tricks. Loses her voice, or so she says. Very convenient."

Charlotte pointed back the way they had come.

"Didn't make it, eh? She'll be annoyed." To Beatrice, who wondered why he never spoke of his wife by name, he said with ungentlemanly satisfaction, "Just goes to show that pride comes before a fall. Must have gone back to lick her wounds. There'll be no talking to her tonight." He took a swig from a hip flask, one of four, judging by the bulges in his pockets, and leaned towards Beatrice, speaking with what he judged to be a flirtatious tone. "And how did you manage to sneak Lucifer out from under my nose, Beatrice? We'll have a talk about that later."

Beatrice laughed. "I was too cunning for you. You know we ladies have to have a Manus-trained hunter."

Waldron's benign expression disappeared. "So I've heard. I was only joking. You're welcome to him." He took a long draught. "Brigadier has a few good years in him yet, so he'll do me." He turned his back. "Time to retrace our steps. Come on, Freddie, and anyone else who fancies a dram at Rafferty's on the way back."

Only Freddie, one of his fellow officers, followed. The rest of the group, cold, tired and hungry, preferred to take the short cut back to the house, to bring them more quickly to the feast and hot whiskeys waiting for them there.

Waldron and Freddie moved off in the direction they had come,

Waldron holding himself in the over-correct posture of someone trying to look sober. On horseback he had no difficulty staying upright. It was when he was dismounting he had a tendency to lose his balance and fall over.

The part Waldron liked best about going to Rafferty's was the way the local men, hunched over their pints of Guinness, looking towards the door when he entered, couldn't disguise their admiration when they beheld him in all his splendour. Their dark clothes acted as a foil to his redcoat military jacket and its shiny brass buttons, his shiny leather straps and boots, and the shiny pouch containing his polished service revolver. The other part he liked was the image of himself leaning on the bar sharing the leisure pursuits of the common man and not making them feel out of place. His fraternising lent authority to any pronouncement he made about his tenants. "I know what they're thinking," he was fond of saying. "Don't I drink with them?" This year there would be an added satisfaction. It would be the first time Thatcher, who had never sat on a horse in his life, would be present at Rafferty's to see at first hand how much the tenants thought of their dazzling landlord.

"Stay with me, dear," said Beatrice to Charlotte. "We'll wait until the coast is clear and then we can take it nice and easy." While they stood quietly waiting until both groups were out of sight, Beatrice, witnessing Charlotte's distress on what should have been her day of triumph, felt a bubble of anger towards Edwina and was constrained to say, "Your mother was very naughty to put you on Sandstorm. On the way I noticed a few times you were having trouble controlling him. He would test a sixteen-stone man, so what chance would a young girl like you have? Not that your mother is a sixteen-stone man, of course, but she has her own methods and Sandstorm knows where he stands with her. You did well to stay on. And to finish. Good girl."

Charlotte didn't think she deserved the compliment. All she had done was stay in the saddle. Her limbs felt weak. The arms of the jacket refused to stay tucked up, making it difficult to hold the reins, now stiffening in the cold. She couldn't feel her feet and, checking to see if they were positioned correctly in the stirrups, had to shake her head to dislodge the tears that continued to obstruct her vision.

"All right, Charlotte, we'd better go now. We'll go the long way so we don't get caught up in the crowd." Beatrice wanted to go back the way they had come in the hope of finding out what had happened to Edwina, but she didn't say that to Charlotte. "Easy does it now."

But when Sandstorm turned for home, he took off as briskly as if it were his first outing of the day, though with more single-mindedness, as he knew where he was heading.

A steady sleet began to fall. The two didn't speak.

They overtook Waldron and Freddie who had dismounted and were retracing their steps, heads down, obviously looking for something one of them had dropped. The men looked up, saw who was passing, and looked down again without a greeting.

Probably lost half a crown, Beatrice thought sourly, and continued to ride abreast of Charlotte.

When Charlotte saw the hedge of Logan's field approaching with its wild hawthorn and four gaps, she felt so ill she thought she might faint. Sandstorm headed for the closest gap rather than the fourth he'd jumped on the outward run. Charlotte's mind was convulsing with vivid, fragmented images.

Beatrice jumped first. When her turn came, Charlotte turned her head hoping to see empty space and no evidence that a clash had happened, but there were horses and people in a huddle beside the wall. Was that Mandrake standing awkwardly? She would know his outline anywhere. One of his legs didn't look right.

"Looks like an accident," shouted Beatrice, already turning Lucifer. "I'll have to go back." She knew Charlotte would have no hope of making Sandstorm change direction. "You go on. You should be all right from here." She kept shouting but the distance between them had widened and Charlotte couldn't hear what she was saying.

25

Miss East lifted the lid off one of the big pots to smell the Irish stew. "Delicious," she said to Cook who was red-faced and perspiring. "It gets better every year."

"Put on the kettle there like a good woman," said Cook, "and we'll have a nice cup of tea before the rush. I deserve a puff of the pipe and a sit down. My legs are killing me. Everything's ready. What time is it?"

"Just after four. They should all be back shortly. I heard a few a while back but they were the children, most likely." Miss East poured boiling water into the teapot. "It's a good sign Charlotte isn't back yet – she must have lasted the distance. I've been thinking of her so much all afternoon you'd think I was riding beside her."

"You're such a clucky hen where she's concerned," said Cook, sinking into her chair beside the range. "You'd think she was your own."

It was the Dowager who had started the tradition of serving a hot buffet to the hunters as soon as they returned and before they changed. The hall floor of quarry tiles, so easily cleaned, allowed them to come in, muck and all, without removing their boots. She said she wanted to hear their stories in their immediacy. If the visitors went off to rub down their horses and then change, they inevitably swapped experiences with each other while doing those things, so when they finally came in to eat the vividness of the telling had dissipated somewhat. The hall, with its double curved staircases, gilt-framed portraits, stuffed animal heads and, best of all, two huge fireplaces on either side burning unsplit logs that at times were so noisy they sounded as if they were talking to each other, the lights and warmth, did what they were meant to do – offered a contrast between the cold darkness outside and the welcome inside that was an embrace and a sensory assault. The trestle tables with their linen tablecloths were already covered with freshly baked breads, steamed puddings, mince pies, cheeses and cream, waiting for the carved roasts of beef, turkey, ham, venison and the lamb stew to be added when the crowd arrived.

From the distance, the sound of barking filtered into the kitchen. The clattering of many horses' hooves on cobblestones had Miss East at the door before she had time to think. She was nearly knocked over by the procession of servers coming to collect the hot part of the supper. Cook jumped up as soon as she heard the noise and, not wishing to miss out on one moment of glory, supervised the removal of the feast.

26

Waldron finally found the silver top of his favourite hipflask, the one that had been used by royalty and as such was his most highly regarded portable possession. He was lucky he had found it when he did as thirty minutes later he might not have spotted it in the fading light. With the help of Freddie he remounted and they cantered on. With the thought of Thatcher waiting at Rafferty's, wondering why he was late, Waldron was keen not to waste any more time getting there.

Freddie, jumping through the second break in the hedge into Langan's field, noticed some mounted figures huddled together near the fourth break further along, and a riderless horse with its reins hanging loose standing apart. He shouted back to Waldron who, after making a clean jump through the first break, would have continued on unawares if Freddie hadn't gained his attention.

Waldron made a wide arc to turn, and identified the riderless horse as Mandrake. Was there something about a last-minute change of mount that someone had mentioned? He approached, lifting his arm to drink from the fourth hip flask to help him concentrate. Mandrake, disturbed, stepped sideways. Waldron saw the bulge of the broken bone poke out against the skin. Something would have to be done about that and he was the right man to do it and he had the means to do it and he would do it as soon as he was ready.

He noticed a fourth person. She was holding on to the wall, leaning over and being sick. It was Beatrice.

Freddie went over to the two mounted girls and one boy to ask who the rider involved in the accident had been, presuming it was one of the visiting Blackshaws he didn't know.

"It was Lady Blackshaw," the older girl leaned over to say in a whisper so that Waldron couldn't hear.

"It was Edwina," Freddie called across to Waldron. "Your wife."

"I know who she is."

"Was she badly hurt?" Freddie asked the others.

"It didn't look good. She was unconscious and her feet were facing the wrong direction," the same girl whispered. "They took her away just a minute ago."

"Her feet were facing the wrong direction," Freddie shouted to Waldron.

"She won't like that." he yelled back.

"They've just taken her away, whoever 'they' are. Get yourself over here so I don't have to act like a parrot."

Letchworth, an older brother of the three young people, had ridden off to get help from the soldiers in the army barracks, the girl further explained. The hope was they would have an available lorry that could be used to transport Her Ladyship to the hospital in Cork. He must have raised the alarm somewhere along the way as a number of tenant farmers and their sons had turned up out of nowhere and had just left, transporting her ladyship on a makeshift stretcher to walk the four miles to the road in the hope of meeting up with the military lorry if one turned up, and if one didn't they intended to walk the twenty miles, taking it in turns to bear the stretcher, all the way to the city. Letchworth was also looking to borrow some type of a firearm so that he could put Mandrake out of his misery as soon as he returned.

"Won't be needed," said Freddie. "Lord Waldron has one on his person."

Sleet continued to fall and daylight was nearly gone.

Beatrice, wiping her mouth and looking distraught, joined the group. Despite approaching quietly, she startled Mandrake, who stepped backwards and faltered before putting his weight on his three sound legs, letting the broken one rest lightly on the ground. She hoped she wasn't going to be sick again.

"Hold him there, Freddie," Waldron commanded.

Freddie had ridden off a short distance to relieve himself and didn't hear. The two girls turned their faces away, and stayed where they were. The boy, aged about seven, hung his head.

"I'll hold him if you like," said Beatrice, "but I think it would be better if we all stayed still. He's not likely to move if you don't make any sudden movements."

"I don't need to be told what to do by a woman, Beatrice, and especially not by you," Waldron said, checking the revolver's ammunition. "Have you any idea who you're talking to? A champion horseman and a crack shot in the cavalry of the British Army for thirty years, that's who."

"Wait for Freddie. He'll be back in a second."

"Are you insinuating I'm not up to the job? Interfering woman, did you take in a word I said?" He began to dismount. "I'll do it myself."

He took his left foot out of the stirrup too soon and swung his right leg too energetically over the saddle, and lost his balance before he hit the ground. The revolver flew out of his hand and landed in the grass. The three young people ducked. Beatrice braced herself waiting for a shot, but there wasn't one. She went over to help up the idiot, as she was calling him under her breath. Mandrake had taken two steps back in reaction to the disturbance, and the broken bone now showed at a more acute angle than it had done earlier.

To stabilise herself, Beatrice held on to Brigadier's mane so that Waldron wouldn't pull her down when she gave him her hand. He made a few false starts before he was able to attain an upright position. Beatrice was tempted to use the revolver herself but from ingrained deference put it back into his muddy hand, then moved behind him out of the line of fire.

A large shape appeared at her shoulder.

"What's happened to Charlotte?" It was Manus, dismounting from Neseen, his father's farm horse.

"Nothing. Charlotte's fine. Lady Blackshaw was riding Mandrake. It was –"

There was a loud bang and an echo. One of the young girls screamed.

Manus had been unaware of Waldron's preparations as the old soldier's back had been turned towards him.

A stream of blood was pouring from one of Mandrake's nostrils. There was a hole in the edge of his blaze, about six inches below the left eye. Those who were watching thought the gelding looked puzzled and sad, shaking his head and quivering. He lurched when he took a step sideways.

Manus flew at Waldron, wrested the firearm from his hand and shoved him out of the way. Waldron rocked backwards, muttering that he wasn't going to let a servant treat him like that and there was going to be hell to pay before the day was out. Everyone ignored him.

By now Manus was weeping, but no one could tell as he was dripping wet and hatless, his hair sodden and plastered over his forehead.

He spoke softly to Mandrake, and Beatrice thought she heard him say "Goodbye, dear friend." Mandrake didn't move when Manus approached him and rested the revolver between the eyes, watching him directly while he aimed it. The hand Manus used to push the hair from his own eyes, and then shield them from the sleet while he took aim with the other, was visibly shaking. He fired, making no mistake, and stayed in that position while Mandrake, motionless for a second, still looking directly at his stable master while he took the hit, dropped down and then rolled on his side, accompanied by the sound of sighing, his broken leg the last to rest on the ground.

Both young girls sobbed aloud.

Manus returned the revolver to Waldron.

"You haven't heard the last of this by a long shot," said Waldron, swaying and holding on to Brigadier for support. "And you can keep your trap shut about this, Beatrice. And you lot as well," he directed at the young people.

"Won't say a word," said the older girl, who couldn't wait to get back to the house to tell her friends what a fool Waldron had made of himself.

Freddie returned, leading his mount. "Job done, I see," he said, looking at the fallen Mandrake and ignoring Manus whom he identified by his clothing as a stable hand. "Didn't notice the nettles and got caught in a bunch of them and couldn't find any dock leaves." He helped Waldron remount, and tentatively remounted himself.

"Will we ever get to Rafferty's with all these blasted interruptions?" asked Waldron, secure in the saddle, deliberately turning Brigadier's rear end towards Beatrice and Manus before riding off with a show of bravado.

Beatrice took Manus's shivering hands in hers. "Don't worry about Waldron," she said.

"I'm not worried about him."

"I'll make sure you don't lose your position at the stables because of this. I have influence."

"Thank you, ma'am, but at the moment I'm not concerned about His Lordship."

"But I am." Let the drunken popinjay better occupy himself showing some concern for his wife and leave Manus alone, Beatrice thought with contempt.

Manus retrieved Lucifer from where Beatrice had tethered him a distance away and, while the young girl held the horse's head, helped Beatrice back onto her side-saddle.

She wanted to get to the house as quickly as possible, not only to tell Charlotte what had happened and to be there to comfort her, but also to reassure Bertie, who must be worried about her by now. Manus signalled that he would stay on.

She joined the three young people and set off in a sad procession back to the house. Looking over her shoulder as she left, she saw through the sleet the silhouette of Manus against the last light of day bending over the fallen Mandrake.

27

Miss East looked up from replacing an empty platter with a full one to see Les picking his way through the crowd. This was most odd – it was unlikely he had ever been in the front hall of the house in his life. He was searching every face intently, apparently unaware of the inappropriateness of his being there. Who was he searching for? Perhaps one of the horses was playing up or injured and he was looking for the owner. That must be it.

Please God, don't let it be me.

When he finally located her and approached, she felt her legs go weak and wished there was somewhere to sit down.

"Is it Charlotte?"

"It is. She's not hurt but she's ran off. I tried to catch her. She's in a real bad state. I'm blaming myself for letting her go."

They headed for the door.

"I blame myself," Les repeated. "I just couldn't say no to her."

Everyone was having last drinks before going upstairs to change, when there was a disturbance at the door. Bertie saw his wife enter the hall and with an undignified cry pushed people out of the way to reach her side.

"There's been a bad accident," Beatrice announced. "It's Edwina."

Someone was heard to say in a low voice, "Thank God it wasn't Beatrice." Answered by, "You can say that again. There's been enough bad luck in that family already." Followed by, "Not to mention the Blackshaws. How unlucky are they?"

Another asked, "How is she?"

"Difficult to say. She's in good hands. On her way to the hospital. Young Letchworth was the hero of the hour. Had a lorry waiting on the main road and four soldiers ready to take over by the time the helpers carried her there."

Sighs of relief and sounds almost like applause came from the crowd, and Frobisher Letchworth's parents felt pride in their son for doing the right thing.

"Where's Waldron?" asked an army subordinate, who had ridden in this hunt for the first time. "He must be worried sick."

"Hardly. He's at Rafferty's. You won't get any sense out of him tonight," said one of the guests.

"And you won't get much any other time either," someone else whispered back.

"*Shhhh!*"

"Does anyone know where Charlotte is?" Beatrice asked.

No one had seen her arrive back.

"One of the stable lads came and fetched the housekeeper a while ago and they went off looking worried. I'd ask her. She'd be the one most likely to know."

"How's Sandstorm?" asked someone from the crowd that had by now encircled Beatrice.

"Edwina wasn't riding Sandstorm," said another voice. "She was on Mandrake."

"That's odd. Why wasn't she riding Sandstorm?" said another.

"How's Mandrake then, Beatrice?" Silence. "I was only asking. No need to look at me like that."

"That's what I have to see Charlotte about – I promised Manus I'd speak to her myself. Mandrake had to be shot."

The crowd gasped in unison, and there were cries of disbelief and pity from sections of it.

Beatrice was finding it difficult to speak. "Worse still, Manus had to do it. After Waldron made a mess of it." More sounds of disbelief,

133

this time punctuated with disapproval. "I must go and find Charlotte and break the news to her. If anyone sees her before I do, please don't say anything until I see her." She disappeared back into the outside darkness in a flurry of sleet that was turning to snow.

Miss East and Les finally found Charlotte in the old nursery curled up in Victoria's cot, sucking the satin trimming of a red blanket and staring straight ahead into the darkness.

Les lifted her out and crouched beside Miss East, who had sunk to the floor. He cradled the child in his arms.

"Was there an accident?" Miss East asked gently, making a guess.

Charlotte nodded, then flung herself into Miss East's arms, burying her face in her neck.

"There, there," said Miss East. "You're all right and that's the main thing. Now let's get you downstairs . . . there, there, don't take on so . . . let's get you out of these wet clothes and find you something nice to eat and warm you up and we'll find out what has happened. It might not be as bad as you think."

The look she gave Les over Charlotte's head was filled with alarm and contradicted the reassurances she was giving.

Beatrice didn't involve the servants in the search – she wanted to tell Charlotte herself in as gentle a way as she could to minimise shock. She was fond of the plain, charmless child with the good seat and sensitive hands who wanted above all to be a champion rider to win her mother's approval, a blameless child whose day of triumph had been wrecked by a jealous mother who would never approve of her, and a drunken father who couldn't shoot straight.

The hot steamy kitchen with servants skidding on the tiles revealed no familiar figure sitting in the corner.

Holly, keeping guard in the new nursery beside Miss East's rooms on the ground floor, was reluctant to open the door until she knew who it was who was knocking. Edwina had given strict instructions that Harcourt was not to leave the nursery that night – she was afraid that Waldron, full of pride at producing a son and heir at last, would command Harcourt be brought in to be displayed to the guests, and in his drunken enthusiasm pick up the baby before anyone could prevent him, raise him high and drop him on the hard floor. So vividly had Edwina outlined the nightmarish sequence of events to her that Holly was taking no chances. No, she hadn't seen Charlotte since this morning. Was everything all right?

"I just want to discuss the hunt with her," said Beatrice, moving off.

Habit, rather than logic, propelled her to the corridor leading to the original nursery, and along its full length she saw Charlotte in between Miss East and Les, coming towards her.

In that moment before she would shatter Charlotte's young life, she wondered which would be harder for Charlotte to bear – her mother's accident or the death of Mandrake?

28

"Have you been to see Manus yet?" Miss East asked.

Charlotte hung her head and said "No" in a small voice. She hadn't seen him since the day before the hunt weeks earlier.

"He keeps asking for you and wants to see you. He's very sad at the moment."

Charlotte made no response.

"Time is running out. You'll be back to school soon."

Her return had been delayed until she regained her voice after the accident.

"Now off you go. Your father wants to see you. He said eleven o'clock and he doesn't like to be kept waiting."

This was the first time Charlotte had been summoned for a serious talk with her father. She expected him to blame her for Edwina's accident and pour scorn on her for being such an incompetent rider. He would probably punish her by beating her, or telling her she could never ride again, or send her to live with the gypsies or the orphans, or have her locked up in gaol.

Waldron informed Charlotte that the family was to vacate Tyringham Park and move immediately and permanently to their house in Dublin. It was Edwina's wish and he could see the sense of it. She would never walk, let alone ride again, and needed to be near medical help, so Dublin – and later, perhaps, London – would be more suitable considering the condition she was in. Living in the depths of the countryside would not be practical.

The implications of what her father was saying didn't register with Charlotte, whose relief at not being blamed for anything overrode other considerations for the moment.

"Your Uncle Charles would like to rent the Park until Harcourt comes of age, so we will all be able to return here to hunt whenever we wish. I shall travel back to India and stay there until my retirement. Your mother's sister, your Aunt Verity Blackshaw, will live with you on a permanent basis, so you will be in good hands. No servant will transfer to Dublin except Holly, who will be needed to look after Harcourt."

"What about Miss East?"

"Miss East? Didn't you know? Lily East has given long-term notice." Waldron was concentrating on one of his military drawings while he was speaking. "She doesn't want her staff to know yet, so we're keeping it confidential until June." He slapped his head in an exaggerated gesture. "Now that I remember, she doesn't want you to know until then, either, so you'd better not let on to her that I told you. Damn. That slipped my mind. Can't be helped. After that date she won't be working for the family any more. Hard to imagine the place running without her, after all these years. She is going to marry that Sid chap and look after his motherless daughter. She wouldn't be needed anyway as your Aunt Verity will be in charge until your mother leaves hospital. Not that any of that should concern you. You'll be back at school shortly." He signed the drawing and swivelled his chair around to face her. "Is all that clear?"

"Yes, Father."

"At least you're speaking again. Will have to think about getting you another hunter. Run along, now."

Waldron was pleased with his interview. Edwina had told him to inform Charlotte of their changed circumstances and not to leave it to Miss East, and he had done as he was asked. He always had a strong wish to please her in the weeks before he quit the country and her company.

One thing he was not pleased about was being forced to keep on Manus as stable manager. Beatrice had had a quiet word the day after the hunt, threatening to spread the detailed story, if Manus was removed, of how a crack shot in His Majesty's service had missed a wounded, stationary horse from four paces and how an underling with no military training at all had to come forward to finish the task.

29

Charlotte, with her arms full of clothes and picture books, flashed Miss East a look of hatred and walked past her out the door of the bedroom they still shared.

What had Lord Waldron said to her to make her act in this way? Miss East wondered with concern, calling out to the child to wait for her.

Charlotte didn't answer, continuing with determined strides along the corridor. Miss East followed. Charlotte walked faster. Miss East caught up and put her hand on Charlotte's shoulder. Charlotte shook off the hand with a violent twist of her body and didn't pause or look back.

"What's the matter, Charlotte dear? You must tell me so I can make it better."

Charlotte continued on until she reached the door of the new nursery, where she dumped her armful onto the floor before knocking. When no one answered immediately, Charlotte looked back to see Miss East advancing, opened the door herself, slammed it closed behind her, and turned the key from the inside. Miss East, helpless, deflated, worried, stood outside and listened. Charlotte's voice was loud and tearful, Holly's soft and coaxing.

After the exchanges died down, Miss East, heartsick, tapped on the door and called Holly's name.

"Don't let her in!" Charlotte's voice shrieked, loud enough for Miss East to hear.

Five minutes of argument back and forth ensued, before the door opened and Holly slipped out. She motioned to Miss East to move further down the corridor where they could speak without being overheard.

"I'll have to be quick," Holly said. "I've left Charlotte in charge of Harcourt and she's not used to it. The news isn't good. Did you know the family is to move to Dublin permanently and Lord Waldron's brother is taking over the Park?"

"No, I didn't." She was relieved the news wasn't worse. "That's devastating for Charlotte, but how has that made her turn against me? It's not as if I had anything to do with it."

"She said you won't be going to Dublin to look after her because you want to look after Sid's daughter instead. I'm sorry, Miss East, but she says she doesn't want to see you again and wants to stay with me instead."

"Lord Waldron shouldn't have said anything about giving notice. I told him in confidence. I wanted to tell her myself about marrying Sid. It was a shame she had to hear all that bad news at once. No wonder the poor little thing has taken it so hard." Miss East's voice shook and she paused until she was able to continue. "She probably thinks it's all her fault. She takes things so much to heart and blames herself for everything that goes wrong. If only I could explain it to her."

"I don't think she's in any fit state to listen at the moment. Leave her with me for a while and I'll see if I can talk her around."

As a farewell gift to Charlotte, Miss East had spent some of her savings on a gold brooch with a glass-hinged front. Behind the glass she'd placed a piece of shamrock and a four-leafed clover, pressed and dried, that the two of them had found on one of their many companionable walks around the estate. She remembered how happy they had been then, and how Charlotte in her innocence had kept asking over and over if she could she stay with her for ever and ever.

Charlotte and Harcourt, with Holly the nanny, were ready to be driven to the station. Their luggage had been sent on ahead. Miss East stood waiting and when she heard Sid's boots on the gravel thought it was the sound of her heart breaking as she looked at Charlotte who had still not spoken to her despite many overtures.

At the last minute, Miss East leaned in with the brooch, folded Charlotte's limp fingers over it and said, "This will bring you luck and remind you I'll never forget my darling girl. I'll be counting every day until you come down for the summer."

Charlotte stared at the brooch, registered what it contained, looked at Miss East and then flung the brooch at her, cutting her cheek, shouting, "*I don't want it!*"

Holly jumped with shock and Harcourt started to cry.

Sid flew out of the driver's seat, opened Charlotte's door, and pulled her out by the arm.

"Pick up the brooch," said Sid.

Charlotte paused for only a moment before picking it up.

"Say you're sorry," he said. "Do you see what you done?"

Miss East, ignoring the blood on her face, was saying don't fuss about it, she didn't mean it, she's upset at leaving, she wants to stay, she's not herself.

Sid ignored her. "Say you're sorry."

Charlotte was trembling. She kept her head down and didn't speak.

"Did you hear what I said?" asked Sid.

Charlotte didn't move.

Miss East placed herself between the two and gestured to Sid to desist.

"There's no need to say anything. I know you feel sorry but you're not able to say it," she said to Charlotte, putting her arm around her.

Charlotte roughly shrugged off the arm.

"I'm not sorry," she mumbled.

Miss East looked pleadingly at Sid not to comment. The three stood waiting until the silence became uncomfortable. Sid was the first to give in as he couldn't bear the look of sorrow on his Lily's face.

"Say 'thank you' anyway," said Sid in a bitter tone. "After all she done for you. And we don't want to miss the train."

"Thank you," said Charlotte.

Sid looked at Miss East who nodded.

"Now come on then, back in and we're off," he said. "That will have to do, then."

"Good luck at school." Miss East held out her arms but Charlotte ignored them and took her seat, turning her head away. Sid closed the door and took his place. As they drove away Miss East saw, from out of Charlotte's window, an arm with a closed hand appear and hang down along the outside of the door. Slowly the fingers opened and the brooch, turning and shining in the light, dropped without a sound into the mud along the edge of the gravel driveway.

PART 2

THE CITY

30

Dublin
1919

Five weeks after the accident, two faces, vivid and unchanged, troubled Edwina if her sleeping draught wore off and she woke in the darkness of the early hours.

The first was Charlotte's at the moment she was told to swap Mandrake for Sandstorm, disbelief and fear replacing her confident expression in a second, and then later the look of panic when she realised she couldn't prevent Sandstorm from jumping in front of Mandrake and clipping his forelegs.

The second was Manus's, bent over her after the fall, his concern barely concealing his disgust, knowing that the horse with the broken leg should not have been Mandrake, and drawing his own conclusions. She knew he hadn't been there and hadn't seen her, but the false memory stayed with her, as clear as a photograph.

She had seen and felt nothing more for a week. After she woke to find herself in a Dublin hospital, transferred from Cork, and grasped the implications of the extent of her injuries, she wished she hadn't woken then or ever. Only thirty-one years of age and her life over.

No more hunting. What was life without hunting? And no going to Australia to find Victoria. Old Beatrice couldn't go on her own, and who else was there to send? Verity had never seen Teresa, Dixon or Victoria, so she was no use, not that she would be much use anyway. There was no one else. It was all so infuriatingly exasperating.

Every night now, instead of waking with relief from constant nightmares of falling, she found reality worse than her dreams.

How did the hunting crowd construe the accident? What had Charlotte said? Had Les told Manus about her training methods? What plausible reason could she give for making Charlotte ride Sandstorm?

Waldron came in. There was lots of news, some recent, some repeated from the day before and some from the day before that. Edwina couldn't turn her head. She lay like a corpse while he spoke to the side of her impassive face.

His brother Charles wanted him down at the Park for one last hunt before Waldron returned to India. Brigadier was in fine fettle. Charles was having trouble with Sandstorm – couldn't believe Charlotte had stayed in the saddle for an entire hunt on such a creature.

Edwina's surgeon was pleased with her progress. She'd be up and about before she knew it. In a chair, needless to say – he didn't work miracles.

Charles had invited Charlotte to the Park for the length of the summer vacation so that she wouldn't lose her touch. Beatrice and Bertie kept singing her praises so often he wanted to see her expertise for himself.

Charlotte had been accompanied home from her Ladies' College the previous day. Expelled for violent conduct. None of the pupils, including Charlotte, was throwing any light on the matter, so the authorities didn't know what had prompted Charlotte to cause the hospitalisation of one of the exemplary senior girls, but such unacceptable behaviour couldn't be tolerated under any circumstances.

Edwina showed as little reaction to this fact as she had to any of the others.

Vetchworth School beside the Dublin Mountains had now agreed to take Charlotte, due to Waldron's influence and their under-standing of the tragic family situation.

"I will be delivering her personally next week after Verity has organised the uniform," he said as if expecting praise for undertaking such a duty. "Oh, yes. Almost forgot," he said. "Got an answer from that artist chap who didn't finish your hand."

Edwina held her breath.

"No luck, I'm afraid. Taking no more commissions for the foreseeable future. Suggests we find someone else. Sounds as if he's got too big for his boots, if you ask me."

Edwina drew in two breaths before she could trust herself to speak. "Did you mention my unfinished portrait when you wrote?"

"Of course I did. I even proposed that he should finish it as part of the commission."

Edwina had to restrain herself from pronouncing aloud that he couldn't expect a favourable reply with a suggestion like that, and what business was it of his to mention it in the first place? Her father was the only one who had that right, even though he hadn't paid for it, seeing he was the one who had commissioned it. She managed to ask in a mild tone. "Did he refer to it in his reply?"

"Not a word, but then what would you expect from a man too successful to accept a prestigious commission? It's not everyone who has the opportunity to paint a Blackshaw. I suppose I'm meant to be grateful that he bothered to answer my letter. Not that he did it personally, I might add. He got some underling to write for him."

"Anything else?"

"Beatrice has asked if she can stay over at the townhouse for the night as she wants to have a chat, mainly about Charlotte."

Edwina tried to look unconcerned.

"Women will be allowed to compete in the Horse Show next year, according to Beatrice," Waldron continued. "Pity it's come too late for you, old thing."

He was meeting someone for lunch in Kildare Street so he'd better head off.

"Probably run into Beatrice on the way out if I don't see her first and get time to duck." He bent over and made a pecking sound six inches from her face. "Chin up, old girl."

Edwina was relieved to see the back of him. As hurtful as Dirk's reply sounded, she wanted to replay it in her mind in case there was a hidden message to her from him. She had followed his career in *Village and County*, which every now and then mentioned aristocrats whose portraits he had painted, and inevitably referred to him as '*a worthy successor to John Singer Sargent*' whose work Edwina didn't know. Occasionally there had been mention of an Irish peer and she had become agitated to think Dirk might be nearby; even passing along the street in front of the townhouse. If there was no hidden message in his reply to Waldron, and if the meaning was as unequivocally dismissive as it sounded, she need never think that again as, now that he had been supplied with her address, he could make sure that he never passed anywhere near the vicinity of the townhouse when he was in Dublin.

By the time Beatrice popped her head around the door Edwina had decided to take the safest way out and say she couldn't remember anything about the day of the accident. This was partly true – she had no recollection of the impact, though everything leading up to it was all too clear. Beatrice had a talent for eliciting information, remembering what one had said previously and applying laws of logic, so it was easy to trip up oneself when talking to her. A convenient memory lapse was the surest way to outsmart her.

After Beatrice, wanting details "for Charlotte's sake", left with no information, and while the nurse attended to her, Edwina remembered clearly how, on the day of the hunt, she had used a special crop with metal spiky tacks she'd pressed in through the soft leather ends. It would give Sandstorm a nice jolt if he became too complacent. But when she, Charlotte and the loose grey were heading for the same space and of the three only Mandrake could be controlled, she gave him an unambiguous crack with the crop, assuming it would give him an extra boost and he would jump safely ahead of the other two. Instead he propped, then half reared, and that was when Sandstorm crossed in front and clipped the two front legs with his back legs. Only she knew what had happened. Charlotte would have no idea why Mandrake had acted in such an uncharacteristic manner, and no doubt she was blaming herself for not being able to obey her mother's commands to get back. No one would think to look for the riding crop in all that sleet in the darkness and, with luck, it had landed in the hawthorn bushes, hidden from view, and would gradually rot away.

31

Charlotte's uniform was ready and her trunk packed in readiness for the hour's drive to Vetchworth Preparatory School near the Dublin Mountains, where the headmistress and matron were eager to take in the notorious child to redeem her and, more interestingly, find out what had happened to cause her expulsion from the exclusive school in England.

Charlotte wouldn't put on her uniform, and alternated between floppiness and rigidity while two servants tired themselves out dressing her. She refused to walk to the car. A male servant carried her in a fireman's lift, and when he placed her on the back seat, she slid to the floor and he couldn't lift her up again as her bulk filled the space and he couldn't find any room for leverage.

Confident that she would behave properly in front of strangers, Waldron accompanied her optimistically to the school, but she made no attempt to move from her prone position. He was forced to walk alone to greet the two women, shake their hands and explain that his daughter was unwell, in fact had fainted, so that it might be better to take her home for the time being. He was sorry to inconvenience them, but he would be in touch. The women exchanged looks of disappointment as he left.

After an hour's silence on the return journey Waldron said, "We'll say nothing of this to your mother. She has enough on her plate. I have decided to hire a private tutor instead, and as it so happens I know just the man for the job."

Waldron was pleased with this decision that seemed to come out of nowhere and reminded himself that retreat was a legitimate form of attack.

Waldron contacted 'the man for the job' as soon as they returned home, where Charlotte immediately recovered the use of her legs and ran into the house and up the stairs before anyone could speak to her. He didn't want to face Edwina with the failed school-entrance attempt unless he had an alternative in place, an option that he favoured all along, he would say, on account of Charlotte's inability to get along with other children.

Waldron's desperation to hire someone who would stay, and lack of interest in what happened after that, along with the knowledge that the atmosphere in the house would hardly tempt anyone to commit themselves, prompted him to make a princely offer to Cormac Delaney, a young Galway soldier from his regiment who had attracted his attention by admiring his military drawings and who had voiced a desire to become a professional painter after his army career had come to an end with the loss of part of his left hand.

While Charlotte was in her room stuffing her school uniform under the bed, Waldron wrote to Cormac, offering generous terms for five hours of tuition five days a week for six years. The young man was to regard the townhouse as his home where he would be free to come and go as he pleased outside school hours. Furthermore, he could choose an empty room for his exclusive use as a studio to pursue his interest in the fine arts and an account would be opened for him in Wilkinsons, supplying him with as many canvases and paints as he required.

The girl's intractable, he reasoned as he wrote, so the terms have to be tempting.

Cormac Delaney wrote back by return post to say he accepted the offer.

Holly was pleased to be asked to supervise Charlotte together with Harcourt from two o'clock in the afternoon, the end of lessons, until bedtime. She thought it would be good for the sister and brother to get to know each other better and, in her kind-hearted way, wanted to make up to the lonely girl for the misfortunes she had suffered in her life so far. Until Lord Waldron asked her, Holly assumed and feared that Aunt Verity Blackshaw would be chosen for the task.

When Cormac arrived, full of enthusiasm, he saw a fat little melancholiac tearing up her exercise books and flicking the paper onto the floor. Charlotte looked up at him with dull eyes when he spoke to her.

I'll have my work cut out, he thought.

Only after he was installed did Waldron tell him about Charlotte's expulsion from the English boarding school and her refusal at Vetchworth.

"On the positive side, she draws well. Takes after me in that respect. Thought that might interest you. That's all I can think of. Ask Nanny Holly if you want to know anything else. Can't bother Lady Blackshaw about such things at the moment." Waldron seemed to be glowing inwardly. "Good man. Good man. I knew I could count on you. I can now make arrangements to return to my regiment, or what's left of it."

"Do what you like," was Edwina's reaction when Waldron, uncharacteristically effusive in his praise of the tutor he had hired, told her what he had decided.

"He speaks French like a native," said Waldron. "That's enough to recommend him apart from anything else. Mutilated left hand put paid to professional army life. Lucky he has something to fall back on, and I don't mean tutoring. He's an artist in his spare time."

"*Artist?*"

"Didn't I mention that? He liked my drawings. That's how I got to notice him."

A nurse came in to turn Edwina on to her left side. Waldron went out into the grounds to have a puff on his pipe.

What's all this about artists, and Blackshaws bringing them in to live with them? And hands? Either there was an irrepressible artistic strain running through both branches of the Blackshaw family that emerged every now and then and should be taken seriously, or else Edwina was going mad and past memories were coming back to torment her.

ROSEMARY MᶜLOUGHLIN

That night in her dreams, visions of disembodied hands and faceless artists painting ugly sitters were so unsettling that for once she was relieved to be woken by the nurses' chatter at the change of shifts.

32

Charlotte woke and looked across to see if Victoria was still asleep in her cot. Around the edges of the drawn curtains, only small strips of light entered the dark room. There was no cot. She sat up and stared at the wall opposite.

No Victoria, no cot. She wanted to call out to Miss East in the next room. She wanted Miss East to rush in, wrap her in her arms and comfort her.

She wanted to be back at Tyringham Park with Victoria asleep in her cot, Miss East next door and Mandrake down at the stables. She wanted Nurse Dixon to take back her curse.

The energetic maid Queenie came in, bringing Charlotte back to the present moment. She said it was time to get up for her first day of lessons with the nice Mr Delaney, and wasn't she looking forward to it?

"No," said Charlotte.

"Are you poorly?"

"No."

"Well, up you get, then. Rise and shine."

"No."

The maid hesitated for a minute, and left the room.

The sound of the word 'lesson' was enough to plunge Charlotte

153

into a state of agitation. The one term she had spent in boarding school exposed her to ridicule, as it was evident she was the only one in the class who couldn't read or write. Declensions, fractions, long division, essays, clauses, punctuation and spelling were all incomprehensible to her. She had felt bewildered and frustrated on a daily basis.

She would stay in bed.

After Cormac heard part of Charlotte's story from Holly, he thought the best plan for Charlotte's education would be to start from scratch. To treat her as a five rather than a ten-year-old.

From Waldron he gathered if Charlotte learned to read and write, add and subtract, speak a bit of French and do some watercolour landscapes, he would be more than happy. Latin and Greek would be wasted on her, being a girl. In fact, if Cormac wanted to play tiddlywinks for most of the day no one would chastise him.

On his first day he arrived at the classroom to be met by Queenie the maid who informed him Charlotte was still in bed and refused to get up even though she wasn't poorly.

Cormac had been expecting some kind of resistance from his young charge. "If the pupil won't come to the teacher, then the teacher will have to go to the pupil, so he will. Lead me to her."

Queenie hesitated. "I don't know if that be allowed," she said. "I'll have to ask Miss Blackshaw."

"Don't you worry. I have to follow Lord Waldron's instructions. I'm here to teach, so I am, and I have to teach someone, or else I'm here under false pretences. You see my dilemma. So please show me the way and announce my arrival so I don't put the heart across the poor child."

Cormac's second time to see Charlotte disheartened him even more than the first. She lay curled in a ball as if all life had been sucked out of her.

His only option, he decided, was to tell stories. He would be fulfilling his side of the bargain by doing something, and she could continue to lie there passively with her eyes closed until she chose to show some interest. He could threaten to wait in the classroom until she was ready to be taught, but what if she took him at his word and never came up, where would he be then? If he didn't give her an order she couldn't disobey him. He badly needed the board and the materials included in his contract until he made a name for himself in the art world and could support himself. Starving in a freezing garret in Paris wouldn't enhance his work in any way – he had already proved that. Besides, he wanted to do his best for the unhappy child and he didn't want to force her into a situation where she would not be able to extricate herself without losing face and he was aware he couldn't afford to lose face himself if he was to earn her respect.

Stories were one thing he knew in abundance.

Taking the chance that 'Little Red Riding Hood' and 'Cinderella' would not be considered babyish by her, he related them first, acting all the parts in an exaggerated fashion. For the first hour when Charlotte looked away he ran around the bed to intercept her gaze and when she turned over, he retraced his steps. When she looked up he loomed over her (that suited the part of the wolf) and when she looked down he knelt on the floor (coinciding nicely with Prince Charming fitting the glass slipper on Cinderella). By the time he began to describe the vain stepmother, jealous of Snow White's beauty and bearing a poisoned apple to kill her off, Charlotte stopped trying to pretend she wasn't interested.

"Snow White, even though forbidden to, opened the front door . . ."

Cormac flung open the bedroom door to find Aunt Verity Blackshaw with a glass to her ear, frozen in the leaning-over posture of an eavesdropper. He took the glass from her hand and held it up.

". . . to find the wicked stepmother in her disguise of an old woman offering Snow White the sweetest apple in all the kingdom and urging her to eat it. Now I'm afraid it's time for lunch." He had spotted Queenie coming along the corridor with a tray for Charlotte. "Would you like to join us later, Miss Blackshaw, to hear what happened to Snow White?"

"Thank you, Mr Delaney, but I'm afraid I have my own duties to attend to. I don't have the luxury of sitting around all day frittering away my time, listening to make-believe." Her colour was still high after being caught in a compromising position. "Not my idea of an education. But then nobody ever consults me."

When Cormac returned after lunch he deliberately left the story of 'Snow White' unfinished, and launched straight into the story of

'Hansel and Gretel', describing in detail the various types of confectionery that decorated the walls of the gingerbread house, assuming from the size of Charlotte that food would be one of her main concerns. She still hadn't spoken a word to him, though he could tell by the way she was reacting to each dramatic scene that she was captivated by the old tales she was hearing for the first time. He didn't ask her any questions, as he didn't want her to get the upper hand by refusing to answer.

"The children of Lir were changed into swans by their jealous stepmother."

What's going on here, Cormac wondered? He had just switched over to Celtic legends and there was that wicked stepmother character popping up again. This stepmother, Aoife, had the grace to feel enough remorse to limit the spell to nine hundred years – not much of a consolation for poor Fionnuala, Aed, Conor and Fiachra, who had to stay on water and were separated from their father and the land they loved, and when they were transformed back to themselves after nine hundred years weren't children any more, but very old people ready to die. "Not very fair, was it?"

Cormac was reading Charlotte's expressions despite her best attempts to disguise them.

As a change from all the gloom brought about by stepmothers, he introduced Setanta, the seven-year-old sportsman and warrior who could take on a hundred and fifty opponents at one time and vanquish them unaided. Charlotte's eyebrows said, "Who are you trying to fool?" but she seemed to revel in the descriptions of Setanta's battle frenzies and the amount of killing that resulted from them. His exploits, both as a boy and then as the renamed Cúchulainn, the hound of Ulster, took them up to two o'clock.

"Must be off," said Cormac, almost running from the room. His mind was teeming with ideas and his hand itching to pick up his favourite hogshair brush that he could already feel loaded with paint. He had eight hours' work ahead of him. Setanta's battle frenzy couldn't be any more powerful than his fever to transfer the images now in his mind to the canvas.

The next morning Charlotte became agitated when Cúchulainn, against the advice of his camp, took on the warrior Queen Maeve and her magic spells and ignored the omens and prophecies that were warning him not to fight. When the faithful horse, the Grey of Macha, began to weep dark tears of blood in sorrow at his master's impending death, Charlotte's lip and chin began to quiver.

Cormac stopped abruptly, abandoning his storyteller's stance. "Are you all right, Charlotte?" he asked, sitting beside her bed.

Charlotte pulled the sheet over her head and broke into loud sobs, banging her heels on the mattress and kicking the brass bed-end.

Cormac leant over to comfort her.

Aunt Verity was on the spot within seconds. She didn't ask what had happened – she must have been listening at the door again. Pushing Cormac aside, she forcibly pulled the sheet away from Charlotte's face. Charlotte wailed more loudly and snatched back the sheet to cover her head.

Cormac had a strong urge to lift Verity up, push her out the door and turn the lock on her but, controlling himself, rang for Queenie and asked her to fetch Holly. "And you look after Harcourt until Holly returns," he said quietly.

Queenie, taking in the thrashing figure in the bed and the intensifying howls, ignored the house regulation of sedate movement at all times and ran to the nursery as fast as she could.

"Control yourself," said Verity, slapping Charlotte's arms in an effort to wrest the sheet from her. Charlotte held on and Verity slapped her harder. "Let go, you wicked girl! Let go, I tell you!"

Holly arrived breathless.

"Holly will take over now, Miss Blackshaw," said Cormac, taking hold of Verity's slapping arm with his good hand.

"Take your hand off me, you uncouth lackey! I'm her aunt," Verity protested, pulling away. "You are only a servant, in case you'd forgotten."

"Lord Waldron's orders I'm afraid, Miss Blackshaw. You will have to take it up with him," he said, knowing she wouldn't. He guided her towards the door. "Thank you for your concern. We'll call you if we need you but I'm sure Holly can manage. Good afternoon, Miss Blackshaw."

Verity, scarlet with temper, said loudly as she left, "You'll never rid her of her wilful habits the way you keep pandering to her. Spare the rod and spoil the child – that's what the Bible says and never were words more truly spoken. You haven't heard the last of this."

When he turned back Charlotte was still sobbing loudly but had relinquished the sheet and was in Holly's arms. Holly signalled to Cormac over Charlotte's head that she would stay and Cormac was free to go.

Cormac visited Holly that evening after the two children were in bed. He had been too distracted all afternoon to paint, thinking of Charlotte's distress and wondering what he had said to cause it. Holly was able to fill him in on Charlotte's past attachment to Mandrake and the awful events surrounding his death.

"No more sad stories about horses then. Thank you for your intervention. All I could think of doing was strangling Aunt Verity. Lucky I have only one hand." He moved off, chuckling to himself.

"Where is she?" Cormac asked the next morning, finding no sign of Charlotte in the bedroom.

"All dressed and ready and waiting for you in the schoolroom. Up like a lark this morning." Queenie was smiling broadly.

Cormac bounded up the stairs.

Charlotte was sitting at her desk, trying to look nonchalant. Cormac entered the room as if her presence there were natural and expected. No more gloomy stories, he resolved. Where to begin?

"Did Snow White eat the apple?" Charlotte asked shyly. This was the first time she had spoken in the eight days of their time together.

"She did," Cormac answered. He finished the story, grateful for the happy ending. "And I know where the house of the seven dwarfs is, the very one, so when you feel better we'll go along to see it."

"I'd like to see it," she smiled, while her eyebrows said, 'Who's he trying to fool?'

They started to make reading charts. "I'll do the letters and you do the pictures," Cormac suggested, looking forward to seeing Charlotte's drawing skills for himself. He took paper, pens, scissors and glue out of the presses.

"What a grand little illustrator you are," he said with pleasure, after Charlotte had drawn an apple, bat, cat, dog, elephant, fish and giraffe. When 'h' came up Charlotte said 'horse'. Cormac said that might be a bit difficult and would she rather draw a hat, but she said she could manage.

While she was adding the bridle to the accurate outline of a horse, she looked up and asked, "What happened to the Grey that cried the tears of blood?"

Cormac hesitated. "Do you really want to know?"

She nodded.

He was tempted to change the ending, but having already mentioned the omens and prophecies, he knew Charlotte wouldn't accept a false resolution.

Charlotte continued to nod.

By the end of the story they were both moved – Charlotte by the actions of the brave Grey of Macha who was mortally wounded trying to defend his master, and Cormac by the dramatic image of the raven sitting on the shoulder of the wounded hero who had strapped himself to a pillar so he could die upright facing his enemies.

"What happened to your hand?" she asked later. "Did it get hurt in battle?"

His index, middle and ring fingers were missing as far as his knuckles, his thumb and little finger as far as his wrist. The rest of his hand and forearm were corrugated with deep scars.

"You could say that." Cormac gave her a sanitised version of the incident that had caused his injuries and she wanted to hear more about the war. The more he told her the more she wanted to know. As with Cúchulainn's story, she was more interested in the animals than the soldiers. He was careful not to include the sufferings of the horses in battle, especially one he couldn't forget who thrashed and roared for what seemed like an age before anyone could get near enough to finish it off.

33

Those who say family life is a crashing bore (most of his regiment) must be going about it the wrong way, Waldron commented to Verity who was following him around to ask him something. After he sorted out each person under his authority, he wrote a short list of directives to leave with his will. If anything happened to him on this trip he wanted it to be known publicly that he took his familial responsibilities as seriously as his military duties.

Blackshaw Townhouse
Dublin. 27th February 1919

1. *Edwina Blackshaw (wife). Ramps to be fitted on ground floor for her convenience, three rooms to be made ready. Two live-in nurses to be employed. Verity can fill in for half days and shift changes to save employing a third nurse.*
2. *Verity Blackshaw (sister-in-law). Chatelaine until Edwina leaves hospital, and after that her companion. To give elocution lessons to Charlotte on a weekly basis to rid her of Huddersfield/Dublin influences. No authority over the tutor who takes orders only from me. To look on the townhouse as her home for the term of her natural life.*

3. *Charlotte (daughter). To be privately tutored until her sixteenth birthday, then to attend a finishing school in Paris for a year.*
4. *Harcourt (son). To attend my old school after his seventh birthday.*
5. *Holly Stoddard (Harcourt's nanny). As one of the million young women with doubtless no prospects of marriage because of the war, she is to remain on in the house for the rest of her natural life. To become Lady Blackshaw's companion after Harcourt quits her care. This is my contribution to the War Widow's Fund, even though Holly is in fact a spinster, not a widow.*
6. *Cormac Delaney. An account has been set up in Wilkinsons to supply Cormac Delaney with canvases, brushes and paints as and when he needs them. There is to be no limit imposed. I have long wished to be a patron of the arts and this is my chosen way of becoming one. Such is my confidence in him, he has my permission to tutor in any way he sees fit.*

Waldron read over what he had written, felt satisfied with it, and signed it. Not for the first time he felt gratitude to his forebears who had made a fortune from the slave trade to the West Indies and had the wisdom to invest it in London property, the proceeds of which enabled him to live the life of a king in India. Tyringham Park could not on its own support such extravagance along with the upkeep of the separate households in Dublin and Cork.

"What do you want, Verity?" he asked, his usual tone of exasperation giving way to amusement, knowing he had curtailed her authority and he would soon be leaving to take his rightful place near the top of the Empire's hierarchy. The way she fussed, one would think she was approaching old age, not her prime, if religious women could be said to have a prime, so circumscribed were their lives.

"It's about the tutor." Standing beside his desk, she appeared intimidated, but driven to do her duty nonetheless. He didn't ask her to sit for fear she would settle in for a long conversation. "Have you known him long?"

"Long enough. Why do you ask?"

"He seems a bit . . ." she faltered, wanting to say 'deranged' but unwilling to admit peeping into the classroom and witnessing Cormac's antics, "a bit *common*. He could fill Charlotte's mind with all sorts of unacceptable ideas and we would be none the wiser." She didn't mention Cormac's manhandling her arm for fear Waldron would make light of the incident rather than give it the serious consideration it merited.

"'Common' is one thing that he is not, dear sister-in-law, and 'none the wiser' is what Charlotte will always be if she doesn't receive some tuition soon. Ten years of age and still illiterate. Need I say more, dear cousin? She is obviously in the right hands – hand – and I expressly forbid you to interfere. Do I make myself clear?"

A flash of hatred flicked across Verity's face before she had time to mask it but Waldron didn't notice. He was rereading his directions and was struck by how his generosity showed through and how smart he was to put it all down in writing.

"Do I?" he repeated.

"Yes, Waldron," said Verity, turning to leave.

"I didn't attain the position of Major General in the army without becoming a good judge of character along the way," he proclaimed to her retreating back.

Waldron travelled to Tyringham Park for a weekend with his brother Charles and his wife Harriet, their four children with their spouses and three grandchildren. Two things struck him. The Park was as full of energy and gaiety as it had been in his father's time, and Manus, rather than being demoted by Charles as he expected, was still head man at the stables and was held in the highest regard.

So, after a four-and-a-half year absence, Waldron set off back to India with a clear conscience.

Verity, on the other hand, full of disquiet about the new tutor, determined to keep a close eye on him, as well as putting her worries in the hands of the Lord. It was confusing at times, Waldron and Jesus sharing the same title.

To break the monotony of the classroom routine and to rid Charlotte of her superfluous bulk without drawing attention to it, Cormac planned excursions to take them all over the city. While they walked, he continued to tell stories, recite poems and speak in French. They visited the house in Stephen's Green where the seven dwarfs used to live; Kilmainham where Rapunzel had been imprisoned; Herbert

Park, which had been cleared of briars since Sleeping Beauty's time; the bridge over the Dodder where the troll lurked before the large Billy Goat Gruff dealt with him; the port where Ali Baba docked, and the Iveagh Gardens where the Selfish Giant once presided.

Each day Aunt Verity waited at an upstairs window for their return, noting how the two of them walked close together, with Charlotte looking up at her tutor with admiration and Mr Delaney reflecting the same regard back to her. The sight of such friendliness between teacher and pupil made her feel quite unwell.

By the time Cormac had depleted his horde of fairy stories and was ready to move on to more mature tales, Charlotte, becoming slimmer by the day, was always the first one ready in the morning and could walk for miles without effort.

Even after she graduated to reading for herself, she would continue to ask Cormac to tell her again about wicked stepmothers, spells and curses, and how the spells were broken and the curses thwarted.

34

"Can I do that?"

Cormac was unaware Charlotte had spoken. He had propped up a work in progress to examine and analyse while she was reading *Little Women* aloud. In less than a year her reading had become so fluent (though she still trailed her finger across the page to keep her place) she didn't need prompting. Cormac's mind wandered from the story, which was just as well as he didn't want to spoil Charlotte's enjoyment by snorting or making cynical comments.

He couldn't help himself. In the middle of a sentence he ran next door to his studio and returned with a brush laden with paint, which he placed on the highlighted left shoulder of the seated blue female nude. He walked backwards while not taking his eyes off the shoulder, then ran forwards, manipulated the fresh paint, ran backwards and stood staring at it for a long period. This he repeated until he was satisfied with the effect.

Charlotte had stopped reading and was watching him.

"Can I do that?" she repeated.

At that moment, both she and Cormac became aware of Aunt Verity's presence in the room.

"Sorry, wrong door," said Aunt Verity, staring at the blue nude.

Charlotte's legs had red squares on them and her face was flushed from sitting too close to the coal fire. The door, often left open, had been closed to keep in the heat. Outside it was a typical January day – cold, dark and raining.

Cormac cursed inwardly. Of course Verity hadn't mistaken the door. In the normal course of events she wouldn't be anywhere near this part of the house, but he guessed she was still keeping an eye on him – he had often been aware of a passing figure during lessons, but now she had caught him doing his own work during class time and he had no excuse to give except his dislike of *Little Women*. Bloody hell.

"Is there anything I can do for you, Miss Blackshaw?" he asked. He wouldn't make excuses.

Aunt Verity, still staring at the nude, began to back out of the room.

"No, thank you," was all she said. She never addressed him by name and during the rare times she did look at him, it was his deformed hand rather than his face that held her gaze.

"Yes, Charlotte," said Cormac, after he gauged Verity was out of hearing range. "You *may* do this. Whether you *can* or not remains to be seen, so it does. I'm nothing if not pedantic. One stipulation, though. We'll paint in French. Agreed?"

It didn't quite work out like that. Soon, Cormac and his 'apprentice', as he now called her, were painting daily side by side for hours, and for long periods didn't speak in any language.

35

Dublin
1921

Beatrice wrote to Edwina telling her how her second son had been recognised by chance by one of his regiment in an English lunatic asylum and how she and Bertie had travelled there to bring him home. They found him in a poor physical state with no memory, parts of his reasoning functions missing, and prone to outbursts of rage, but they were glad to have him back under any circumstances and hoped he would soon be restored to his former health now that he was in familiar surroundings.

Her next-door neighbour on the other side had been burnt out during the year by rebels who claimed he was sheltering British troops there after their barracks were destroyed, she continued.

> *Our estate and Tyringham Park are still intact (except for your gate lodge which was uninhabited as usual, making the burning look like a token gesture), no doubt due to the influence of someone we both know high up in the organisation, not mentioning any names. One can't be too careful these days.*

Letting on she had inside information about the nationalists, as usual. Unlike Tyringham Park which had a policy of not taking on local people as servants, Beatrice and Bertie employed them exclusively on their 12,000 acres, and were supporters of Home Rule. Beatrice, particularly, was vociferous in her wish to rid Ireland of British colonial rule. Waldron called her a traitor to her class.

We seem to be at Tyringham Park a lot these days. Bertie was friendly with your brother-in-law when they were younger and their friendship has been renewed to mutual benefit – they have so much in common. Charles's wife Harriet and I took to each other straight away. The place is so lively with three generations happily living there you'd hardly recognise it.

Was Beatrice deliberately rubbing salt into her wounds? Edwina was more annoyed than saddened to think that that might be the case.

As it so happens, last time I was there I ran into both Miss East (can never think of her married name) and Manus, who has just had his first child, a son. I think I told you in my last letter that he married a girl from the locality. Marriage must have loosened his tongue. You know how shy and unassuming he was.

Oh, God, how can I bear it? Beatrice setting herself up as an expert on Manus when she obviously knows so little about him – talking about his first child. His *first*? How little she knows! And Manus, when he sees the emptiness of his attachment to his local bride, must mourn the loss of what he had with me – a relationship closer than a marriage. Each day of those years, already full of interest, coloured by our rivalry, our opposing philosophies on training fought over with exhilarating intensity. How could Beatrice know anything of that, when she and Bertie saw only his superficial skills each time they dropped by to pick his brains?

Both of them asked after Charlotte. Miss East said she thinks of her every day and even little Catherine (her stepdaughter in case you've forgotten) can't touch the part of her heart reserved for her. Didn't she word that very nicely? Manus is training the colt Bryony who has the same breeding as Mandrake, and would love Charlotte to see him and perhaps take him over. They both hope she will visit her cousins and come to see them while she's here. One can see how both of them are genuinely attached to her. I promised I would pass on their messages so that you can relay them to Charlotte.

Charlotte. Charlotte. Always Charlotte.

Beatrice ended the letter with effusive wishes for Edwina's good health and happiness.

No mention of calling in if she ever found herself in Dublin. Four years and four Horse Shows since they'd seen each other face to face. Did Beatrice not realise she was hungry for news, especially now that women were eligible to compete in the Show? The *Irish Times* printed the results, but she wanted to know the inside story behind each event.

Edwina saw Charlotte approaching with her usual nervousness.

"Tell me, Charlotte, did you ever hear from Miss East since you left?"

"No, Mother."

"Or Manus?"

"No, Mother."

"That's a little disappointing, don't you think?"

Charlotte squirmed and shifted her weight from one foot to the other.

"Well, don't you?"

"Yes, Mother."

Charlotte was now fourteen and already tall. She moved the folder of paintings she had brought to show her mother from under her left arm to her right and looked unsure of what to do next.

"Have you brought something for me to look at?"

Charlotte nodded, and a flicker of pride showed on her face.

"Put it on the table over there and I'll cast my eye over it later when I have time."

"Well, what did your mother say?" asked Cormac.

"She didn't say anything about them because she didn't look at them. She said she'd look at them later."

"Never mind." Cormac could feel Charlotte's disappointment. He realigned his easel with two sharp kicks to the base. "Perhaps she was busy."

"Doing what? She never does anything except play bridge, and she can't do that all day long."

Lady Blackshaw hadn't shown the slightest interest in Charlotte's education all the time Cormac had been at the townhouse so it was difficult to keep a judgmental tone out of his voice.

"Perhaps she wanted to look at them when she was on her own. In fact, she's probably looking at them right now."

"Very likely," said Charlotte with heavy sarcasm. She picked up her brush and made some strong slashing strokes across the canvas.

"That's the girl," Cormac cheered. "Don't hold back."

Five days afterwards, he saw Charlotte carrying the folder that enclosed her paintings.

"Well, what did your mother say?" he asked, holding his breath.

"She didn't even look at them. They were in the exact same place . . ." Charlotte couldn't finish the sentence. She dropped the folder, kicked it, and ran out of the room.

Cormac bent down, picked it up and opened it. "So help me God, I could swing for that woman," he said as he spread out the work he so admired.

36

Dublin
1925

Harcourt went off to school at the age of seven. Holly, turning down Waldron's offer to stay on as a companion for Edwina, travelled to County Down to take up another post, leaving Charlotte doubly bereft. She had grown attached to Holly, and her departure brought back memories of her rupture with Miss East. When Harcourt was escorted from the house by a tutor who accompanied the new boys to England, she went to her room to weep secretly both for Holly and Harcourt, and the memory of little Victoria.

Two years earlier Aunt Verity, either through weariness or fear of Waldron, told Charlotte she was now old enough to stay unsupervised after Cormac left at two.

So while Cormac was working in secret, Charlotte did the same in the empty classroom, hiding her work at the end of each day in one of the many empty cupboards. Dublin was forgotten, and life at Tyringham Park became her subject matter. She ignored Cormac's view of narrative as an outdated and usually moralistic device and painted the story of her early life. He would never see them so she wouldn't have to justify herself to him. Besides, she called them frozen moments rather than narratives. Whether she would keep them hidden or destroy them at a later time was of no immediate concern to her.

She continued experimenting with different painting techniques and, after two years, arrived at a method that yielded the end result she wanted. She would wait three weeks for the basic layout of a painting to dry, so that if the final fluent, single brushstrokes were not to her liking, she could scrape them off and do them again without disturbing the underlying layers of paint. Sometimes she redid them as many as ten times until she arrived at the exact effect of immediacy and spontaneity she sought.

"You call those highlights?" Cormac often teased her.

The subdued pigments she favoured – black, white and grey as the dominant ones, with bare hints of siennas, ochres and muddy blue-greens – were in direct contrast to his approach of pure colours applied straight from their tubes.

"You'd be blinded looking at yours if you didn't half close your eyes," she would counter with affected scorn.

It was moments such as these that made Cormac feel his tutoring had been a success. She had been guided by him early on but was now following her own path and the only aspects of her work that now showed his influence were the exuberant brushstrokes and impasto, which they both favoured but used differently.

When she was with Cormac she left aside Tyringham Park as a theme and concentrated on urban subjects – streetscapes, bridges, locks, façades, railings, warehouses, gravestones, churches, interiors, houses – but came in so close with her viewpoint that it was difficult to identify exactly what the subjects were, as they looked like puzzles of abstract rather than concrete shapes, with the close tonal values and limited palette infusing them with a quiet harmony.

"There," she said, sighed, put her brush into the turpentine and placed the painting at a distance, staring at it with her head cocked to one side. "Would you say it's finished?"

"I would, and it's masterly. That's the only word I can use to describe it. Masterly. This area on the left is a touch of genius."

Charlotte couldn't hide her pleasure.

He continued to stare at the painting and Charlotte was gratified to see his expression was one of undisguised admiration. He was a severe critic so a look like that meant a lot to her.

"What a gifted little party you are." His voice had turned serious. "Just think. You have exceptional horsemanship, so I've heard.

That's one. An ear for languages – you're now speaking French like a native. That's two. And now, to top it all, you're passing me out as an artist. Would you not think that's an embarrassing excess of riches?"

"You forgot to mention being useless at arithmetic and English composition and having two left feet and being tone deaf."

"Accept the fact that you have talents and be grateful for them and stop running yourself down. That's my lecture for the day. Now I have a surprise for you."

"Another foreign ship in the docks that we have to visit?"

"Nothing like that this time. Something completely different. How would you like to give me four of those sombre, boring cityscapes of yours –"

"Not to be confused with those contorted, garish, chopped-up nudes of yours . . ."

Cormac laughed. He encouraged, even goaded her to be outspoken, and enjoyed it when she was, though he warned her that this was acceptable only in the classroom. Outside it she would be wise to exercise restraint and decorum, and speak in the way Aunt Verity instructed her.

"For exhibition. To mark your sixteenth birthday."

"Me? Exhibit? Do you mean it? How is that possible?"

Cormac told her that the Society of Emerging Painters had secured an extra room this year for their annual exhibition.

Charlotte already knew of the Society, as Cormac was a member of it and had exhibited with it for the last six years, but couldn't see what news of it had to do with her.

To fill the extra space, Cormac explained, each member could invite one young student of promise and genuine merit to hang in the show, giving greater publicity to an already popular event.

"So of course I thought of you. Who else? A parting gift to you before you go off to Paris. Well, what do you think?"

"I don't know." Charlotte looked excited and apprehensive in turns. "I think I'd like it. What would I have to do?"

"You wouldn't have to do anything except paint the pictures. I'll arrange everything else."

"What if I'm not good enough and everyone laughs at me?"

"Trust me, my little apprentice, no one will be laughing. Madly jealous, more like."

Charlotte's frown deepened. "I don't think my mother would allow it."

"She doesn't have to know. I'll deal with everything. It's not as if you're a child any more – you'll be married in a couple of years' time, for God's sake. I'm sure your father will give his permission now that he's back home."

"My father?" She was so used to not considering him, it was now an effort.

"Remember how he and I met?" Cormac went on. "I told you. The War Office. His drawings all over the place. We got talking. Later he asked me to become your tutor as he didn't want your artistic gifts going to waste."

"Did he? You never told me that before. I didn't know he'd seen any of my work."

"Apparently your old housekeeper kept everything you did and showed it to him."

"But I was only a child."

"He said he could see the promise even then."

"Well, imagine, I never knew, but I still don't want him to come because that means Mother and Aunt Verity would come as well, and I couldn't bear that."

"If that's the way you feel, we'll leave it as it is. Just me exhibiting as usual. They've never been interested in my work before and completely ignore my invitations every year, so you're safe enough. Pity in a way. I think your father would enjoy it." He smiled at her. "Can I leave you then to do three more on a similar theme to the one you've just finished, to be ready in eight weeks?"

Charlotte looked at Cormac with open gratitude.

He was moved, and on impulse, in the manner he always greeted his young siblings, put his good arm around her shoulder and kissed her on the top of the head. "Just as well I'll be leaving soon," he said, "before my little apprentice overtakes me and becomes my teacher, filling me with resentment. Come on now – back to work. Good Lord, it's two o'clock already. I'm off. See you in the morning."

Back in his studio, he thought to himself how lucky he'd been to have been given this position six years earlier, allowing him time to discover a distinctive style and amass over two hundred works that would be invaluable to him when he returned to Paris.

How lucky, as well, that Charlotte had a natural aptitude and that their personalities suited each other so that his years spent as a teacher were enjoyable in their own right.

He could hardly believe she was the same person as the fat little melancholiac he'd seen on his first day at the townhouse. She could never be described as beautiful or even pretty, but after maturation had brought a pleasing balance to her features, she had acquired something more significant than either beauty or prettiness – a striking, arresting originality that would excite admiration in anyone who saw her.

37

"What will I wear?" asked Charlotte on the day of the opening.

"Anything you like," said Cormac. "You're an artist now, don't forget, so you can get away with anything, though a few woman painters I know seem to favour floaty, colourful things, probably to match their paintings, if that's any help to you. I presume that means you should wear black and grey armour."

"Very funny. I'll have a look through all the classic stuff in the trunks upstairs and see what I can come up with. Are you sure no one knows?"

"Quite sure. I said to your aunt it was a group show the same as always and tried to make it sound as boring as possible. I didn't tell a lie – just an omission of fact. I didn't say 'Charlotte won't be hanging' or anything like that."

She was losing track of the conversation as she was becoming jittery.

"It would have been safer not to give any invitations," he went on, "but then by Murphy's Law they'd surely find out from someone in this small city, and then I'd be in strife. Better this way. If they –"

"I'll run up and change," she cut across him, even though it was only four o'clock.

By half past five she was ready. Her outfit was black, white and grey. Purely coincidental, she said.

"You look great. Really great. You did ask if you could come with me, didn't you?"

175

"Yes, I asked Aunt Verity and she said she couldn't see any harm in it at this hour and it being only three streets away, though she did look at me in an odd fashion."

"No change there, then. Come on, what are we waiting for?"

"I'm so nervous." She kept dropping the hem of her cloak and tripping on it. "What if everyone's paintings except mine are sold?"

"That won't happen, but even if it does, no one knows who you are, so just look unconcerned."

"What if people are standing around them and laughing?" She looked up at him. "What's the big grin for? Do you know something?"

"Just nerves," he said. "It never gets easier, you know. It might be my seventh showing, but I'm on tenterhooks, just as you are. Wait until you have a solo show and then you'll know what nerves are all about."

They arrived and looked through the front Georgian window.

"There aren't many there," said Charlotte, finding it difficult to speak as her mouth had gone dry.

"Give it time. It's only a quarter past six, and it's on until eight. Some people like to miss the opening speech in case it's too long-winded. Come on, now. Deep breath." He pushed open the door.

There were bright lights and a din of voices, even though there were only about twenty people there.

"Where are yours?" asked Charlotte, looking for her own.

"Upstairs – I have a whole wall to myself. I was in this afternoon to check. But let's look around here first."

Charlotte pretended to look at the other paintings but they merged into a blur. She couldn't scan the whole room at once because of alcoves, partitions and people, up to forty in number by now.

"There you are, Cormac," said a voice behind them.

It was David Slane, the elected President of the Society for the year and, as such, curator and arbiter of this exhibition. "Did you get a glass of wine yet?"

"No, not yet. We thought we'd have a look around first. David, this is Charlotte Blackshaw of the grey urban landscapes. Charlotte, David Slane, President of the Society."

David's face lit up. "An honour to meet you. You're causing quite a stir. All sold. Come and see for yourself."

"Does he really mean me?" Charlotte whispered to Cormac.

"Of course he means you," Cormac smiled. "Don't look so surprised."

David led them to the right-hand wall where Charlotte's four submissions were grouped in a square with red dots on the white cards beside each one.

"I had a buyer in this afternoon who threatened my life if I didn't let him buy all four before the opening, he was so afraid of missing them, and since then there have been three disappointed clients who've made me promise to let them know as soon as you show any more of your work. Congratulations and well done. Hard to credit you're only sixteen – people don't believe me when I tell them. You're in good company, you know. Think of the amazing Turner for one, exhibiting at the Royal Academy when he was only fifteen."

"Damn," said Cormac. "If I'd known that I would have entered you earlier."

"Not to mention Velázquez, painting 'Old Woman Cooking Eggs' when he was nineteen. Can you think of any other early bloomers, Cormac?"

"Not off the top of my head," said Cormac. "I didn't study art history. I had to pick up bits as I went along."

"You did well with the bits you picked up, then, judging by your pupil here, and your own work, too, of course." David turned back to Charlotte. "Think what you'll be able to achieve in a lifetime, following in their footsteps. Now I must leave you to meet our guest speaker. Congratulations again to both of you. Enjoy the night." He disappeared into the crowd that was now up to sixty.

Charlotte couldn't stop smiling and stayed facing her paintings until her smile contracted to a normal width.

"Did you hear that? Turner and Velázquez, no less," Cormac beamed. "Now do you believe you're talented?"

"He was talking about age, not skill, so let's not get any inflated ideas. You knew about the sale, didn't you?"

"I did. I happened to be here this afternoon when the deal was done. Your purchaser is a famous collector, apparently, who used an agent to do the negotiations so he couldn't be identified. Even David Slane doesn't know who it is, or if he does he's not saying."

"Imagine. I'll be spending the rest of my life wondering who it could possibly be. And what about yours?" Charlotte really did care about Cormac's, now that her own were accounted for. "I suppose you know already?"

"He didn't buy any of mine if that's what you're asking. Come and see."

"Why didn't you tell me earlier and put me out of my misery?" asked Charlotte, as they made their way up to the next floor, while other people were coming down to hear the speech.

"And spoil that moment? Would you really have wanted that?"

Charlotte was wondering why she had been so worried in the first place. "Probably not."

Cormac's eight works, much larger than hers, had the gable wall to themselves.

"Only seven sold," teased Charlotte. "Oh, dear." She noticed one of his commanded the same price as four of hers.

While they were watching, a Society member excused himself when he walked in front of them to place a red dot on the eighth one. "Well done, Cormac," he said when he turned around. "Full house."

Cormac grinned at Charlotte. "That makes two of us."

The crowd was being shushed to listen to the speech. Most stood with their heads bowed as if in prayer until it was over. After polite applause, the noise level rose again.

"Let's go down and get a glass of wine," said Cormac.

It took them a while to negotiate the stairs, as so many were ascending. On the second last step Charlotte's heel caught in the hem of her skirt and Cormac grabbed her arm to steady her. She was pushed against him by the force of the crowd that now filled the room.

There was some kind of movement attracting attention at the door.

"Can you believe it?" said Charlotte, disappearing behind a screen and pulling Cormac after her. "What are we going to do?"

Aunt Verity had seen them, she was sure. Waldron was busy negotiating the wheelchair and hadn't looked up yet. Edwina couldn't be seen through the crowd. With difficulty, space was being made for her and her wheelchair.

"Is there a back door out of here?" asked Charlotte.

Cormac was saddened to see Charlotte so unnerved. "They know we're here, Charlotte, so there's no point in hiding. Your Aunt Verity must have had her bloodhounds out. Come on. What have you got to feel guilty about?" Cormac made his way through the crowd and Charlotte followed with reluctance.

"Oh, there you are, Cormac," said Lord Waldron. "We wondered if we'd find you in this crush. Evening, Charlotte. Are you enjoying the show?"

There were comments and greetings all round.

"Where have all these people come from? Who would have thought art could be so popular?"

"It will thin out any minute, Your Lordship, now that all the business has been done."

"Mr Delaney's are upstairs," said Charlotte, staying on the side of the group to cut off their view of the right-hand wall where her pictures were hanging. "All sold, too. A wall to himself. You simply must view them."

"Clear the way then, Cormac."

"That means I won't be able to see them," said Edwina.

"Nonsense," said Waldron. "Cormac, get another pair of hands."

Cormac caught the eye of one of the helpers, called him over and mimed what he wanted him to do.

"Hold on there, old thing," said Waldron, who held the handles of the wheelchair so there'd be no tipping backwards or forwards while Cormac took one wheel with his good hand and the helper took hold of the other. People reversed back up the stairs to make room.

"There!" the three of them said together when they reached the upper floor and placed her down in a smooth movement.

"Love the Blackshaws . . ."

Waldron and Verity turned towards the speaker whom they couldn't locate in the moving groups.

"Was someone talking about us?" asked Verity.

"That's what I thought but there's no one I recognise," said Waldron.

"I didn't hear anything," said Edwina.

"One's own name always stands out, so it's a wonder you didn't hear it," said Waldron. "Now, let's take a look at yours, Cormac."

Cormac's paintings were now facing them: all nudes, five female and three male, in undiluted colours of purple, orange, green, red, yellow and blue, toned down only when they overlapped or seeped into one another. He had avoided the averted heads and anonymity of the bodies being favoured by his contemporaries. Each subject looked straight out from the canvas with an expression of intense engagement with the viewer. A minimum of brushstrokes had been used, forcing the viewer to interpret the artist's suggestions rather than merely absorbing his statements.

"These Delaneys deliver a punch," said a man beside them in evening dress to his companion. "All sold. Pity. I was hoping to add another one to my collection."

Waldron wondered if the man was joking. For his own part, he didn't know what to say. He liked anatomically correct paintings of horses, and landscapes that looked like photographs, and not much else. His subordinates praised his drawings of battle scenes so effusively that he secretly considered himself a real artist, and should have felt the confidence to denounce Cormac's work as untidy, unrealistic and unfinished, but he was held back by a fear of appearing uninformed in a world in which he wasn't the master. To fill in time until he could think of something quotable he said "Interesting. Very interesting," half-closing his eyes and nodding.

Cormac caught Charlotte's eye and winked.

The little group around the wheelchair heard the Blackshaw name mentioned again and gave themselves up to unashamed eavesdropping.

"First time showing, so I heard. One to watch, definitely."

"I wonder who he is?"

"No idea. Never heard of him."

"Come on, let's have another look at them on the way out." The party of about ten moved off.

"A bit of serious competition there, Cormac," said Waldron, "judging from all those comments."

"All to the good. The higher the general standard, the better for the reputation of the Society and its members, though I have to say I haven't seen such a response to a newcomer before."

"Well, let's finish looking at yours first. Charlotte, you're very jumpy. Control yourself and stand still. Verity, what do you think of the nudes?"

"You call that art?" she scoffed, rising to the bait. "If it wasn't for the disgusting subject, a child could do that. Look at the length of that face. Have you ever seen a face shaped like that?"

Charlotte gave her a poke in the ribs and, when she caught her eye, put a finger to her lips.

"And don't think you're going to silence me, young lady! If this is what you've been exposed to all these years, I dread to think of the consequences."

Cormac and Charlotte exchanged looks behind Verity's back.

A new wave of people arrived and the name 'Blackshaw' was mentioned again.

Cormac looked over at Charlotte and made a thumbs-up gesture. She put her hand on her heart in response. Verity noted the exchange.

"Let's hope this person everyone's talking about is a relative," said Waldron. "We'll claim him anyway."

He was in high good humour and even Edwina seemed to be affected, looking around with interest and studying every face in the room.

"I hope to get some private lessons from you, Cormac, now that your stint with Charlotte is up. I have time on my hands," said Waldron, who privately thought he could teach Cormac a thing or two. "Drawn all my life but would love to attack the nuts and bolts of painting. Come and see me tomorrow and we'll arrange a time."

"I'll look forward to that," said Cormac.

"Where's Charlotte gone?" asked Verity.

"I think she's gone to the . . . outside. She's gone out for some fresh air, I think." He'd noticed how Charlotte had become paler and more agitated each time the name 'Blackshaw' was mentioned, and had seen her slip away. He expected her to be missing for some time.

"Verity, go off and look for those paintings everyone's talking about. We'll wait here for a bit until the crowd thins out."

"Shouldn't be long," said Cormac.

"So you show your work here all the time?" asked Waldron.

"For the last six years. Lucky to join the Society. Had my first one-man show two years ago."

"You should have told us. I'd like to have seen it."

"You were away, sir."

"Did you do well?"

"Very well, thank you."

"Really?" asked Waldron, surprised. "I'm not surprised."

Verity arrived back, puffing. "Nearly everyone's gone," she said.

"We can hear that," said Edwina.

The painting beside him caught Waldron's eye. It was a still life

181

painted in a naïve fashion in gaudy colours. "No wonder that didn't sell. If I can't do better than that after a week I'll shoot myself. Now, Cormac, fetch that assistant again and we'll see these Blackshaw paintings for ourselves. Where's Charlotte? She shouldn't miss out on this."

They all dutifully looked around but she hadn't returned to the room.

"No point in waiting any longer," said Waldron.

The stairs were negotiated again by the three men, and Edwina ended up facing the grey paintings, though from her chair she could only see the top two above the heads of the people viewing them.

"They're lovely," she said spontaneously.

David Slane waved over at Cormac and indicated he would join them shortly.

Cormac had never before been in the predicament of having to introduce his employers. What on earth was the correct procedure? And what was Aunt Verity's title? Did one follow the gender and age rule only or were there added refinements to confound the uninitiated? Or did one simply not introduce them and let them make themselves known if that's what they wanted?

As David approached he turned to face him and, shaking his head slightly as he pointed to Charlotte's paintings, hoped that David was quick-witted enough to heed the warning to proceed cautiously.

"Lady Blackshaw, Lady Verity, Lord Waldron," Cormac said, taking a chance. It didn't sound right, but it would have to do, "I'd like you to meet David Slane, President of the Society."

"How do you do?" said Waldron and Edwina.

Verity registered her disapproval at not being given her correct title by remaining silent.

"You're very welcome," said David. "I hope you're enjoying the exhibition." Because of Cormac's warning, he was careful not to ask any questions. "Opening night always creates a flurry among the buyers. Anyone with money can buy an established name," he went on to explain, "but what excites a serious collector is identifying a new talent before anyone else does. It shows he has an eye. Taste. Discernment. That's why there's so much chagrin here tonight about missing out on a Blackshaw."

"By a strange coincidence," said Waldron, "that's our family name and we're curious to know who he is and if by chance he could be a relative of ours. It's not as if it's a very common name."

Puzzled, David looked across at Cormac for guidance and was silenced with a look.

"Well, let's have look," said Waldron. He left the chair at the back of a group of people and went in front of them to check the signature on the paintings they were studying.

"It's signed 'C. Blackshaw'," he said to the group when he returned. "I'm still none the wiser. I'll look up the family tree when I get home."

David's expression now said 'Help me'. Cormac had mentioned there might be some family animosity to Charlotte's showing publicly, but he didn't know they didn't know. "Just excuse me for a minute," he said with a meaningful glance at Cormac. "There's something urgent I've forgotten to attend to." He hurried across the wooden floor through a door marked 'Private' at the far end of the room.

We won't be seeing him for a while, thought Cormac.

There was no one now between the Blackshaws and the paintings so Waldron promptly moved the wheelchair forward, Verity following. They quietly absorbed the twenty shades of luscious greys made from complementary colours and not black and white, but accented by black and white and containing subtle hints of colour.

"This one's called 'The Fish Market'," said Waldron at last, reading the card beside it. "'Oil on canvas, 24 inches by 24 inches'."

"Oh yes, I see it," said Verity, as the abstract shapes became fish, boxes, shelves and stacks receding into a distant window.

"I don't see it," said Edwina.

Waldron couldn't either but he wasn't going to have anything pointed out to him by Verity. "Stand back, now. It will be easier to interpret from a distance," he said as he wheeled Edwina back into the middle of the room. "There!"

The paintings' stillness subdued them again.

"They're wonderful," whispered Edwina.

"That sense of design and composition," said Cormac. "Perfect. What an eye! And the depth. It's as if there's another world under the one we're seeing." His speaking first without being spoken to by his employers would normally be unthinkable but in this room on this night his natural ascendancy went unremarked.

"Quite ambiguous and restrained," said Verity, who'd been waiting to use those words since they arrived. "Not like some of the others we've seen tonight," she added, looking meaningfully at Cormac.

"It's the textures and tonal values I love," said Cormac, trying to make sure he gave Charlotte as much praise as he could while he had the chance.

He saw her standing at the far end of the room. She raised her eyebrows. He made a circle with his thumb and forefinger to signify a good reception, and shook his head, to indicate they didn't know. She advanced slowly.

"Charlotte, there you are," said Waldron. "You took long enough. Come here and take a look at these."

"I think 'The Lock' is my favourite of the four of them," said Verity.

"What about you, Mother? What do you think of them?" Charlotte asked hesitantly.

"I like them all equally and would love to have the set hanging in our study. They have a strange power. I feel as if I could move in and out of all those shapes."

The four stared at her, as they'd never known her to have any interest in the visual arts, and the use of the word 'move' touched them all with its double meaning.

Waldron wished he could say something original, but couldn't think of any phrases. There was nothing in the work he could identify – not a person or an animal in sight – but, in the presence of all those red dots, he thought it prudent to look wise and say nothing.

Charlotte looked helplessly at Cormac. "Will I say anything?" she whispered.

"It's bad manners to whisper in company," said Verity.

"We'll certainly be claiming C. Blackshaw as one of ours," said Waldron, smiling. "I wonder what the 'C' stands for. Cameron? Christian? Don't remember any of those as family names."

Cormac was given a sign by Charlotte.

"How about Charlotte?" he said.

38

All through dinner that night, Charlotte was warmed by the reality of her triumph despite the chill in the atmosphere. Every now and then she smiled to herself.

"What's that supercilious look in aid of?" Edwina, eyes narrowed, asked from her place at the end of the table as the main course was being tidied away.

The temperature in the room dropped a further few degrees.

Charlotte sat still while her plate was being removed and acted as if she hadn't heard her mother's question.

"I said, young lady, what does your supercilious look signify?"

"Oh, are you talking to me? Sorry. I couldn't tell from the question and you didn't address me by name." Charlotte's tone was mild and her look inoffensive. Cormac's encouragement and advice were shielding her like a suit of armour.

"Don't use that innocent tone with me. One minor success and you've got above yourself already –"

"Hold on, old thing."

"I won't hold on. The superiority flaunted by artists makes me sick to my stomach. Just wait until I tell you what I think of artists, seeing no one has bothered to consult me about my daughter's turning herself into one behind my back."

A manservant rushed over to refill Waldron's glass that he had emptied in two gulps and was told he and the others could leave for the night.

"We will serve the cheese and port ourselves. Just pass over that opened bottle of red before you go."

"Artists think they are a cut above everyone else," continued Edwina before the door had closed behind the servants. "They think ordinary rules of conduct don't apply to them. They wreak havoc in the lives of others and it doesn't cost them a thought. They don't defer to their betters because they don't think they have any. According to them their authority comes from their talent and they're not impressed by any other kind – just because their works live on after them, giving them immortality . . ."

Verity was becoming fidgety.

". . . they think their calling is higher than the law, the Church, the Army, politics, the Civil Service, the Diplomatic Corps, even the Monarchy. Where did such an idiotic belief come from?"

"I don't know where it came from," Verity said, taking a deep breath to give her courage, "but I believe it to be true. I think they *are* superior."

"You *would* think that, wouldn't you, seeing you were madly in love with one."

Verity blushed scarlet. "So were you."

"Now we're getting to the nub of things," Waldron said with satisfaction. "Are we by any chance talking about that chap who doesn't complete his work? What was his name?"

Charlotte looked at each face in turn – all this was news to her – and remained still, hoping they would forget she was there.

"There's no need to mention names because I'm not talking about one artist in particular," said Edwina. "I'm talking about artists in general. For all the high-flying notions they have of themselves, they're nothing but tradesmen."

"Never!" Waldron looked as if he was taking personal offence.

"Nonsense." A flinty look came into Verity's eyes.

"There's no difference between an artist and a peddler – they both offer a commodity and people can choose either to buy or not. What clearer definition of trade can there be than that?"

"There's something wrong with your logic," said Waldron, "but I can't put my finger on it. Give me a minute."

"We don't have a minute. Charlotte's pictures are to be taken down before that place opens in the morning. I can't have her peddling her wares in public and dragging the Blackshaw name into the mud. And Mr Delaney should be shown the door for overstepping the mark – he had no authority – encouraging her in such a sly fashion. That's the last I have to say on the matter."

Waldron lurched to his feet. "I hope it *is* the last you have to say – I've never heard such poppycock in my life. Charlotte, leave the room and don't listen outside the door. I have a couple of things I need to sort out with your mother, and it can't wait."

Verity made as if to depart as well, but Edwina commanded her to stay as, by the sound of Waldron's tone, she might need a witness.

Charlotte quietly entered the darkened storeroom next door, reassuring herself that what she was about to hear couldn't be any worse than what she had already heard about herself over the years.

"The wrong daughter disappeared," was Edwina's often-repeated lament to Verity after she had drunk too much port. "It's a pity you never saw Victoria. You would have been captivated by her. Such a pretty child, with her soft dark curls and blue eyes. You'd never think she was Charlotte's sister to look at her. And so sweet-natured. Yes, that Teresa Kelly knew what she was doing when she stole Victoria and left me with the wrong daughter."

At this point Verity would take her cue and cluck in sympathy. "All Charlotte's life, nothing but one disappointment after another. You've done well to cope."

As was her habit, Charlotte rested her head against the wall where the hole she had made years ago was hidden on the dining-room side by a large gilt-framed portrait, conveniently leaning outwards so that very little sound was blocked. It was the first time she'd had the chance to eavesdrop on her father.

Waldron was in the process of forbidding his wife to either dismiss Cormac or revisit the salon to insist on the removal of Charlotte's paintings. Edwina demanded to know why she should be cast as the villain and what right had Waldron to give orders when he had been an absentee husband, father and landlord all their married life and now that he had retired he was still absent.

"Not this again," Waldron moaned.

And when he was around he was usually in various stages of inebriation, so wasn't much use anyway. And they had all managed very well without him. And how dare he push her out of the gallery when she was in mid-sentence to that David Slane chap.

Waldron asked if she would allow him to answer her accusations and she said it would be interesting to see how quickly he could make up excuses to justify himself. She was all attention and he had the floor, so carry on.

The reason he'd chosen Cormac as a tutor in the first place, Waldron said, was because he was an artist and Waldron knew Charlotte was good at drawing horses even at a young age and presumed she'd inherited it from him, and she might as well paint as do needlepoint.

Charlotte was grateful the dining-room table was twenty feet long – she wasn't missing a word as they projected their voices at each other to cover the distance.

From what he could see, continued Waldron, Cormac had done wonders for the girl. Anyone could see how slim and happy and accomplished she had become under his tutelage. This evening he had been jolly proud of Charlotte's success and appearance and thank goodness Cormac hadn't asked permission as, if he had, it wouldn't have been granted and they might never have found out about Charlotte's talent.

"Finished?" asked Edwina.

"Of course I'm not finished," answered Waldron, refilling his wineglass. "Just warming up."

"In relation to Mr Delaney, there's something I should mention," said Aunt Verity in a small voice. She sat at the far side of the table, opposite Charlotte's place, and had to twist her neck backwards and forwards to follow the arguments.

"Is it important?"

"I think it's very important."

"What is it, then?" asked Waldron, his voice full of exasperation.

"I just happened to be passing the schoolroom the other day –"

"I thought I told you to stay away from there."

"Oh, shut up, Waldron, for a minute and let Verity speak. What did you see, Verity?"

"The door happened to be opened. I saw him kissing her. And they walk close together when they're out on excursions."

Waldron laughed. "Is that all?"

"That's not the response I'd expect from a father."

"What response do you want me to make?"

"If that's your attitude I'll keep the rest to myself."

"No, go on. Sorry. I can't wait to hear more," said Waldron.

Even Charlotte could hear the playful tone in his voice. He was enjoying this.

There was a pause.

"Well," Verity continued more reluctantly, "he had his arm around her at the exhibition and she pulled away when she saw us. Then later she looked at him in a special way with her hand on her heart. She removed the hand when she saw me looking. If that's not a sign of guilt, I don't know what is."

"And that proves Cormac has wicked designs on Charlotte?" Waldron laughed.

"I don't know why you find it so funny," said Verity in a voice that trembled as if she was about to cry.

"My apologies, dear sister-in-law and cousin."

"Why don't you address Verity by her name?" said Edwina. "It would save time and be less irritating."

"There are lots of Veritys in this world, but for me only one sister-in-law and cousin, that's why. I'm sorry about the laughing. Of course you're right to concern yourself with Charlotte's virtue, dear cousin. Just where did Cormac kiss Charlotte, presuming your eyesight is good enough to give an accurate account?"

"My eyesight is perfect, thank you. It was in the classroom."

"I mean on what part of her person did he kiss her?"

"On the top of her head, no mistake."

There was an explosion that was a cross between a sneeze and a splutter, followed by coughing.

"Ring for a servant, Vee, to clean up that mess."

"Stay where you are," said Waldron with difficulty. "They can do it later."

"Perhaps you could desist from drinking until we've finished this discussion. Red wine obviously doesn't do your reasoning or the table any good."

Waldron's voice was back under control. "There's nothing wrong with my reasoning. It's not my drinking causing the trouble, it's your sister's witticisms."

There was the scrape of a chair. "I know when I'm being made a fool of," said Verity with tears in her voice.

"Sit down, Vee, and behave yourself, Waldron," Edwina snapped. "Though I can't really see why we're bothering to talk at all seeing there's no way we can come to any agreement. I think Mr Delaney should go, Waldron thinks he should stay. I think the paintings should be removed, Waldron thinks they should stay."

"I'm not looking for agreement," said Waldron. "And why are you speaking to your sister as if I'm not in the room? I'm commanding you – Cormac Delaney stays and the paintings stay. I forbid you to go back to the salon to badger and hector that poor man who is only doing his job."

Charlotte could hear him taking big gulps of liquid. She couldn't imagine the expression on her mother's face, as she'd never heard her spoken to in that way before.

"Why can't you let the poor girl experience a bit of joy? Don't bother answering. I'll answer for you. Because you're jealous of her, that's why. You can never resist a dig. You've always been jealous of her."

Edwina snorted. "That's preposterous. What's there to be jealous of?"

"Her riding ability for one. Bertie couldn't praise her highly enough, and everyone who saw her at the hunt was amazed by her horsemanship. All this talk of superiority and a trade – it's all balderdash – silly arguments to cover up your jealousy. And you never pass the chance to make snide comments about her every time her name comes up in conversation. Just remember that if it wasn't for you she'd still be at the Park riding Mandrake as happy as the day is long."

Charlotte's heart somersaulted.

"Let's clarify this." Edwina's tone was slow and menacing. Charlotte shivered to hear it. "Are you saying I'm to blame for my accident?"

"Well, of course I am. That's exactly what I'm saying."

"I don't believe I'm hearing correctly. It was Charlotte who jumped in front of me and knocked Mandrake's legs from under him."

"She was only nine, for God's sake, and who instructed her to ride that treacherous, pig-headed, half-mad mongrel of a horse with no mouth when she had a perfectly safe one of her own?"

"Half-mad mongrel? How dare you? I trained Sandstorm myself."

"Exactly. Ruined him, more like."

"So that's it. Now it's all coming out. Showing yourself in your true colours. Admit it. It was you who was always jealous. Of me and my horsemanship."

"Jealous of you? There's a laugh. When did you ever hear yourself described as a good rider?"

"I've had plenty of compliments."

"Yes, I've heard them. Fearless, tough, strong, but never *good*. Any word except *good*."

Verity contributed. "She's been told she rides as well as a man."

"What man?" Waldron scoffed. "The mad major who sits on a horse like a sack of potatoes? Or Marcheson, who wears out his mounts before they turn eight? Or Partridge, who crippled his prize filly? Not me, anyway. No, it was you, jealous of Charlotte. Why else put her on an unmanageable mount and then blame her for not being able to manage him? Don't interrupt. I haven't finished. Charlotte has a rare ability that you don't have, and because of you it's wasted. *Wasted*. There was no need for her or Harcourt to be relocated here. It's not as if you ever see them. They should have stayed at the Park. It's their birthright. Charles always said he would love to have them. It was spite that made you do it. Nothing but spite."

"Now I've heard everything," Edwina screeched. "The next thing you'll blame me for is Victoria's disappearance."

"Now that you mention it. Let's put it this way – if you were in the army you'd be court-martialled. It happened on your watch. Nothing you can say can alter that. *Your* watch. Responsible."

"You've gone too far. Vee, would you mind? I can't stay here another minute. We would have all been a lot better off if you'd stayed in India. We've managed perfectly well without you over the years. Come on, Vee."

"Managed perfectly well? Looks like it. Harcourt is still only a child and he's all right so far," Waldron slurred. "Give it time. You'll think of something."

The door banged and the women were in the passageway. "Drunken loud-mouth. Twisted liar. If he thinks he can tell me what to do he's got another think coming," said Edwina, loading each syllable with venom. "Charlotte, Charlotte, always Charlotte!"

"He might be a lord, but he's not your master, Edwina. There's a higher authority than his so you don't have . . ."

Charlotte strained to hear more but the swish of the wheels of the chair obscured the fading voices.

So it wasn't my fault? Could that possibly be true? Her father had said the most beautiful words she'd ever hoped to hear and he sounded as if he knew what he was talking about.

Until she was twelve she'd believed Nurse Dixon had caused Mandrake's accident by screaming the curse, 'Mandrake will die,' but after Charlotte outgrew her fascination with fairy stories and accepted with sadness that they were all make-believe, she had to conclude that curses fell into the same category as the stories and had no power, just as Miss East and Cormac had repeatedly told her. So if it wasn't the curse, she had to accept it was her poor horsemanship that had caused the clash. Until she heard her father's pronouncement through the wall tonight, the conviction that it was all her fault hadn't wavered during those years.

There was a thud and sounds of shattering glass next door and then more sounds of fumbling and smashing.

She heard the sound of footsteps entering the dining room and recognised the voices of two male servants.

"There now, easy does it, sir," said one. "Just put your arm around my shoulder."

"There we go, sir," said the other.

Wishing to avoid what would obviously be slow progress, Charlotte slipped out of the dark room, silently closed the door, and disappeared around the corner. She could see herself staying awake all night – so much to think about and so much to tell Cormac in the morning when he returned from his night of celebration. He would be pleased to hear how her father had stood up to her mother over the matter of exhibiting. About Mandrake she would say nothing.

39

It was five o'clock in the afternoon when Cormac arrived back from his revels to find Charlotte waiting for him in the classroom.

"She did it, my little colleague," he said. "She did it. Can't call you 'apprentice' any more after last night. She did it. Blast her, anyway. Sorry."

"She?"

"Your mother. Afraid so. Paintings gone. Wait till I sit down and I'll tell you the story, then I need to go to bed for a long time."

According to David Slane, Edwina and Verity were waiting at the door at opening time. Edwina insisted the paintings be removed as her daughter was underage and had not been given permission to participate. A few other members of the Society tried to talk her out of the decision, saying if only she knew what a sensation the paintings caused she would be bringing more in, not taking them down. They said not being an artist herself she couldn't appreciate how difficult it was to sell one piece, let alone four, especially if you weren't an established name and not regarded as an investment as yet. Charlotte was the talk of the town already, showing such talent at a young age, and when word spread there would be a lot of people turning up to see them and leaving disappointed. Did she have any idea that the Society was considering offering her daughter full membership at the next meeting – the youngest member ever – and what an honour it was?

"No luck, then?" said Charlotte.

"Not a bit. The more they argued the more intransigent she became. But David had to stand firm in not declaring the sale null and void – said it was out of his hands. That collector won't be able to believe his luck. David said in the end it was the wheelchair that won the day – you can't argue with a person with a disability — and he gave in about taking the paintings down. But he was upset. Now he has to face people who weren't lucky enough to be at the opening pouring in to get a look at this artist's work, and all they'll see is a blank space. He's going to have to make up some story to placate them but it won't be easy and he's not looking forward to it. Your four masterpieces are hidden away in the back of his office where they'll have to stay for three weeks until the exhibition is officially over and the owner's agent can come and collect them. That's how the system works. David begged me to try to get your mother to change her mind."

"No chance of that," said Charlotte, relating what she'd heard in her hideout the night before.

"You'll have to try to look at it in a positive light seeing as you have no choice. In a strange way she might have done you a favour. The city will be buzzing with the story by the end of the week and the demand for your pictures will grow out of all proportion. To capitalise on it, you can work hard and build up your stock and then when you come of age you can burst back into the limelight and your mother won't be able to do a thing about it."

"But that's five years away."

"It will pass quickly." He leaned over and put his good hand on her head as if to bless her. "Promise me you won't fritter your life away in trivia like most of your lot. Promise me you'll use those years to experiment. Try new approaches."

"I don't have to promise," Charlotte said.

"Of course you don't. I know I can count on you. Good girl." He removed his hand and stretched as he yawned. "Now I really must go and pass out. Great night – pity you were too young to join us."

"Just as well, actually. I heard last night that Aunt Verity thinks your ways are too informal with me and you're not her idea of a

194

schoolmaster." That was the most innocuous way she could rephrase Verity's accusations.

Cormac laughed with genuine delight. "Does she now? And she'd be an expert, would she? You'll have to enlighten her that I never claimed to be a teacher. A soldier who took orders from his superior, that's all I was." He gave her a mock military salute. "But we did all right, didn't we?"

"Better than all right," Charlotte smiled.

"So there you are, then. Congratulations on last night. You were great, so you were. Now go and tell your Aunt Verity I'll hardly be seeing you at all over the next six months as I'm expecting your father to be a hard taskmaster, so she can relax." He stood up and took a few seconds to steady himself. "And after that I won't be seeing you at all, unless you come to see me in my bohemian area of Paris. Now *that* would give your aunt something to pray about."

40

During the six months while Waldron was resisting any attempts by Cormac to change his rigid ideas about art, Charlotte painted conscientiously. Cormac dropped by every afternoon to follow her progress and tell her how terrific she was. "You're on your own now," he told her. "There's nothing more I can teach you. When I come back to check on you in a few years' time, I expect to be even more dazzled by your singular vision than I already am."

After Cormac finally left the townhouse for Paris Charlotte was gripped by a sudden and terrible loneliness. Deprived of his exuberance and support, she slid into a state of inertia. Her old sense of worthlessness returned as if it had never left. Week by week, the walls of the safe Dublin world that Cormac had created around her began to crumble and fall and she felt as if she was trapped in a basement, cut off from all sources of light. The speed of her loss filled her with the same sense of helplessness and fear she had felt as a child when Nurse Dixon was in authority over her.

Along with the desolation there was a perverse sense of comfort in reverting to a state that was familiar to her. She had lived in a dark basement for a long time in the past and was now returning to it. It was as simple as that. Cormac's good opinion of her that had buoyed her up for six years had been fuelled by his own optimistic outlook and bore no relation to what she knew to be her own lack of value.

Victoria, her face contorted with pain, appeared in a dream, holding out her hands in an appeal for help. Charlotte tried to run to save her but her legs wouldn't function, and she could only look on while Nurse Dixon seized Victoria and slammed her against the nursery wall to punish her for being such a cry-baby. Charlotte woke, disorientated with sick disgust at not being able to protect her little sister.

After staying hidden for so long, Charlotte asked, why have you chosen to show yourself now, Victoria, when I haven't the strength to help you?

Charlotte stood in front of a finished painting and was suffused with a hatred for it and for all her work. Cormac had told her not to waste her life on trivia, but what could be more trivial than this useless object when one compared it to the actuality of a lost sister? Daubs of colour on a canvas, arranged this way and that and then framed and hung on a wall, achieving nothing. Decoration. Nothing but decoration. How could she take herself seriously? Two of her favourite brushes lay on the easel ledge, hardened by paint she had forgotten to rinse out with turpentine and she didn't care. All those various shades of grey were pathetic in their lifelessness. She took up a tube of vermilion, squeezed it on to the canvas and spread it around with the palm of her hand, but felt no release of frustration.

If she didn't get a stretch of sleep soon she would become ill, if she wasn't already ill. Victoria's supplicating hands hovered on the borders of consciousness, not even waiting until Charlotte had sunk into a deep slumber before reaching out to ask for help.

"I'll make a deal with you, Victoria," Charlotte wept, sitting upright in her chair, trying to avoid sleep to escape her nightmares, her neck sore from snapping each time she nodded off. "It won't make up for the past, but it's the only thing I can think of to try to make amends."

She would not dedicate her life to art, as she had promised Cormac. Instead she would take her year in the Paris finishing school seriously, so that she would emerge polished and ladylike, ready to marry the first man who asked her. She would have a baby immediately, and she would dedicate her life to it and make sure it never came to any harm, looking after it herself with no nanny to help, not following the aristocrats' tradition of using boarding schools to gain social advantage, and sending it to day school instead so she could study its face at the end of each day and discern if there was anything troubling it, and if there were she would find out what it was and would fix it. That was her objective – to replace Victoria with a child, preferably a daughter, who would, due to unstinting vigilance, survive fearless and happy into adulthood.

Victoria must have accepted the deal as she didn't intrude on Charlotte's dreams again for years.

41

Sydney
1925

Two years after the Waratah was refurbished, Norma Rossiter, encouraged by her husband, had thought she'd better start a family before she ran out of time – no point in working all the hours God sent to build an empire if there were no little Rossiters to inherit. Mrs Sinclair had then left the Waratah to help her daughter in the house, confident that Elizabeth Dixon, now Head Receptionist and Head Bookkeeper, had learnt everything she could teach her.

In a rival bank, a block away from the one Mrs Sinclair introduced her to, where she lodged the hotel's daily takings, Dixon had opened a second account under the name of 'Beth Hall' to avoid confusion.

The Rossiters had gone on to have three children during which time Dixon received thirty-six proposals of marriage: ten from drunks, seven from octogenarian widowers, five from married men whose wives didn't understand them, six from lonely men who recanted the following day, six from simpletons and two from underage boys. A desirable eligible man near her age with all his parts intact was such a rarity she hadn't seen one, and even if she had she wouldn't have accepted him because he wouldn't be able to hold a candle to her memory of the divine Manus.

Her dislike of other people's children was reinforced every first

Sunday of the month when she visited the Rossiters and was repulsed by their brats who grew worse as they grew older, hanging on to their mother, making demands and interrupting the conversation. If she could have them on her own for a week she'd be able to straighten them out. It was all she could do to restrain herself from leaning over to give them a good slap when their mother wasn't looking. They even pestered Mrs Sinclair while Norma, red-faced and breathless, being made a fool of by the middle one, was tending to their needs in the kitchen. Mrs Sinclair was as bad as her daughter in spoiling them, wearing herself out when she wasn't really up to it any more. It was obvious her health was failing but the children didn't take account of that. Why didn't they pay someone to look after the brats? It wasn't as if they were short of money.

She held the youngest child's sticky hand away from her to prevent it touching her new frock and hoped it would go away before she lost patience and bent back the little fingers with more force than was necessary to teach it a lesson.

Some days, after Dixon returned from the Rossiter home, she would think how lucky she was to be treated as one of the family by people she admired so much, and how lucky she was to be able to walk away from all that noise and confusion when it got too much for her, returning to her organised office in the Waratah. On other days she would race to her bedroom and howl into her pillow at the injustice of Norma having a lovely mother, an admirable husband (though not as admirable as Manus), and three children (who would be of a superior mould if they were hers), and a beautiful house, whereas she had no one and nothing except a growing bank account. Was the pain she was feeling the pain that old Lily East and middle-aged Teresa Kelly had suffered? Was this the child hunger that she had been so scornful of when she had been young and in love with Manus?

42

Paris
1927

In the finishing school in her eighteenth year Charlotte was in a class with fourteen other aristocratic girls who all knew each other and were socially confident. She tried to take an interest in flower arranging, etiquette, table settings, personal grooming, fashion, deportment, curtseying, dancing, sketching, the use of watercolours and spoken French, skills that would help catch an aristocratic husband provided there was money to go with them. During all these classes she kept seeing Cormac's mocking smile, especially when she was painting botanical specimens in a constrained, ladylike way, and could hear his voice urging "Don't hold back. Let fly. Get stuck in," and knew how unacceptable those words would be in this establishment. The girls were resentful when they heard how fluent her French was, so she became hesitant in her delivery and used incorrect words at intervals to appease them.

She became isolated and unhappy and took larger portions of food to console herself. Her cheekbones and jaw line began to lose their definition again. All this she could bear as she knew the year would soon be over and it was necessary for her plan, but what she couldn't bear was how she had unwisely confided in her roommate and suffered the consequences. Having read in books that confiding was an essential ingredient in friendship and, never having had a friend to know if this were true or not, she took the theory on trust and told her roommate that she intended to marry the first man who asked her so that she could have a baby as soon as possible to replace her lost sister to please her mother whom she was responsible for crippling. Instead of praising her altruistic ambitions, the girl screamed that she couldn't stay around a person who was cursed with such bad luck, called her a freak, and picked up her things and went off demanding to be allotted another room.

While her former roommate was socialising with the other girls after dinner she lay on her bed, looking at the ceiling, imagining how much louder the girl's screaming would have been if she had told her the full story.

The next day one of the other girls came up to her and said, "I know who you are. I thought I'd heard the name before. Everyone knows about the lost Blackshaw, but they didn't make the connection. You're her sister, aren't you? And it was you who was expelled from school in England for attacking a girl and putting her into hospital."

For taunting me. For accusing me of crippling my mother and being such a bad rider that my horse had to be shot. That pupil deserved what she got, Charlotte believed, staring dumbly back at her accuser.

"We don't want your sort around here. Why don't you go back to the bogs where you belong?" the girl concluded before returning to join her group.

To avoid the risk of repeating her past behaviour, Charlotte packed her bags and returned home, telling her mother the course bored her and she had no intention of returning. Edwina knew from experience that there was no point in trying to force her to change her mind.

Charlotte learnt her lesson. From now on she would never again confide in anyone. She would block the past from her mind and keep her old secrets hidden so deeply that even she wouldn't be able to gain access to them.

When her turn came to be launched into society at the traditional ball she didn't know how to behave around men. The joking informality that she used in her conversations with Cormac caused them to look askance at her, so she switched to speaking in the clipped cadences favoured by her mother. Before she had time to gauge if that yielded more success, she noticed three girls from her finishing school mingling easily with the established crowd and knew any chance she had of finding a husband in this company was now gone. She saw the girls looking towards her as they whispered, and noticed the horrified looks on the faces of those who listened to them. After she wasn't asked for a single dance during the length of the ball, she admitted defeat and retired from the social scene.

43

Dublin
1934

When Charlotte turned twenty-five she came into the fortune left to her by her paternal grandmother, the Dowager. She wished the old lady had had the sense to specify eighteen rather than twenty-five as the age to inherit, to give her marriage prospects some chance before she had become a joke. By now she was the only girl of her rank and age still unmarried.

Washington Square, whose plot had been related to Charlotte by Aunt Verity as a cautionary tale, became Charlotte's guide. The heroine in that novel would have been better off taking a chance and marrying the fortune-hunter she loved, Aunt Verity believed, rather than settling for the colourless, dreary life of a spinster, filling her life with dutiful tasks and second-hand experiences under the eye of a sneering parent. All one had to do was look at the inconsequential life of poor Aunt Verity to agree with that conclusion.

Any suitor who approached Charlotte now that she was rich would, by definition, be a fortune-hunter. When such a man presented himself, she planned to accept him. All she had to do was wait for the news of her vast wealth to reach the receptive ears of the appropriate man.

She didn't have long to wait.

Peregrine Poolstaff, with his lack of purpose and wit, had reached the age of thirty-eight unhampered by a wife. If the large bulge on his forehead had been filled with brains he would have been a genius, but since it evidently wasn't, it was regarded instead as an example of nature's propensity for irony. His estate in County Donegal was much in need of funds – if nothing was done soon he would have to sell off more land and art treasures and eventually be left with only the house, and even that was in jeopardy. His younger, married friends convinced him that marriage needn't alter his way of life – he could still lead the life of a bachelor, just as they did. Meanwhile, they would coach him in the finer points of courtship and induct him into the secrets of what made a man irresistible to a woman. He was no oil painting, but then neither was Charlotte in her present blown-up state.

Everything went according to their plan. Peregrine became a frequent and welcome caller to the townhouse. Charlotte wondered why everyone had been so dismissive of him when, after she got to know him, she could see he was entertaining and insightful. He even charmed Edwina who said looks weren't everything and beggars couldn't be choosers. Waldron was impressed by his family lineage.

An engagement seemed imminent, and the night of the Hunt Ball at the RDS an ideal place to announce it.

The pair agreed to arrive separately and meet there. Charlotte was accompanied by her cousins up from Cork and her brother Harcourt, seventeen years old, six feet tall and strongly built.

Peregrine arrived during a lull between dances in the company of two young, handsome, jocular men and a thin, pretty, unknown woman, not the wife of either, whom he partnered in the next dance. She must be a visiting cousin of one of them, Charlotte thought, and he is being well-mannered, doing his duty. The woman's gown, similar in style and fabric to all the other silky creations being worn by all the other women at the ball, was sleeveless, low-cut at the back, and had an elegant drape to it. Her own long-sleeved outfit of stiff grey satin with its high neck, made by an eighty-year-old dressmaker who charged very little, was unfashionable and unflattering by contrast. Why did she assume she knew what was suitable to wear without consulting anyone? Why didn't she have a friend of her own age who could advise her? Considering she was now wealthy, why hadn't she thought to seek out a modern dressmaker who used expensive fabrics and flattering patterns? In agony during the space of three dances, she waited for Peregrine to deposit the girl and claim her, but he continued to dance with the stranger and didn't once look her way. He was the only one who didn't. All the others – she recognised two finishing-school contemporaries who had married Irish peers – were watching her to see how she was taking it. She tried to avoid their scrutiny by staying backed up against a column. Choosing not to dance in a show of solidarity, Harcourt and the cousins stayed beside her in a tight protective ring.

When the fourth dance began Charlotte felt ready to expire and indicated she wanted to leave. She didn't even go to the cloakroom to collect her stole. Silence followed the little group as it left the ballroom.

"That cad deserves a jolly good hiding," said Harcourt.

"No, no. It's not his fault. I must have misread the signals." Charlotte was holding herself as if she were in severe physical pain. Her plan to replace Victoria would never come to fruition. She was a failure. Even her mother couldn't like her, so why would anyone else?

At the door of the townhouse she thanked Harcourt and her cousins for their support and urged them to return to the ball as she didn't want to spoil their entire evening. She closed the door on them, went to her rooms and rang for Queenie to come and help her take off her dress. When there was no immediate response, she continued to ring the bell at intervals for a long time, crying with frustration, thinking Queenie could hear the bell but was deliberately and selfishly not answering it. In the end she took a firm hold of the tapestry bell pull and, employing her full weight, yanked it from the wall. Charlotte heard the sound of crunching and of metal snapping, before she landed on the floor on her rear end with the detached bell pull in her hands. She lumbered to her feet, reached behind her back and tore at her dress, until all the button loops down the back ripped open, and she was able to step out of the monstrosity and hold on to it until she fetched the scissors and cut it into pieces. While she had the scissors in her hand she let down her long brown hair and hacked it all off.

She didn't hear that Peregrine had been relieved of his dancing partner by a rival after the fifth dance and had received a thrashing in the early hours of the morning by an unnamed assailant and that his two friends were disgusted that he had thrown away the chance of an advantageous marriage just because he wasn't man enough to be seen in public with an overweight woman in an unfashionable gown.

An overweight woman in an unfashionable gown who happened to be extremely wealthy in her own right.

PART 3

THE STUDENTS

44

Dublin
1937

Charlotte's lunch hadn't been delivered. She opened the door of her sitting room for the fourth time to see if the tray was in its usual place on the side table in the anteroom, but there was nothing there.

Since the disastrous Hunt Ball three years earlier she had lived in self-imposed isolation, with her maid Queenie as her only contact with the rest of the house. Today was Queenie's day off so Charlotte had no way of finding out why the tray hadn't been delivered. She hadn't had her bell reconnected as she couldn't face the thought of having a man coming in to fix it. She was fully reliant on Queenie calling at her fixed times.

Six hours until the next meal. What would happen if the cook were sick or absent and dinner wasn't delivered either? How could she bear to miss two meals in a row? With Queenie away there was no way of finding out if there was anything amiss in the kitchen. Of course, later she could sneak down to the kitchen using the back stairway, but she made a point of never moving out of her rooms during the day for fear of running into her brother who shared the corridor with her. He hadn't as much as laid eyes on her for months and she wanted to keep it that way.

She imagined her tray being delivered by a new maid to the wrong door. All the doors along this corridor were identical and the upper floors of the house looked much the same. Tuesday's offering of roast lamb with rosemary and garlic accompanied by onion gravy and mashed potato followed by bread and butter pudding with custard might be unclaimed and spoiling in the wrong anteroom.

She picked up last week's paper to finish the crossword but still didn't have answers to eleven of the clues. A paragraph about the war in Spain caught her eye but she was bored by the time she started the fourth sentence. *The Ambassadors* was in the same place beside her chair as it had been for the last month – reading a page at random, she didn't take in a word. White smoke from her fourteenth cigarette of the day mixed with grey smoke from one already smouldering in the ashtray.

Would she chance a quick trip to the kitchen? Harcourt would be studying for his exams, but would he be doing it at college or at a friend's house, or here?

She opened the sitting-room door and stood in the anteroom, listening for footsteps. Silence. Each time she put her hand on the doorknob she lost her nerve and stood to listen more intently. After what seemed an age she heard the familiar sound of Harcourt's footsteps.

Hearing them fade away and thinking she was safe, she opened the door and found herself looking up at the most handsome face she had ever seen.

For a second his beauty made her forget her fear of being on display. He looked back at her, and inclined his head in a friendly way as if he were about to speak. She saw him clearly, even though he was standing in front of a long window and the back lighting was creating a halo effect around his dark hair, putting his face in soft shadow.

A second face, similarly lit, appeared beside him.

"Manus, what are you doing here?" she said at the same moment as the face said, "Christ Almighty, Charlotte. What have you done to yourself?"

She whipped the door closed and leaned against it.

"Charlotte, let me in to talk to you," a voice called gently from the other side. "It's me. Harcourt."

Harcourt, not Manus? How could she have made a mistake like that? The three years of isolation must have addled her brain. But the shape of the head and the way it sat on the shoulders? She couldn't be mistaken. She remembered the outline so well.

"Not now," she managed to answer. "I'm not prepared. But soon, I promise, soon."

"I'll hold you to that," Harcourt replied. "Come on . . ."

Charlotte didn't catch the name of the friend.

There was a murmur of voices, and then the sound of footsteps retreating along the corridor.

Turning away from the door, she hit her shin against an antique tub chair and gave it a kick for being in the way even though it had been in the same place for years.

Six hungry hours later, Charlotte retrieved the tray from the anteroom after the cook's maid tapped on the inner door to let her know that high tea had arrived — there would be no dinner tonight, the cook's maid said, as the cook was feeling poorly and young Florrie had to fill in and this was the best she could do.

"Tell her she's done well," said Charlotte, not knowing or caring who Florrie was, concentrating on controlling her impulse to snatch the tray out of the maid's hands. "Put it down there, thank you, and close the door after you."

Charlotte felt so ravenous after missing lunch that as soon as the door closed she ate two sausages and one rasher before she even lifted the tray. With her free hand she manoeuvred the soft fried eggs, flicking them on to thick slices of toast that had already soaked up the savoury juices. She sat and devoured the egg on toast. Grease trickled down the front of her dress. A sausage rolled from the plate onto the floor. Charlotte looked at it with regret but didn't attempt to retrieve it as bending was too difficult – Queenie could pick it up in the morning.

After she finished the meal with a cup of tea and her thirty-second cigarette of the day she stretched out on the couch for an after-dinner nap. Usually she dreamed of banquets, but tonight she experienced the terror of falling in slow motion from a cliff. An archangel with dark hair and enormous wings swooped down to catch her in his powerful arms but was unable to take her weight and let her slip through his hands. He flew off without making a second attempt to save her, and she was left only seconds away from crashing to the ground before she woke.

45

Queenie looked as if she was about to start purring. "There's someone to see you, Miss."

"Who is it?" asked Charlotte.

"He told me not to give his name."

"Then tell me what he looks like."

"He asked me not to say anything."

Could it possibly be Harcourt's friend, curious to meet her after their wordless exchange the previous day?

"Ask him to wait a minute, will you please, Queenie?"

"Shall I open the curtains, Miss?"

"No, leave them. I can do without all that glare."

She tried to comb her hair into some kind of shape. Since the night of the Hunt Ball she had kept it short, snipping away at bits that annoyed her, not caring how it looked. She now tried to hide the gaps and jagged edges under a band, but they poked out no matter which way she tried to arrange them.

In the end her impatience to see Harcourt's friend again overrode her desire to look presentable. "You may send him in now, Queenie," she said.

She positioned her arms so that her still slender hands could be seen to their best advantage.

It was not Harcourt's friend, but an older, greyer Cormac who came through the door.

Charlotte looked up at him with a blank face as Queenie slipped out, smiling.

"Afternoon, Miss," he said to Charlotte. "Nice day. Looks as if the rain is holding off."

Why is he talking to me like that? "Yes, but not for long. Would you care to take a seat?"

"I'll wait until Miss Charlotte arrives, Miss, if you don't mind." He motioned towards the large canvas hanging on the far wall. "Meanwhile, if you'll excuse me, I'd like to have a closer look at that."

"Please feel free to do so."

Two can play at this game of pretending we've never met before, she thought.

Cormac stood in front of an abstract of luscious greys, one of her early works similar in concept to the four she had exhibited when she was sixteen.

"Amateurish, isn't it?" said Charlotte. "Wouldn't you think she'd choose to paint something interesting like a bit of horseflesh in a summer landscape rather than those dreary, colourless shapes?"

"I suggest that if you let in a bit of light you'd be better able to see it properly and be able to make a more accurate judgement."

"I've seen it in bright light and it looks worse. Are you a close friend of hers, pretending to like it?"

"I am her friend and I'm not pretending. I was her tutor until I left twelve years ago and I taught her the rudiments, but she soon left me behind." His face was inches away from the canvas. "Masterly. Masterly. I'd forgotten how good she was. Will she be long? I'm impatient to see her, so I am."

"Your impatience must be easily controlled if it's taken you twelve years to come to see her."

Cormac looked back over his shoulder and stared directly at her for a second. "You must be related. You have the look of her and your voice is very like."

"We've been told we look more like sisters than cousins, but that's where the similarity ends. Our natures are quite different."

"I've already noticed." Cormac resumed his close study of the painting.

"I remember feeling sorry for you when I heard you'd been lumbered with Charlotte who was notorious for being miserable, not to mention quite dense. I presume you had a tough time of it."

Cormac flushed. How did one fake a flush? "You presumed incorrectly. Charlotte was none of those things. She was bright, good-natured, courageous, quick-witted and a joy to teach."

Charlotte was moved by his words even though she knew they were only part of a game.

"High praise, indeed. One would never suspect all that by looking at her."

"If you were in any way perceptive you would, even on short acquaintance. I liked her from the start and couldn't have wished for a better pupil. I was blessed. And such talent. It's not often you come across talent like that and I was lucky to have seen it, so I was."

"All of that admiration must have gone to her head."

"Not in the least. I had to keep boosting her confidence. She had no idea how good she was."

"I'm beginning to think you are making all this up to incite some cousinly jealousy."

"Why would I waste my breath doing that?" He looked at his watch. "How much longer do you think she'll be? I've an appointment to see her father in ten minutes."

"He won't mind waiting. It's not as if he has anything else to do. This is my only chance to hear about Charlotte as I'll be moving back to Belgium shortly and it will be years before I see her again. Where are you stationed now?"

"Paris."

"Paris? How convenient. Perhaps I could travel down to see you and you could give me some art lessons. I've heard that talent runs in families."

"I don't give lessons any more." Cormac looked alarmed. "And I may not be in Paris much longer." As if his life depended on it, he bent to study two small paintings hanging beside the large one.

"Pity. You'd find me a very agreeable pupil, not like Charlotte with her temper and her sulks."

216

"You've not been listening to me. She had no major character faults. If you are looking for a juicy bit of scandal to spread around the family, I'm afraid I can't help you. I couldn't think of a bad word to say against her even if I tried."

Deeply moved by his words, Charlotte was annoyed to find tears welling up, and opened her eyes wide to disguise them. "The thing is, can your word be trusted? I heard you led Charlotte astray, painting misshapen nudes all day long."

"Did you now? No need to ask where that story came from. God preserve me from narrow-minded craw-thumpers and from uninformed gossips who listen to them." Cormac turned to face Charlotte for the first time and spoke with rising anger. "You were in Belgium being fed tittle-tattle by a woman who knows as much about art as a flea, while I was here for six years in Charlotte's company, and I can tell you without fear of contradiction that Charlotte was one of the most admirable and gifted people I ever had the privilege to meet. If it wasn't for the fact that I am so keen to see her new work I'd leave immediately and come back to see her when she has no disloyal cousin sitting there in her chair spouting bile. Shame on you!"

Charlotte felt a surge of love and affection for Cormac. She tried to speak but made a sound like a honk. Tears spilled over and began to fall.

"And don't try those crocodile tears on me. If you dish out dirt you can't expect to get bouquets of flowers back in return."

"Joke," Charlotte wept, praying that this indeed was a joke. "The joke's over."

"What joke? What are you talking about?"

Charlotte wiped her eyes and looked into Cormac's face. She felt a coldness spreading over her body and kept staring at him. He stared back, waiting.

"Have I changed so much?"

"How would I know? I've never met you before, and after today I hope I never see you again."

"Cormac, I'm not a cousin. I'm Charlotte."

"And I'm Brian Boru. I thought you said the joke was over, Miss."

"It is me," she said, swamped by feelings of unspeakable shame.

"Or should I say in front of my old, dear teacher 'It is I'? The same teacher who said that artists must above all things be observant?"

Cormac half-laughed, then abruptly stopped and focused on her as if he needed to weld her image onto his memory. His mouth dropped open.

"Christ Almighty, Charlotte. Oh my God, Charlotte, what has she done to you? Jesus, Mary and Joseph, of course it's you." He looked as if he'd been punched. "Bloody hell. I wasn't really looking. That bad-mouthing cousin of yours had me distracted. And this gloomy room. I couldn't see you properly." He rushed over and pulled back the curtains. "There. Now no one could mistake you."

"You can't bluff your way out of it, Cormac, but thank you for trying. I know I'm disgusting."

"No, no. Don't say that. It was the dull light and the short hair and the fact that I wasn't really looking at you that threw me. You look fine. Reubenesque."

"That's one way of putting it. All those nice things you said . . ." Her eyes filled up again.

He pulled a footstool up beside her and took her hand with his good hand.

"I only said them because I knew it was you all along," he laughed. "Now do you want to hear my real opinion?"

"Too late. You can't talk your way out of it now. I never knew you thought so well of me."

Cormac's face became grave. "Every word I said was true. You were all that and more. We've so much to talk about, but first, I want to see your work. I have been imagining you going in so many creative, original directions. Come on, let's go and see them."

Charlotte began weeping in earnest. "I didn't last," she managed to say. "It all just slipped away. Without you around I couldn't motivate myself. It all seemed so pointless." She looked at him and let out a loud sigh. "I'm sorry I let you down."

"You didn't let me down. Never think that. It was I who let you down, I can see in hindsight. I shouldn't have left before I pushed you into the Society – they would have looked after you and encouraged you, and stood up to your mother."

"They could have tried, but it wouldn't have done any good."

"But you're not sixteen any more. You're a young –"

218

"Not so young."

"Take it from me, you're young. Why don't you come back to Paris with me now and make a fresh start?"

"Paris? I couldn't."

"Why not? What's to stop you? You're over twenty-one and independently wealthy. You're obviously wasting your life here."

"I can't go to Paris. I can't even walk from here to the door without running out of breath. I've been in these rooms so long I don't think I can cope with other people. I've no energy and no purpose."

"Trust your old tutor to look after you. You'll soon make up for lost time. You already have the advantage of the language." He became more animated with each word. "Don't sit around thinking about it. Just do it. I can walk the legs off you like I did when you were a girl and you can regain your health. You can always return if it doesn't work out."

"I lack the courage. You described me as courageous but you were wrong. I'm really a coward. There's a certain comfort in rotting here – no decisions to be made."

"You'll soon change your attitude when you're mixing with like-minded people. It's sinful to give up on life before you've lived it."

He was making so much sense she had to side-track him.

"I'll tell you what, Cormac, I'll make a deal with you. Give me a year and make the same offer. I'm just not mentally prepared for it at the moment."

"I hope you're not saying that to fob me off and keep me quiet."

"Of course not." The image of the archangel from her dream the previous night flicked across her mind.

"All right then. I'll take your word for it. One year from now. Shake on it."

They shook hands and grinned into each other's faces.

"So you didn't marry either?"

"Me? No. Never. I'm married to my work. I always thought creativity and domesticity didn't mix."

"When I was a child I was hoping you and Holly would marry."

"Did you now?" Cormac enjoyed that remark. "Lovely lady, but even she couldn't tempt me. You know yourself. Can you imagine being immersed in a masterpiece and being called away to fix a leaking tap or shift furniture? God preserve me from that. But I'm not holding back –

I don't want to bring a blush to your maidenly cheeks so I won't say any more. One year, then. It was wonderful to see you again. Can't say the same about your nasty cousin." He kissed her on the top of her head, and she felt immediately lonely. "Now I'm off to see if your father's failing eyesight has had a beneficial effect on his brushwork."

46

Charlotte listened for the two sets of footsteps passing her door, waited for a short while, and then made her way to Harcourt's rooms. She took her time so she wouldn't be out of breath when she arrived. Down to the end of the corridor and along a short hallway – she should be able to make it. She was conscious of herself – her arms stood out from her sides like the gunslingers she saw on the covers of westerns her father left lying around the house. The skin on her inner thighs was already chaffed, causing an increased feeling of discomfort with each step, and her joints ached. She adopted a rolling action to minimise the friction on her flesh.

She stopped for breath – not even at the stairs yet. To give herself courage she told herself it was a scandal she hadn't visited her younger brother for years. He had made overtures to her up until two years ago, but had finally given up after she rejected his offered friendship once too often.

The long pause she took outside his door was necessary to slow her heartbeat and to rehearse what she was going to say.

Harcourt opened the door in response to her knock. With light shining directly on his face, the likeness to Manus she had noticed the week before in the dim corridor wasn't so marked, but it was still there.

"So you meant it. I'm pleased. Do come in." He looked happy to see her. "Wait until I pull over a seat."

The one he chose was too small. Charlotte pointed to a large leather armchair.

"All right if I take this one?"

"Of course." Harcourt immediately saw his mistake.

"Thank you."

"You're well?" he asked.

"Very well, thank you. And you?"

"Very well, thank you."

"Are the exams over?"

"No, two more weeks."

"And will you be going to Tyringham Park again for the summer?"

"Yes, Uncle Charles has given me an open invitation. Says he likes me to keep Giles company."

"You're lucky to have a cousin your age."

"I certainly am. But they keep asking for you and want you to come and stay. For as long as you like."

"That's very kind. They have invited me before but I'd rather not go."

She had never told anyone about the shame she felt whenever she thought of Tyringham Park. To think she had thrown that brooch at Miss East and cut her cheek. Miss East, the woman she wished was her mother, the saviour she longed to see. It still made her feel sick to think about what she had done and she hated her younger self for having done it. And Manus. How could she face him, the man who had to shoot Mandrake because of her incompetent handling of Sandstorm? He wouldn't chastise her but his kind, sad eyes would say it all.

There was a long silence. Charlotte was looking at her brother, liking him and wishing she knew him better so they wouldn't now be speaking to each other in this stilted fashion.

There was a sound of a door opening and closing behind her.

"Charlotte, this is a friend of mine, Lochlann Carmody. He's in the same year and we shame each other into studying during the end-of-term panic. Lochlann, my sister, Charlotte."

Charlotte turned and held out her hand to her earthbound archangel – for it was he whose face had appeared in her dream – and couldn't imagine that he would be the type to let anyone slip through his hands and fall to the ground.

Cormac's visit had energised Charlotte. How could she have wasted all those years after she had failed in the matrimonial stakes and reneged on her deal with Victoria? She must contact David Slane – she knew he genuinely liked her work and would point her in the right direction.

The fact that Cormac hadn't recognised her had deeply disturbed her. The cakes and pies Cook laid out for her each night since then were left unclaimed, and Queenie had been commanded to bring only cigarettes from the stores. When the contractions of hunger gripped her, all she had to do was remember the shocked look on Cormac's face to lose her desire for excess food.

On a subsequent visit to Harcourt's rooms they had talked about Manus, and Charlotte studied her brother's face closely while they did so, once again noting the similarity between the two men. Charlotte wanted to know if Manus had aged well – he used to be so handsome, she said. Hard to say, Harcourt answered. He had so much facial hair it was impossible to tell. Charlotte said she couldn't imagine him with a beard as he had been clean-shaven when she knew him.

"Do you like him?" she asked.

"Very much. He makes sure the city boy on holidays is trained to ride like a son of the estate."

In the end it was Harcourt who brought the visit to an end, saying they needed to prepare for the physiology exam and couldn't afford to waste time. Lochlann directed a special smile at her as she was leaving and said that her visit certainly wasn't a waste of time. He had enjoyed it, and hoped they would meet again soon. Charlotte waited until the door behind her was closed before she moved off – she didn't want the students looking at her slow, waddling progress.

"Does your friend have a girlfriend?"

Charlotte couldn't trust herself to say the name 'Lochlann'.

"Who? Lochlann? No, but he'd like to, and he will. Niamh McCarthy's her name."

"Is she a medical student too?"

"Yes, one of the three females in our year."

She must be very unfeminine to want to study a course like that, Charlotte thought. Aloud she said, "What's she like?"

"Lovely in every way. Lochlann's not the only one in the class who has his eye on her, but the rest of us don't stand a chance with him around. They're drawn to each other like magnets." Harcourt began to smile. "You should see the two of them walking down Grafton Street together. They look like film stars. People trip over themselves trying to get a good view of them."

Niamh's boyfriend back in Co Mayo had given up the chance of a university career to look after his five younger siblings, Harcourt went on to explain. Niamh admired him for that but, after three years, the separation was beginning to take its toll. The boyfriend kept commenting on how citified she'd become, and besides it was obvious to everyone she fancied Lochlann.

"It's only a matter of time," said Harcourt.

"What does her father do?"

"He's a doctor, and Lochlann's parents are both doctors. Most of the class are like that – it seems to run in families. I'm the odd one out in more ways than one."

"How did you two become friends?"

"Well, we're in the same year, obviously. Then we found ourselves walking home the same route after lectures every day. Found no shortage of things to talk about so it went on from there."

"Where does he live?"

"Two streets over. Bostobrick Road."

"Which end?"

"This is turning into a bit of an interrogation. The end with the double-fronted red bricks. The southern end."

"Yes, I know the ones. They're very nice. Quite roomy." About a fifth of the size of the townhouse, but still regarded as roomy.

"Why do you want to know?" Harcourt smiled.

Charlotte smiled back. "Just curious."

For the summer vacation Harcourt, as usual, went to Tyringham Park to spend it with Giles. Lochlann, with three of his old school friends, travelled to Boston to work in a country club.

Charlotte had four months to reinvent herself before she saw

Lochlann again. She planned to lose a large amount of weight and give up smoking at the same time.

The energy she was feeling after years of torpor must be a manifestation of love. Could these strange unfamiliar feelings of joy and optimism come from anything else? The romantic fiction she read seemed to indicate they were, and she had nothing else to go by.

She filled her days with walking and painting, concentrating on semi-starvation, and keeping a constant image of Lochlann in her mind to strengthen her resolve.

By September she could walk a mile without becoming breathless and could fit into clothes she hadn't worn for years. Her hair had been professionally cut and she wore it in a style that accentuated her re-emerging cheekbones and jaw line.

All the romantic clichés were true – she felt as if she loved the world and it loved her. Food and sleep were peripheral, life was lived on a higher plane and she finally was convinced that she understood the secrets of the universe.

Two years. The students would graduate in two years' time and disperse to hospitals all over Ireland and abroad to do their internships. Until then she was assured of regular exposure to Lochlann's company. She intended to enjoy every second of it.

Lochlann, tanned from a summer in the outdoors, seemed pleased to see her when he returned from the US, and tried not to show how astonished he was at the change in her, but she could tell he was impressed.

Lochlann came to Harcourt's rooms from the commencement of term, though the serious studying wouldn't begin until after Christmas. They spent a lot of time just talking, invariably about medical matters, in an animated and analytical way. Sometimes other students joined them. Charlotte, warmly welcomed on her earlier visits, took it for granted that she would now be included in the gatherings. For most of the time she was happy just to sit and listen. The eight-year age gap that existed between her and them she tried to dismiss as unimportant.

Her flimsy excuses for calling, the lengths of her visits and the ruses she employed to inveigle Lochlann to her rooms were becoming embarrassing to Harcourt, though Lochlann gave no hint of exasperation or impatience. Her window was stuck, she couldn't reach the box at the top of the wardrobe, there was a spider in the bath, she needed to move a bronze sculpture.

"I'll come," Harcourt offered more than once. "No need to bother Lochlann, Charlotte."

"No, I'll go. It's no bother and won't take a second."

"You're too good to her. Don't let her take advantage," Harcourt often said to him after Charlotte had left and was always answered with, "It was so little to do it's hardly worth mentioning."

47

Dublin
1938

It took four years for Peregrine Poolstaff to summon the courage to visit the townhouse again. If he didn't have news of Cormac Delaney as an excuse to call, he wouldn't have dared, then or ever.

He gave Queenie his card and asked if she would be so kind as to inform Miss Charlotte he had visited Cormac Delaney's studio in Paris and had purchased a painting from him that Miss Charlotte might like to see. What he requested was advice on where to have the canvas stretched and framed – he didn't know how to go about it or who else to ask.

Queenie's stare of hostility unsettled him, as he assumed she was reflecting her mistress's attitude, but he continued with his rehearsed speech, making a mental note to caution Charlotte, at a later date, about being too intimate with servants. It irked him to have to tell Queenie so much of his business but he knew that if she didn't have these tempting messages to relay he had no hope of gaining admittance.

Would Miss Charlotte kindly grant him a few minutes of her time and – here was the bit he knew she wouldn't be able to resist – allow him the opportunity to relay a private message from her former tutor?

Queenie didn't invite him inside to wait but closed the outside door in his face and left him standing on the street facing the Square while she passed on his words to Charlotte. Peregrine had to accept the servant's insolence but determined that if his plans came to fruition, and there was no reason why they shouldn't with Charlotte now considered unmarketable because of her age and past history, the first thing he would do would be get rid of Queenie.

After a thirty-minute delay, during which time Peregrine had to suffer the stares of passers-by, Queenie opened the door to report that her mistress would see him in three days' time at four o'clock. There was no mention of an alternative arrangement if that day didn't suit him.

"More than gracious," Peregrine said, his bulging forehead throbbing because of the indignity the servant was making him suffer. Would she please inform Miss Charlotte he would be honoured to attend to her then as her most obedient servant?

Queenie smirked, and took satisfaction in again closing the door in his face, using even more force than she had used earlier.

When the time came, Charlotte received Peregrine civilly enough. With a gravitas that he hadn't possessed when she knew him earlier, he told her how he had travelled to Paris with an aunt and uncle. During a tour of the studios there, he had come across Cormac Delaney by chance and had admired his work so much he felt compelled to purchase a canvas. Would she like to see it?

"Very much so." Of course she would. Why else had she allowed him to visit?

When he retrieved the painting from the anteroom where he had left it with his hat and coat, Charlotte had to restrain herself from snatching it out of his hand. She stood back while he rolled it out on the table and leaned forward to examine it.

"I knew it," she said, "I knew it," not bothering to tell Peregrine what it was she knew.

Cormac's style had changed, influenced by the Cubists. For all that he'd said about staying apart from the Paris scene during his six years at the townhouse to develop a unique style, he hadn't resisted their power. A suggestion of a hand and the shape of a small head were all that was left of a human figure amongst the geometric shapes. Colour, and the use of overlapping rather than perspective, created space and depth. The painting vibrated with cool colours against warm, light against dark, and didn't yield up all its significance in one look.

"You bought well," she said, admiring Cormac's skill in the details.

It was wonderful, though she wished he had continued on his own path, taking a different route from Braque and Picasso, giants who would overshadow anyone following their trail.

How big was his studio? How many completed works did he have on offer?

Peregrine snapped to attention with pleasure at questions he could answer, followed by more. What sizes did he favour? Were they all in a style similar to this one? He faltered. No, there were a few brightly coloured nudes . . .

"Ah-h."

And others, but he didn't have the technical terms to describe them. He worried he hadn't chosen wisely. At the time, he and his aunt and uncle couldn't agree, and finally he let Cormac make the decision for him. Surely the artist couldn't be wrong.

Did he look well? What was his message?

Peregrine puffed up. "He told me to make sure you didn't forget your promise. The year is nearly up. He said you'd know what he meant."

She did, and smiled in anticipation of Cormac's next visit. Would he be able to believe that her appearance and attitude had changed so much in less than a year, and would he like the new paintings she had done, stacked in the old classroom?

Queenie brought in the tray for afternoon tea and subjected Peregrine to a disdainful glare. Peregrine looked over at Charlotte to see if she had noticed, hoping she would chastise the servant in front of him, but she was eyeing the cakes and didn't witness Queenie's flagrant show of disapproval.

Things have changed, thought Peregrine, as Charlotte allowed herself one thin cucumber sandwich, leaving all the cakes for him. During his earlier courtship she had shown no hesitation in scoffing everything in front of her.

Peregrine held Charlotte's attention by mentioning the work of other artists he'd seen in Paris. It was obvious he had put a lot of work into preparing for this visit. One wouldn't have to be an astute reader of people to realise he was trying to hide his desperation while presenting himself as a serious suitor. An apology for his previous behaviour was implicit in his eagerness to ingratiate himself and, to give him the benefit of the doubt, perhaps delicacy prevented him from mentioning it.

The visit lasted over an hour and, despite the fact that there were no awkward silences and Charlotte showed nothing but friendliness, Peregrine could sense that she wasn't interested in him. If, to secure her affection, he had to fall on his knees and beg forgiveness for the public humiliation he had inflicted on her at the Hunt Ball, he would, and if she demanded marriage as compensation he would gladly accede, but one cue after another failed to elicit a response.

Charlotte's fortune could be used to fix his Big House's leaking roof, crumbling stonework, mildewed rooms, gaping window frames and rotting tapestries. And she could furnish him with an heir, tall healthy-looking woman that she was. What a fool he had been to let her go. The most galling thing of all was that he really liked her and was impressed by her improved appearance. If only he could turn back the clock!

Peregrine didn't expect a second invitation, but he was determined to ensure that the townhouse wouldn't be permanently closed to him.

"If there's anything I can do for you, *anything*, just say the word and consider it done," he said with a tremor of sincerity. "At any time for whatever reason, I am at your command. Promise me you will remember that."

Much as Charlotte was loath to part with Cormac's painting, she rolled it up and handed it to Peregrine so that he wouldn't 'forget' it to engineer another visit. It did cross her mind he might have offered it to her as a gift, but he was flustered, trying to leave with dignity, a skill he'd never mastered.

She wouldn't tell her parents of Peregrine's visit. His title and lineage were so impressive they would pressurise her to encourage him, especially as it wasn't likely she would get another offer. But he was too late. Under normal circumstances she would give him another chance because of her lack of choice, but since her sighting of Lochlann she had no interest in any offer he could make. She would rather settle for small portions of Lochlann's company than the lifelong commitment of marriage and children with Peregrine, isolated on his distant County Donegal estate where she might never set eyes on Lochlann again.

48

Whenever Charlotte visited her brother's rooms she took the chair next to Lochlann's, and during the next hour her knee or arm would touch his 'accidentally' and her excitement when that happened was obvious to Harcourt, though Lochlann didn't seem to notice. Sometimes when Lochlann was speaking, he would place his hand on Charlotte's forearm for a minute or two to emphasise a point and Harcourt could see her change colour and radiate happiness. She even ventured to put her hand on Lochlann's when he was talking but, surprisingly, had the sense not to let the touch linger too long.

On Friday nights it had become a tradition that whoever went to Harcourt's rooms ended up having too much to drink. It became the highlight of Charlotte's week. The two glasses of wine she allowed herself loosened her tongue and heightened her feeling of wellbeing. Lochlann, surrounded by clusters of friends, would always draw her in and she would stand close to him. Later, when the members of the group moved away out of politeness, some raising their eyebrows in disbelief and others smiling in amusement, she had exclusive access to him for long periods while the rest of the company talked about subjects that didn't interest her.

It was disconcerting to discover that after she had made efforts to sound witty and affable in her conversations, quoting things that

Cormac had said, Lochlann couldn't remember one word the next day. She was forced to learn how to identify the point of inebriation at which he lost his memory so that she could save her best lines until the early part of the evening the following week and not waste them.

He spent Saturdays and Sundays with his family and school friends. Charlotte spent those hours wondering what he was doing and wishing Monday would come soon.

In this unvarying fashion one academic year slid into the next.

The medical students' final year was uneventful except for Niamh McCarthy's news. Her boyfriend at home had met a girl at a dance and had fallen in love. It took him a long time to tell Niamh as he was afraid of causing her pain. She took it well and, to his relief, was instantly forgiving. He hoped she would meet someone who would suit her as well as this new girl suited him. She didn't tell him she already had.

Harcourt relayed all this to Charlotte, while flicking through *The Irish Times* to make it look as if the news he was imparting was of little consequence. He felt sorry for her, but was relieved he had something definite with which to dash her unrealistic expectations. Her flirting during the Friday night socialising was becoming increasingly blatant.

Niamh now sometimes joined Harcourt and Lochlann in their study sessions. From the first time she met her rival, Charlotte analysed her looks, conversation and mannerisms, looking for flaws, trying to identify the ingredient that made her so attractive to men. She thought Niamh's laugh was 'common', though it seemed to be one of the many characteristics Lochlann liked. There was no doubt the girl was friendly, but not as good-looking as Harcourt had led her to believe. Was she a little bit too long in the neck?

Niamh invited Charlotte to a performance of Bach's 'Mass in B Minor' where she would be part of the choir.

"Good enough to be a soloist," said Lochlann, "but went the medical route instead."

Niamh laughed her big, throaty, common laugh. "He would say that. No, the amateur status suits me – all the enjoyment and none of the responsibility. Besides, I wouldn't be good enough, so don't mind him."

At the performance Charlotte sat with Harcourt on her left and

232

Lochlann on the other side. The shared chair-arm on the right occupied her more than the singing, which she found boring, all sounding the same and no distinguishable melody to be heard. "Sorry," said Lochlann when the pressure on his arm made him think he was taking more than his share of space. He folded his arms and Charlotte felt bereft. When he once again became lost in the music, his arm returned and this time Charlotte made sure the contact between them was so light he wouldn't notice, though it was enough to keep her in thrall until the end. Harcourt could see what was going on in the semi-darkness, and felt mortified on his sister's behalf.

49

Dublin
1939

In the months approaching their final exams Harcourt, Lochlann and Niamh studied together daily. Charlotte tried to disapprove of Niamh but was disarmed by her friendliness and lack of guile.

Cormac belatedly paid his promised visit and after one look at Charlotte didn't need to be told that she wouldn't be returning with him to Paris. "Who's the lucky man?" he teased.

Charlotte painted with renewed dedication. Nominated by David Slane, she had become a member of the Society and was promised a solo exhibition within three years.

"Come and see what you think of this," she was now able to say at any time to Lochlann, having run out of other inventive ways to coax him to her rooms. Harcourt and Niamh were included in the invitation so it wouldn't appear too obvious, and as it turned out, Niamh was the most knowledgeable and appreciative of the three. Charlotte then resorted to using larger canvasses so that she could single out Lochlann to ask him if he could move or hang them, tasks she was well able to do herself. He always obliged without hesitation. Charlotte avoided looking at both her brother and Niamh as she left Harcourt's rooms to follow Lochlann to give him instructions.

An informal party to celebrate the final exam was held in the townhouse. Harcourt was the only one who had enough space to accommodate the whole year. Everyone came. Charlotte was the only non-medical person there.

"That's not like you," Harcourt said, watching her gulp down a third glass of wine. She usually stopped at two. He hadn't been very welcoming to her when she first arrived.

"You're right. It's not like me. But then this night is not like any other night." She filled her glass for the fourth time and avoided looking at his scowling face. "It's the end of a chapter."

"Good riddance to all that cramming is all I can say. Roll on, the next chapter."

The next one for you, perhaps, thought Charlotte, but there's no next chapter for me. It's all over.

After tonight the students would disperse and she would never be included in their company again. By September Harcourt would be relocated in London to specialise in neurology – did he hope to make Edwina walk again? – while at the same time Lochlann and Niamh were due to become engaged before they headed off to Boston together to specialise in surgery. Who knew how long it would be before they would meet again?

After her fourth glass Charlotte felt fortified enough to join the crowd that was gathered around Lochlann and Niamh. Niamh drew her into the centre and introduced her to the people Charlotte didn't know and then talked exclusively to her for half an hour. Lochlann broke in to excuse himself, saying there were some classmates leaving early that he wanted to see before they disappeared out of his life for good. Niamh excused herself as well and went with him. Charlotte was left standing beside a female — one of three in the room besides herself — who did her best to think up things to say to a non-medical person. Charlotte kept tracking Lochlann and Niamh as they made their way from group to group. The female beside her was claimed before long and was absorbed into the crowd. Everyone had a lot to say to everyone else. Some of the conversation became maudlin. Charlotte picked her way through the revellers and took her fifth drink to a chair that had been pushed into a corner.

A young man backed into her, turned around and said, "Sorry. Are you all right? Is there anything I can get you?" and when she said she was fine, thank you, just taking a rest, he turned back to his friends and she heard him whisper, "Who's she? I've never seen her before."

By two o'clock Niamh had fallen asleep while sitting on the couch with Lochlann by her side. She had been revising until late the night before and had only managed to have a couple of hours' sleep. She had wanted to stay awake as it would be her last night with Lochlann for some time. She and her parents were leaving for Africa the next day for a three-month tour to celebrate the completion of her degree.

The wine wasn't helping Charlotte's equanimity. She was finding it difficult to keep her mind off the dark days that would follow this night.

When someone vacated the place on Lochlann's left side, she slid in quickly before anyone else had a chance to take it. Lochlann welcomed her and put his arm around her. He was already three parts inebriated and in the height of good humour. She looked over at Harcourt and caught his steely, disapproving look.

By four in the morning she was the only person in the room who wasn't asleep. Most students had left by then but there were about a dozen slumped on chairs or stretched out on the floor. She was glad that Harcourt's suspicious gaze wasn't trained on her as she shook Lochlann awake and, with difficulty, pulled him to his feet and, motioning that there was something in her room that needed attending to, guided his unsteady progress along the corridor.

Just one hour with him, that's all she asked. Niamh couldn't begrudge her an hour when she was going to have him for the rest of his life. Just to lie beside him on the bed, not doing anything, not that he was in a fit state to do anything, moving in really close, putting her head into the hollow between his shoulder and head, and pretending, just for an hour, that he belonged to her. It wouldn't hurt anyone, and no one need ever know. Lochlann, true to form, wouldn't even remember, so what difference would it make to anyone?

50

Lochlann received a letter from the teaching hospital in Boston to say his application had arrived two days too late, making him ineligible for enrolment until the following year. There was no system for redress as all places had been filled.

Damn. Damn and blast.

Niamh had sent her application in on the same day, so she would have missed out as well.

He should have learnt his lesson about the consequences of late applications the time he arrived back from a holiday in Italy. By a week he missed enrolling at Earlsfort Terrace where all his friends had gone, and had to settle for the Royal College where he knew nobody.

What to do?

He and Niamh had talked about working in Africa as volunteers with the Medical Missionaries and delaying their further training in Boston for a year. The nun they had spoken to about it said they couldn't work in the same mission unless they were married, to prevent giving scandal to the pagans the Church was trying to convert. Seeing they intended to marry in a year's time anyway, they didn't see that as an obstacle. In fact, it gave the option an added appeal.

They could take up that alternative now. In Niamh's absence, knowing her as well as he did and assuming she would agree, Lochlann took it upon himself to inform the Mother Superior that they would travel to Africa and would be married before they left. He then wrote to Niamh telling her what he had done, sending the letter poste restante, hoping it wouldn't arrive too late for her to collect it. He would like to have included a description of the erotic dream he'd had about her on the night of their final exams, but it was too intimate to commit to paper, so he only hinted at it and said he would describe it to her in detail when she returned. He had wanted to tell her about it the morning after the celebrations, but by the time he went to seek her out, she had left the townhouse and he hadn't seen her since. How he'd ended up in Charlotte's bed he had no idea, but presumed it was habit that had propelled him there when he needed to sleep. It was with relief he had seen he was alone in the bed when he awoke in the late morning.

His arms felt superfluous without Niamh enclosed in them. Four more weeks until her return. Their wedding night couldn't come soon enough as far as he was concerned.

51

"Her Ladyship sent me down to tell you that you are obliged to attend dinner tonight, Miss, poorly or not. Her exact words."

Charlotte retched into her handkerchief. Queenie picked up the basin beside the bed and held it under Charlotte's chin. Charlotte heaved a few more times without producing anything, then sank back onto her pillows.

"Can't possibly. The thought of food makes me feel ill. Tell her that."

"I already did. She said if you don't come, she'll send out for a doctor, seeing as Harcourt isn't here to have a look at you."

Charlotte wailed "I can't let her do that," and wept into her already sodden pillow.

Lady Blackshaw had wanted to know every detail about Charlotte's indisposition and Queenie, alarmed that Charlotte was set against seeing a doctor even though her condition hadn't improved after three days, told Her Ladyship about the retching and the weeping, information she would normally keep to herself out of loyalty to Charlotte but was now relieved to pass on. Had any gentleman been calling on Charlotte? Lady Blackshaw wanted to know. Lord Peregrine was the only one, Queenie answered, but that was over a year ago. Was she sure he hadn't called more recently? As

239

sure as she could be, but then she wasn't in attendance all the time so she couldn't swear to the fact.

Looking down at the prostrate figure on the bed, Queenie was glad she had passed the responsibility for Charlotte's health on to Lady Blackshaw. Things were looking serious.

Lord Waldron and Harcourt's places at the dining-room table were vacant as they were spending the summer in Tyringham Park. Harcourt had left the day after the end-of-term party as he wanted to make the most of his last long holiday before beginning his internship in London.

Charlotte sat opposite her mother, beside Aunt Verity. As soon as the soup was served, Charlotte put her handkerchief to her mouth, pushed back her chair and ran from the room.

Charlotte yelped when she saw Harcourt standing beside her bed, and covered her face with her hands. "What are you doing here?"

"Mother sent for me. She thinks you've disgraced yourself with Peregrine Poolstaff and wants me to find out. I don't know why she couldn't ask you straight out herself and save me the journey." Harcourt slammed a chair beside the bed but didn't sit on it. "Well, have you?"

"No."

"That's that, then. Wasted journey. Just as well, I might add. His wedding was in the *Times* last week. Quiet affair. Married his rich cousin. It's a wonder you didn't see it. His roof must have fallen in. Mother clearly doesn't know about the marriage and so got the wrong end of the stick."

Charlotte turned her face to the wall. "Not exactly. I *have* disgraced myself, Harcourt. I'm glad you came. You're going to have to help me. What am I going to do? I don't know what to do. I wish I were dead."

There was a heavy silence. Harcourt stared at his sister and said with venom, "If you're telling me what I think you're telling me, then I can only wish for the same thing."

Edwina's initial mildness on hearing Harcourt's report vanished when she heard that the man responsible for Charlotte's condition was not a still-single Peregrine Poolstaff as she had assumed, but someone she had never heard of called Lochlann Carmody. The fact that he was Harcourt's friend who had been coming to the townhouse for five years didn't soften the antipathy she felt at the mere mention of a name that didn't belong to anyone in her circle. She assumed Lochlann was a social climber from the peasantry with an eye on the Blackshaw fortune, that Charlotte had lost all sense of propriety in her desperation to be married and that the family would become a laughing stock when the facts became known. If the facts became known.

A servant from the townhouse delivered a note to Lochlann from Lady Blackshaw, requesting his presence at his earliest convenience.

Despite Lochlann's frequent visits to the townhouse over the years, he had rarely encountered Harcourt's mother who generally confined herself to her apartments on the ground floor. He had often wondered at the fact that every member of the Blackshaw family lived a separate life and could avoid seeing every other member of the family from one end of the year to the next if they so wished, as evidenced by poor Charlotte's bizarre three-year-long self-imposed internment. Reception rooms took up the whole of the second floor, Harcourt and Charlotte occupied half the third floor each and shared a corridor, Lord Waldron lived on the fourth floor when he was in residence, and the servants were either down in the basement or up in the attic. Now Lady Blackshaw had peremptorily summoned him, and he felt both puzzled and apprehensive.

It all came clear to Charlotte. She would break ties with her family, travel to England with Queenie, take on a new identity, have the baby there, keep it and rear it, and never return to Ireland or have any contact with anyone here ever again. What a mistake it had been to tell Harcourt who by now would be informing their mother, who would then inform Lord Waldron.

While she was waiting for her next wave of nausea to pass, Charlotte imagined what it would be like to be married to Lochlann. It would be a heavenly state, in which she need never fear abandonment again. Her mother had handed her over to Nurse Dixon, her father was never at home when he was needed, Miss East had chosen Catherine and Sid over her, Holly left the townhouse after Harcourt went to school even though she had been offered an alternative position in the house, Cormac opted to live in Paris and didn't contact her for twelve years, and she never saw Manus. If Lochlann were legally tied to her for richer for poorer in sickness and in health until death did them part, all the hurt she had suffered in the past would be cancelled out. In the same way Cormac had done, Lochlann would enclose her in a warm orbit and keep away her nightmares.

There was really no need to worry about Niamh. According to Harcourt, half the men in the year, including himself, were in love with her. She would soon find someone else. She had a large pool to choose from, whereas Charlotte, part of a dwindling number of aristocrats in the country, had so few. Niamh also had the advantage of having time on her side.

A beautiful dream.

Plenty of time to fantasise when she was miles away, living on her own. Charlotte picked up a pencil and started to make a list of what she needed to take with her to England. Not much. She could buy what she wanted there. It was some compensation to know she would never have to worry about money.

52

When Lochlann was shown into Lady Blackshaw's presence after being summoned by her he was struck again by how much Harcourt looked like her, and how little Charlotte did.

He felt the chill of her personality even from a distance.

She didn't greet him or call him by name before she accused him.

Lochlann felt as if a cannonball, fired at his chest, had gone right through his body, taking all his vital organs with it, leaving a gaping hole.

No recollection whatsoever of the action he was accused of came back to him. He had a vague memory of being in a bedroom sometime during the night after a deliciously erotic dream about Niamh, and it was only after waking later that he identified the room as Charlotte's. Distaste at the thought of intimate relations with that lonely woman was his initial reaction, but what could he say in his defence? Everything that happened after eleven o'clock on the night of the party was either a blur, a dream or a blank.

Harcourt brought the news that Lochlann had agreed to marry her so there was no need for any dramatic resolutions as the family honour had been saved. He looked at her as if he hated her.

"That's not what I wanted. You must know that."

"Don't insult me by lying. Besides, you have no choice. It is all arranged."

"What if I refuse to marry?"

"I don't think that's an option unless you want to spend the rest of your days locked up in a lunatic asylum. Mother has already threatened that and you know she's not to be trifled with." He backed out of the room. "You are not to receive anyone in case pressure is brought to bear on you, and you are not to leave the house. Mother's orders. Now don't expect me to speak to you ever again from this moment on."

Lochlann's mother cried and prayed for three days, his father felt unmanned by not being able to save his only son from a life of certain misery, and his sister Iseult, from her perspective of twenty years, was revolted at the thought of her twenty-three-year-old brother marrying an old woman of thirty. His friends thought he was making a joke in poor taste when he told them he was going to marry Charlotte.

"You've fallen for the oldest trick in the book," one of them said bitterly, when Lochlann explained the circumstances. "Poor, innocent, sacrificial lamb."

Edwina needed a favour. Mr Kilmartin, the specialist who had looked after her since she had been transferred to Dublin after her accident, was the only person she could think of to ask. Would he find a position for her future son-in-law whose one desire all his life had been to travel to the outback of Australia and work there for a couple of years? The fares were to be a surprise gift from her – he was penniless – and the position would have to be arranged at once. Could Mr Kilmartin contact one of his many colleagues who had emigrated there (he had often referred to them) by cable – letters would be too slow at this late stage – and let her know?

Mr Kilmartin said he would be only too delighted to help. He had never seen his brave, resigned patient look so vital and animated. She must think a lot of her future son-in-law. He was pleased to inform her within a fortnight that a friend of his had found advertised in a medical journal a small twenty-bed hospital serving a small town in the midst of a large area on the top of a plateau 400 miles from

Sydney. At present it had no doctor, which wasn't surprising, as it was an isolated, cold, rainy place, quite unlike the sunnier parts of the country that most people favoured.

"That sounds ideal," said Edwina, and asked if Mr Kilmartin would send a telegram to the hospital, accepting the post on behalf of Dr Lochlann Carmody.

Edwina then bullied the local priest into officiating at a wedding ceremony three weeks hence, a speedy resolution by anyone's reckoning. To ensure the contract would be legal and binding by Lochlann's standards, she swallowed her prejudices and opted for a Catholic service. Let them try to get out of that one. Finally she booked two one-way tickets from Southampton on a cargo ship. By registering Lochlann as a doctor, she was not charged for the fares.

Satisfaction all round. The Blackshaw name rescued, Charlotte off her hands. What did she care if Lochlann was a fortune-hunter and not of her class if the pair of them were living 12,000 miles away? She could tell everyone a baby had been born five months later than it had in reality and there would be no one in a position to contradict her.

Lochlann didn't try to contact Charlotte – seeing her on their wedding day would be too soon. Being married to her loomed like a sunless, bleak, never-ending winter. And there would he be, wearing neither shoes nor coat, standing on ice in a treeless landscape.

If only Niamh could return from Africa so he could hold her in his arms one more time and have her press her dear hand against the wound in his chest so he could forget for a moment the nightmare that was sucking the spirit out of him and colouring his future in various shades of black.

With relief, Charlotte changed her mind about escaping to England. She was too weak in her dehydrated state to undertake a journey, and besides, when one came to think of it, did one have any right to deprive a baby of its father or a man of his own flesh and blood?

She thought not, and perhaps things might not turn out so badly. She could be the most generous benefactor as well as the best wife and mother in the country if she put her mind to it. Her fortune would enable Lochlann to study in the best hospitals in Europe and America if he so wished. In time he would be able to set up his own private clinic, enabling him to fund wonderful research that would change the face of medicine and, with her contacts, have no shortage of influential patrons and patients. It was even possible that one day he might bless the moment they met, and publicly acknowledge his good fortune in having married her.

The fact that Niamh McCarthy's life might be destroyed by Lochlan's betrayal of her was something she wouldn't think about right now. Protecting her unborn child from the effects of dark and depressing thoughts must be her priority from now on.

53

Sydney
1939

Dixon placed her bunch of keys beside the copy of *Middlemarch* on her rosewood desk. Her office was behind Reception – through the glass panels she could keep her eye on activities in the foyer. Some guests were signing in, some leaving. She knew them all by name. Two more pairs of handmade shoes on account were being delivered to her. The head chef's weekly projections were ready for her assessment. Five young girls were sitting outside her door waiting to be interviewed for the waitress vacancy.

She walked from her office to the reception desk to look over the register. Guests and staff passing greeted her with deference, and those to whom she spoke the extra word felt honoured by being singled out. Now that she was past her prime, respect acted as a satisfactory substitute for admiration. If her fiancé had lived, she would be a lady of the manor by now, the story went. Just look at the size of those diamonds. She'd stayed true to his memory all those years, you have to give her credit for that – heroic and romantic at the same time. Worked hard. A good listener, a keeper of secrets. A real battler, and you can't give higher praise than that.

She was expecting a promotion she knew she deserved that would make her the first non-family female to become the manager of any hotel in NSW. As she completed one task after another she rehearsed the speech she would make after the promotion was announced.

There was a visitor for Dixon at Reception. It was a journalist from the *Woman's Monthly* who wanted to write an article about her. About how she had transformed the Waratah from a basic watering hole into a comfortable hotel and become a legend herself in the meantime, rumoured to be about to make history. The dead aristocratic fiancé and the pieces of fine jewellery he had given her before he left for the front would add glamour and pathos to the story.

Dixon agreed to give an interview and be photographed provided they didn't mention the promotion as it hadn't been made official yet.

If only the Matron from the orphanage and Manus, Miss East and Teresa Kelly could see me now, she thought as she posed, making sure her best features were facing the camera.

54

Dublin
1939

Edwina's orchestration of the matrimonial merger was swift and thorough. In exchange for the wedding taking place at such short notice and in a Catholic church (though at a side altar and not the main one) plus a promise that all their children would be reared as Catholics – even Edwina couldn't make the parish priest back down on that one – Lochlann agreed to accept the post in Australia. With Niamh lost to him, Siberia or the Arctic would have done just as well.

The night before the wedding Lochlann wrote a long letter to Niamh and entrusted it to Iseult to give her when she returned from Egypt in three days' time. Iseult dreaded that task almost as much as she dreaded attending the wedding.

"This is the last time we'll talk like this," Lochlann said to his sister.

How he would live without Niamh he didn't know. As best he could, he supposed, now that there was no option. At least he had a profession he loved and would soon have a child of his own – there were a lot of people worse off.

He wanted to put on a good front for his parents' sake.

The two embraced in sorrow, before parting to prepare for the ordeal.

Iseult felt so ill on the morning of the wedding that she asked her father for some calming medicine to help her cope with the farcical ceremony she would give anything not to have to attend.

The mother refused anything, in case she might be needed.

The father was filled with an awful hopelessness at being forced to witness the procedure as if it were a normal occasion. Try as he might, he couldn't blame Charlotte for insisting on the marriage – it was her right to give her child a father and a name. He could only lament the unfortunate background to it, and his son's part in it.

Edwina didn't even tell Waldron about the wedding, and Verity was sent off to Tyringham Park for the week to get her out of the way. Only the Carmodys were in the pews, with Edwina in her wheelchair alongside, when the silent, unsmiling Harcourt supported an unsteady, weakened Charlotte into the little side chapel. Charlotte kept her head down when she reached Lochlann's side. She was heard to say "I'm sorry." Lochlann didn't turn to look at her and didn't acknowledge the apology.

While they said their vows Charlotte felt the presence of the absent Niamh and shivered. Lochlann turned to look towards the door as if expecting a late arrival.

After the ceremony Edwina beckoned to Charlotte and indicated that she should wait until the others had left the side chapel. Charlotte sat in a pew beside the wheelchair and waited.

She's going to tell me I look nice and that Lochlann is a worthy addition to the family, she thought.

Edwina drummed her fingers on the arm of the wheelchair. "I want to make two things clear before I give you your tickets, so listen carefully and don't tell me later that you made a mistake because you didn't hear what I said. Are you concentrating?"

Charlotte nodded.

"Under no circumstances are you to write to me when the baby is born. Let five months elapse before you do."

"Then how will you know about it?"

"I am quite capable of restraining my curiosity for five months. I've made it easy for you to remember. A year to the day from today – you'll hardly forget your first anniversary. I don't want to risk anyone knowing the real date of birth and turning me into an object of ridicule."

"But all Lochlann's family and friends know the circumstances, and they will be informed."

"That is hardly a consideration to me seeing their paths and ours are unlikely to cross ever again. I made it clear that there will be no social contact between the two families from this day forward." Edwina's face twisted in a grimace of unholy triumph. "I think I can say with certainty they won't talk out of turn after what I've said – well, 'threatened' might be a more accurate word. No need for you to know the details. You can thank me for knowing how to save the family honour."

Charlotte was filled with cold displeasure at her mother's attitude and had no inclination to thank her.

"So you don't even want me to write privately to you?" she asked.

"No. Decidedly not. Verity collects the post every day and she's likely to steam open your letter, she's so desperate to know what doesn't concern her. There's been talk. The fact that you'll be abroad and they won't be able to count the months is frustrating the gossips and Verity would love to claim her moment of glory by uncovering the truth and spreading the word. She's far too weak to keep a secret and your father can't be trusted to keep his mouth shut when he's drinking, so Harcourt and I are the only ones who know. Unless you've been talking."

"Of course not. Why would I? What's the second thing?"

"I want you to find your sister. That is why I picked Australia for your exile. I would do it myself if it weren't for this accursed wheelchair. I would have travelled there twenty years ago if the accident hadn't happened – Beatrice and I had it all arranged. As you know, I have made some attempts to advertise in Australia – to no avail – and I hired that private detective who did nothing but pocket my money I suspect, apart from verifying that a Teresa Kelly arrived in Australia. But it's a common name. He could not confirm that Dixon arrived, for lack of a first name, though several female Dixons entered the country around the time. And so I have to rely on you to find Teresa Kelly and Victoria for me – or, failing that, Nurse Dixon. It is my belief that they are together."

"I won't waste my time." Charlotte's disappointment at her mother's attitude to the baby cancelled the usual caution she adopted when speaking to her. "I never believed Teresa Kelly took Victoria, nor did anyone else except you – she would never have done anything so selfish."

"I'll thank you not to use that tone of voice with me. How would you have the faintest idea what that woman would do? You were a mere child at the time she was at the Park."

Charlotte stiffened. "I have to go. They'll be waiting outside. Harcourt is ready to take us to the train. We can't afford to delay as we might miss our later connections. Is there anything else you want to say to me before I go?"

"Just remember who you are and where you come from. Now take these."

Charlotte accepted the tickets her mother held out to her and thought it only fair to thank her for being so efficient at organising the wedding.

"Think nothing of it. Have a good trip." Edwina remained rigid as if to stave off any last-minute show of affection. "I'll stay on here until you've gone."

"Goodbye, Mother." Charlotte's mind blanked when she tried to think of something significant to say. To cover the awkward moment she flicked through the tickets and looked at the itinerary – Cobh, Southampton, Canary Islands, Capetown. "This says our destination is Capetown. Why are we going to Capetown?"

"Because of the short notice that was the nearest destination I could find. Cooks assured me you won't have any trouble securing a passage between there and Sydney."

Charlotte's eye came to the last entry: *Return – Void.*

"But these are only one-way tickets." She looked at her mother in disbelief.

"Yes?"

"I thought a couple of years – three at most – would be sufficient."

"Do you personally know anyone who has returned from Australia? Now off you go and remember everything I've said. I'll send you your instructions in the post."

Lochlann was standing with his family in the graveyard beside the church. He didn't seem to notice when Charlotte joined them and clutched his arm with too much force. His solemn expression made him look even more handsome than usual, but older.

"I've said my goodbyes," he said in a flat voice. "I told them we would slip off without any fuss." There had been no wedding breakfast arranged by the Blackshaws.

The pair followed an equally serious Harcourt, who had kept his word about not speaking to Charlotte. Lochlann looked back at the last minute and raised his hand in a gesture of farewell to his mother, father and Iseult, but they had already started to walk off with their heads lowered and didn't see him.

PART 4

THE EXILE

55

Australia
1939

Scottie Cunningham guessed who the two strangers on the platform
were when he arrived to collect the mailbags. He was looking
forward to hearing their story, which by the look of them, would be
no ordinary one.

The overdressed woman was flushed and damp from the heat.
Looking as if she was about to pass out at any minute, she was
leaning against the paling fence in the shade, her eyes closed. Her
companion, who must be her husband though he looked too young
for the role, was trying to keep the flies away from her face with the
vigorous flapping of a folded newspaper. If their clothes and luggage
didn't already signal them as newcomers, that action with the
newspaper did – give them a few weeks and they would be taking the
presence of flies for granted. If the woman removed her tweed jacket
and undid the buttons on the high neck of her blouse she would be
less likely to be suffering from heat exhaustion. It made Scottie, in his
shorts and singlet, feel uncomfortable just to look at her.

The stranger checked that the woman beside him was in a
comfortable position, before coming forward with his hand
outstretched to meet the mailman.

"Scottie Cunningham?"

"That's right, mate. I was just about to make myself known. You
the new doctor?"

"I am. Lochlann Carmody. How did you guess?"

"We've been expecting you." He grinned. "Plus your accent."

"The stationmaster said you would be able to give us a lift."

"Happy to oblige. The lady feeling crook?"

Lochlann hadn't heard 'crook' before but guessed what it meant.

"She is. She's prone to travel sickness. The boat trip over was a nightmare for her and the twelve-hour train trip from Sydney didn't help. Couldn't sleep."

"She'll be as right as rain once we get her up the mountain where it is cooler. Talking to Matron only yesterday. She said she'd send someone down to meet you if she had any idea when you were due to arrive."

"We had no idea ourselves. No one seems to have heard of Redmundo and we didn't have a clue."

"We're a bit off the beaten track, all right, but that's how we like it. Greatest little place on earth."

The men heard a moaning sound and looked over to see Charlotte slipping sideways. Lochlann was by her side in a second and eased her back into a sitting position.

When Scottie was introduced to Charlotte and heard her plummy accent he was convinced that their story wouldn't be a straightforward one. His wife Jean would be dying to be the first to know. He was confident he would find out during the next few hours – it was amazing how much people would tell you in the intimacy of the cabin of a truck that they would never divulge under ordinary circumstances.

"Has your wife anything lighter to put on before we start?" Scottie asked Lochlann in a low voice.

"I beg your pardon," said Charlotte, overhearing. She pulled her jacket more tightly around her.

"No offence, Mrs Carmody. Take advice from an old hand. I've seen a few in my day become crook from wearing wool in this climate. Especially black wool – it absorbs the heat. The consequences can be serious. Even you mightn't know that, Doc, being new. We can't afford to stand on ceremony here."

"So I see." Charlotte, who had learnt from her father how important it was that British colonisers wear formal dress even in the tropics to demonstrate the superiority of their civilisation to the natives, wasn't about to let the side down on her first day. "I am perfectly all right, thank you."

"Have it your own way, then. Come on, I'll give you a hand."

The two men supported her between them. Scottie had to reach in through the window to open the passenger door as the outside handle had broken off.

"In you go," he said, standing on the running board to get better leverage as Lochlann passed her up. He could tell by the look on Charlotte's face she didn't like being handled by him, but in her fragile state she didn't have much option.

"Did you bring some Irish bullion with you?" asked Scottie, picking up one end of the trunk. "This weighs a ton."

"No such luck," said Lochlann, taking the other end to help lift it over the tailboard into the back. "Reference books. Thought I'd better bring the lot seeing I won't have any colleagues to confer with."

"You can say that again. We couldn't even rustle up a retired doctor these last few months." Scottie was now warming to his favourite role – introducing someone from the Old World to the hardships of the New. "Forty miles in one direction, sixty in the other before you run into one. Taking the state of the roads into account, you can double that distance. Are we glad to see you!" He fastened the tailgate with a lever on one side and a loop of barbed wire on the other, gave it a slap and beamed at Lochlann. "Rightio, then. We're off."

Charlotte's face was bright red. Her blouse, soaked with perspiration, had black smuts dotted across the front of it, souvenirs from their trip on the steam train.

"The humidity's what gets you," said Scottie, sitting on the towel that prevented the seat from burning the backs of his bare suntanned legs. He accelerated as smoothly as the old vehicle would allow.

Lochlann, holding Charlotte with her head on his shoulder, felt the heat radiating from her and, concerned, began to slip off her jacket.

"Don't," she mumbled in her half-awake state, shrugging off his hand.

"Sorry, doctor's orders," he said, continuing with the task as if she were a child. "There, now. Isn't that better?"

While Scottie concentrated on making a right-hand turn Charlotte rearranged her smocked maternity blouse.

They had been delayed for three months in Cape Town. England declared war on Germany the day they arrived and they had to wait their turn for a berth. Lochlann sent a telegram to Redmundo to explain his delay and was lucky to be offered a short-term post at the Cape as a locum, saving himself the embarrassment of having to wire home for funds, or worse still, having to ask Charlotte for money, something he vowed he would never do.

"I'll only be a tick." Scottie pulled up in front of a produce and hardware store and went in to collect goods ordered by his customers.

Charlotte stirred.

"Nearly there," said Lochlann softly. "Go back to sleep."

Charlotte twisted her head deeper into the hollow between his neck and shoulders, enjoying the closeness enforced on them by the limited space in the cabin despite the extra heat generated by having her body so close to his. If the journey went on for hours she would be well pleased.

"Still out for the count. That's good," said Scottie, re-occupying his seat and banging the door after him. "Rang the wife to get your house ready. Only two more stops before the mountain."

Now that Charlotte was in a deep sleep, Lochlann turned his attention to the countryside. Everything was in such sharp focus and the light so strong he had to squint to cope with the glare. The sky was startlingly blue: he wondered if he'd ever seen a truly blue sky before now.

"Father Daly will be pleased to have two more recruits for his congregation," Scottie said with a question in his voice.

"Only one. My wife is Church of Ireland. Anglican."

"Ahh."

"And where are you from originally yourself?"

"Aberdeen. Brought here when I was two. Fifty years ago this year. Living up the mountain suits me. Couldn't take that coastal heat for long. Daresay that applies to you as well." He looked meaningfully at Lochlann for too long and hit the ditch. "Don't worry, Doc," he laughed, making a quick corrective swerve. "You're in safe hands. I could do this trip blindfolded. My life wouldn't be worth living if I lost the doctor on his first day. I'd be taken out and shot. Now, where was I?" To Lochlann's relief he faced forward as he continued to talk.

They crossed a long wooden bridge over the Gillenben River that divided the flat coastal region from the mountain range.

"Wait till you get an eyeful of this," Scottie said proudly. "Bet you won't have seen anything like it back home. My favourite stretch of road in all the world. Not that I've travelled the world, but who would want to when they can live in a place like this?"

Scottie double-clutched down to low gear as the rise became steeper. "We go up three thousand feet in seven miles. Must be some sort of Aussie record."

The road had been carved out of an escarpment covered by a rainforest. Rocks and trees above them seemed to be held in place by some gravity-defying mechanism. On the other side, Lochlann leaned forward to see bluey-green eucalyptus trees receding in successive drops hundreds of feet at a time into the pale blue distance that led ultimately to the Pacific Ocean.

The labouring engine precluded conversation. Scottie concentrated on the bends, one of them a horseshoe and all of them blind because of the steep banks. At one time he had to pull over into the gutter to allow a bullock team pulling a load of cedar logs to pass.

Halfway up the mountain they stopped at a waterfall to give the radiator a chance to cool. Lochlann extricated his arm from around the still-sleeping Charlotte. He crossed to the other side of the road the better to see the top of the fall, but it was so high up it looked as if the sheet of water was coming straight from the sky. The first thing he must do after they settled in was buy a camera. Not that a photograph could ever do justice to the sight in front of him, but he would like an image to bring back the memory of it after he returned home.

Scottie was filling a can from a spring which gushed out of the rocks and into a stone trough beside the road. Lochlann joined him. He noted with interest that the overflow from the trough ran into the same pipe that drained the falls under the road.

"Have a taste of that," Scottie called to Lochlann over the sound of the falling water, with a jerk of the head towards the spring. "Can't get purer than that. Straight from the bowels of the earth."

He went back to the truck and used a cloth to twist off the

261

radiator cap in such a way the rusty, boiling water didn't spit on him. He emptied the contents of the can into the steaming opening and screwed the cap back on.

Lochlann cupped his hands and drank from the ice-cold spring, and made a sign of approval to Scottie.

The men, damp from the spray, returned to the cabin, sitting on either side of Charlotte. Scottie drove on, constantly changing to low gear with a double shuffle to make it over successive crests, and dealing with the boiling radiator one more time. The temperature kept dropping.

The steep incline gave way to a more gradual slope and then finally the road flattened out when they reached the top of the plateau. Lochlann's first impression was one of space and light from the cleared pastures, with land disappearing into the horizon, and the second was the unreal vividness of the luscious red-ochre colour of the soil banked up on either side of the road.

The engine, now cruising along in top gear, was quiet enough for Scottie to speak without shouting.

"Nearly there." They passed a little wooden church on the left. "Yours," said Scottie, pointing. "We're coming into the town now. Population, one thousand. Main industries timber, cattle, potatoes, dairy. Butter factory and a bacon factory. And there's your hospital. Twenty-two beds. Plenty for our needs. Matron's highly qualified – salt of the earth and all that, but a bit of a wowser."

"Can't say I know that word."

"You soon will. Belongs to a bunch of misery gutses who don't drink, smoke, gamble, dance, or want anyone to have a good time. Matron's very strict. We're all a bit afraid of her, but as I say, highly qualified."

The truck picked up speed on the steep slope into the town, which consisted of two wide intersecting streets with a war memorial in the centre.

"I'll just unload all this and then I'll drop you off at your house. Might be an idea to wake up the missus now."

Charlotte shivered when she woke. Lochlann helped her on with her jacket.

"Relief to get away from that coastal heat," said Scottie, putting on a cotton shirt before he drove on. "Smell that air. Can't get any fresher than that. Fit for the gods."

They were met at the door of their three-bedroom weatherboard house by a welcoming Jean, Scottie's wife, who had lit the fire in the stove, filled the water fountain – a tall cast-iron container with a tap that sat on the edge of the stove and kept water hot – put flowers on the table and brought in essential provisions, as well as her own lamb casserole.

"Just give us a shout if you want anything, Doc," said Scottie as he drove away. "Chalk and cheese," he said to his wife beside him, answering the question before she could ask him.

Jean wasn't surprised when he couldn't answer subsequent questions, knowing that he would have done most of the talking.

"Did you find out when the baby's due at least?" she asked finally.

"What baby?" asked Scottie.

56

Lochlann held Charlotte's arm to steady her. She was swaying as if she were still on board either the ship or the steam train. Every now and then the feeling of being in motion came back to disconcert him as well.

"Let's get you settled first," he said. "Would you like a cup of tea and something to eat?"

"Nothing thanks. Couldn't face a thing. Still feel ghastly."

He guided her to the freshly made bed. They could smell the sunlight off the sheets when he turned back the covers. He retrieved her nightgown from the trunk and helped her undress. By the time he found a tap to fill a glass of water for her, she was asleep.

Before attacking the casserole he went outside to have a look around. There were verandahs on three sides of the house. At the back were trees, on the left a water tank on a high wide platform, under which was parked a Buick, on the right the surgery, which was attached to the house but had a separate entrance, and to the front was a street and above it on the hill, the hospital. One of the sheds in the yard was full of chopped wood, and beside it a smaller open structure enclosed in wire netting, which he presumed was a hen house without hens. He couldn't identify the birdcalls or the shrubs or plants or the trees. Despite his weariness, he felt a stirring of interest in the unfamiliar nature of everything that surrounded him.

He re-entered the kitchen, looking forward to a bowl of lamb, with bread to soak up the juices, and strong sweet tea to finish.

There was a whirring sound in the hall. He identified the telephone on the wall and lifted the earpiece.

"Is that Redmundo 145?" asked a female voice.

"I'm not sure," he answered, leaning into the mouthpiece. "I've only just arrived."

"Are you the new doctor?"

"Yes, I am."

"Putting you through. Go ahead, Matron."

"Thank you, Cheryl."

The matron was really sorry. She had seen Scottie drop them off and realised they must be feeling dreadful after their long trip but she had an emergency, a young man in excruciating pain with an appendix that might rupture. There wasn't time to send him on to the next town and there was no one else to call. If there was any way the doctor could see him . . .

"Of course, I'll come straight up."

"You know where it is?"

"Yes, Scottie pointed it out. I can see it from here. I'm on my way."

As he walked with speed up the hill he hoped he would be equal to the task ahead and that he'd paid attention to the demonstrations he'd watched as a student. If he were in a city hospital he wouldn't be doing unsupervised surgery for years.

He had reason to be grateful to Matron Grainger that day and every day afterwards. She was a stickler for cleanliness and procedure and was expert in the administration of chloroform. Her age (mid-thirties) and cold seriousness were the only impressions he had time to register before he scrubbed up.

"Thank you, Matron," he said many times during the operation as she anticipated what was needed. "How many times have you assisted at one of these?"

"I've lost count. Over thirty at least."

He didn't tell her it was his first, and she may not have guessed, as everything worked out with textbook precision. He would have been unnerved by the unfamiliarity of the theatre if she hadn't been there to guide him and deal with the practicalities.

"Just think," Matron said, tidying up and collecting all the instruments to be sterilised while Lochlann stitched the wound, "if you hadn't arrived when you did young Billy Ericsson here wouldn't have made it."

"He's obviously destined for great things. We'll have to follow his progress from now on to see what he achieves."

When Lochlann arrived back at his house, replaying the operation in his mind, he looked at the shape in the bed, and for a second couldn't think for the life of him who the person under the coverlet could possibly be. He stood disorientated, swaying on his feet, trying to concentrate his mind and ignore his exhaustion. It was with a sickening jolt he remembered it was Charlotte.

57

After three days Charlotte felt well enough to leave the bed, and her determination to be a wonderful wife resurfaced. Groceries, milk, bread and meat were delivered to the door, so she didn't have to face meeting any of the townspeople. She turned down Lochlann's suggestion of bringing a woman in to help her.

"It can't be too difficult with just the two of us," she assured him. "It's not as if I've never seen the inside of a kitchen."

He lit the wood stove in the morning before leaving to do his house calls. Arriving back at one o'clock he saw a concerned man hovering at the gate wondering if he should rush in with a bucket of water. He found Charlotte standing in the middle of the kitchen, her eyes streaming from the smoke, bewailing the fact she didn't know what to do. Water in the vegetable and potato saucepans hadn't come to the boil, and lamb chops were lying cold in the pan. She had forgotten to stoke the stove earlier and had crammed in too many pieces of wood at the last minute, cutting off air from the few embers that remained.

"I'm sorry. I thought I'd watched Cook so often I'd know what to do, but she had a range run on anthracite and this is so different."

"Never mind. It will only take a minute." He coaxed back the flame with kindling, an open flue and better placed wood, and was only thirty minutes late for afternoon surgery.

During the next week she shrivelled a joint of roast beef in an over-heated oven and burnt two saucepans dry. Potatoes welded to the bottom of one of them wouldn't soak off, so the pan had to be thrown out. She scorched her hand picking up the metal tongs from the top of the stove, and dropped many slices of bread into the embers while trying to make toast. After a cast-iron baking dish slipped on to the floor and splashed scalding fat over her legs, she told Lochlann she had changed her mind about not accepting help. Lochlann, for safety's sake if for no other reason, was relieved and employed Mrs Parker who had worked for the previous doctor and was thrilled to be asked. She started with two hours per day, but after adding shopping, cooking and gardening to her cleaning duties, was soon doing a full week.

Every day, after their morning tea and a chat, with relief Charlotte took herself off to the back verandah where she sat on one wicker chair and put her feet up on another. Sometimes she read, but more often she stared at the trees and the blue sky and contemplated her impending motherhood with satisfaction.

Mrs Parker felt honoured to be privy to the secrets of the house and especially enjoyed sharing the midday meal with the couple.

Many people were curious about the doctor's wife. Only Scottie the mailman, and his wife Jean, had spoken to her since she arrived, and both reckoned she was putting on the dog. Mrs Parker was proud to enlighten them that the doctor's wife was not putting on the dog. Her accent was genuine, she explained. She was the daughter of a Lord. The reason she didn't see anyone was not because of snob-bishness, but because of anxiety about her approaching confinement, especially since she had been so ill for all those weeks on the trip on the way over. Mrs Carmody, as Mrs Parker called her, refusing to address her as 'Charlotte' seeing she was the daughter of a Lord, was ideal to work for as she never interfered or told her what to do. Mrs Parker didn't add that Mrs Carmody seemed to know so little about running a house she wouldn't know what orders to give – her loyalty to her employers precluded giving out any negative details.

"Would you like to be my receptionist instead?" Lochlann asked Charlotte, thinking she might be bored. "It would be a good way for you to get to know the townspeople." The startled look she gave him made him add, "It's light work. You'd be sitting in a cubicle beside the phone so you wouldn't have to move about or be on display."

"I wouldn't know what to do. I've no experience." Her eyes pooled with tears. "I'm sorry. I didn't think anything like that would be expected of me."

"It's not. It's not," he rushed to reassure her. "It was for your sake I was suggesting it. I thought you might be looking for a bit of diversion since painting has been ruled out." Her paints and brushes remained unpacked as she said that, in her condition, even the thought of the smell of linseed oil and turpentine made her feel sick. "I already have someone lined up if you're not interested, so don't think I'm putting you under any pressure."

"That's all right, then. I'd rather not expose our unborn child to infections brought in by shopkeepers and farmers when I don't have to, if you don't mind."

Lochlann told her to think no more about it – he sympathised with her misgivings. The position could now be offered to Marie Dawson, a kind intelligent widow whose children were reared and whose warm personality would be popular with the patients.

Charlotte detected relief on Lochlann's face after her refusal, and saw him jump the front gate when he returned to the surgery for the afternoon.

"Someone's in a good mood," smiled Mrs Parker, watching from the kitchen window. "Oh, for the energy of youth!"

58

Charlotte was glad of Mrs Parker's presence in the house when Wombat Churchill came into the yard uninvited and began to split logs that had been thrown over the fence early that morning by Billy Ericsson's grateful father.

Mrs Parker took out a pot of tea and some Anzac biscuits to share with Wombat while they sat together in the shade on the side verandah under a passion-fruit vine. His disfigured face made Charlotte shiver, and when he laughed – at least it looked as if that was what he was doing though it was hard to tell as his mouth had restricted movement, and there was no sound emerging – he showed a few blackened teeth among the gaps and looked as if he wasn't the full shilling. He kept looking towards the kitchen window.

Later, Mrs Parker asked Charlotte if she could spare the time to meet Wombat as he was too shy to come to the door.

"I'd rather not," Charlotte answered. "What if his disease is catching?"

"He doesn't have a disease," Mrs Parker explained, keeping her voice low so that Wombat wouldn't overhear. "He fell into a fire when he was four and was lucky it was only his face that was burnt. Hasn't said a word since that day."

Charlotte experienced a flicker of fellow feeling.

270

"No one knows if his vocal chords were damaged or if it was pure fright that struck him dumb, poor coot. Wouldn't hurt a fly."

Reluctantly, Charlotte went out and offered her hand. Wombat didn't take it, miming that his hands weren't clean, and made an odd little bow instead.

Next day she saw a dozen one-day-old chickens in the fowl pen, and a week later a pink and grey galah in a cage appeared on the verandah. Mrs Parker said to Charlotte that Wombat must have taken a shine to her.

"I wish he hadn't."

Charlotte was feeling vulnerable. Used to being surrounded by servants, thick exterior walls, upper storeys, anterooms and separate entrances, she couldn't get used to living in a six-room wooden bungalow where every window could be looked into from the outside and where the paling fence, only waist high, left the garden exposed. "It's not as if we want those things."

"He's the town's Good Samaritan," Mrs Parker explained. "Helps out everyone who needs it with gardening and chopping wood in his spare time after he's done a full day's work at the butter factory. The town would be a poorer place without him." Mrs Parker voice had taken on a pleading tone. "Still lives at home. Parents are real battlers."

When Charlotte was young, Nurse Dixon rarely bothered to tell stories, but when she did they were always about ugly people who did nasty things to children. Looking at Wombat, the fear Charlotte felt back then returned unbidden and paid no heed to her adult reasoning.

Keen to justify herself to Lochlann for rebuffing Wombat's overtures of friendship, she said she was worried about the effect Wombat's presence around the house would have on the baby. "What if it's born deformed?" she asked.

"That's not possible. Pre-natal influences don't work like that." He did think her nervous attitude might be harmful, however, so asked Wombat if he would fence off a section behind the surgery, the part furthermost from the house, and plant a vegetable garden there. A project dear to his heart, Lochlann said, hoping it would keep the affectionate man occupied and out of Charlotte's sight until after the baby was born. Wombat was grateful to be asked and was reluctant

271

to accept payment. The pink and grey galah was removed by Mrs Parker when Charlotte complained about its noise.

Charlotte could now sit undisturbed, picturing the look on her mother's face when she returned home triumphant, enjoying the respect that would then be due to her as a mother.

Standing back so she couldn't be seen, Charlotte looked through the front window. Lochlann was at the gate in conversation with someone she didn't know, which wasn't surprising as she'd only met four people since she'd arrived. Lochlann was talking, gesticulating, listening intently, and every now and then throwing back his head and laughing. His eyes were lively and his body relaxed as he leaned against the gatepost.

Charlotte's heart contracted. It was the old Lochlann she was seeing, the light-hearted one she remembered talking to Harcourt while she looked on at him, drowning in adoration, desire and hopelessness, never thinking that one day he would be hers. Legally hers. And here he was, soon to come through the door, and she would have exclusive access to his company for the night.

He took leave of the man he was talking to and, still smiling, closed the gate, and walked up the short path. On the verandah he paused, and the smile left his face. He took deep breaths while standing staring at the door.

He hates coming home, Charlotte acknowledged with sadness. He's bracing himself.

She stepped further back so he wouldn't know she had been watching, then waited to greet him. I don't even possess a tenth of him, she thought. He's inaccessible to me.

He turned back to look at the hospital on the hill and then the park to the right of it. He's like a condemned man, she thought, taking his last look at the outside world before being forced to return to prison.

It will be different when the baby comes, she reassured herself. Everything will be better then. We will become a tight little family unit, cut off from the rest of the world. Secure. Happy. Exclusive.

59

Offer a reward, Edwina wrote in her first letter to Charlotte. *One substantial enough to set someone up for life. There is no honour amongst thieves – those two women from the lower orders will trample over each other to be the one to claim it and, once you have either one of them, you have Victoria. Advertise in every newspaper, magazine and periodical in the country. I realise there will be difficulty with the names, all changed since they left here either through marriage or deviousness, but they will recognise their original ones and rush for their reward. The name changes are a trial. Because of them there is no point in looking through the voting registers, which list every adult over twenty-one in the country. If only they were men, it would be so easy to find them because of the compulsory voting system there. I have done my research. There is no point in looking up Department of Immigration records or port entry records as they wouldn't tell you where they went after they got off the boat and that's the bit we're interested in – in any case the private detective I hired already did that or so he claimed. No, a reward is the only solution, and I presume you can see why you are the only one who can do it. Every con man, trickster and gambler in the country will be after it and will try to claim it fraudulently. Only you know what Teresa and Dixon look like even after the lapse of years, and you would recognise Victoria because of the family resemblance. I'm confident you can do it. Just don't stint on the reward.*

Your father has become a hypochondriac since he suffered palpitations and breathlessness two months ago. He panics when he feels any irregularities in his heart rhythm, which he says is often. He is afraid of having a heart attack during the night, so has employed that ex-soldier Thatcher to sleep in the same room. What help he'd be is a puzzle as the few times I've seen him, he's been as drunk as his master.

I expect to hear from you with results in the near future.

Charlotte crumpled the letter, opened the door of the stove and pushed the pages into the flames.

60

The Hogan children, curious and expectant, hung back as Lochlann approached Spike, one of their larger, stronger stock horses. When he managed to mount without falling off the other side or collapsing on the gelding's neck they looked disappointed. He smiled at them, and they shyly ducked their heads. One of the younger girls giggled.

"So you have ridden before," said Dan Hogan.

"I'd hardly call it that. Walking, trotting, high-trotting around an arena with eight other children for two hours on a Saturday for four years. It's my wife who's the real rider."

"So Scottie was saying."

"She was only eight or nine at the time of her first hunt."

"She won't have lost it, you can be sure of that."

"Good. I'm hoping she'll get back to it after the baby's born."

"Something to look forward to. Ah, here's Scottie. What kept you?"

"Couldn't get the damn horse to move – until young Mick picked a switch for me. Now it's a different story." He gave Dixie a flick to demonstrate, and she jumped sideways and forward.

"No mustering today," said Dan. "Just looking for a cow that's due to calve. Probably hiding in the bush. An easy day, then."

Lochlann had already met Nell Hogan – she had cried in his

surgery about her seventh pregnancy when she brought in her sixth child to be immunised. "It's not as if I don't love them, Doctor. So many mouths to feed, that's the worry." Her next child was due around the same time as Charlotte's first in six weeks' time.

Charlotte had been invited to the farm as well but refused, as he knew she would. Lochlann made sure Matron Grainger was on duty at the hospital and that Mrs Parker would spend the day with Charlotte, so that if anything did happen, which wasn't likely, she'd be properly looked after.

Dan rode with the reins held loosely in the left hand, so Lochlann did the same. The eldest boy, Kevin, rode bareback and kept a little way back from the three men covering extra ground when he became bored. Lochlann learned later that they had only four horses and three saddles so all the children couldn't ride at once. This would sort itself out naturally, as Kevin was due to go to boarding school on a bursary next term and they would all move up one, so the three-year-old would begin on the quietest pony.

They rode in a single file down to the creek, and crossed over the wooden bridge. On either side of the water lay the red earth exposed, due to years of erosion, and deeply grooved by the hooves of cows making daily tracks over and back. The water was a greeny-brown colour, not the clear trout stream over pebbles found locally, but mud-based and churned up by the movement of the animals who came there to drink.

Going up a steep hill was easier than going down, Lochlann discovered. He didn't like the feeling of the horse disappearing in front of him, whereas leaning forward and having the horse's head higher and nearer was more reassuring.

The grass was green, the creek was full and the cows through the fence in another paddock looked fat. Four inches of rain had fallen during the previous three weeks, putting everyone in good humour.

"Our last remaining cedar," said Dan, pointing to a lone tree beside a spring over the next rise. "The farm used to be covered with them."

The three could now ride abreast and talk. Kevin rode off to look at the monkey vine which swung between the earth and high branches above in the scrub. It was on the way back to join the men he saw the cow, who had calved only a few minutes earlier by the look of it. Kevin couldn't disguise his pleasure when he was the first one to spot it.

By the time the men got there, the calf was on its wobbly legs and sucking, its coat rippled from the mother's licking.

"Good mother, that one. Managed well by herself again. I thought I might have to enlist your help, Doc, if she got into difficulties."

The sky was cobalt blue, and the sunlight so strong the shadows were sharp-edged and black. There was stillness and silence except for the hum of insects, the singing of birds and the 'swat, swat' as the men flicked small branches to disturb the flies on their faces and arms.

"Son, you can bring in the cows." Dan then turned to explain to Lochlann and Scottie: "It might be a bit early for them, but saves making a second trip."

Kevin leaned over to open the gate. Not easy with one of the hinges broken. Because he took them for granted Dan didn't remark on the skill and balance of the boy, the training of the horse or the poor condition of the gate, cobbled together with barbed wire and fallen to one side, but Lochlann took in each detail with interest.

While Nell and the four older children did the milking, the three men drank the whisky Lochlann had brought.

"Just as well the truck knows the way or we mightn't make it home," said Scottie when the time came to leave and they had clambered into it.

"You're all right out here, but be careful close to town in case the police are out," said Dan.

"They'll be in bed by then," said Scottie, "and they can't very well take away the licence of a mailman. What would they do without me?"

"I wouldn't bet on it." He grinned at Lochlann. "You'll be eating your tea off the mantelpiece, tonight, Doc."

"I don't feel a bit sore."

"You will."

After saying their goodbyes with promises to repeat the day before too long, Scottie and Lochlann took off in a spray of gravel and dust.

"You'd think those Hogan kids were your brothers and sisters, they look so like you with their dark hair and blue eyes," said Scottie. "You must be related."

"Oh, it's a common Irish colouring – we call it 'black Irish'. But perhaps we are related. I know there was a Hogan back there somewhere. My father says he'll do our family tree when he retires but it could be difficult with so many records destroyed in the twenties. And none kept during the worst parts of the Famine." He was speaking slowly with long pauses as he was nicely inebriated.

"Wouldn't that be a coincidence if he found a mutual forebear?"

"Not really. Ireland is a small country. It would be more of a coincidence if he didn't, when you come to think of it."

It would please Lochlann to be directly connected to the Hogan family as he had taken a liking to all of them. Dan was hospitable and sociable in some ways, but on the whole he was locked into his family and kept his distance from neighbours and relations. Nell was self-effacing, confident in her own home but shy outside it. The six children were all athletic, bright, capable and attractive.

"Will the missus be cranky with you when you get back?" asked Scottie.

"Can't think why. This is my first drink and first day off for months."

"There you are, then. You can't speak fairer than that. Jean had the mother visiting, so she was glad to see the back of me. I won't come in. Give the missus my best."

61

After taking a while to open the door, Lochlann almost fell against Charlotte who was poised as if waiting for him.

"Have you been drinking?"

"Of course I have," he beamed at her, bending to give her a kiss but missing the mark. "Best day I've had in ages. Scottie declined to come in, sends his regards. Drove well, considering. Only went into the ditch twice." He manoeuvred himself into his chair and grinned up at Charlotte. "There's a lot to be said for living on the land. Perhaps we'll buy a few acres and run a couple of horses."

"Is that the drink talking?"

"No, I mean it." Lochlann's speech slowed with every word. "They gave me one of the children's horses – not a pony, mind you – and nobody laughed. Too polite. Can't wait for the next time."

"You're going again? Leaving me here all on my own?"

"You weren't on your own. Mrs Parker was here. Besides, you were invited. You could have come."

"I'm not moving until the baby's born. You know that."

"That's your own choice. There's no medical reason for you to stay put."

"So you keep saying, but I'm not taking any chances. And what would I do out there anyway while you were playing cowboys?

279

Talking to the saintly Mrs Hogan, and her million children with all their germs?"

"Six and another on the way. Hardly a million. And they're exceptionally healthy." He eyed the covered plate on the back of the stove. "Dan told me I'd be eating off the mantelpiece tonight, but I think I can manage the table."

Charlotte picked up the plate with the meal Mrs Parker had prepared earlier, lifted it high and dropped it on the floor, saying, "Looks like you're both wrong."

Lochlann examined the mess of the broken china and splattered food as if it were intrinsically interesting.

"I think this calls for another drink," he said at length, his face clearing as if he had solved a mathematical problem. He moved unsteadily across the room to take a glass and the whisky bottle from the dresser.

With a pulse throbbing wildly in her neck Charlotte left the room and slammed the door behind her. She lay fully clothed on the bed, trying to calm herself for the sake of the baby. Why had she done that? she chastised herself. Why couldn't she control her temper? Dropping the plate on the floor was the sort of thing Nurse Dixon would do and she swore long ago she would never follow her example.

Lochlann was singing. Was he trying to remember the words or was he having mouthfuls of whisky during the intervals when there was silence?

As Charlotte quietened, she saw the unfairness of her outburst. Today was the first time he'd taken a drink since their arrival in Redmundo, either because he took seriously his responsibility as the only doctor, on call twenty-four hours a day, or because the consequences of his last bout had been so catastrophic. It wasn't that she was against his drinking. She'd actually always liked to have him drunk. It made him more approachable. What she didn't like was the evidence that he enjoyed himself so much when he was out of her company.

"*But come ye back when summer's in the meadow,*" Lochlann sang with feeling.

Indeterminate sounds and humming followed.

"*For you will bend and tell me that you love me . . .*"

The singing trailed off.

Was he overcome by the meaning of the words? Crying into his drink? Passing out? Pouring another drink?

After a long period of quiet Charlotte tentatively opened the kitchen door. Lochlann was asleep. By the soft light of the kerosene lamp he looked so handsome Charlotte felt a clutch deep in her gut. Was it wrong to love someone's looks so much? Could the divine harmony of his features be enough to satisfy her, as they might need to if Lochlann's policy of no intimacy continued? Was he being cautious until after the baby was born, and would he love her as a wife after that? Did he ever burn in the bed beside her in the same way she burned beside him?

"For you will bend and tell me that you love me . . ."

If it were possible she would give up everything – her social position and her fortune – to be able to believe that he ever would bend and tell her that he loved her.

She collected an eiderdown from the spare bed and placed it over him. Kneeling beside the chair she turned his face towards her and kissed him gently at first, and when he didn't wake, deeply and at length, positioning her head so she could breathe easily while she explored his mouth with an abandon unthinkable when he was awake, the taste of whisky bringing back the memory of another time, and firing her desire even more.

She cleaned up the smashed plate and scattered food.

The next morning Lochlann couldn't understand why he was so hungry. He apologised to her for leaving her alone for the day in her condition, then went next door to the surgery, hoping there wouldn't be too many patients to disturb his hangover.

If only he would argue with her. His kindness was indifference. His caution was indifference. His indifference was indifference. Even when he was drunk she couldn't puncture his composure.

She reconsidered her fanciful notion of exchanging her social position and wealth for love. What an absurd idea it appeared to her only hours after she had entertained it. Common sense, in the face of her desire for Lochlann, must have temporarily deserted her, for in the cold light of reason she knew that without her status and fortune there would be little left to love.

62

Australia
1940

Charlotte was aware of the date but thought it best not to draw attention to it. First wedding anniversary, and the day she was allowed at last to mention the baby in a letter to her mother. The only difficulty was she'd have to get out of bed to find a pen and paper and she didn't think her legs would obey a half-hearted command. No energy. If she rang the bell on her bedside locker Mrs Parker would come in to ask her what she wanted and she could tell her to bring in a tray with paper and a pencil on it – she wouldn't have to sit up to write with a pencil. She could imagine her mother's disgust at receiving a pencil-written letter, but she couldn't have it her own way at every turn. It was either that or nothing at all.

Perhaps she would think about it a little longer. Her mother had said not to write before this day, but she hadn't specified an exact date to write. What difference would a week make? Or a month? It wasn't as if Edwina was on tenterhooks waiting for the announcement. The only news she wanted to hear was that one of the old servants had come forward to claim the reward for locating Victoria, but seeing Charlotte hadn't put any advertisements in the papers offering it, there wasn't much likelihood of that happening.

At seven she had pretended to be asleep when Lochlann left to do house calls before surgery. She hoped he didn't remember the significance of the date. She wouldn't remind him.

After these last weeks in bed her limbs ached, and her hips and shoulders were sore to the touch. And now, lying on her back to ease her side, her heels were beginning to object to the pressure.

Would this day be as long as yesterday and the day before yesterday? Sleeping passed the time but she'd already slept eighteen hours out of the last twenty-four, so she might have to settle for closing her eyes. She must ask Lochlann to leave the blackout blinds down all the time to keep out all that bloody sunlight. If she heard that kookaburra laugh once more outside her window, she'd go mad. Yesterday when she had asked Mrs Parker to throw something at it, the older woman had looked horrified at the suggestion and hadn't done anything. Cutting up a handkerchief and stuffing bits of it in her ears might solve the problem of intrusive noise. Where were the scissors? She must ask Mrs Parker, and tell her at the same time to change the sheets as they felt limp, and there were crumbs in the hollow of the kapok mattress.

She looked at the clock, wondering if it was lunchtime yet. It said five past ten. Must have stopped. She lifted it up, squinted her eyes, and saw that the second-hand was moving. Leaning over to replace it she let it slip – a miscalculation of distance – and heard the sound of breaking glass.

Lochlann came in smelling of health, antiseptic, wood-smoke and sunshine.

"Up you get," he said. "Doctor's orders. Mrs Parker has packed us a picnic." His voice was full of enthusiasm, or at least the pretence of it. He reached down to pick up the clock and didn't comment on the cracked glass front.

"I don't want to go anywhere," said Charlotte through the sheet.

"I'm afraid you've no choice if you want to celebrate our anniversary with me and who else could you spend it with? I have to make a house call to old Mrs Humphries out Ober way, and there's a waterfall there the like of which you've never seen before." He bent down, lifted the sheet and kissed the top of her head. "Happy anniversary."

How could he even say the words? The irony was hard to bear.

"I haven't the energy," she said, keeping her eyes closed. "You go. I'll stay here."

"It's such a beautiful day it would be a shame to waste it. Come on. You don't have to talk, eat or even get out of the car. Just come for the spin to mark the occasion. I can help you dress or get Mrs Parker to if you'd prefer." He headed towards her wardrobe.

"Don't touch anything," she said, then added with weariness, "I'll come. I'll dress myself."

"That's the spirit."

She didn't move.

"I'll wait in the kitchen."

He'd rather go on his own, she knew. What would she add to the journey?

Nothing.

She heard the voices of the two talking quietly in the garden, as they often did. "How is she today?" was the opening question – she waited for it – but after that she couldn't distinguish any words. Invariably they walked towards the bottom of the garden, ostensibly to look at the self-sown potatoes and pumpkins, but really to make sure she couldn't overhear them.

The flicker of energy she felt when Lochlann came into the room died as soon as he left. He would probably give her ten minutes to dress herself before coming back to check, so there was no need to make any move yet. She didn't have to go on this outing. No one would think any the worse of her – Lochlann hadn't run out of patience yet, Mrs Parker thrived on her role of nursemaid, and there wasn't anyone else who knew about the anniversary.

Except those back home, of course, but they didn't count. Her mother would be expecting news, now that the day had come. There was a lot to be said for living so far away. If she stayed in bed all day her family wouldn't be any the wiser. She could write that there had been a party, a dinner or a trip to the coast to celebrate the day, and they would never know the difference.

On second thoughts, she would ask Lochlann to write the letter. He would be better able to explain how the baby had died, seeing as he did the delivery while she was unconscious for the final few minutes. But even he couldn't answer why, as he didn't know and if he didn't know, who would? He could tell them main facts: the baby was a boy and had lived for ten minutes, during which time Lochlann had baptised and named him Benedict, hoping that the "blessing" in the name might prompt the failing infant to rally, but it hadn't.

Only the priest, Father Daly, and Lochlann, who carried the white coffin, were present at the burial on top of the windy hill above the church. She remained in hospital for a further week, next door to Mrs Hogan who had given birth to her seventh healthy child, and she would have stayed longer if she didn't have Mrs Parker to care for her when she returned home.

She rocked to give herself enough momentum to sit up and, with difficulty, swung her legs onto the floor. She felt dizzy, so stayed still until that feeling passed. Taking her time, she stood up and wobbled. Was she losing the use of her legs? She held onto the brass bed end and called for Mrs Parker who came in straight away as if she'd been waiting at the door, and asked if there was anything she could do to help.

"Yes," said Charlotte. "I've decided to go on the picnic with the doctor. If you would be so kind as to get me my French navy maternity dress out of the wardrobe. I think it's the only thing I have that will fit me." She sat down heavily on the side of the bed while Mrs Parker collected the clothes and then began to dress her as if it were a great honour. By the time Mrs Parker slipped on the court shoes, Charlotte was exhausted.

"Come on now," encouraged the housekeeper, taking her arm and guiding her into the kitchen where she passed her over to Lochlann. "A day out in the bush will do you a world of good. You can't beat a bit of fresh air."

"There's plenty of fresh air on the verandah," said Charlotte. "I don't need to go elsewhere to find that."

"A change of scenery, then. Here you are." She handed Lochlann the basket. "Wait till you see what I've prepared for you. There won't be a skerrick left for the wildlife."

"By the weight of it, you didn't skimp on anything. Good. I'm hungry already," said Lochlann. "Come on, careful now."

Charlotte slipped on the shiny lino. "Leather soles," she said to Mrs Parker.

"Do you want me to roughen them for you?" asked Lochlann.

"Hardly worth the bother. I'll be staying in the car, so there's really no need. Thank you, Mrs Parker. You're a treasure. I don't know what we'd do without you."

"You Irish and your blarney," smiled Mrs Parker. "You'd give me a big head if I believed everything you said."

"It's no blarney," said Lochlann. "If anything we're holding back. We won't be late, but still won't see you until tomorrow. Good luck and thanks again."

I bet she thinks that he is the one who needs the good luck, thought Charlotte, watching the ground as she tentatively put one foot in front of the other.

"Would you look at that view!" said Lochlann, a few miles into the journey. "Those blue mountains. And that has to be the sea in the distance. Hard to believe. Must be forty miles away."

Charlotte politely turned her head to the left, trying to concentrate on what he'd said. Yes, the mountains were indeed blue, and that blur in the distance could indeed be the sea. Was there anything else she was supposed to look at? Turning back to stare straight ahead again, she forgot to ask or comment. As usual, her thoughts turned to her mother and how she imagined she'd respond when she received news of baby Benedict's death.

"Don't say I'm with you," said Charlotte, when Lochlann turned into Mrs Humphrey's driveway, all mud and tussocks. "Park the car behind that tree in case she sees me."

"I was going to anyway, for the shade."

Two dogs ran out to dance around Lochlann and bark. Charlotte was relieved when they followed him to the door.

A flock of parrots, so brightly coloured they looked as if they were designed for paradise, squabbled in the trees in front of her. The sky was cerulean blue and the frostbitten grass, yellow ochre. If she decided to paint again, she would have to give up the greys she favoured when she was younger as they would look dead in this luminous brightness. Not that she had any intention of painting while she was suffering from this bone-wearying lassitude – the act of picking up a paintbrush was as alien to her now as the thought of riding to hounds.

She liked this weather – warm days followed by cold nights which were conducive to sleep. It was sleep she craved, both to fill in the time and to lose her conscious self. She wished humans were hibernating animals who could pass months at a stretch in a dark place.

After leaving the main road Lochlann needed to concentrate to avoid the water-filled potholes and the soft mud that might send him into a skid.

"A bit of an obstacle course," he said. "Not surprising with all that rain last night."

He followed the track for about a mile before turning the car and parking it on an incline in case the battery or starter gave trouble when they were leaving. It would be unlikely that there would be anyone around to give the car a push if either of those failed – in all the times Lochlann had been coming here he hadn't run into another human being. Fishermen favoured the pools upstream on the other side of the main road.

"Would you just look at that?" Lochlann breathed in reverence.

Charlotte was already looking.

The shallow trout stream had swollen to a churning brown and white tumult of water, carrying branches with speed along the central flow, which was split at intervals by trees and rocks.

Charlotte remembered with a jolt another flooded river that had broken its banks at the time Victoria disappeared, but quickly pushed the image out of her mind. Today of all days she wouldn't think about her lost sister. Too many losses to take in at once.

"Damn. I forgot the camera. The falls should be spectacular today."

"Haven't you enough photographs of waterfalls? You must have a hundred by now."

"That's not many when you consider how many there are around and how different they are from each other and how different they look at different times."

He threw his door open with an exaggerated flourish. When he came around to her side, she said she wasn't leaving the car – she had made that clear earlier – and besides, she couldn't walk in her shoes, and he said "Well, we can't get any closer than this by car," and he opened her door and bent down and slipped off her shoes and scored the soles with a sharp stone. She was conscious of his hand on her ankles as he replaced the shoes.

"Come on. You'll regret it later if you don't. Here, give me your hand." He stood, confidently smiling down at her. "No pressure. It's just that I would hate you to miss one of the wonders of the natural world."

She pretended reluctance as she gave her hand, and nonchalance as his long fingers closed over hers, but the contact sent a charge through her that she couldn't disregard or minimise, even if she wanted to. For such a long time now, every touch of his had had a medical intent: taking her pulse, feeling her forehead, listening to her heart with his ear on her chest – joy that he did that instead of using his stethoscope – and leaning over to shine a light in her eye, a position she welcomed as a near embrace.

"Well?" he continued to smile, tightening his hold on her hand.

For her, the anniversary was well celebrated in that moment.

"I'm not sure," she said. "I don't know."

"We could picnic over there by that tree if you like and give the waterfall a miss. How's that for a compromise?"

She agreed and, holding on tightly, placed both feet on the running board and then stepped down, leaning heavily on him.

"Don't worry, I've got you."

By the time they reached the tree she, surprised by how strong she felt, agreed to walk the extra four hundred yards following an animal track. She picked her way under a canopy of gum trees, with peels of eucalyptus bark, logs and sticks crunching underfoot, all the time being supported by him, with the roar of water sounding closer with each footstep.

Before they reached the lookout spot, Lochlann put his hands over her eyes and guided her into a clearing. "Look left first," he said, putting hands on either side of her head to direct her.

The earth fell away so sharply and so deeply she couldn't see the extent of the drop except in the distance. The mountains were so far away one couldn't see where the furthest, palest ones merged with the sky.

"How strange," she said, wanting to fall to her knees in a pagan-like worship of the beauty before her, but knowing the ungainliness of her action would cancel out the effect she wished to portray. "The mountains are lower than we are, and yet they look so high."

Straight ahead, across the deep gorge, trees one hundred feet high appeared to be less than an inch, riding on the top of a cliff that showed its geological history, with rock formations layered from top to bottom, looking like a carelessly assembled cathedral put in place by an unrestrained stonemason.

She could see the white spume of the falls in her peripheral vision, despite Lochlann's hands on the side of her face acting as blinkers, but when she caught his hand and finally turned to look at the water directly she wasn't prepared for their magnitude and burst into tears at the impact of their grandeur. She turned to Lochlann and saw that he was pleased by her response. She remembered him saying, "That's one thing we have in common at least," while they enjoyed a thunderstorm together, and now here was a second one.

The expression on his face was one she hadn't seen before and didn't know what it signified. Their eyes locked for a few seconds before he broke the contact.

"I'm glad I came," she said, as if no look had passed between them.

They both turned to worship the splendour of the falls, so profligate in their generosity, putting on this show at this moment for just the two of them and, after they left, no one, and to think it had done this for millions of years, perhaps unseen even by the aborigines who might never have stood on this exact spot when they wandered free across the land during all that time before the white man came and dispossessed them.

One could see by the rock formation that the falls were formed on two levels, but such was the volume of water after the rain, the drop of hundreds of feet looked like one solid mass. Charlotte would love to be able to stand closer, to feel the spray on her face. Having no fear of heights, she made to step forward but Lochlann held her back.

"Don't go too near the edge," he said, raising his voice to be heard over the din.

He was being over-cautious, she thought. They were at least ten feet from the edge, but he had his reasons. Earlier, he had told her about a boy walking his dog along the cliffs near Tramore in Co Waterford, wanting to see the Metal Man up close, who fell to his death when the ground gave way. The sea had worn away the base of the cliff so the ground he stood on, so solid-looking to the eye, was only six inches deep and couldn't take his weight.

"Sit over there in the sun," said Lochlann, "and I'll go back for the basket. You must be exhausted."

"Surprisingly enough I'm not. Just pleasantly tired," she answered, but when he pulled over a large branch she was glad to sink down and rest her back against the warm bark of the tree.

"Shouldn't be long," said Lochlann, heading back the way they had come. She tried to follow his progress, but he was soon lost in the trees. When she leaned to the right she could see the sun reflecting off the emblem on the bonnet of the car but couldn't see him anywhere near it.

Becoming conscious that it was time Lochlann returned, Charlotte leaned over as far as she could in either direction but couldn't locate him. Putting her arms on the tree behind her, she was able to push herself into a standing position, then move closer to the edge where there were fewer trees and the view opened up. She saw him, surrounded by rocks, standing on the lip of the gorge right beside the waterfall where the river first fell away from the land. He looked into the wall of the water, then looked back to where she was, but when she waved he didn't wave back and she realised he wasn't looking at her but the cliff beneath her. He crouched, then leaned, then edged his way further out, and for some reason she stepped back so that he wouldn't see her if his gaze shifted. The rim of the gorge between them was in the shape of an arc, so that he would be able to see if the drop beside her was straight, or curving inwards, or sloping outwards, just as she would be able to see how his cliff was formed if she went far enough out to look over the scrubby growth that blocked her view from where she stood.

Lochlann moved forward, stopping and checking every few yards. Even from this distance she could see the concentration in the tilt of his head and the stillness of his contemplation.

Distracted for a minute, she turned to watch an eagle riding the thermals over the gorge, and felt her spirit lift and join in union with it. She felt that something was about to happen. The stupor of the last five months (five years?) was over, to be replaced by she knew not what. A resolution? Confrontation? Reality?

Would her wronged husband finally bring her to account in this isolated, beautiful, frightening place? Is that why he had brought her here?

Lochlann was back in the position she first saw him, staring at the wall of water at his feet.

She heard the spluttering of an engine. Lochlann was either too lost in thought or too close to the thunder of the water to hear it.

After an interval the driver of the car came up behind the doctor and waited at a distance, obviously not wishing to startle a person so close to the drop. Lochlann finally turned and saw him, registered surprise then walked towards him. They moved away, talking, out of Charlotte's view.

She didn't realise how expectant she had been until she felt the disappointment of an action deferred with the arrival of the man. When she sat back down on the branch and leaned against the warm trunk she felt as if she'd walked a mile, rather than just standing up and sitting down again.

Fifteen minutes later Lochlann returned with the basket and a square of tarpaulin. She searched his face for clues but he was his usual unreadable self.

"Just ran into Wombat Churchill. He came to look at the falls from the bottom up. Going to climb down."

"How could he tell you all that when he can't speak?"

"Easily enough." Lochlann acted out the words in exaggerated sign language that would have made her laugh if she hadn't been feeling so overwrought.

"Isn't that a bit dangerous? After all that rain? On his own? What if he falls and breaks a leg down there? No one would ever know. Except you, but it's only pure chance that you are here."

"No. He told them at the pub where he was going. They would send out a search party for him if he didn't return. Funny man. Pity you took against him."

After eating Mrs Parker's specialities – rare roast beef and horseradish sandwiches, pork ribs baked in her secret sauce, and rhubarb crumble with cream, Lochlann stretched out in the sun and fell asleep, giving Charlotte the opportunity to admire his features openly and avidly.

How young he looks, she thought. And how old I feel.

One look, exchanged in a corridor of the townhouse when she first saw him had altered her life's course, and even now when she remembered that look it still sang in her consciousness and made her wonder at its power. Thousands of glances later, she knew she would never see that open, trusting gaze directed at her again. It's not that he had become furtive. 'Impervious' would describe it better. She had no hold over him stronger than any human being's hold over another. This thought returned again and again to torment her. He was tied to her by convention, not feeling. In his role as her doctor during her confinement, and even more so since its harrowing aftermath, she couldn't fault his care and sympathy, but she had never felt at any moment that it was personal.

Using a twig to flick off the ants that found their way on the tarpaulin, and her hand to keep away the flies from Lochlann's face, Charlotte enjoyed the luxury of sitting close to her husband, and feeling the warmth of his forearm through her skirt against her thigh.

She must have been over-stimulated. Conjuring up fantasies. A man with a face as wonderful as that, and an expression as innocent as that could not have entertained what she, in her madness, had thought he might be considering – murder or suicide, guiding her on to an overhang, and like the boy in Tramore, have the earth give way beneath her weight – or worse, jump himself, leaving her the victor, free to tell whatever story she chose.

Had Wombat Churchill, the man she treated so badly, been her unwitting saviour?

She must keep a tight rein on herself so she wouldn't end up like other women she'd heard of who lost their minds after the death of a child.

Lochlann woke, blinking and disorientated, and for a second looked at her with pleasure and smiled, and then the smile faded. It wasn't of her he was dreaming – the fading smile said it more clearly than words.

Lochlann kept his grieving face lowered as he gathered up and repacked the picnic basket, taking his time, folding the tarpaulin exactly. He stood for one last look into the chasm where the evening shadows were making patterns on the rocky mass on the far side and leaving all but the top of the falls in shade.

Charlotte was the first to break the silence on the way home. "I know what you mean about this place taking you out of yourself. It's done me the world of good. I'm feeling a lot better. Less gloomy. More energetic."

"Good. I'm glad." Lochlann's voice was dull and flat. "Because I want to talk about going back home as soon as you're well enough to travel."

She was unprepared. "I don't think I'm as well as that," she flustered. "It could be a long time before I could face that long trip."

"You'll be surprised at how quickly you'll rally now that you've made the first steps. We've stayed away long enough to save your mother's reputation. That was the agreement, remember? Besides, I want to enlist."

"But you can't. Ireland's neutral," was the first objection that came to mind.

"Thousands of Irish have joined up. Haven't you been reading Harcourt's letters?"

She had, but she always skipped the war bits, searching instead for any hidden messages from Niamh being relayed through Harcourt to Lochlann.

Did he consider her wifely claim on him now null and void, seeing there was no shared responsibility of a baby? Did he consider his vows to love, honour and obey until death were made under duress and were never morally binding? Did he dislike her? Or even hate her?

She must pull herself together. All that staring and concentration he had engaged in at the falls – it was evolution he was thinking of, not hatred and death. He was looking at the rock formations exposed in the gorge, that's all. His probing into evolutionary theories and his projections about how white Europeans would live in this mostly unsuitable hot dry land, apart from their intrinsic interest, saved him from having to talk about anything personal to her.

A wallaby hopped across the road in front of them. Lochlann braked and the engine cut out while he waited for the mate to follow.

"I must have another baby," Charlotte found the courage to say while they were distracted watching the marsupials crossing. "Or else it was all for nothing."

Lochlann swung out of the driver's seat and cranked the car with unnecessary force, before returning to take his seat beside Charlotte. Sneaking a look at his bleak expression, she wished she hadn't blurted out what must have sounded to him like an ultimatum, ruining what on the surface had been a perfect day. Why didn't she have the sense to wait for a more opportune moment? After he'd had a few drinks, for example, when he'd lowered his defences?

He turned to look at her. Her plea for understanding remained unspoken when she confronted the calm hostility in his gaze.

"It *was* all for nothing," he said. "There's no other way of looking at it, but that's no excuse for continuing to make things worse."

That afternoon nine-year-old Sandy Turner, camping with his father, an itinerant rabbit trapper, was bitten by a tiger snake when he put down his hand to collect wood for the campfire and didn't see the snake camouflaged amongst the sticks and grass. The father made a tourniquet for the boy's upper arm from the rope he used as a belt, the first thing he could lay his hands on. He hobbled his son's horse and left it at the camp, then put the boy in front of him on his own mount and held him tightly for the fifteen-mile ride to the town in the dark.

"I'll take him," said Lochlann, reaching up when the pair finally arrived at his door, roused by the father calling out and rattling the gate with his foot.

The father found it difficult to loosen his grasp as his arm had become stiff and numb. He handed down the slender boy, barefoot, suntanned and golden-haired, and Lochlann carried him into the surgery.

"I got here as quick as I could," said the thin man with the leather face and gnarled hands. He took off his hat, leaving an indent across his forehead and, blinking, came into the light.

The doctor had his ear to the boy's chest and his fingers on his neck. He had taken the tourniquet off the bloodless right arm.

"Is he going to be all right, doctor?" asked the father. "Did I do the tourniquet properly?"

"You did it perfectly. I couldn't have done it better myself."

"Is he going to be all right?" the father repeated.

When the doctor didn't answer, the man looked down and saw tears dropping on to the boy's chest.

Word got out that the new doctor, just back from an outing with his wife to the Ober falls, had cried when young motherless Sandy Turner was brought in dead by his father.

"He must have been reminded of his own loss to take it so hard," said the town sage, who had never before heard of a doctor being so upset at the death of a patient.

63

Every indication that she wasn't completely valueless came too late, Dixon reflected, sitting in the hotel garden in the shade of a wattle tree listening to the currawongs and kookaburras. How different her life would have been if she had known then that she was good-looking and clever, not ugly and stupid as she had been told.

One day, at the age of sixteen back in England, she had been trusted to escort a twelve-year-old girl inmate to the dentist for an extraction. During that walk along the busy streets she noticed that both women and men were staring at her.

As a child she had been convinced she had a freakish facial irregularity. There were no mirrors allowed inside the orphanage, vanity being considered a worse sin than blasphemy, whatever that was, so she'd only ever seen her image distorted in rippled glass or convex shiny surfaces. When prospective parents came to choose a girl for adoption the matron, obviously to spare Dixon's feelings, knowing she'd never be picked, hid her away until they'd left with some other more attractive child. Later, on her first excursions outside the orphanage, when she caught sight of her reflection in shop windows and once briefly in a mirror in a doctor's surgery, she realised she looked quite normal and was left to wonder why Matron always hid her away.

"Everyone's looking at you," said her young companion.

"I can see that." She couldn't understand it. She dropped her head to hide her face in the folds of her scarf.

If it was her feet that they were looking at she could understand it, as Matron had surpassed herself on this occasion by choosing from the second-hand store an even uglier pair of shoes for Dixon than she usually did. Already she could feel the pain of blisters forming on her heels as the backs of the ill-fitting shoes flapped up and down, scraping her flesh with every step she took.

"I wish they'd stare at me," the young girl continued. "But then I'm not beautiful like you."

Dixon tried to detect sarcasm in that remark but found none. It was the first time she'd had that word applied to herself and she wondered if the girl could be trusted to know what she was talking about.

"Everyone wants to look like you. Even Matron. I heard her say it."

There was little bleeding when the young girl's tooth was removed as it had long been disengaging from its socket. The dentist told her to come back when she was due to marry and he would remove her remaining twelve teeth and fit her with a nice set of dentures so she'd be no bother or expense to her husband.

"How is it we haven't seen you before?" he asked Dixon. "Let's take a look while you're here." He examined the inside of her mouth. "Splendid," he said. "You must have good heredity to survive the diet up at that place. Something worthwhile from your mother or father, though I presume you've little else to thank them for." He tilted up her chin. "Even a face as beautiful as yours would be spoilt if you had gaps in your mouth. Mind you look after them."

It had taken sixteen years to discover she was beautiful and twenty-six to find out she was clever, in her ignorance missing out on adoption, education and marriage during that time. To think she could have had a home with a mother and father to love her if Matron hadn't prevented her from being adopted; she could have gone to school and become a teacher or a writer; she could have married Manus and been the envy of all the females in Ballybrian and had beautiful children of her own. She could have been saved from working at the Park where she was hated by Charlotte and humiliated by Lily East, who had cast her out into the world with not one person to call her own.

The women's magazines that Dixon read advised people not to indulge in regrets as they were a waste of time and didn't alter anything. Dixon didn't agree. Her regrets were her constant and valued companions. They mightn't change the past but they could flavour the future, spurring her on to revenge, the prospect of which comforted her. When the opportunity presented itself, she was making sure she would be ready by having a substantial amount of money in her bank accounts to give her the freedom and the power to wreak the havoc she so desired.

64

Four letters. One bulky one for Lochlann from his lawyer friend Pearse. Charlotte knew the handwriting. Would he be sly enough to enclose a secret letter from Niamh? She'd find out soon enough – Lochlann left his letters in his desk drawer and she read them when he was at work. So far, to her knowledge, Niamh and Lochlann hadn't communicated. The only information about her had come through Harcourt, who said she had, after two months at home in County Mayo, joined the Medical Missionaries in Uganda for the agreed year, after which time she would decide what to do next.

Waldron's palpitations seemed to have disappeared, Edwina wrote, since that soldier, Thatcher, had taken over nursing him. She was losing her patience waiting to hear if the offer of a reward had flushed out the two women.

Charlotte crumpled the letter, poked it into the fire and later replied to it, saying that neither Teresa Kelly nor Nurse Dixon had contacted her.

Next morning she opened Lochlann's desk drawer to read Pearse's one-page letter.

"*I've done the research,*" he began, "*and it looks as if you have a strong case.*" It went on to outline the grounds for obtaining a civil as well as a religious annulment that would prove the so-called marriage had been null and void from the beginning. Her frightened eyes flicked over the words *consummation, coercion, intent, duress, maturity, freedom, mental incapacity*. Tucked into a pigeonhole was a folded document that hadn't been there the previous day. She took it out and saw that it was an application form for a civil annulment. That was what Pearse had enclosed, not a letter from Niamh, though she had a feeling that the two were connected.

65

A Red Cross dance was held to raise money for the overseas troops. The organisers chose a night with a full moon to make it easier for the townspeople to walk or cycle to the showground pavilion in the night light. People from outlying areas either rode or crowded into vehicles to make their way there. Everyone who could come did come.

Lochlann thought the night out would do Charlotte good. It was now eight months since the birth and death of Benedict and one month since their anniversary outing which had lifted her out of her depression but plunged her into another form of gloom. "Not yet," was her answer to any suggestion made by Lochlann or Mrs Parker to involve her in any outings. A day at the beach with only Lochlann for company was the one thing she fancied, but that wasn't feasible seeing the car's petrol use was restricted to official business. Not that anyone would begrudge his poor depressed wife a trip to the coast but he didn't want to give himself a special dispensation.

Lochlann was determined to leave for Dublin as soon as a replacement could be found. He wanted to enlist immediately after dropping Charlotte safely back at the townhouse and what happened after that he didn't much care. His hopes rested on a doctor coming out of retirement for patriotic reasons. A practitioner in his nineties with failing eyesight and a shaky hand would be better than no doctor at all. Lochlann had sent his resignation to the Medical Board in Sydney, asking at the same time if it had any suitable candidate on its register, and had put a notice in the *National Medical Journal*.

One trained nurse had to be on duty at the hospital on the night of the fundraiser. The young nurses expected Matron Grainger to put her own name down when she was doing the roster, seeing she must be thirty-five if she was a day and was a killjoy into the bargain, but the name of a younger nurse appeared on the notice board leaving Matron free to attend.

"It's not fair," said the unlucky one who had been selected. "She's a complete wowser and thinks dancing is an invention of the devil."

Lochlann had told Charlotte that if she was sure she hadn't changed her mind he would put in an appearance to support the function but would return as soon as tactfully possible. He didn't intend to drink as he expected his services to be needed before the night was out but, in line with local custom, brought along a bottle of whiskey to share around.

"Just the one then," he said, joining Dan Hogan and a group of men outside the pavilion in the moonlight. Dan went inside to have the Pride of Erin with his wife, then returned. It crossed Lochlann's mind that he hoped dancing would be the only activity the Hogans would engage in that night – he didn't want Nell crying in his surgery in a few weeks' time with number eight on the way. The full moon, now high above the pine trees, was ravishing enough to put ideas into the minds of even the most inveterate cynics. He must remember to warn the incoming doctor to expect a rise in births in nine months' time, and most of them "premature" babies.

Lochlann reluctantly took leave of the men to enter the hall – one dance with Nell Hogan should be enough to fulfil his duty. The band, consisting of a fiddle, piano and drums, was playing the schottische. In the dim light coming from one central bulb in the ceiling, he saw the women sitting in benches along the side walls talking to each other while keeping an eye on the few men standing around the door. He spotted Nell Hogan going into the side room to help prepare the supper, and asked her to dance. After they executed a few turns he noticed Matron – he had to look twice to make sure it was she – crossing the floor and standing in the spot vacated by Nell. It was a surprise to see her there as he knew she disapproved of dancing. She must have made an exception so she could support such a worthy cause as the Red Cross. He would have to have the second dance with her, and then he could leave, duty done. Placing herself where she did meant he wouldn't have to search her out amongst the other women, all patients of his.

One man standing at the door was Digger Flintoff from the west slope of the Plateau. He had been secretly in love with Matron ever since the day he had been admitted to hospital two years earlier, his right leg broken by the limb of a falling tree. Under her care for weeks, he had watched and admired her crisp manner and gentle touch and thought the sound of her voice sweeter than eucalyptus honey. But they came from different ends of the spectrum – he was afraid of her rules and strictures and didn't think for a moment she would consider a drinker and a larrikin like himself. So he stood at the door, watching Dr Carmody escort Nell Hogan back to where he found her and continue to chat to her until the music started up again.

Foxtrot. "Ladies' Choice." Matron was in position to ask Lochlann before the MC had completed the announcement and Nell was free to return to the supper room.

"Not letting the grass grow," someone whispered.

Two young nurses nudged each other, and a few of the older women exchanged knowing glances.

Digger was transfixed by Matron. She was dancing with grace and expertise, laughing up at the doctor, her hair swinging loose and the silky, chiffon skirt of her dress floating in time to the music. It was a revelation. No trace of starch anywhere. Perhaps he had misjudged her. As the Ladies' Choice came to an end, he started to make his way across the floor so he would be in position to ask her for the next dance, all the while promising God he would become a saint if only she would look at him the way she was now looking at the young doctor.

Waiting for the next dance to be announced, he hovered near the pair. Matron, with her eyes riveted on Lochlann's face, didn't notice him over Lochlann's shoulder, even though he was only a fraction outside her direct line of vision.

The Viennese waltz came next. Digger excused himself and made his request but Lochlann, thinking it would be bad manners not to return the compliment of being picked for the Ladies' Choice, had already asked her. He offered to stand aside. Digger wouldn't hear of it, especially when he saw the look of alarm on Matron's face. She promised him the next dance, which was the one before supper, and he was content with that. As the doctor and Matron moved off, many pairs of eyes looked beseechingly at Digger, hoping he would ask them, but he stayed where he was, staring at the dancing couple laughing as their twirls became wider and more exuberant. Other dancers on the floor were tripping over themselves trying to take in the sight they thought they would never see – a glamorous Matron dancing with the best-looking man in the hall, while the most eligible one waited on the sideline to claim her.

Lochlann, satisfied that no more was expected of him, joined the men outside again and when supper was called after the Canadian Three Step, told them that he would give it a miss and head for home. They persuaded him to have a couple more for the road. Out of a sense of tact, no one asked after his wife. The fact that she never showed her face and was the mother of a dead baby restricted their enquiries as much as it would restrict his answers, so to be on the safe side they said nothing.

They felt sorry that such a young sociable man was saddled with a wife who, from what they could see and what Mrs Parker didn't say, was a complete dead loss.

At ten o'clock Lochlann reluctantly took leave of the men and during the quarter mile walk hoped that Charlotte would be in bed asleep by the time he arrived home.

"You've been drinking," Charlotte said without lifting her head from the book she was reading at the kitchen table.

Lochlann closed the door behind him with exaggerated care. "Of course I have. Couldn't expect to feel as good as this sober. Only half cut though. Obviously not legless or I wouldn't have made it up the hill."

Charlotte laughed despite herself.

"It's a pity you didn't come. You would have enjoyed it." He leaned on the table and tried to get her attention in a teasing fashion. "Couldn't have left any earlier. Had to have a couple of duty dances."

He straightened up and moved around to stand beside her. She continued to stare at the pages of the book. He started to hum 'Danny Boy' just as he had in the old days when he arrived at this mid-point of intoxication. Bowing, he took her hand, turned the book face down on the table and said, "One more duty dance to finish the night. May I have the honour?"

Charlotte, choosing to ignore the insult implied in the word "duty" and trying not to look too eager, allowed herself to be pulled from the chair. Lochlann gave only a small stumble as he took up the dancing position and held her close against his chest.

"*But come ye back . . .*" he was singing the words, as if he was taking them to heart, "*For you will bend and tell me that you love me . . .*"

He moved his head away from hers and sang to the ceiling.

The smallness of the kitchen and the bulkiness of the furniture restricted their movements. After Charlotte banged her hip on the corner of the table, she moved closer, and when Lochlann backed into the dresser and rattled the crockery she put both her arms around his neck. They shortened their steps to avoid any more collisions and soon were barely moving their feet at all.

The aftershocks of the dance became apparent during the following weeks.

When Nell Hogan realised she was pregnant with her eighth child she didn't visit the doctor then or during the subsequent months. The Hogans had no vehicle of their own and she didn't like to ask the neighbours for favours when there was no emergency.

Matron and Digger had a shotgun wedding at the two-month stage. "Don't bother getting in a large incubator for me," she laughed. "Everybody knows and I don't care." A perceptive person might say Digger had warmed his hands at the fire lit by another man, but whatever the beginnings of their union the two considered themselves fortunate.

The third was a young woman from North Redmundo.

Charlotte was the fourth casualty.

"And before you say anything," she said to Lochlann, even though he was making no sign that he intended to speak, "under no circumstances will I undertake to travel in this condition. I am sure

304

being seasick for weeks on end on the way out had an adverse effect on Benedict. And I don't care if you are a doctor and don't agree with me. I'm not moving from here until the baby is born and that's my final word on the matter."

"It didn't cross my mind to ask you to," said Lochlann gently. "I know everything will go well this time. It will be something for both of us to look forward to."

Dr Merton, aged eighty-two, had written to say he would like one more stab at trout-fishing in the town of his birth before he died and would like to fill the position until the end of the war if he lasted and it didn't go on too long.

Lochlann wrote back to thank him for his application but, regretfully, had to inform him that the position was filled, then wrote to the Medical Board to report his change of plans.

66

Charlotte suffered an anxious pregnancy. Early on she came up with the theory that there was something intrinsically wrong with her, owing to the fact her parents were cousins, and it was an inherited deficiency rather than the seasickness that had caused the death of Benedict. Lochlann's reassurances didn't help as he still didn't know why Benedict had died, and he couldn't categorically say that the same misfortune wouldn't happen again, though he said it was highly unlikely. He didn't tell her that it was medical practice to advise women who had had two stillbirths not to try again as the likelihood of having another one after that was too great.

There was some consolation for Charlotte in the fact that Edwina and Waldron weren't first cousins, but not enough to pacify her as she lay awake in the middle of the night imagining a second disastrous outcome.

Hating to be left on her own, she would have no one but Lochlann or Mrs Parker to keep her company, ending up exhausting them both, as well as herself, by the time she went into labour. Lochlann drove her to the hospital and she begged him not to leave her until after he had delivered the baby.

Matron had given birth to a son nine days earlier and had already returned home. The acting matron, Sister Townsend, had completed her general training but had not done the midwifery course, though she had assisted at many births and was considered experienced. With personnel shortages all over the country, it was not unusual to have under-qualified staff in charge. Hospitals, especially small ones like Redmundo, were grateful for whomever they could get.

Lochlann had offered to take Charlotte to Pumbilang's large hospital with better facilities forty miles away, but she became tearful and refused to go, saying she didn't want to be among strangers or have anyone but him deliver the baby, and if the deficiency was in the blood better facilities would be of no benefit.

At five o'clock in the morning Nell Hogan arrived unaccompanied. She had come into town before her due date to stay with the priest's housekeeper at the presbytery. The younger children were distributed among the relatives and the older ones stayed at the farm to help Dan with the milking and poddy-feeding. She had walked down the frosty hill in the dark without a coat, carrying her bag. A lonely sight, Lochlann thought. He loosened Charlotte's tight grip on his arm, promised to return within minutes, and went to the reception desk to greet Nell and check her in, and then hand her over to Sister Townsend.

At eight o'clock Sister Townsend, who hadn't slept in thirty-six hours, saw with relief her replacement, Sister Fullbright, arriving for the day shift. She waved to her but didn't stay to fill her in as she usually did – Dr Carmody could do that seeing he was on the premises – and left, thinking only of her bed, hot-water bottle and a ten-hour sleep ahead of her.

"Good God, Pam, what's the matter with you?" Lochlann asked Sister Fullbright when he saw her.

"I feel a bit crook at the moment, to tell you the truth, Doctor. Coming down with a cold, I reckon," Sister Fullbright croaked. "But don't worry. I'll be fine as soon as I've had a nice hot cup of tea."

"I think it will take a lot more than that to cure you." He went through her symptoms with her – headache, sore muscles, tiredness, sweating, shivering. "And fever," he added, putting his hand on her forehead. "It's off back home with you immediately and into bed and don't get out of it until I see you. Full-blown influenza is what you have. No doubt about it."

Sister Fullbright was loath to leave him with only a nurses' aide and a cook, especially when she heard that both Mrs Carmody and Mrs Hogan had come in. Lochlann said she would be more of a danger than a help spreading the highly infectious strain of influenza around the hospital – the last thing he wanted. She suggested calling Sister Townsend and asking her to return – it wouldn't be the first time she'd done a double shift – but Lochlann said she hadn't slept a wink between the last two. She would be of more use that night seeing he was holding the fort during the day, and the patients wouldn't mind a bit of neglect if they could have her fresh and well rested for the night shift.

Sister Fullbright was glad the doctor had made the decision for her – she hadn't looked forward to dragging herself around all day. It would be a pity, though, to miss the birth of Charlotte Carmody's baby – it was as if the whole town and district was holding its collective breath hoping for a happy outcome for the poor depressed recluse and her long-suffering husband. And Mrs Hogan's eighth. She would be sorry to miss that as well as it should be an easy delivery. But she was feeling so rotten it was a relief to be told to go home.

Lochlann settled Nell Hogan in the labour ward when her time came nearer. She lay quietly suffering, trying not to be any trouble and apologising for taking up Lochlann's time. All she asked for was chloroform in the final stages – she'd had it for all previous births and without the promise of it might lose her courage altogether. The nurses' aide dropped in to see her whenever she wasn't dealing with the needs of the other patients in the general wards.

Nell gave birth to identical twin girls at four fifteen and four twenty-four. Lochlann weighed them – five pounds two ounces and five pounds twelve ounces – before swaddling them in cotton hospital blankets and placing them in cribs in the nursery next door to the labour ward. He gave Nell a little extra chloroform while he waited for the placenta to come away.

Charlotte Carmody delivered a dead baby girl at six thirty in the room next door to Nell's. Lochlann baptised it, cleaned it up, swaddled it, and put it in a crib beside that of the twin girls. He gave Charlotte a second whiff of chloroform to extend her not knowing and his not having to tell her.

He was on his own all this time.

When it was all over, he sought out the nurses' aide and asked her to see to the needs of the mothers while he concentrated on the babies, as one of them was slow to breathe and needed oxygen.

Sister Townsend, reporting back for work at eight that evening, refreshed after nine hours' sleep, noticed how dreadful Lochlann looked and immediately thought there was bad news about Charlotte. He wearily told her what had happened in her absence. He had taken his wife home straight after delivery to be looked after by Mrs Parker, he said, to lighten the workload on the nursing staff, with Sister Fullbright out sick.

He took her into his office and asked her to fill in the death certificate, which he would sign later. The doctor appeared drained and sombre to the nurse, who had been on duty the day the doctor's son Benedict had died and had hoped never again to be in the vicinity of such a painful event.

She blamed herself – an acting matron should be prepared for days like today. It wasn't her fault, Lochlann said, finding it difficult to enunciate the words. How was she to know Sister Fullbright was ill, especially when she'd seen her arrive for work? It was just one of those things, he said sadly.

The first thing Sister Townsend did was ring her fiancé, the young policeman on duty, and ask him to drive out to Taltarni to ask Shirley Dudgeon, who had no car and no phone, if she could come in and help out in the morning.

"Don't take no for an answer," she said, filling him in on what had happened that day. She didn't want to be unfavourably compared to Matron 'Wowser' Grainger who had ruled here so efficiently for ten years. "Arrest her if you have to – or charm her – that would be more down your alley – but don't come back without her. Tell her she can stay with me. Thanks, love. You too."

Charlotte was sitting up in the bed, her head bent, adoring the dark-haired baby at her breast.

"I think I must be the happiest woman in the world," she said, beaming up at Mrs Parker.

"You probably are at this moment," agreed Mrs Parker.

"I thought I might never be lucky enough have a live, healthy baby. It's the only thing I ever really wanted. I can't believe it's happened at last. What did I do to deserve such good fortune?" She stroked the little hand fluttering in the air. "I suppose everyone says that."

"No, not everyone. I have to say you look like an experienced hand, Mrs Carmody. A real natural."

"Do I really?" Charlotte looked pleased. "That's reassuring. I was worried that I wouldn't know what to do."

"You could have fooled me. You really look like an old hand. Have you settled on a name yet?"

"Finally. The doctor said that he didn't want any of those la-di-da long names, and I said I didn't want one of those Irish names that most people can't spell or pronounce, so I think we'll settle for something plain and simple, like Mary Anne, after various forbears, if he agrees to it." She had wanted to call her Victoria but was afraid Edwina would be hostile to the idea.

"Very nice," said Mrs Parker. "The sort of names that never go out of fashion." She didn't know if Lochlann had told her about Mrs Hogan's stillborn twin. "I wonder how Mrs Hogan is getting on," she said to put out feelers, and when Charlotte's smiling expression didn't change, presumed she didn't know.

Maybe that was one of the reasons why the doctor had brought Charlotte home immediately – to take her away from a situation that could only evoke bad memories. Meanwhile, she would take his lead and not say anything, and let him be the one to tell her.

Mrs Hogan determined not to break down when Sister Townsend pulled up a chair beside the bed.

"Dr Carmody baptised her and called her Dolores," she said after many false starts at trying to speak.

"That's good. So you have a little angel in heaven," said the nurse, using an expression she'd often heard.

Mrs Hogan didn't ask if there was any reason for the baby's death – she accepted it as one of life's mysteries. She had seen plenty of that kind of thing on the farm and never got used to it. Not that you could compare humans and animals, though to hear a cow bellowing for her separated calf, it was hard to believe they didn't feel the same as humans. Sometimes she wondered should she be a farmer's wife at all when she was so soft-hearted and squeamish.

"I'll just go and fetch your little girl," the nurse said. "What have you decided to call her?"

"Alison, after my favourite aunt."

"That's nice. Your aunt will be pleased."

"I hope so. She's on her last legs, poor thing. I don't think there's a Saint Alison so I'll give her Rose as a second name just in case."

"That's nice. What does that make it?"

"Five boys and four girls." Nell started to cry. "Three girls."

Sister Townsend was annoyed with herself for asking such a tactless question.

In the privacy of his office, Lochlann wrote to the old doctor, eighty-three by now, to say the offer was open again and, if he was still available, he could take possession of the house and the practice within the month. He then applied for a position on a troop ship – he still had the original forms. As he walked in the darkness to the Post Office to post the two letters, he wondered if he'd ever have a peaceful night again. From this day on he expected never again to sleep the sleep of the just.

Lochlann later assured an anxious Father Daly he had baptised the child correctly with due procedure, relieving the Hogans of the worry their little girl's soul would be consigned to Limbo. He thought it better not to mention that the child had been lifeless when he poured the water on her forehead and said the words.

Was there ever such a blackguard as I am? Lochlann asked himself, amazed at how easily the lies rolled off his tongue.

Nell stayed in hospital for the usual two weeks. Lochlann visited her on his daily rounds and, if he was hoping for redemption by her admitting it might have been just as well the twin had died as she didn't think she could manage two on top of the number she already had, he was disappointed. She mourned little Dolores as if she were her first. Worse, she told him before she was discharged that her sister-in-law in Sydney had asked could she adopt Alison as, after six miscarriages, she had given up hope of having a child of her own and thought that the Hogans, with their eight healthy children, would be

311

pleased to give one of them a huge financial advantage and a secure future.

"What did you say to that?"

"Didn't consider it. Not for a minute. Dan and I both agreed we couldn't part with our own flesh and blood, and that if God has willed us to have all these children, He will provide. Poor Cat will have to settle for being godmother. Not that that will be much consolation to her, poor unhappy woman, but it's the best we can do. God's will can be very unfair at times, Doctor."

The sister-in-law would have to steel herself against further instances of unfairness, Lochlann reckoned. Nell was only thirty-three and Alison was unlikely to be the last. That projection didn't give him any consolation either.

The old doctor wrote to say he could take up duties within the month and hoped he wouldn't be cancelled this time as he was looking forward to coming back to his old stamping ground.

If Nell and Charlotte continued true to type, Lochlann believed, the next four weeks should pass without the two women meeting each other and comparing babies. Nell, living twenty miles out with no transport, didn't come to town except for emergencies, and Charlotte never left the house. His mother's dictum that all good-looking babies look alike and all ugly babies look alike didn't console him. Identical twins would be too particular to be covered by that generality.

67

Charlotte's handling of Mary Anne astounded both Lochlann, who since their marriage had only ever seen his wife dispirited and idle, and Mrs Parker who had been expecting to do most of the childminding but found she wasn't asked to do any.

Charlotte was alert to Mary Anne's every signal, tuned in to her every change of mood. She found herself talking to her in a language that she thought came naturally to her until she realised it was an imitation of the way Manus used to speak to the horses, especially the foals. It worked for the foals and it worked for Mary Anne, who proved to be contented and placid.

"Why wouldn't she be?" Mrs Parker told her friends. "Mrs Carmody doesn't allow her to cry. The little one's hardly ever off the breast, and is always in her mother's arms. Mrs Carmody has moved into the spare room so the baby can sleep beside her and not disturb the doctor."

Lochlann was trying not to think or feel or become attached in case some all-knowing arbiter swooped down to pick up Mary Anne to return her to her true family. He couldn't believe he could get away with it. If only the twins had been fraternal, rather than identical, he wouldn't have to live in constant terror. If only they could leave town immediately.

Two days before their departure date, Nell Hogan rang to say Alison had a chesty cough and a temperature of one hundred and two degrees and what would she do? Would she ask a neighbour to give her a lift in? Was it serious enough for that?

"I'll tell you what," said Lochlann. "I have a call to make to old Chippie at the mill, so I'll call in to you. Just leaving this minute. No trouble at all. No, I mean it."

Old Chippie was surprised to be visited by the doctor, as he hadn't contacted him and was feeling well.

"Will you have a drink with me, Doctor?" he asked, rinsing out a dirty glass.

"Just the one. A farewell drink. I'm heading back home in three days' time to enlist."

Chippie was the first to be told, the Hogans the second.

After he attended to Alison, and supplied medication to bring down the temperature, he told them he was leaving the town. They showed their disappointment and said they must organise a send-off for him. No fuss, said Lochlann, and there was no time now as he was dreadfully busy with the preparations to leave – as was his wife. That was why he wasn't telling anyone until the last minute.

He would need to stand guard over Charlotte and the baby until they left, he thought, for fear Dan Hogan would consider it proper to visit to say goodbye.

"You may come back after the war," Nell said with feeling.

"Please God," said Dan.

Lochlann asked if he could have some photos of the family. They were flattered to be asked. He made sure Alison was centre stage.

For my eyes only, Lochlann thought.

He wanted to tell them how much he owed them, but thought it might sound peculiar. They would think nothing of the days he'd spent on their farm on horseback.

He didn't offer to keep in touch and didn't give them his home address – they wouldn't have expected either. He left a box of gifts and money for the children, and the irony of the paltriness of it wasn't lost on him. If only he could give much more. Half of everything he would ever own wouldn't come anywhere near paying off his indebtedness to them.

68

Lochlann and Scottie packed the luggage into the back of the mail truck.

"By the way, if you're looking for a hotel in Sydney," said old Dr Merton, settled in since the previous day, "I can highly recommend one. My dear late wife looked on it as a home away from home and I can swear by it. The Waratah. Run by two friendly Pommie women."

"Thank you," said Lochlann, "but I don't think we'll be needing one. We expect to be allowed to embark early."

"In these uncertain times you can't be sure of anything and you might be in for a long delay. I kept a magazine article with all the details. Now, what did I do with it?" He foraged in his black bag. "The younger one used to be a real stunner – part of the attraction of the place – and was still a good sort last time I saw her though my dear late wife told me I needed new glasses. I think she was a bit jealous, not that she had any cause." He produced a folded piece of paper and handed it to Lochlann. "No harm in hanging on to it just in case. Don't want to see you stranded. The Waratah will take the pain out of the disruption if your ship fails to turn up."

"Thanks, but I hope we won't need to avail of it." Lochlann slipped the page into the breast pocket of his jacket. "I'll read it on the train."

The few townspeople driving by at this early hour swivelled their heads when they saw evidence of departure. Lochlann had told only a few at the last minute that he was leaving to forestall any plans for an official send-off. The risk of Charlotte's parading Mary Anne around to be admired, especially by the Hogans who would make the effort to attend, made Lochlann feel sick at the thought.

Wombat, on his way to the butter factory, pulled over when he saw the little group, his face showing as much surprise as it was capable of registering. He joined them and held out his arms for Mary Anne. Lochlann, remembering Charlotte's fear of him, made as if to intercept, but Charlotte gave the man a full smile and, handing over the baby, said, "You brought me luck, Wombat." She pulled back the shawl so he could get a good look at the baby.

Lochlann wondered what she was talking about.

Wombat examined the baby, looked from it to Charlotte and Lochlann, and then back again.

"Twin," he mouthed.

Lochlann was the only one who knew what he was trying to say.

"Heard you were out at Hogan's place yesterday, giving Dan a hand," Mrs Parker said in the clear tones reserved for the handicapped. Despite her fondness for him she didn't like looking at his mouth, so missed his observation. "You'd be an expert on babies after that," she smiled around the little circle.

"Twin," Wombat repeated soundlessly.

"Wind," Lochlann said, taking Mary Anne gently from Wombat and patting her on her back while he held her over his shoulder.

"I thought he said 'twin'," said Charlotte.

"No, it was 'wind'. I talk to him a lot and I'm an expert at knowing what he says, aren't I, Wombat?" Before the man could answer Lochlann guided him to his vehicle, jabbering at speed, thanking him for all the work he'd done in the garden and telling him he'd never tasted such vegetables, shaking his hand and saying he would never forget him, good man himself, all the while feeling as if he was about to vomit and have a brain haemorrhage and suffer a heart attack, all at the same time.

Charlotte appeared at his shoulder. She took Wombat's hand and kissed him on his scarred cheek. "Thank you for everything," she said. "I'm frightfully glad I didn't miss seeing you before I left to thank you for the good fortune you brought me in the end."

Wombat shuffled his feet and hung his head to hide his pleasure before swinging into the driver's seat.

What was all that about? Lochlann wondered, with no intention of asking. "Sound man," he said, his voice husky, returning to the group, hoping that none of them had noticed how fearful he was when he'd rushed the poor man off in such a rude fashion. They hadn't, and they presumed the catch in his voice was due to the sadness of leaving.

Charlotte waved to Wombat until he was out of sight and said to Mrs Parker, "You were right. He is a Good Samaritan."

Mrs Parker said her final farewells, and Scottie arranged a day's fishing with Dr Merton.

"Sorry to be going, Doc?" Scottie asked as they took their seats and waved to Mrs Parker and the old doctor.

"Very." He put his head down, willed the truck to move off before anyone else came along, and kept his head lowered until the truck was well clear of town.

He hoped Nell Hogan wouldn't come into town for at least a year so that Mrs Parker's memory of Mary Anne would have faded sufficiently for her not to make a connection between the two little girls born on the same day and looking so much alike. And he hoped Wombat would begin to doubt what he'd seen, and that the towns-people would continue to treat him with indulgence, believing that his brain as well as his face had been damaged in the fire and, if he did regain his voice, they would take no notice of his belief that Charlotte Carmody's baby and Nell Hogan's baby were twins.

"Can't believe that you've only been here for just over two years – seems longer," said Scottie.

Like ten years, Lochlann thought, with so much happening.

"Remember the first operation you did on the day you arrived?"

"The appendix. I remember it well – felt half dead and didn't know where anything was. I was lucky to have Matron Grainger assisting me."

"You said he must be destined for great things. Billy Ericsson. Well, he wasn't. Heard last night he was killed in action. What a bloody waste. You needn't have bothered."

"I hope that wasn't the case."

Beside him Mary Anne was asleep in Charlotte's arms and Charlotte was in her usual pose of smiling down at her.

317

"Wombat definitely tried to say 'twin', Lochlann. Seems to have confused me with Nell Hogan," Charlotte said. "I don't think I look anything like her, do you?"

"Not a bit. Would you like me to take Mary Anne to give you a rest?" asked Lochlann, desperate to change the subject.

"Perhaps later. I don't want to disturb her sleep just now."

"Speaking on behalf of the town, seeing you wouldn't have a send-off," Scottie said with uncharacteristic seriousness, "you'll be missed."

"Thank you," said Lochlann. "It's a special place. I loved being here and I'm sorry to be leaving."

If only they knew, he thought. If they were told that of all the hypocrites in the world I must be the worst, would they believe it? No, not without proof, for when they'd look at me they would see their own goodness reflected back at themselves.

And of all the people in the world who are in a position of trust, I must be the one who has proven to be the most treacherous.

What mitigation for acting out of pity, with no premeditation, tightening my shackles in the process?

None. None.

What solace from any divine or human source?

None. Not an iota.

If there is a God, and I hope there isn't, there will be no forgiveness for me as I'm still in possession of my neighbour's treasure and have no intention of returning it. No recompense, no absolution. That's the rule.

Snuggled against Lochlann's shoulder, Charlotte fantasised that one day she and Lochlann, with their four children, would be celebrating their Silver Anniversary in Tyringham Park, for that's where she pictured herself living after Harcourt inherited and was speaking to her again. And she would ask Lochlann, with just the right touch of lightness in her tone, if he remembered their first anniversary and if it had crossed his mind then to push her into the abyss seeing she was such an albatross around his neck at the time. She could imagine him looking back at her as if she'd just lost her mind, or laughing, and saying 'Where did that idea come from?' and then he would take time to search his memory before he would say, 'Why would I be thinking of such a thing? I was studying the

318

geological make-up of the planet and marvelling at the origins of the universe, not contemplating an insignificant thing like murder.' And she would be able to smile back, as their relationship by then would be easy, and say, 'I know that's what you were thinking. I was the one with the black thoughts. Imagine if that had happened, little Mary Anne would never have been born and that doesn't bear thinking of. How could I have known then how happily things would turn out in the end?'

PART 5

THE HOMECOMINGS

69

Dublin
1941

Aunt Verity took it upon herself to meet the mail boat and the first thing she told the returned emigrants was that Harcourt had been wounded, how seriously they didn't know. The telegram with the news had been delivered to the townhouse three weeks previously.

Lochlann reached out to take Mary Anne in case Charlotte became weak, but she held the child closer and said she was fine.

"That means he'll be coming home, won't it?"

When her brother saw what a good mother she had turned out to be and how happy Lochlann was now that he was home, he would forgive her for her past machinations and admit that it had all turned out for the best.

"We're waiting for word. Did the nanny travel on a different deck?"

"No, we've been able to manage without one."

"Oh."

Aunt Verity was relieved when Lochlann shepherded the pair to the car and settled them into the back seat, as she was afraid someone she knew might see them. To her, the sight of a woman of her class carrying an infant was as distasteful as one balancing a heavy weight on her head or kneeling to scrub floors.

"You don't look too well, Dr Carmody," she observed while they were waiting for the chauffeur to finish collecting and stowing the luggage.

"I'll be all right in a moment." He averted his face. "It was a long trip."

"Of course. How silly of me to forget that you are a good friend of Harcourt's and must share the anxiety with the family. We can only wait and hope and pray."

"How are Mother and Father?" asked Charlotte.

"Stoic, as you would expect. You'll find they haven't changed one bit, still taking the opposite view to each other on principle. It's wearing on me in my role of peacemaker. Now, let's have a good look at the little one."

Charlotte took off Mary Anne's bonnet, loosened the shawl and faced the baby towards her aunt.

"Goodness me, what a little beauty! I have to say, Charlotte, she's the image of Dr Carmody."

Charlotte looked over at Lochlann to see if he enjoyed the compliment, but he continued to stare out the window. She had to remind herself that her aunt had never seen Victoria, so couldn't be expected to make the comparison she so longed to hear.

"Just as well you gave birth to her yourself or one would doubt you were her real mother." She laughed at her own wit. "When her time comes she'll be the debutante of the decade and break a lot of hearts and marry an earl."

'Unlike her mother' was the unspoken end to that observation, Charlotte thought.

"So you returned," Edwina said through tight lips, "without doing the one thing I asked you to do. The one thing. It's not as if I ever asked you to do anything else. Did you make any effort at all?"

"I made a frightfully large effort," Charlotte answered. "But I didn't get one answer to my queries."

"You've dropped a fine filly there," boomed Waldron, squinting through his spectacles, "and no need for a steward's enquiry either by the look of it."

On first sight, Charlotte had hardly recognised her mother, looking older at fifty-three than the mottled-faced Waldron who, despite being eighty-two, appeared fit and energetic.

After lunch was announced, mindful of the house rule that no child under twelve was allowed in the dining room during mealtimes, Charlotte passed the baby over to Queenie with the stipulation that she must come and fetch her immediately at the first sign of fretting.

Edwina rolled her eyes up towards the ceiling.

Charlotte thought Mary Anne's dark hair and pretty face would have her mother exclaiming over a likeness to Victoria. In fact, she had expected her mother to register a degree of stupefaction when she saw what could have been a reincarnation of her favoured daughter, but Edwina merely glanced at the baby for a few seconds and said nothing.

Lochlann came in, his hair damp from the bath he'd just taken and Charlotte thought she would burst with pride at his handsomeness, his easy manner and his polite lack of deference. He shook hands with his parents-in-law and commiserated with them on the news about Harcourt.

Edwina placed him beside Verity, on the opposite side of the table from Charlotte who felt there was much to celebrate despite the bad news about Harcourt. It was Lochlann's first time to share a meal with the Blackshaws as part of the family, her first in the townhouse in her role of a new mother, and the first time her parents had been introduced to their first grandchild. Not to mention a homecoming after two years abroad.

"I was thinking of going to the Club this afternoon," Waldron said after the first course had passed in silence and the roast beef was being served.

"There was an article in the *Times* about the Japanese threat to Darwin," Verity said to Lochlann on her right.

"Would you pass the horseradish, please, Verity?" asked Edwina before Lochlann had time to comment. "I hope it's better than the last lot we had. Cook has a habit of overdoing the vinegar."

"The Club's not what it used to be. They're letting all sorts of riff-raff join these days."

"I was trying to remember how many hospitals there are in the Dublin area," said Charlotte, making an attempt to bring Lochlann into the conversation. "Lochlann was the only doctor within a forty-mile radius of the hospital he was in charge of."

"So you said in your letters," said Edwina. "Will you be able to make up a fourth for bridge this afternoon, Vee? Tilly claims her cold has gone to her chest."

"I'll check my diary after lunch to see if I'm free. Did you see any snakes while you were away, Dr Carmody? I've always been fascinated by poisonous snakes, even though I've never seen one."

"I saw a couple," said Lochlann. "One was –"

"I'll take Thatcher with me in case my palpitations return," said Waldron. "He can wait outside while I check who's there."

"One of Lochlann's patients, a young motherless boy, was brought in already dead from snake bite," Charlotte said, hoping to hand over the telling of the story to Lochlann.

Waldron wasn't listening. "Last time I recognised fewer than a quarter of the members."

"Tilly probably has nothing more than a sniffle," said Edwina. "She's a frightful hypochondriac."

Verity said in a tone that sounded deliberately mischievous, "Just think, we now have an Australian Catholic in the family for the first time in four hundred years. Two novelties in the one child."

Charlotte and Lochlann looked up at the same moment but their eyes didn't meet.

"It's of no consequence what she is, seeing she can't inherit," Waldron pronounced.

"What do you mean, can't inherit?" Edwina shot back. "If Harcourt doesn't return, she will automatically become the heir – heiress – after Charlotte. There's no reason why she couldn't change her name to Blackshaw."

Charlotte didn't dare look at Lochlann.

"That shows you how little you know about the law, which a bit of name-changing won't alter. Charlotte's daughter can never inherit, and you know that as well as I do."

"That was British law. Why should that apply now that we're a Free State?"

"It still applies. If Harcourt doesn't survive, the land and title will go to my brother Charles after I die, and if he predeceases me, to his eldest son. That's Giles's father," he explained to Lochlann. "My brother was only in his twenties when he married." He turned back to Edwina and his voice took on an irritable tone. "If Charlotte's daughter wants to live at the Park, she'll have to marry her cousin like you did and change her name, which you didn't have to do. That's the only way she can become a real Blackshaw."

Charlotte addressed the tablecloth. "Can we talk about this another time? It's hardly a matter of urgency."

Waldron turned to address her. "You're right, it's not, but your mother won't let it rest. You know why she champions the female line, don't you? To spite Charles and Harriet who are too popular and successful, that's why. Their children and grandchildren keep winning prizes at the Horse Show and point-to-points around the country whereas Harcourt never won one. How anyone could expect him to when he was city reared is beyond me."

"That's not the reason," said Verity. "It's the unfairness that galls her."

"I can speak for myself, Vee. Charles gave Harcourt inferior mounts to ride. That's why he never won prizes. It rankles to this day. He had more natural ability than Giles, and Charles couldn't stomach it."

"As if Charles would be so petty or devious," scoffed Waldron. "It was the city rearing that handicapped Harcourt, not my brother, and besides, no amount of allegations against Charles, false or otherwise, has anything to do with the case in hand. Private grievances aside, male primogeniture must prevail. It's the only system that makes sense. Where would the Blackshaw name and the House of Lords and the British Empire be without it? Answer me that."

"Certainly not as powerful as they are today," Verity chimed in.

"Exactly. It's the only way to keep power and wealth in the hands of those bred to wield it, preventing catastrophes like some female marrying a nobody without a fortune . . ."

Charlotte looked studiously at her plate, but could see that Lochlann had stopped eating.

". . . and him squandering the lot in the space of one generation."

They've had this argument before, Charlotte realised. Verity is prompting Waldron so that he will repeat it in front of us.

"Anyway, I'm not dead yet and Harcourt isn't dead yet, and the Park isn't what it used to be with all the acreage sold off. Still, there's plenty for Charlotte besides the Park thanks to the foresight of my forefathers." He refilled his glass.

Lochlann quietly replaced his knife and fork.

"That's a good one – 'the foresight of my forefathers'!" said Waldron. "It's almost poetry. Here's to the townhouse, the West Indies, Kensington and the City." He raised his glass. "Thanks to my forefathers – note, not my foremothers – jolly smart chaps that they were."

Lochlann pushed back his chair and stood up. All heads turned towards him and they waited for him to raise his glass.

"Excuse me," said Lochlann, leaving his glass on the table. "Seeing this is a private family matter I won't intrude any longer. I'll take the opportunity to call over to my parents' house to see my own family."

"I'll come with you," said Charlotte, already half out of her seat. They'd agreed earlier they would make their first visit to the Carmodys together. "I won't wait for trifle."

"No, stay where you are. There'll be plenty of time after you've contributed to this important issue." He gave her no sign of solidarity or any hint of a smile to soften the sarcastic tone – the first time she had heard him use it – before he left the room.

Smarting from Lochlann's rebuff, she had to be addressed three times before she noticed Queenie standing beside her.

"Excuse me, ma'am," the servant said. "The baby needs to be fed."

Edwina waved her hand as if to shoo her off. "You know I don't tolerate interruptions at mealtimes. You and Cook deal with it."

"They can't very well," said Charlotte, leaving the table.

When Lochlann hadn't returned after two hours, Charlotte saw no reason why she shouldn't make her own way around to see the Carmodys and be the one to revel in their admiration of Mary Anne and, by association, herself. She could imagine them now, talking, drinking and laughing in celebration, while Lochlann and his sister Iseult teased each other about the comparative excellence of his daughter and her son, Matthew, born two months before Mary Anne.

She asked Queenie to fetch Harcourt's old pram. "You and I are taking Mary Anne for a walk," she told the delighted servant.

"It's already scrubbed and waiting," said Queenie, rushing off.

When she returned with it, Charlotte nearly let the baby slip out of her arms.

The first thing she saw was the tartan quilt, and then the scratched acorn emblem half worn away. Queenie wasn't to know – she'd never been to the Park – that it was the one in which Victoria had been sleeping before she disappeared.

"This isn't Harcourt's," said Charlotte with difficulty, keeping her voice calm. "Why is it here?"

"Someone left Harcourt's out in the weather behind the potting shed for years and it rotted and rusted away. Her Ladyship asked for this one to be sent up from the Park last week to be ready for you."

Charlotte, weak with anger, slumped onto a chair. How unfortunate that her parents' distaste for 'new' money and their reluctance to spend old money coincided with their convenient preference for shabbiness.

"Take it away," she ordered the concerned Queenie. "Dr Carmody will buy a new one tomorrow. We'll put off the walk until then. I'll have a rest with Mary Anne instead."

She held herself in check until Queenie wheeled the offending article out of her sight.

Charlotte's mother-in-law Dr Grace Carmody rang at eight that evening to welcome her home and to say how sorry they were she hadn't come over with Lochlann. They were impatient to see her and little Mary Anne, but she understood from Lochlann that urgent family business had prevented her from accompanying him. There was no trace of irony in her voice. Please God they would see her and Mary Anne tomorrow.

Why is Lochlann allowing his mother to make this call? Charlotte asked herself, a familiar feeling of rejection swamping her.

"Unfortunately, dear, Lochlann overdid it and has fallen asleep in his old room. He was so excited at being home he lost the run of himself. Doesn't seem to be any point in disturbing him. He was so jaded from the trip that we probably wouldn't be able to wake him, anyway, and you know what he's like after a few drinks."

No irony there, either. "It would be a lot less trouble to leave him where he is and let him sleep through until the morning. I didn't want you to be worrying."

Charlotte thanked her and said she would bring Mary Anne over to No 7 as soon as Lochlann returned to accompany them. She hung up the phone with a dejected heart. What she had feared was already happening on their first day back – Lochlann's old life coming to claim him, leaving her out in the cold. Tomorrow it would be his best friend Pearse, then other school friends, then college friends, and then more relations. She thought of their little wooden house in Redmundo where she'd had him all to herself for most of the time, and wished they hadn't left it.

70

The trip to Tyringham Park that Charlotte had set her heart on had to be ruled out, as Lochlann received his posting within the week.

She was already planning their long-term future there, picturing Mary Anne under Manus's tutelage, Lochlann safely back from the war, practising as a country doctor, newly converted to country pursuits, herself painting in between hunts, and Miss East in her old age being treated like a queen to make up for all the years she hadn't gone to see her.

It saddened Charlotte to see the suppressed excitement in Lochlann's bearing on the day he was due to leave to join the Medical Corps in the British Army. She tried not to read too much into it. The male love of adventure was the least hurtful interpretation she could put on it, the most his wish to find Niamh – perhaps she had left the Ugandan mission by now to join the war effort.

"I'd like a photograph of you with Mary Anne," Charlotte said minutes before he was to leave. The words 'Just in case' were suspended between them. "Where did you put the Brownie? I'll go and get it."

"No, I will. I know exactly where to lay my hands on it."

Bloody hell. He had forgotten to deal with it.

Charlotte, with Mary Anne in her arms, followed him into the bedroom. The camera was in his unpacked trunk with all the unsorted letters, souvenirs and documents he had brought with him from Australia. Only four photographs had been taken on the last reel, which featured the Hogan family with Alison Hogan, Mary Anne's twin, in the foreground.

He delved into the trunk and pulled out the camera. "Right . . . here it is . . . let's see . . ." He pretended to examine the camera, then glanced up and smiled at the baby. "Look at the birds, Mary Anne," he said, pointing out the window. "They're chirping just for you."

"She might be a genius, but I don't think she understood what you said," Charlotte laughed, taking the child to the window and supplying a few bird noises of her own.

Lochlann turned away, quickly rewound the film, took it out of the camera, slipped it into his breast pocket and, glad to discover a distraction there, pulled out a folded page.

"Dr Merton's two friendly Englishwomen running a Sydney hotel," he said, handing it to her. "Do you want to read about them?"

"Not really. What's the point? It's not as if we'll be going back."

"True enough." He flicked the page into the trunk. "A pity but there's no film in the camera. I'll have to rely on you to take snaps of Mary Anne and send them to me so I can follow her progress."

Lochlann was tender when he kissed Mary Anne goodbye, and brotherly when he enclosed Charlotte in a hug and told her to mind herself and take good care of the little one.

On the mail boat crossing the Irish Sea Lochlann summoned up, he hoped for the last time, the three little faces that kept haunting him. He had tried to leave them behind in Australia, but they had embedded themselves in his brain and followed him across the seas.

Did Nell Hogan ever allow herself to acknowledge, as she tended Alison during winter nights or took her around with her while she milked cows and fed poddy calves, that it was fortunate that Dolores hadn't lived, as she was finding it so difficult to cope as it was? And when child number nine and number ten came along would she be relieved Dolores had saved herself and Dan the worry of having an extra mouth to feed and the problem of finding money for boarding-school fees when the girl reached the age of twelve and had to leave her isolated one-teacher bush school if she wanted a secondary education and didn't win a bursary?

Three little newborns in three little cribs. Two alive, one dead. Could he hope for forgiveness because what he did wasn't premeditated? Because his hands had frozen before they moved to lift up the live child so that he wouldn't have to witness Charlotte's stricken face for the second time?

No.

Would he do it again under the same circumstances?

Yes, he would.

So there was no hope for him, for not only was he a sinner, but an unrepentant sinner at that.

Now he had been given the opportunity to make some kind of amends and he intended to use it. Giving no thought to his own welfare, he would court danger, work himself into exhaustion and be brave to the point of foolhardiness in an effort to dislodge those tiny little faces from his brain.

71

Dublin
1943

How could she have known how easy it was to love and care for a child? Why had no one told her how all-consuming and satisfying tending to a child could be? Charlotte had feared she would be as cold and distant as Edwina, as resentful and cruel as Dixon. Where was the exasperation, the grimness, the nastiness, the screaming, the beatings? At what age did the child have to be before one turned on it, to frighten it and break its heart and spirit?

Every once in a while she thought of Mrs Hogan in Redmundo in Australia with her seven or eight children and she wondered how she was able to cope with all of them, as well as run the household and the dairy, while with only one child she found her day overcrowded.

As she tended to Mary Anne's needs with gentleness and delight, she often had memory flashes of the way Dixon used to drag a comb through her knotted hair, snapping her neck, and then calling her 'Cry baby' when it brought tears to her eyes. Bath time was a particular dread. When Victoria was old enough the two children were put in an almost cold bath together. Dixon would roughly lather their faces and hair and when Victoria cried out because of her stinging eyes, Dixon would slap her and leave a handprint on her wet, naked skin. The rinsing off was the worst – a bucket of cold water was thrown on both of them and Dixon took her time drying them with towels that were small and threadbare and gave no warmth or comfort. Charlotte dressed herself, but Victoria had to subject herself to Dixon's rough handling – arms twisted to fit into armholes, chin snapped as a jumper with a too-tight neck was tugged over her head, nails dug into her scalp as Dixon dried her hair.

Charlotte often thought of the shivering Victoria as she wrapped Mary Anne in a warm towel after her bath and cuddled her close, in front of the coal fire.

News of Harcourt's death came as a shock. So much time had elapsed since his wounding that the family in the townhouse had grown confident he was recovering. Harcourt's superior, Colonel Turncastle, who had been a subordinate of Waldron's in India, made a detour in his recruiting trip a fortnight later to sympathise with his old commander.

Harcourt hadn't died from his original wounds, the colonel told the assembled family. The young doctor, not properly healed himself, volunteered to travel to France to bring back a valuable Special Operations Executive agent who had been captured, severely tortured, and left for dead. Because of the presence of three ladies in the room, the colonel gave only the bare outline of the facts. He would fill in the details for Waldron later if the old soldier indicated that he wanted to hear them.

Harcourt tended to the agent until he judged him well enough to be flown back to England without a doctor to accompany him, then he stayed on and became caught up in one of the projects the agent was working on at the time. He assisted a Resistance explosives expert in blowing up a bridge at the exact moment a trainload of German soldiers was crossing it. Over a hundred perished. The Germans put a price on the head of the perpetrators. Harcourt and fifteen Resistance members were betrayed, rounded up and shot.

"So you can see why I wanted to travel over to tell you myself. 'Killed in action' would give you no indication of the extent of Harcourt's bravery."

The colonel stayed for dinner and during the course of it outlined a new development in the war. While he was talking, Charlotte had the feeling he was appealing directly to her.

The authorities had decided to recruit women agents in the field in France, he explained, holding her gaze, because so many male agents had been lost to capture or death. Each agent had to work alone: no uniform, no back-up, and no protection under the Geneva Convention. If caught, agents were regarded as spies who could be eliminated, rather than prisoners of war. Those were the rules, or lack of them, under which Harcourt had been executed.

Double agents were the biggest danger. It was suspected one of those had been responsible for betraying Harcourt. So many Special Operations Executive agents had recently disappeared within their first week of arrival, it was assumed there was at least one who was privy to the secret workings of the organisation. If the Germans seized a wireless they could torture passwords and codes out of the agent and, using that same wireless, send misleading information back to Britain.

Charlotte pictured herself taking up the challenge of finding the double agent. How thrilling and important that would be. It could avenge her brother's death and might even change the course of the war. Think of the lives saved, the false information stopped at source. The colonel could give her the details and she could enlist tomorrow.

"Young Charlotte here would be perfect for the job. I hear she speaks French like a native," he said as if reading her mind.

"She does, thanks to the tutoring she received from Cormac Delaney, a protégé of mine –"

"Is that what you called him?" interrupted Edwina with heavy sarcasm.

". . . and the time she spent in finishing school in Paris," Waldron concluded, ignoring his wife's comment.

"I would love to go. More than anything in the world," said Charlotte, meaning it. "But I have to think of my daughter. I can't leave her without anyone to look after her."

"What do you think nannies are for?" Edwina exploded. "Only common people look after their own children. I was sent over from India at the age of four to go to school and saw my parents only twice after that up until the age of eighteen, and before that I was looked after by a nanny – and it never did me any harm."

"Nor me," chimed in Verity.

"If Hitler wins the war your child won't have much of a future, full stop." The colonel leaned towards Charlotte as if to add emphasis to his words. "Thousands of women have already sent their children to places as far away as Canada and Australia for years so they can concentrate on the war effort."

"Any idiot can look after a child," said Waldron. "In my opinion they all turn out the same way, no matter what you do to them. Even though you are only a female, you would be much better employed serving your King than hiding away in the nursery, Charlotte. There is a lot of family honour resting on your shoulders now that you are the last Blackshaw."

Verity rushed in with, "What about the Cork family?"

"Not the same. They've been diluted. They don't have Blackshaw blood on both sides."

To preclude Waldron from using a more offensive term than 'diluted', Charlotte didn't state the obvious – that Mary Anne was the last in the line at the present moment.

"We all have to make whatever sacrifices are necessary," the colonel continued, fixing Charlotte with his unblinking stare. "Think of Harcourt's example."

"I'm glad Harcourt took a few down with him before he went," Waldron glowed. "This medical patching-up business is all very well, but a few dead Huns are more helpful to the cause."

They all think I'm a coward, using Mary Anne as an excuse to stay at home, Charlotte thought, anguished.

The two men went back to talking about the mechanics of war until the end of the meal. Before leaving, Colonel Turncastle gave Charlotte his address and said when she changed her mind and contacted him, he would, because of her background, make sure her name was put on the top of the list.

Charlotte determined to remain unmoved and bear any disapproval directed at her for the sake of Mary Anne.

Lochlann's letters were censored, and he himself was so cautious that the only thing she knew for sure after reading each letter was that he was alive. As wonderful as it was to know that, Charlotte wanted to know more – where he was, how he was, what conditions he was working under and, most particularly, if any female doctors were working in the vicinity. All letters from war zones were collected and taken back to London to be posted, so she didn't even know in which country he was serving. Each time she asked the question "Have you run into anyone you know?" it was left unanswered.

Without fail, she wrote to him every day, sometimes enclosing one of the many snapshots she had taken on the Brownie, concentrating on two main topics – Mary Anne's development, as could be traced in the photographs – and the friendship that was flourishing between herself and his sister Iseult. The two women saw each other every other day and, in contrast to previous times, had no shortage of things to talk about. The playful tone that Charlotte adopted when describing how much more intelligent and advanced Mary Anne was than Iseult's Matthew, despite his being older by two months, was a cover for how seriously she held the belief that Mary Anne was indeed superior to her cousin and to all other infants she came into contact with.

Charlotte's world had narrowed, but in many ways she felt as if it had expanded. If Lochlann returned from the war to join her, not only out of love for Mary Anne or a sense of duty to her, but in the certainty of having made a correct choice, she would consider herself the most fulfilled of all women and would look forward to supplying Mary Anne with a brother or sister.

72

Elizabeth Dixon received a letter from Teresa Kelly, postmarked Coogee, a suburb of Sydney.

I couldn't believe it when I saw your photo in an old magazine in my doctor's surgery. I would have recognised you anywhere, Teresa wrote. *You haven't changed a bit. How unfortunate we didn't know each other's whereabouts when we've been so near each other for over twenty-five years. I didn't end up marrying the farmer with the sick mother. It's a long story. I will tell you all about it when we meet which I hope will be soon. Now that I've found you at last I can't wait to see you. I sent my new address to you, but the letter was returned with 'No longer at this address' written on it, and I was at a loss to imagine what had happened to you. I presumed you would have married Manus as that was your plan when I left. I wrote to my brother but he didn't reply. His witchy wife must have intercepted the letter and I didn't write again, so I've heard no news at all from Ballybrian. What year did you quit the Park and what news have you of everyone there, if you're still in touch?*

Dixon was vibrating with excitement by the time she had finished reading.

At last she would see her old friend again after years of thinking they were lost to each other forever. Teresa had signed her name as 'Kelly' so she mustn't have found a replacement for her old farmer. Who would have thought that both she and Teresa, with their glittering prospects, would end up in the same boat as pitiful old Lily East with her spinsterhood and her child hunger?

At least she and Teresa would have each other from now on. That wouldn't make up for their lost chances but it was something to be glad about.

"I've a big crow to pick with you," were the first words Dixon said when she met her old friend.

"That's a fine greeting after all these years," Teresa laughed. "I'm surprised you can remember. You look wonderful. That photograph in the magazine didn't do you justice at all. And look at this office. So impressive."

Dixon couldn't hide her pleasure at hearing such praise from someone from her former life. Secretly she thought Teresa's face looked like untreated leather and her hands like a workman's but she complimented her all the same. "Before I pick the crow," she said, "I want to know why you left that poor old farmer high and dry with no one to look after his dear old sick mother."

"Don't mock. I felt guilty about that. I've had to work my fingers to the bone over the years to pay him back the money he sent for my fare. I thought it the least I could do under the circumstances. He must have felt a terrible fool after he told everyone to expect a respectable, pious Catholic lady, and I write from Sydney – didn't have the neck to travel any further – to tell him I had changed my mind but didn't tell him why. I didn't think his heart would bear the strain of hearing the truth and he, poor man, ends up with all that wasted time and money and no one to call a wife at the end of it."

"You can tell me. My heart's in good shape."

A waitress came into Dixon's office and placed a tea tray on the low table between the two women. Dixon said she would pour and told the young girl to leave.

"First things first," said Teresa, falling back into her old role as the one who naturally took the initiative. "That can wait in case you throw me out when you hear what I did. I want to keep your good opinion for as long as possible. Tell me, what did I do wrong that you have to pick a crow with me? I can't imagine what it could be."

"You came up to the Park that day you were leaving," Dixon explained, "and didn't bother to seek me out, that's what you did wrong. Do you remember? Don't you think I have a right to be peeved?"

"Of course I remember, but you won't be cross when you hear the circumstances. I didn't really have time to go to the Park that afternoon – I was peppering all the way there and back, terrified I'd miss my lift and be too late for the boat – but I thought I would have bad luck if I didn't collect that beautiful leather diary you all clubbed together to buy me, and I couldn't risk bringing bad luck on myself with the long journey ahead and a new life awaiting me." Her face showed anxiety recalling it. "All the way up the stairs I was worried someone had seen it and moved it, thinking I thought so little of it that I didn't bother bringing it with me, but there it was on my bedside table where I left it, so I wasn't delayed, thank God."

"Did you see *anyone*?"

"Only Peachy. The little timid chambermaid, if you remember."

"I do. She told us. That's how we knew you'd come back that day."

"I called out to her but neither of us stopped. It was after the time when everyone goes to the walled garden, so I didn't expect to see a soul. Does that answer your question to your satisfaction?"

"It does. It does." Concentrating on keeping her voice steady, she asked "Did you happen to see Victoria?"

"I did."

"Where?"

"As I passed the stables."

"Was she asleep?"

Teresa's voice broke with emotion and she averted her eyes. "No. She was wide awake, the little sweetheart."

Dixon leaned forward, concentrating, waiting for Teresa to compose herself. Perhaps Teresa was about to supply the missing piece in the jigsaw of Victoria's disappearance. She must have been the last person to have seen Victoria so whatever she said could be invaluable in solving the twenty-five-year-old puzzle. And as she didn't know what had happened after she left, Dixon would be the only one with the information to fit all the pieces together.

"It was because of Victoria I knew I had to have a child of my own, and that is why I agreed to marry the old farmer. I wanted a child just like her."

"But you didn't marry him. Did you miss out?"

Teresa shifted in her chair and looked embarrassed.

"Don't tell me there was another child involved," said Dixon. "Is that why you knew the old farmer wouldn't accept you?"

Teresa flushed. "Yes, there was," she said. "I was trying to work up the courage to tell you. How did you guess?"

Teresa had become pregnant on the way over on the ship, attempting to comfort a wounded soldier who had died happy a week later. "So much for being an example of virtuous Catholic womanhood," Teresa laughed. "My main feeling was annoyance at missing out on so much when I was young. What a waste! Obviously I couldn't turn up to greet my straight-laced prospective bridegroom in that condition, so after I wrote to tell him I had changed my mind, I went and stayed with my friend from Cork until my son was born."

"Your son? You have a son?"

"Yes. Joseph. The best thing that ever happened to me. You'll have to come and meet him when he returns from the war. I bought myself a wedding ring and passed myself off as a war widow, which I suppose I was in a way, so that I wouldn't be forced to give him up for adoption. The ship I came out on was sunk on the way back, so with all the records lost I had a good excuse for not being able to produce a marriage certificate. I told everyone I was married on board and they all thought it terribly romantic."

"And no daughter?"

"No, unfortunately. Joseph was my only fling and I was lucky to squeeze him in at the last minute. So, I never had a girl replace little Victoria Blackshaw in my affections. I often try to picture what she looks like now."

"Me, too. You said Victoria was wide awake in the baby carriage when you last saw her. So you saw her through the open doors of the stables as you cycled past?"

"No, no – it was on my way back I saw her – wide awake – being carried by Charlotte. She didn't see me which was just as well. She and Charlotte were just turning the corner of the stables onto the river bank as I went past and neither of them noticed me. I didn't actually see you, but I knew they must have been following you, which at the time struck me as a bit odd as I knew you never took the girls anywhere near the river."

Dixon felt as if a giant had suddenly materialised in the room and was landing punches in the region of her stomach.

Teresa was smiling at her memories and didn't notice the change in Dixon's expression.

"It was so sweet seeing the older sister looking after the younger. It was all I could do to keep cycling and not stop to say goodbye to them, and you of course, but I was so late I couldn't. Besides, I didn't want to upset them by putting them through another sad farewell. The day before was bad enough. Near broke my heart, and theirs too by the looks of them."

Dixon gripped the sides of her chair. "Charlotte carrying Victoria, you said?"

Charlotte at the stables? Not building a bridge behind the east wing?

"Yes. In quite an expert way." Teresa smiled dreamily as if she was replaying the scene in her mind. "I wished I had a camera with me to take my last image of them."

"Along the side of the stable and then turning the corner beside the river? Are you sure it was on that day?"

"Of course. How could I ever forget the last sighting of my darlings? It's seared into my heart, but I still would have liked a photograph. Why do you ask?"

"I remember distinctly how sad I was that day, imagining you getting ready to leave home." Dixon felt as if she must keep talking to cover the confusion that must be showing on her face. "I think I got my times mixed up. I was out of sorts all day, and so were the girls. We hoped you would change your mind at the last minute and not go. I was thinking of poisoning your sister-in-law or something drastic like that to persuade you to stay. Those two days of heavy rain didn't help my mood. The girls kept listening for your footsteps on the stairs so I took them down to the river to see the floodwaters to distract them but it . . ." She could gabble on no longer as her mouth had turned dry and her throat felt constricted. She stood and picked up the tray, then left the room barely managing to croak "Excuse me a minute."

Teresa's concerned enquiry after her health was lost in the clatter of china and cutlery as Dixon dropped the tray on the reception desk.

"Are you all right, Miss Dixon?" asked the young receptionist, looking up in alarm and rising from her chair.

Dixon motioned to her to sit down, then smiled and nodded to indicate that there was nothing wrong. She walked away sedately until she was out of sight of the girl, then put her handkerchief to her mouth and ran up the stairs to her bedroom.

73

Charlotte! So it was Charlotte all along. No one had suspected. Dixon herself didn't guess, not for one second, and she knew better than anyone else what a wicked child Charlotte was. How could she have been so blind? When she came upon her that day, sitting in the mud, building one of her bridges out of stones and bricks, it didn't cross her mind that she had been anywhere else during the last hour. Certainly not down by the river disposing of her sister. Mad with resentment, of course, at her mother showing an interest in Victoria and rejecting her older daughter. It was so obvious she could kick herself for not working it out at the time. If she had thought for one minute that Charlotte would defy her by going to the river and if Lady Blackshaw hadn't fixated on Teresa right from the start she might have come up with the solution, but she had led herself down the wrong track and would still be there if Teresa hadn't dropped her bombshell a few minutes earlier.

She sat on her bed, trying to bring her mind under control. Her head felt as it was rotating. All her previous conceptions were shifting at an alarming rate. She wanted to lie down and try to sort them out. Should she send a message to Teresa to say she was unwell and could they continue their conversation another time? No. No. She must pull herself together and see it through. With her talent for acting a role, she should be able to cope.

A sip of brandy would help. She kept a bottle in her bedside locker for emergencies. The oblivion of drinking had never tempted her – she preferred to stay alert at all times, listening to the secrets of drunks, but never giving away any secrets of her own.

Teresa had no idea of the significance of what she'd seen because she had left Ballybrian before hearing of Victoria's disappearance.

If Charlotte, all these years later, thought Dixon, has persuaded anyone to marry her, hiding her true nature behind her social standing, and if she has a child, wouldn't her husband need to be told for the sake of the safety of that child what Charlotte had done?

Not that Charlotte would ever admit to any wrongdoing, of course. The broken vase, the spilt milk, the soiled clothes, the lost hairbrush never had anything to do with her. She could hear her claiming that Victoria's drowning was not her fault, it was an accident, Victoria had slipped and she had nearly fallen into the river herself trying to save her.

Then why didn't she run for help? Her mother and Manus were around the corner. If she had alerted them straight away Victoria could have been saved and Charlotte would have been hailed as a heroine.

It was no accident. That's why she didn't run for help.

It was guilt that kept her quiet.

How cunning of her to sit in the mud, building a bridge, to provide an explanation for her wet and muddy clothes, and how cunning to pretend she had lost her voice so that she couldn't trip herself up when she was questioned by that nice constable.

The brandy was working, moistening her throat and taking the edge off reality. Twenty minutes had passed since she'd run out of her office. Teresa would be wondering what had happened to her. Dixon stood up, breathed in deeply and, feeling in control of herself again, went downstairs to join her old friend.

"Are you all right?" asked Teresa with concern when Dixon came back into the office. "I was wondering if I should send someone to look for you."

"Sorry about that. I've had a tummy upset and cramps for a couple of days but I'm fine now."

A waitress brought in a fresh tray and flashed a worried look at Dixon before leaving. Dixon poured a cup for Teresa.

"Please help yourself," she said, motioning towards the lamingtons, "and continue what you were saying before I so rudely ran off."

"You're still pale. And look at you – you're shaking."

"I'm fine, really. Carry on."

"If you're sure you're all right. Where was I? Oh yes. Regretting I couldn't stop to talk to the girls. I had to keep going. I looked back when I turned to cross the bridge but couldn't see you or them for the trees. I was hoping Manus was with you. Was he? Tell me, did he ever declare himself?"

"He did," Dixon lied.

"I knew it. It was obvious he had taken a fancy to you but was too caught up with politics and the horses to do anything about it. So why did you turn him down?"

"Religion," Dixon continued to lie. "He wouldn't marry me unless I turned, and I refused."

"Oh. Oh. So you never married?"

"No, I never felt the need." She hurried on in case Teresa questioned her in more detail. "I was lucky enough to meet Mrs Sinclair . . ."

She could tell the story of the last twenty-five years without deviating from the truth.

Dixon was beginning to feel queasy again and she wanted to be on her own to try to assimilate the enormity of what Teresa had revealed, but Teresa continued. "Wouldn't you love to know if Manus ever married and wouldn't you love to know how Charlotte and Victoria turned out? Just think, they're all probably married by now. I wonder who to. If only we could be flies on the wall just for a day."

Dixon fixed her face in a solemn mask and let the silence lengthen between them. There was no way she was going to share what she had deduced from Teresa's information with her.

"I'm afraid there is something I can tell you and it's not good news," she said.

Teresa's apprehension became visible at once.

"Little Victoria died less than a month after you left. Pneumonia. We cared for her around the clock. Everything that could have been done was done but it wasn't enough." To add verisimilitude she added, "Dr Finn wore himself out trying to save her. He was in a terrible state over it. We all were."

Teresa looked at Dixon as if she'd never seen her before. Tears welled in her eyes and followed the cracks down her weather-beaten face.

"Poor pretty little Victoria," she said softly. "The little darling. I loved that child. Poor sweet little girl." She shook her head in disbelief, then replaced her cup with what she thought was care but it clattered against the saucer. "And poor, poor Manus," she added softly as if talking to herself.

When Teresa came out of her first wave of crying, the receptionist was standing beside her and Dixon was gone.

"Excuse me, but Miss Dixon said I'm to show you around the hotel, as she has something important to do for the next half-hour, and then she'll join you in the dining room for lunch."

Over lunch, Teresa explained she had been lucky to find work as a live-in housekeeper to a kind family who had allowed her to keep her son with her, but in the end it meant that she had ended up with no home of her own.

"Like me," said Dixon.

"Except that you're not retired."

"No, that's true. And I'll never be homeless. Jim and Norma, the ones I told you about, think the world of me and treat me as one of the family, so I expect they'll take care of me until I fall off the perch." Dixon refilled Teresa's wineglass and with a feeling of satisfaction offered her a job working in the hotel. Now that she had found her friend again, she wanted to keep her close, basking in that remembered warmth of her personality.

"But what would I do? Wash pots?"

"Not on your life. No friend of mine washes pots."

"But I'm not trained in hotel work."

"I'll fit you in somewhere. It would be wonderful working together again. Remember the good times we had at the Park?"

"Ah, yes, I do, but the two little girls were with us then. We could never bring those days back, try as we might." Teresa's voice wobbled for a second until she checked herself. "You must be very high up if you can offer an unskilled person like me a job without having to consult anyone."

"I'm not just an ordinary member of staff," Dixon couldn't help boasting. "I have been head bookkeeper and assistant manager for years, and should have been manager, but in the end they lost courage and wouldn't give that position to a woman, even though I could do the job with one hand tied behind my back. Well, what do you think?"

"It's a tempting offer, and it's lovely of you to think of me, but I'm afraid I can't accept. I'm already committed to helping my daughter-in-law and little grandson until my son returns from the war, and after he comes back I'm going to move in to live with my Irish friend whose late husband left her comfortably off. She's quite a bit older than me and needs the help and company."

"Sounds as if she wants you to look after her in her old age." Dixon couldn't keep the bitterness out of her voice.

"Probably," Teresa agreed without rancour. "That seems to be my destiny in life. My father and now my friend. But I'm not complaining. It's wonderful not to be among strangers in my later years."

"All very convenient and cosy," said Dixon, deflated. "Never mind. It was just a thought. I didn't really expect you to be available."

"Perhaps you'll come to visit me at my son's house and meet my daughter-in-law and grandson."

"Perhaps I will," said Dixon, who had no intention of doing any such thing. Let you go off with your devoted family and your old friend and let you all have a lovely time and don't give a second thought to me who has no one except poor old Mrs Sinclair who isn't even a relation and who is at death's door, anyway, and isn't much use to me now. See if I care.

Dixon could feel herself cooling towards Teresa, who had achieved motherhood after all and who had brought Manus's name into the conversation when there was no need, just to show off how well she knew him. The temperature in the room was dropping as if in a southerly wind, and a familiar greyness was being painted over her bright image of two equal friends working together side by side for life.

"Did you ever regret leaving Ireland?" she asked, scrambling around for something civil to say.

"No, not with my yearning for a child and the way things were with my brother. And then being blessed with a baby at the last minute. I love it here. I think I have been very fortunate in my life."

"How lucky for you," said Dixon, jealousy clawing away at her insides. "Tell me." She leaned across the table in a confidential manner. "Tell me. There's one thing I always wanted to know, and you can tell me now, seeing the Park life is over for both of us and we won't be going back."

"Of course. Ask me anything."

"I can't believe I didn't think of it at the time, but as the years went by it seemed glaringly obvious. You can clarify it for me now. Did Miss East employ you with instructions to spy on me?" The idea had come to her only in the last few minutes, but now that she'd put it into words, she believed it to be true.

"Whatever gave you that idea?" Teresa picked up her glass and swallowed a large mouthful of wine. "She thought you could do with a hand after Victoria was born, that's all."

Dixon studied Teresa's face. Its heightened colour and downcast eyes convinced Dixon she was lying.

Half an hour later Dixon paid for a taxi for Teresa to be rid of her, and stood on the pavement waving her off with the intention of never seeing her again. She then went to her room and howled into her pillow for a long time, tearing at the pillowslip with her still perfect teeth.

74

Dublin
1943

Charlotte received a parcel from Ballybrian in the post. While she read the letter that had been inserted under the second layer of brown paper, she allowed Mary Anne to take out the tightly scrunched balls of paper that were packed around the object in a large cardboard box.

> *Dear Milady,*
> *My name is Robyn Parsons. You probably won't remember me, but I was a housemaid when you were a little girl at the Park and I saw a lot of things that upset me at the time but I was too green to do anything about them, like the time Nurse Dixon didn't know I was watching when she took your doll from you and punched and slapped you as if you were her size and not a little girl and when she saw me she dragged you inside and I heard your screams and I still cry about how I didn't try to help you, but at the time I didn't think I could because Dixon was in charge of you and kept you away from us servants. I pray every day for . . .*

Charlotte paused in her reading.

Mary Anne squealed with joy when she lifted out a further handful of paper balls to reveal what was under all the packing in the box.

Charlotte continued reading. The last paragraph of the letter said:

I found something hidden in the old nursery you might like to have returned to you, better late than never, now that you have a little girl of your own. I hope I have done the right thing. It's so hard to know what to do for the best.

Charlotte glanced up and screamed when she saw, tucked under the arm of her twenty-two-month-old daughter with her pretty face and dark soft curls, a yellow-haired porcelain doll wearing a sapphire-blue dress. The doll that had once belonged to her and had been confiscated by Dixon. The companion piece to Victoria's red-headed one, the one she had been holding on the day she disappeared.

Charlotte dropped the letter.

She couldn't breathe. She felt as if she would suffocate. Her ribcage heaved as she tried to force air into her lungs.

Mary Anne looked up and began to cry in alarm to see her mother's contorted face.

There was roaring in Charlotte's ears, and a sensation of pain in her chest. She was finally able to draw in a honking, rasping breath, the sound of which increased the volume of Mary Anne's wailing.

Five minutes later Queenie found Charlotte in a state of near collapse and told her she would run straight for the doctor and not to worry. Charlotte made feeble gestures with her arms, signalling Queenie to get the child out of the room.

"I'll take Miss Mary Anne to her aunt's for the morning," Queenie said and knew she had made the right decision when Charlotte nodded and tried to smile. "And I'll fetch Dr Grace on the way back. Don't panic. I'll be here again before you can say Jack Robinson."

Queenie put the sobbing child, still clutching the yellow-haired doll, sitting up in the pram she was now too big for and wheeled it with speed across five streets to Iseult's house, where she told Iseult that Charlotte had a throat infection and didn't want Mary Anne to catch anything. Three streets back she called to the Carmody house and rang the bell of the surgery at the side and, when there was no answer, banged on the knocker of the front door. Dr Grace answered and, as soon as she could make out what the breathless servant was saying, said she would come over straight away. On being questioned, Queenie said she had no idea what had brought on the attack or fit but it must be something drastic if ma'am was so out of sorts she couldn't attend to Mary Anne.

"Has this happened before?" Dr Grace asked, picking up her coat and medical bag and pulling her door closed behind them.

"No, not that I've ever seen."

"Is there someone with her?"

"No, there isn't."

Queenie wanted to run ahead, but had to wait for the doctor so she could guide her to Charlotte's rooms by the back entrance to avoid being spotted by Lady Blackshaw. While they hurried along the street Queenie tried to answer the doctor's questions as accurately as she could.

Hours after Dr Grace had sedated her, Charlotte tried to rouse herself but found it difficult to keep her eyes open. There was someone asleep in the chair across the room, she noticed, and the curtains were drawn, so it must be night. Where was she? What had happened? Why were her arms too heavy to lift?

She saw a child standing beside the bed. It was Victoria. Not the distressed one of her dreams who didn't leave until Charlotte had made a deal with her, but a happy one, holding a redheaded doll. Charlotte turned with joy to welcome her lost little sister in her white linen dress.

"Thank goodness you're alive," Charlotte whispered so as not to wake the person in the chair. "I knew you'd come back one day to see me."

Smiling and confident, the child held out her free arm.

"Come closer, my little darling, so I can take your hand," Charlotte said in a coaxing voice.

Victoria moved forward one step, hesitated, then started to cry.

"Don't cry, my pretty pet," Charlotte pleaded, feeling a terrible anxiety overwhelming her. "Come to me and I'll kiss you better." She tried to move so that she could rise from the bed to comfort the child, but her head wouldn't lift from the pillow and her legs remained leaden. Her arms ached with the desire to enclose the figure, hold her close and keep her safe.

"I have a little girl just like you, with curly hair and a pretty face. You'll be able to meet her in the morning when she wakes."

"Is there anything the matter, ma'am?" asked the figure in the chair.

Charlotte's eyes snapped wide open at the sound of Queenie's voice, and Victoria vanished.

"What did you do that for?" Charlotte wailed. "You frightened her away. Come back, Victoria, ignore Queenie! I have so much I want to say to you." Her voice rose to a shrill pitch. "Come back and I'll explain everything."

Queenie rushed over to her side. "Take some more of this, ma'am," she coaxed, lifting up Charlotte's head and pouring liquid into her mouth. "Dr Grace said it will calm you down."

"Get back – get away," Charlotte spluttered, trying to spit out the potion, but ending up swallowing most of it. She turned her head away from the servant to avoid being given a further dose and said with as much force as she could summon, "I don't want to be calm. I want to talk to Victoria. You go away and she might come back. Go on, leave immediately and don't dare return unless I ring for you. Do as you're told. Go!"

Queenie ran from the room and kept running until she reached the Carmody house for the second time that day and told the sleepy Dr Grace to come quickly as Charlotte had definitely lost her mind this time.

Charlotte looked at the space vacated by Victoria and pleaded aloud for the child to return but was met with emptiness and silence. The energy she had felt while talking to Victoria was dissipating. Her body was becoming heavier. That damned medicine Queenie forced her to drink was sending her to sleep. She called out to Miss East for help, but there was no answering voice.

A familiar person leaned over her and she felt the sting of a needle being injected into her arm.

The next time Charlotte woke she stayed still and didn't speak so that Queenie, keeping vigil, wouldn't rush over and pour that opiate down her throat.

There was a strange sensation in her head. It was as if her mind was a hundred-roomed mansion that was falling apart, each wall as it crumbled revealing its individual secrets to all the other rooms until the house was a single pile of rubble with all its furnishings and artefacts exposed.

She was eight years old again, back at Tyringham Park. Her mother was wheeling the baby carriage towards the stables. Charlotte, as was her habit on the daily walks with Nurse Dixon, began to follow.

"Not you," Lady Blackshaw snapped at her. "I don't remember including you in the invitation. Nurse Dixon, take her off."

"Of course, ma'am." Dixon reached out for Charlotte's hand. "Come on, Charlotte, dear. We'll go back to the nursery and do something nice."

As soon as Edwina was halfway down the hill and too far away to hear, Dixon turned to Charlotte and said: "Go and make yourself scarce, Uglyface. I've enough on my plate without having to look after a nuisance like you. Why don't you go off and build one of those bridges you're so fond of? And straighten up them shoulders!"

Charlotte slumped towards the walled garden, but doubled back when the two adults were out of sight, and made her way towards the stables.

By the time she arrived and pushed open one of the double doors, the baby carriage was placed against the wall in the shade and the courtyard was empty. As she sidled along the wall she noted the sleeping Victoria and felt a sting of hatred for the sister she loved, before heading towards the voices she could hear coming from Manus's office.

She put her ear against the door but wasn't able to make out what was being said. The voices became softer and softer until the talking stopped altogether. The following silence was punctuated by odd sounds. She risked peering in the small side window and couldn't believe what she saw.

Her mother and Manus weren't wearing all their clothes and her mother's hair was hanging loose and the two of them were lying on a horse blanket on the floor doing funny things to one another.

Charlotte watched for a few minutes with the same fascination she had experienced when she came upon Sid drowning a litter of kittens in the freshwater barrel.

Charlotte snatched the sleeping Victoria and her doll out of the baby carriage and passed under the arch through the open door which she had left ajar. She walked around the stables, following the narrow earthen path that hugged the stable walls, and headed to the river. The muddy verge was slippery from all the rain. She skidded. The jolting movement she'd made to prevent herself from falling woke the child, who was immediately alert, gazing around her to take in the unfamiliar surroundings.

As soon as they turned the corner onto the river bank and Victoria saw the rushing water, she wriggled to show she wanted to be placed on the ground. Charlotte put her down and took her hand.

Both sisters were conscious of the novelty of the two of them on an adventure without any adult supervising them. A forbidden adventure. Walking alongside the river, which had a deep Dark Waterhole and was always out of bounds.

Victoria was almost shy of her big sister, holding her hand and smiling up at her.

"Mummy's pet," Charlotte said sadly, not returning the smile.

Victoria, wearing a white dress and carrying her doll, walked confidently. She was advanced for her age, as Nurse Dixon never tired of pointing out, steady on her feet at ten months, whereas Charlotte, the dummy, hadn't taken her first steps until she was sixteen months old.

They continued on a little way to where a section of the bank had eroded, taking half the crumbling path with it. Victoria tripped on a dislodged lump of rubble and would have fallen into the water if Charlotte hadn't held her tightly. The doll flew from Victoria's hand and landed on the bank, its hair trailing in the flooded river.

"Stay back," Charlotte shouted as they bent at the same time to retrieve it. "I'll get it for you."

Victoria ignored her and, snapping up the sopping doll with a squawk of relief, clutched it to the bodice of her white dress.

"Now look what you've done, getting muck all over your front. Give the doll to me so I can wash it so we don't get into trouble."

"No," said Victoria. Mud was now dribbling all the way down her skirt.

"Did you hear what I said? Give me the doll."

"No."

"Give it to me."

"No."

"I'll give you one more chance. Give it to me."

Victoria looked bewildered and clutched the doll more tightly to her side. "No, no, no," she said, shaking her head for emphasis.

"Give it to me or you'll cop it. Teresa Kelly can't help you now. She's gone for good. Vanished."

Victoria stepped back. Charlotte leaned forward, grabbed the doll by the hair and wrenched it out of Victoria's arm.

Victoria toppled backwards inches from the water. Charlotte pulled her to her feet. Victoria wailed and tugged at Charlotte's skirt.

"Stop that noise." Charlotte held the doll above her head and tried to pull her skirt free.

Victoria held on tighter and wailed louder.

"Shut up or they'll hear you."

Victoria's howl rose to a full-blooded screech.

Mummy's pretty little favourite didn't look so pretty now with all that mucus running down her screwed-up face.

Charlotte lowered the doll. Victoria let go of the skirt and reached up to claim it. Charlotte held it within an inch of Victoria's desperate, fluttering fingers.

How easy it would be to give it to her and watch her clasp it close, cease her caterwauling, and look with pleasure again at her older sister, who could take her hand and lead her back to the courtyard, the dangerous adventure safely over. Easy, but not good for her, getting her own way just because she made a lot of noise.

With the dangling doll remaining just out of reach, Victoria's frustrated screams rose to an even higher pitch and her contortions became so extreme she looked as if she was about to turn herself inside out.

Her face was so devilish it didn't look like Victoria's. Her voice was so harsh and piercing it didn't sound like a child's.

"I said shut up. Don't you understand plain English? Do you want to be caught near the river and get beaten? Shut up! Shut up!"

Charlotte gave Victoria a straight-armed shove that shot her small frame, arms flailing, backwards into the river.

The white dress ballooned out around the child before the swirling water turned her slowly and propelled her away from the bank into the swift current where the water was deepest. Shock registered on her face. She re-emerged once downstream, her eyes and mouth wide open, her arms thrashing. Seconds later she disappeared from view, and Charlotte followed the course of the river with such unblinking concentration that her eyes flicked in and out of focus.

It would have been so easy to give back the doll.

But you can't give in to children like that. It turns them into spoilt brats, Nurse Dixon's voice scorched through her mind.

But Victoria is not a spoilt brat, Charlotte shuddered to realise, holding the doll out to her little sister now, too late. Offering it to the empty space where the pretty darling had stood a second earlier.

Charlotte felt a taste of vomit in her mouth. Her boiling temper had cooled in an instant as if it had been quenched by an upturned barrel of icy water.

"Come back, Victoria! Come back!" she called, with the doll dangling uselessly from her proffered hand. "I didn't mean it!" Her leg muscles had turned soft but she forced them to move, all the while repeating, "Come back, Victoria! Come back! Please, Victoria, come back! I don't mind if you're the favourite. You're my favourite too. You can have the doll. Look, I'm giving it to you!" She ran downstream past the bridge, hoping to see Victoria's dress snagged on the branch of an overhanging tree, and Victoria holding out her arms and crying out to her. What wouldn't she give to be able to reach out and unhook the dress and pull her to safety? What wouldn't she give to have her beside her on the bank again?

She would give up her jealousy and her misery and promise to love her mother and Nurse Dixon and even give up riding Mandrake and never go back to the stables or see Manus again if only Victoria wasn't drowned. She would join in admiring her pretty face and wouldn't be relieved if Nurse Dixon was being cruel to her rather than to herself.

Perhaps below the weir where she'd often watched a ball or a tin can dance on the churning water, trying to guess how long it would stay there before being swept along, she would find Victoria wedged at the bottom of the fall, held by opposing forces.

With the large volume of water passing over the weir there was no fall of water. Only a bulge and then a straight run.

To gain height she stood on the bridge and looked as far downstream as possible. All she saw was brown water and flickers of white that gave her hope for the second before she realised they weren't Victoria's dress but froth created by the tumult of the flood. Upstream was the deep Dark Waterhole that swallowed up young children, according to Nurse Dixon. Perhaps Victoria was lying on the bottom of it, held down by strange creatures always on the lookout for naughty children who didn't do what their nannies told them.

Consumed by a terror of being discovered by her mother and Manus, who might by now have realised that Victoria was missing, she staggered along the path by the river, bent over so she would be hidden by the vegetation, until she was out of sight of any of the estate buildings, before circling back to the rear of the Park. Knowing Nurse Dixon was in the nursery, she went only as far as the ground floor where she stuffed the doll under the stairs – she would retrieve it later and hide it in a better place – and then went outside again where her energy deserted her and she fell beside a channel that drained water from the house where for weeks she had been building a bridge. While her mind filled with a silent, long drawn-out scream she rearranged the stones she had collected for her construction and it was there some time later Nurse Dixon had found her sitting in mud to tell her Victoria was missing and everyone was needed for the search party, including her, though God knew why, seeing she was so useless.

75

Iseult kept Mary Anne with her until Charlotte had recovered sufficiently to take her back. Mary Anne had been happy enough during the day, but cried for her mother at night.

"Please don't tell Lochlann about this little episode," Charlotte begged her sister-in-law. "It will only worry him and besides it was nothing. I think I've been overdoing things and not getting enough sleep. I'm fully recovered now."

Dr Grace, visiting at the time, murmured sympathetically as if she believed her, but secretly worried about the state of Charlotte's nerves and wondered if she suffered from a deep-seated condition that could erupt at any time. Iseult feared that Charlotte had inherited a family madness that might be passed on to the child. One had only to remember that she had locked herself away for three years and eaten herself into the size of a barn to realise she might be a bit unbalanced. Neither woman confided her fears to the other, but both determined to keep a closer eye on the unfortunate woman whom they had grown to love and admire.

During the next few weeks both noticed that Charlotte didn't recover her confidence and joy in the handling of Mary Anne. She was sad and tentative and prone to lapses of concentration, sinking into deep thought at intervals, oblivious of her surroundings.

Mary Anne became clingy, registering unease if Charlotte moved even a short distance away from her side.

Charlotte wrote to Colonel Turncastle to say she had given a lot of thought to what he had said, especially the part about securing the future for all children, and was applying to join the SOE as soon as possible.

76

Sydney
1943

It was half past five in the morning and the heat was already unbearable.

"Elizabeth."

The whispered name woke Dixon from a deep sleep. The room was in darkness.

She was slow to react, having lain awake for hours the previous night, and many nights before that, trying to make sense of the explosive information Teresa had unwittingly given her. She was consumed with planning who to write to first, what to say or hint at, and how best she might revenge herself on those at Tyringham Park who had wronged her, especially the little tell-tale, Charlotte.

"Elizabeth." A little louder this time, accompanied by tapping.

Lady Blackshaw would be first – that was only fair – she had already written a letter to her at Tyringham Park and would post it later in the day. Charlotte, Miss East, Manus and Dr Finn would have to wait until she heard back from Her Ladyship.

"*Elizabeth!*" said for the third time, loudly and impatiently, finally drew Dixon from her bed.

It was Jim Rossiter's voice. Mrs Sinclair must have died and he had come around to tell her and to bring her back to the house to include her in the funeral rituals. Thoughtful as ever.

She pulled her dressing gown around her, clutching it at her neck with one hand while she opened the door with the other. Her face was already fixed in an expression of sympathy – Jim was exceptionally fond of his mother-in-law, and she of him.

"Is it Mrs Sinclair?"

Jim pushed past her, flicked on the light switch and closed the door behind him.

"No. It's not her. She's still hanging on. It's you. What I want to know is what have you done with the bloody money?"

Afterwards, Dixon couldn't remember in what order Jim had made his accusations, but "robbing me blind for years" was the phrase he kept repeating.

"Pack your bags. You'll never see this place or Norma or her mother again. I'm making sure of that."

Dixon felt as if she wasn't standing in the middle of her bedroom, bare feet firm on the carpet, but falling backwards out of an open window, her fingers losing their grip on the slippery frames while a freezing wind snapped at the shroud-like curtains. She experienced a flashback to the time Miss East and Dr Finn came to the nursery together and she knew by the look on their faces that her time was up.

Jim upturned her mattress and emptied the contents of her wardrobe on to the floor. He accompanied her to the bathroom and waited outside while she washed and dressed. At one point while he was questioning her he came near and she put up an arm to defend herself from an expected blow, but he said he had never hit a woman in his life and wasn't about to start now. He held her shoulders, looked into her face and said in a reasonable voice that it would save him a lot of trouble if she would tell him where the money was. The physical contact comforted her and she didn't pull away. With hands like those steadying her she would never have to fear falling backwards through an open window.

After everything the family, especially Mrs Sinclair, had done for her, Jim continued, telling him where the money was hidden was the least she could do. She must have had an aberration. It could happen to anyone handling all that cash, being tempted, giving in during a weak moment, afraid to own up, not knowing how to undo it. He understood. It wasn't too late to make it right.

An image of Charlotte Blackshaw keeping a stubborn silence came to mind. She would do the same. He couldn't trip her up if she didn't say anything. Look at what Charlotte had got away with.

He waited, but she held her nerve, looking downwards so she wouldn't be influenced by his expectant expression.

"We all thought the world of you, Elizabeth," he said, dropping his arms. "Just shows you how wrong you can be. I'll find the money, believe me, even if it means lifting up floorboards and tearing the place apart, and putting the hard word on every bank manager in Sydney."

Apologising for having to check her handbag, he took it to examine the contents and found amongst her personal things a wad of high-denomination notes fitted into an empty cigarette packet. The money was for her Beth Hall account. She had intended to deposit it later on in the day after she'd done the hotel banking, but she couldn't very well tell him that.

"The mother of your fiancé?" he asked, reading Lady Blackshaw's address on the unstamped envelope of the letter she had written. "I would offer to post it for you, but I have a better idea. You'll hear about it in a minute."

He replaced everything in her handbag, including the money. "You'll need that where you're going to tide you over," he said. "It's the big stuff I'm after, not this piddling amount. I can't have you ending up on the streets. It's not that I don't appreciate what you did for the Waratah, but you have to admit you were well paid." His voice sounded more sad than angry. "There was no need for you to put your sticky fingers in the till."

From the top of her wardrobe he retrieved her suitcase, opened it, and felt around the linings and pockets where he found the necklace, rings and bracelet she had stolen from Lady Blackshaw. "Mrs Sinclair mentioned these. From your fiancé, she said."

Dixon made a grab for them.

"I'll keep them," he said, putting them in his pocket as he side-stepped her. "Compensation. Go on. Pack. I'm not taking my eyes off you until we leave."

It was Peter Molloy, the new manager, who had noticed something wrong, Jim said. "Get a professional to look over the books," Peter had advised after he'd been there for six months. "Something isn't adding up."

The young pup had never liked her. He must have thought all his Christmases had come at once when the auditor found deficits going back twenty years.

The mistake she'd made was increasing her percentage after Peter, a hotelier with little experience, had been appointed manager over her when she knew the position was rightly hers. Passed over because she was a woman and a spinster. She knew there was no malice in what Jim did – he often acknowledged how she and Mrs Sinclair had done wonders wooing customers and how she had held on to them after her patron had left. He thought being manager, even of a respectable establishment like the Waratah, was no job for a woman, and he would have considered it the gentlemanly thing to do to protect her with a male superior.

He was going to deport her at ten o'clock precisely. It was either that or inform the police, and he'd made the executive decision to send her back to England, from where she could cross over the Irish Sea and deliver her letter to Lady Blackshaw by hand and save on the postage. He would personally escort her to her cabin and wait at the gangplank until it was raised and the ship pulled away to make sure she didn't disembark at the last minute.

"You'll have the status of a stowaway," he said, "except the captain knows you're there. This no-speaking lark will come in handy for the trip."

He couldn't bring himself to involve Norma while the investigation was going on, he continued, and didn't look forward to telling her before the next first Sunday of the month to explain Dixon's absence. As for Mrs Sinclair, she would go to her grave without knowing her protégé had disgraced herself.

Jim didn't allow Dixon to enter her office, speak to the night porter, or leave any written notes or phone messages before she left the hotel.

A young sailor was expecting them at the quay and led them to a cabin the size of a cupboard with '*Quarantine*' fixed to the door.

"I gave your name as 'Jane Brown', not that anyone will be talking to you. Remember to stay out of everyone's way – I don't want my old mate cursing the day he did me a favour. You won't be seeing him. He has more important things on his mind than social chitchat, like trying not to be sunk by a German U-boat, for instance." He placed her case on the bunk. "You're a cold fish, aren't you? Did we ever know you?"

He put his hand in his pocket, retrieved her pieces of jewellery and, taking Dixon's hand, folded her fingers over them. "Keep them," he said. "I can't dishonour the memory of your fiancé who wasn't as lucky as I was coming home from the Great War in one piece. Just make sure you never show your face around here again. If you do I'll personally break your bloody neck."

With that, he left.

77

Dublin
1943

Edwina placed the music box on the low table beside her chair and hoped that Charlotte would choose to pay a duty call during the day. With things so strained between them she couldn't make a specific request to see her.

Around midday she heard the familiar footsteps and her heart quickened. Charlotte came in with her usual sour face, pulled along by Mary Anne, who was all set to explore the familiar things in the room. Her favourite item was the piano which Charlotte would not allow her to bang on, holding down the lid and saying, "Don't annoy your grandmother" – a phrase she used constantly. Edwina always wanted to say 'Leave her. I like to see her enjoying herself,' but the words refused to form in her throat when she imagined the disbelieving scorn on Charlotte's face if she said them.

During a visit three days earlier, while Charlotte was distracted reading the paper, Mary Anne, all trust and affection, had climbed on to Edwina's lap and begun to play with her necklace. Edwina found herself affected by the touch of the little fingers as they lifted the brightly coloured beads in turn. When Charlotte looked up and saw the interaction she gave a cry of dismay and ran to scoop up the child, saying, "Don't annoy your grandmother," before carrying her to the far side of the room.

Edwina, feeling hurt, said, "My arms still function, you know. I wouldn't let her fall," wanting to add, 'Let her stay. She's no trouble. I like having her here,' but was once again unable to say the words.

Edwina admired Mary Anne's slender limbs, pretty face and dark, soft curls – no trace of Waldron or Charlotte there – but most of all she admired her spirit: she was not afraid of an old woman, ugly and immobile.

The maid had been sent out to buy something that would definitely appeal to a child approaching two years of age. Anything with moving parts that made a noise was irresistible, the shopkeeper had assured her. If this worked, Edwina would buy more and would even engage a toymaker to design novelty items that would tempt Mary Anne to visit more often and stay longer. A magnificent rocking horse had already been commissioned from a master carver to be ready for Christmas, and even though lap dogs were anathema to her, Edwina had ordered a Yorkshire terrier puppy as the ultimate enticement. In a year's time she would buy a few acres outside Dublin and keep some ponies there so that Mary Anne could begin her training to ride better than a man, thereby compensating Edwina for not quite reaching that standard before her accident. Manus, for old time's sake, could be inveigled up to oversee the initiation. How could he turn down a request from her after all they had shared in the past? To top all that, she would invite over Sir Dirk Armstrong, by now the most famous and most expensive artist in the British Isles, to paint Mary Anne's portrait. Her letter to him would not be hectoring like Waldron's had been, inviting rebuttal, but persuasive, recalling past intimacies that he was now too old to be threatened by, and she wouldn't even hint at the possibility of a discount.

Edwina reached down to open the lid of the music box. Mary Anne heard the tinkling of 'Greensleeves' and followed the sound to the table beside her grandmother. The child stood staring at the twirling figure in a white tutu, reflected in mirrors angled in a semi-circle around it. When the music and figure slowed and finally halted, Mary Anne pointed at the box and looked up at Edwina.

"How interested she is," said Edwina. "What advanced concentration she has!"

Charlotte hovered suspiciously. Edwina lifted up the box, rewound it, placed it back on the table, and opened the lid again to release the twirling figure. Mary Anne, laughing and jigging, could not restrain her excitement.

"I've never seen that before," said Charlotte. "Where did it come from?"

"I bought it," said Edwina.

"You *bought* it?" Charlotte lifted up the box and examined it, noting the price written on the base.

Mary Anne made gestures signalling she wanted to hear the music again. Charlotte put the box back on the table and sat down to watch the interaction. For five minutes Edwina continued to wind up the box, and Mary Anne didn't tire of it. At one stage she put her finger gently on the figure of the ballerina, pulled back at the feel of it, and then repeated the move. Charlotte noted the pleasure on her mother's face. She picked up Mary Anne, saying, "I'll take her down to the garden before she gets bored and restless," and left.

That night Verity reiterated Charlotte's faults, the main ones being her over-familiarity with servants, spending too much time with her sister-in-law drooling over babies, and worst of all, nursing – she couldn't bring herself to use the more descriptive term – a practice abhorred by Queen Victoria who forbade her daughters-in-law to do it, and if the dear Queen didn't know what was right and proper, who did?

"I blame that one-armed, Communist, French-speaking artist Delaney for the way she turned out. If she'd had a refined female tutor instead of that mad Irishman, she wouldn't have ended up spurning her class and its military traditions," she concluded.

Usually Edwina countered with, "I blame Waldron. He should have forced her to go to that school and there wouldn't have been any need for any kind of a tutor," but she had lost the heart for this conversation in its entirety and remained silent. She even had an urge to speak up in Charlotte's defence, and not just to annoy Verity.

For Edwina had fallen in love with her granddaughter. She couldn't understand how it had happened, and with things the way they were between herself and Charlotte, couldn't admit to it. One thing she did know was she would have to disarm the mother to get access to the daughter. How she would go about it would require a lot of clever planning and she didn't want Verity clacking away in the background while she was trying to think.

78

Dublin
1943

Before travelling to County Cork, Elizabeth Dixon opened two accounts in two different names in two separate banks in Dublin and signed the forms to have both her accounts in Sydney transferred, marvelling at herself while she was doing it that she was able to do it. How far she had come! Influential and all as Jim Rossiter was, as his father had been before him, courted by all the bank managers in Sydney vying for his business, Dixon was convinced he wouldn't find her money.

But he did.

Who would connect Elizabeth Dixon and her pin-money account in one bank with Beth Hall and her sizeable amount in another, when no one from the Waratah Hotel knew she was a customer at the second bank, and no one from the second bank knew her real name?

He did.

When she returned to the banks to see if her money had come through, the teller in each establishment had looked at her oddly and told her that her account in Sydney had been frozen.

"Frozen?"

Both of them?

If she had any enquiries about the matter, she could make an appointment to see the manager, said both tellers.

Dixon said that wouldn't be necessary. She would sort it out herself.

It wasn't fair. All her legitimate savings as well as her stolen hoard had been hunted down by Jim Rossiter, leaving her penniless. There would be no sorting out. Where was her hope now of buying a house of her own and having enough money to support herself into her old age? Or, if the worst came to the worst, finding a respectable position?

Who would want her at her age and who would employ her when she had no way of producing a recent reference?

79

Charlotte laid out what she considered to be her forty-two best oil paintings – completed before her marriage – ready for David Slane to assess. He had undertaken to oversee the framing and hanging of her first solo show, booked to take place in three months' time. Cormac Delaney promised to travel from Paris to attend the opening night.

On the last occasion David Slane had contacted her, he was so excited he had to slow down and repeat himself before Charlotte could make sense of what he was trying to say. Sir Dirk Armstrong, the most famous artist in the United Kingdom, would be in Ireland at the time and, although he had at first declined to open the show, citing an overcrowded schedule, had changed his mind when he heard the artist's name was Blackshaw.

To prevent a repetition of Edwina's earlier unwelcome antagonism, David suggested that Lady Blackshaw should not be told about the show until an hour before the opening.

Later on the same day, Charlotte drew up her last will and testament with Mr Dunwoody, the family solicitor, in which she stated that her mother would never have any hand, act or part in Mary Anne's rearing. The outward fondness the old woman was showing the child didn't fool her and the amount of money she was spending to win the child's favour was beginning to appear sinister and cynical.

Lochlann was to be her main beneficiary. If he pre-deceased her, then his sister Iseult would become Mary Anne's legal guardian, and a generous slice of Charlotte's fortune would revert to her, the rest being held in trust for Mary Anne until she came of age. Mary Anne's name was not to be changed legally from 'Carmody' to 'Blackshaw'. A bequest of five thousand pounds each was to be left to Miss East (now Lily Cooper), Manus, Cormac and Queenie.

Because she made a point of not looking directly at Waldron, Edwina hadn't noticed that his skin was turning yellow. Verity did, and expressed concern as she took her place between the two of them at the dinner table. Edwina forced herself to raise her eyes. When had the yellow managed to displace the purplish-red tones that had predominated when she last looked at his face?

He's showing his age at last, Edwina thought. The military bearing and slim figure are gone, replaced by a stoop and a paunch. His voice lacks authority. And what does it signify that his hands are restless, constantly scratching at himself?

Charlotte was five minutes late taking her place. "Sorry," she said. "Mary Anne took a little longer than usual to settle tonight." She didn't say it was because the child kept trying to return to her grand-mother's room to play with the new toy monkey and his clashing cymbals.

"This letter came for you in the afternoon post, Charlotte," said Aunt Verity. "It's postmarked 'Ballybrian' and it's quite bulky. I don't recognise the handwriting."

"Thank you. I'll open it later," said Charlotte, whose pulse quickened, thinking that Miss East or Manus must have something so important to tell her that one of them had decided to write to her at last.

While the rack of lamb was being served Charlotte slit open the envelope with a knife and, under the table, flicked to the second page to reveal the signature, *"(Nurse) Elizabeth Dixon"*, written in a clear, well-formed hand.

Both sisters registered the look of dismay on her face as she pushed back her chair and, without giving a word of explanation, ran from the room.

"Is the doctor dead?" asked Waldron, looking up in time to see an envelope flutter to the ground and his daughter, clutching sheets of paper, making a dramatic exit.

"It could be anything or nothing. Charlotte makes a habit of running from rooms," said Edwina, who had seen her do it twice.

Charlotte waited until Mary Anne was asleep before moving to the next room to read the letter so that the child wouldn't be contaminated by anything that had any connection to Nurse Dixon. Aunt Verity dropped by to ask if everything was all right and left aggrieved when she didn't get any information out of Charlotte.

If only Lochlann were with me now, giving me courage, Charlotte thought as she positioned herself beside a lamp and forced herself to read:

Ballybrian
23 July1943

Dear Charlotte, or should I now call you Mrs Carmody?
   I hope this letter finds you as well as it leaves me. There is something important I want to do before it is too late. The last time I saw you I put a curse on you and now I want to take it away. I have been staying in Ballybrian waiting for a sign. I have not visited the Park yet, but I met some of the maids who told me what happened to your mother and Mandrake, and more recently, your brother. That shows how powerful the curse is and that is why I am worried that something terrible will happen to you. I have just returned from Australia after many years to hear that you were there as well for a time. What a pity we didn't meet then. At least we can make up for it now.
   Lily East or Mrs Sid Cooper whose husband died recently, supposedly of natural causes, doesn't know I'm here. I want to keep it as a surprise, so I'm relying on you not to say anything. She has been told she has to vacate the cottage before the New Year even though she has nowhere to go. The maids say she is in a state about it.
   Curses are hard to control, so I have to be sure to do it right. My worry is that yours might transfer to your daughter.

Unfortunately I wasn't in time to help Dr Finn who died a slow and painful death five years ago – all his pills and potions didn't help him. I would have liked to have saved him from that cruel end.

You and I will have to meet in the old nursery. I've been given the sign. Your relatives will be away next week, which means we can go about our business without anybody noticing. There is still no one living in the gate lodge as it wasn't rebuilt after it was burnt down, so we'll be able to come and go as we please.

I was sorry later that I had cursed you all, but at the time I didn't know what else to do when Dr Finn and Lily East came to take you away from me when I wanted to keep you. They had no right. Everything I did as your nanny I did for your own good. I'm sure you can see that, now that you have a child of your own.

I expect to see you in the nursery at 3 p.m. on the Tuesday of next week. I have checked that the train is due in at noon, and that there are plenty of jarveys there to meet it. I don't know what the war restrictions are like in Dublin, but there is no petrol available here so all vehicles have been forced off the road. The noon train should allow you plenty of time, unless of course you travel down the previous day to make doubly sure you don't miss our meeting. I worked as a businesswoman while I was abroad and am used to organising things. It will be a great relief to me to distance you from danger. It has played on my mind all these years.

If you don't turn up, I will travel to the address on this envelope and stay there until I see you.

Yours sincerely,

(Nurse) Elizabeth Dixon

What kind of a fool does she take me for? was Charlotte's initial response to what she read. Does she think I am still eight years old and credulous? If she really believes in the power of her curse why doesn't she withdraw it straight away, rather than wait to set up a dramatic charade at the Park? Does that final sentence about calling to the townhouse contain a threat?

I'll have to travel to the Park to see her. I can't risk having her anywhere near Mary Anne, putting her evil eye on her.

She must have fallen on hard times. That's why she wants me to travel down. All that mumbo-jumbo about a curse is a trick to make sure I turn up. One thing I can guarantee – she doesn't intend to do me a good turn. She wants something. Why else would she contact me? Even she wouldn't have the brass neck to be asking for a position at the Park, so it must be money. I can't think what else it would be. I'll leave Mary Anne with Iseult and go down and face her on my own. That would be the best thing to do. I'm not afraid of her any more. What harm can she do to me at my age?

80

Ballybrian
1943

Elizabeth Dixon dressed for the performance of her life. Her well-cut costume, silk stockings, handmade shoes, opal hatpin, kid gloves and crocodile handbag all proclaimed to the world her success and refined taste. Even with Jim Rossiter looming over her while she packed a single case, she had chosen well. It was a pity she couldn't wear her jewellery. Now that she was back in Ballybrian, she feared it might be recognised.

Turning the compact mirror to reflect light on her face, she had to admit she was still a fine-looking woman. The Australian sun's damage to her skin was slight because she had stayed indoors most of the time. The two months enforced rest at sea had rejuvenated her, though it had taken until the final fortnight for her strength to return, such had been the shock to her system of being found out and deported.

She applied red lipstick – the final touch. She didn't know what would thrill her more – the shock Lily East and Charlotte must get when they saw the change success and education had made to her bearing, or their reaction to the fact that she and she alone had solved the longstanding mystery of Victoria's disappearance, a solution so unexpected that apparently no one, including herself, had thought of it during all those years of conjecture. Or, after all that, the satisfaction she would experience at extracting a pile of money out of that rich Charlotte to replace what Jim had stolen from her.

She had been staying under her alias, Beth Hall, in a room in a guest house in Ballybrian, visited by a trio from the Park staff who had been invited in by the young proprietor, Mrs O'Mahoney, to meet her. Fascinated by Dixon's stories of the old days, they accepted her as one of their own and gave her uncensored versions of all the happenings since then, the most affecting being Lady Blackshaw's accident, the most fortuitous, the death of Mandrake and the most hurtful, Manus's marriage to a local girl. Sid's death didn't mean anything to her. She'd had little to do with him when she was at the Park and the only memory she had of him was that he never liked her. Who would that little tyrant Lily East get to fight her battles for her now that Dr Finn and Sid were both gone?

Dixon swore the Park employees to secrecy about her presence there, not divulging her real name for added security, stressing how much she looked forward to surprising her former colleagues.

She couldn't help but notice that the calibre of servant had altered since her time. The new breed seemed to be either physically deformed or mentally deficient, or both. In her day the Big Houses were filled with bright talented people with unrealised potential, who could have done better things if they hadn't been held back by history and lack of education, through no fault of their own. Mrs O'Mahoney from the boarding house explained to Dixon that since the Great War young people would no longer accept the low wages, long hours and isolation of the estates, preferring factory work in the city. Besides, the power and influence of the Big Houses had declined along with their numbers. The way of life the landlords had imposed on Ireland for centuries was fast dying out.

She thought she might faint when she first saw Manus in the village. Her belief that he was hers by right was as strong now as it had been during those eight years of waiting for him to declare himself. Standing at her window, hidden behind lace curtains, she stared and stared, willing him to cross the street so she could have a good look at him, but he stayed on the other side. He was walking home after Sunday Mass when she spotted him. There was a female imposter walking beside him and four children accompanying them. Two boys, two girls. How perfect. The eldest, a boy of about twenty, looked the dead spit of how she remembered Manus looking when she first met him.

The unfairness of it. Those four children should have been hers.

The younger daughter said something and Manus and his wife laughed. The wife had no dress sense and was on the plump side, the typical shape of someone who had let herself go. After Manus met Dixon again, would he regret turning her down when he saw how well she had preserved her looks and kept her figure?

She wondered what description Jim had given the bank to ferret out her Beth Hall identity. 'Outstanding-looking woman, middle-aged but looking thirty, fashionably dressed, impressive manner, air of authority'? Yes, something along those lines.

She straightened the seams of her stockings, pulled the veil down over her face and smoothed on her gloves. It was one o'clock. Making her way down the main street of the village, and walking the half mile to the Park gates, past the shell of the lodge, and then along the beech-lined avenue, was an experience she wanted to savour, every second of it. As she passed by she expected to dazzle the locals with her finery. It was the first time she had put herself on display since her arrival. Would they be able to judge, simply by looking at her, that she would have been wasted if she'd stayed in this backwater? And when they heard her speak, if they dared speak to her, would they be surprised to find she could now outshine Lily East in the use of long words and correct grammar, though she stopped short of the la-di-da accent Lily affected as it tended to put people off?

It gave her pleasure to hear from the current servants that Miss East had given up her position of head housekeeper to become ordinary Mrs Sid Cooper, living in Sid's small cottage (from which she was soon to be evicted), rearing his daughter Catherine until the young girl was old enough to leave for Dublin to become a nurse, all the time doing good works, making ends meet and leading an uneventful life.

That last bit was about to change.

The stables came up on Dixon's left. The double doors were open, but there was no sign of Manus, which suited her as she didn't want to see him face to face until the following day. Best get Lily East and Charlotte out of the way first so she could give Manus her full and undivided attention when the time came.

She stared at the spot where Lady Blackshaw had left the baby carriage, and at the corner where Teresa had glimpsed the two little girls for the last time, not understanding the significance of what she'd seen. Dixon wouldn't be the only one looking at those areas with heightened interest when her story was told.

As the huge stone house came into view, snippets of the optimistic, romantic notions she held when she first arrived here at the age of eighteen and gazed up at it as if it were a magic castle, made her cringe at the naïvety of her misconceptions, almost as naïve as the belief when she was in the orphanage that one day her mother, whoever she was, would call by to reclaim her.

The vicar of her Huddersfield parish in England had told her she would be nanny to a very grand family on a very grand estate. Her mind had filled with images of beautiful women with tall hair in exquisite clothes and men in embroidered coats with buckles on their shoes – she had seen pictures of such people in the few books of fairy tales at the orphanage. What a disappointment the life at Tyringham Park had been. Lady Blackshaw never dressed for dinner when Lord Waldron was abroad, which was most of the time, staying in her male riding clothes all day and evening. No parties, no balls, no visitors, no occasions. The last hunt that Lord Waldron had hosted on his way back from India before he joined the War Office in London was so thrilling she knew what she was missing. After seeing all those stylish people dressed for the dinner and the dance, she had become more dissatisfied than usual, sitting in the dark, wearing flat, mannish, lace-up shoes, dressed in her uniform that she wore seven days a week, entertaining sour thoughts in a cold nursery with a whining child for company.

At the back of the house she passed the door that led to the nursery wing and it took all her strength of purpose not to open it and go straight up the three flights of stairs to confront Charlotte who would already be there waiting, expecting to be saved, unaware of the sharpness of the axe that was about to fall, splitting her life apart, separating her from her daughter, and serve her right the little tattle-tale and liar who had told Lily East that Dixon had hurt Victoria. As if she would have hurt a pretty little thing like that. Dixon had tripped, that's all, and accidentally dropped Victoria against the slats of the cot. It could happen to anyone. And as a result of Charlotte's lie, Dixon had been cast out, deprived of Manus, the only love she had ever wanted.

Let Charlotte wait and stew.

First, the former Miss Lily East had to be enlightened.

The rowan trees in front of Sid's cottage had grown so thick she couldn't see the building, but she remembered where it was and followed the path.

One thought persisted. If Miss East hadn't taken it upon herself to get rid of her, she would have made Charlotte speak that time and, who knows, might have forced the truth out of her. She estimated she was only two days away from starving her into submission. But the old witch had come along with her jealousy disguised as concern and, with her friend to back her up, had cast Charlotte as the innocent victim rather than the child murderer that she was.

She saw a bent figure kneeling on the ground digging holes and separating seedlings. Moving closer, she stood to take in the scene and deliberately let her shadow fall across the woman and the flowerbed.

What a comedown, she thought. Instead of the neat, spotless figure with her set of keys jingling with each brisk step she took along shining corridors as she inspected her domain and gave orders, here was a dumpy old widow with clay on her hands, wearing shabby clothes and not a servant in sight to do her bidding.

Lily Cooper couldn't turn her stiff neck to see who was casting the shadow behind her and struggled to get to her feet. Dixon took her arm and with a strong grip pulled her to a standing position. The old woman looked up at her helper.

"Well, Lily East," said Dixon. "I can't think of you as Mrs Cooper, so I'll stick to Lily East if you don't mind." She paused, pleased with her cool delivery. "You may call me Elizabeth, my proper name. I'd be upset if you didn't remember me. And what are you doing putting in flowers that you won't be around to see blooming?"

Recognition flared in Lily Cooper's eyes. She stepped back, treading on the seedlings she had just planted and held on tightly to the picket fence behind her for support.

"There's no need to back off like that. I'm not going to bite you." She held out her hand.

Lily kept clutching the fence and ignored the outstretched arm.

"Have it your own way, then. I think what you need right now is a nice cup of tea. Or perhaps something stronger after you hear what I've come twelve thousand miles to tell you."

81

Tyringham Park
1943

Charlotte's shoes clattered on the wooden stairs. She could feel a heaviness bearing down on her head. Around the return and up the second flight she found it difficult to lift her feet as more weight seemed to press on them. Her mind told her she was moving upwards but her perception was that she was sinking into a basement.

At the top of the third flight she stood on the landing and looked over the banister into the dark stairwell, hearing Nurse Dixon's voice shouting: "Come away from there! It's dangerous. If you fall over and break your legs, don't think you can come running to me to complain!" cackling each time at her tired joke as if she had just thought of it and was saying it for the first time.

Charlotte was eight years old again, standing in trepidation outside the nursery door, wishing she didn't have to enter. Wishing she could go back to the kitchen and stay there all day with Cook. Or sleep on a bench in the tack room with a horse blanket over her for warmth, waiting for Manus to arrive in the morning. Or in the servants' quarters with Miss East who always looked at her with a kind face, but to whom she wasn't allowed to speak as Nurse Dixon said she was a witch. Charlotte knew that she wasn't as she didn't have a lump on her nose or a pointy hat or chin but she stayed away from her all the same to avoid Nurse Dixon's wrath.

Looking back it seemed as if she had spent hours wishing she were anywhere else but here, on this landing, delaying for as long as possible having to face Nurse Dixon, but knowing in the end she had no option as there was no one at the Park willing or in a position to take her part.

She turned the handle of the nursery door. It was a surprise to see the light coming through the windows dazzling her when she looked in, as in her memory the nursery was always dark. She had to remind herself she was now an adult, tall and strong, and had nothing to fear, but the eight-year-old inside her was full of apprehension, waiting for a punishment that could fall on her at any moment for no reason at all except to satisfy a whim of Nurse Dixon's.

Victoria's cot and her own bed were still in their original positions, unused for twenty-six years and covered in dust. There beside the window was the rocking chair that Dixon slept in for most of the day while Charlotte was forced to keep quiet or, as she grew older, go off and amuse herself. Charlotte, who until recently had been able to block out all memories associated with this place, could now see Victoria sitting in her small chair beside the low table, as clearly as if no time had passed.

With anguish borne of her new sensibility as a mother, she remembered the day Dixon's indulgence towards Victoria changed to anger when Victoria refused to eat a portion of particularly disgusting-looking steamed liver. It pained her to picture Dixon forcing open the child's mouth and pushing in a spoonful. Victoria spat it on the floor and ran away laughing, thinking it was all a game. "You won't make a fool of me, young lady," Dixon growled, seizing her and yanking her back to the table with an action strong enough to stretch a ligament in the child's shoulder. Victoria looked towards Charlotte, bewildered and frightened into silence by the pain of the rough handling. Closing her mouth and twisting her head from side to side was futile after Dixon scraped up the liver and forced it back into Victoria's mouth. Victoria spat it all out. Dixon slapped her and repeated the procedure. Victoria gagged. Dixon slapped her again and screamed: "Open your mouth." Victoria refused. Dixon used force to shove in three pieces. Victoria panicked and made choking noises and the three pieces flew out. "Don't think you'll get the better of me," growled Dixon, picking up the wet liver.

How powerless Charlotte had felt, and how well she knew without being told that none of this was to be mentioned to Teresa Kelly when she returned from the village where she had gone to pick up a length of lace. Worst of all, though, was her shameful reaction, a quivering gladness that it was Victoria rather than herself who, for a change, was being attacked.

After Dixon failed to impose her will, she lifted Victoria high in the air and threw her from a distance into the cot, ignoring the loud crack the child's head made against the side and, not checking to see if the impact had done any damage, left the room. Charlotte, now flooded with genuine sympathy for Victoria who had blood pouring from a gash on her scalp, ignored one of Dixon's rules and climbed in beside her sister who turned and put the unhurt arm around her in a tight clasp, and quietened her hiccupping sobs. Charlotte pressed the red blanket against the cut and cuddled Victoria until the little one stopped quivering and fell asleep. It was one of the sweetest memories of her life. After Dixon came back and found the two of them in each other's arms, it turned into one of the bitterest.

That episode which occurred a month before she disappeared marked the end of Victoria's babyhood. Every day after that the two little girls held themselves suspended, listening for the sound of Teresa Kelly's footsteps, knowing that Dixon's manner would change at the sound, after which time she would pretend to be as good-natured as Teresa herself. A reprieve would be won for only as long as Teresa was present.

"I'm sorry, Victoria. I wish I'd known what to do," said the adult Charlotte to the memory of her sister. "I did tell Mother but it got worse after that. She told Dixon what I'd said and Dixon called me a sneak and a tattle-tale and said if I ever told anyone anything again, worms would grow inside me and they would eat my tongue and heart and grow so big my tummy would explode all over the room and I would die, and I believed her and I never said another word about her."

When Dixon told them Teresa Kelly was leaving for good because they had become too wicked for her to tolerate any longer, Charlotte could see only bleakness in the future. Worse for Victoria than for herself, as Victoria would have seven more years to endure, whereas Charlotte would be escaping to boarding school in September, only three months away – or so she thought at the time.

When Teresa came to say goodbye, she and Victoria clung to her, weeping, begging her not to go. Teresa joined in the tears. Dixon stood by, grim-faced, and later punished them for being so undisciplined. At her orphanage no one was allowed to show any sadness when any of the girls left, either for adoption or employment, and she didn't see any reason why that rule shouldn't be applied to this nursery.

The day she saw Teresa descend the nursery stairs for the last time before heading off to Australia, Charlotte remembered, was the day she completely lost hope.

Before Dixon arrived, there was something she must do.

She entered the room beside Dixon's that had been permanently out of bounds for as long as she could remember. It was filled with hundreds of years of accumulated broken and discarded items – toys, books, clothes, lamps, shoes – such small shoes – cribs, baby carriages, sporting gear for cricket, swimming, tennis, rugby, and football, burst and perished balls: heaven for a bored child on a rainy day, but a place deemed dangerous by Dixon. The smell of damp was stronger than she remembered. All the objects to the right were covered by thick mould, the cause of which was easy to see – a missing slate from the roof that had let in years of rain. It crossed her mind that she should tell someone about it before the whole room and the two rooms below it were destroyed. She should but she wouldn't.

She lifted up objects and stacked them to the side as she made her way to the back corner, which looked relatively dry. As a child, she was able to crawl under or over, but that wasn't an option now. No one had been there since then, she could tell by the uniformity of the thickness of the dust and the uninterrupted pattern of the widespread mildew.

Reaching under a small wicker chair, she pulled out an object wrapped in an embroidered cushion cover, cold to the touch, but not damp. She let the light from the hole in the roof shine on the cover as she partially unwrapped it to reveal a doll's red hair. Breathing deeply to control her nerves – she didn't want to have another attack – she pushed the doll in its cushion cover into the bottom of her bag, where she covered it with her cardigan, scarf and gloves. Halfway across the Irish Sea, on her way to London after she received the summons bound to come from Colonel Turncastle, she would drop

385

it over the side of the mail boat and never have to think of it again.

Closing the door of the storeroom behind her, she returned to the nursery to wait for Nurse Dixon's arrival, expecting to stay only as long as it took to tell her how much she hated her. What she really wanted to do was give her a hard slap on her face. Better still, eight hard slaps, one for every year Dixon had made her life a misery. But she wouldn't do that, lowering herself to Dixon's level. She would control her outrage and keep her dignity.

Then over to the cottage to see Lily East at last. To apologise for not coming down to see her, to ask forgiveness for throwing the brooch at her, to thank her for saving her from Dixon, to beg her to come and live with her in Dublin, where she would live in luxury with the family, being treated like royalty, until they all returned to Tyringham Park together.

After that, down to the stables to see Manus and tell him about Harcourt's heroic end. Presumably her mother hadn't bothered to write to tell him the details he would be so avid to hear.

But first she had to endure this meeting with Dixon. She had nothing to fear, so why did she feel so afraid?

It wasn't as if anyone had forced her to come. She had come of her own free will to face her old tormentor. After today she would never think of her again.

82

Lily sat slumped at the kitchen table as if winded. She had seen pure joy on Sid's face when his first grandchild had been placed in his arms, on Sinéad Quirke's face the day she married Manus, hardly able to credit she had finally secured the man she had been in love with for years, and on Manus's face when Charlotte completed her first clear round on Mandrake, vindicating his method of training to Lady Blackshaw. Now she saw a look of joy in a distorted form on Dixon's face as she headed off to ruin Charlotte's life.

Lily wanted to run after her to hold her back, but she couldn't run and if she were able to catch up with her, Dixon would swat her off like a fly, the way she had done all those years ago in the nursery before Dr Finn had to come to her rescue. If only Sid were here to stand by her and support her.

"Charlotte expects me to remove my curse," Dixon had said before she left, "but she'll find she's going to cop a lot more than she bargained for, and leaving the curse where it is will be the least of it, as you now know. No doubt she'll come running back to you after I've finished with her, so that you can kiss her and make it all better. That should test your motherly skills, kissing away murder and making it better."

Poor Charlotte, Lily grieved, pitted against this heartless

adversary, with memories of her mother's accident and Mandrake's death making her credulous.

Not for one second did she believe that Charlotte had deliberately pushed Victoria into the river. Dixon was making assumptions. The little one must have slipped and poor Charlotte must have witnessed the drowning, then lost her voice with the fright of it all and then been too afraid of Dixon and Lady Blackshaw to allude to it then or ever. If only the terrified child had come to her. She would have enveloped her in sympathetic understanding rather than bringing the wrath of vengeance down upon her innocent little head.

"I'll take the train back to Dublin in the morning after I've given my report at the police barracks to that Inspector Declan Doyle, who I remember had a soft spot for me," Dixon had continued. "I'll call to Lady Blackshaw tomorrow afternoon. I was going to post my letter to her on the way up here but I decided I'd rather shove it in front of Charlotte's face first – together with the one I'm posting to her husband – to show her I mean business. It gives me goose bumps to think of meeting Her Ladyship and telling her in person." She smoothed down her dress and adjusted her hat. "I think this is going to be a satisfying week. Pity old Dr Finn isn't still around to see it. He always had a soft spot for me despite your efforts to turn him against me. Just make sure," she threatened, wagging her finger, "that you don't come over sticking your nose in or you'll make it all the worse for Charlotte."

As she left, she looked back over her shoulder to fully enjoy the old woman's powerlessness.

Things couldn't be worse for Charlotte, Lily grieved, checking the time on the kitchen clock, but if that evil woman thinks I'm going to sit here and leave my darling to her mercy, she's got another think coming. I'll wait until she's out of sight and then I'll go and find Manus.

Despite being cocky about knowing all the secrets of the Park, Dixon won't be able to tell Charlotte everything because there was much she wasn't aware of at the time, Lily thought with satisfaction while she waited.

Every adult on the estate except Nurse Dixon and Lord Waldron had known about the liaison between Lady Blackshaw and Manus. Many had seen the telling signs of attraction between the two, despite Lady Blackshaw's conviction that she was being discreet. By commanding the servants to use the most desirable part of the demesne, the walled garden, for the purpose of limiting the range of their prying eyes, and by giving the three stable lads every Friday afternoon off so they would take their prying eyes off to a shebeen in the village, she thought her movements had passed unobserved.

Lily would gladly sacrifice the remaining years of her life to save Charlotte from knowing why Victoria had been the favoured one and why Lady Blackshaw had spent so long in Dublin for her last two confinements, a necessary subterfuge to falsify the actual dates of birth of Victoria and Harcourt.

Most explosive secret of all was that Harcourt was conceived, not in London as Lady Blackshaw was at pains to assert, but earlier, in Manus's office, perhaps sometime in the forty-minute interval during which Victoria disappeared. The sums added up for someone who didn't believe everything Lady Blackshaw said and who, as head housekeeper, didn't go to the walled garden on Friday afternoons with all the other servants but, from the cover of the trees in the arboretum, a favoured sanctuary of hers, was often able to observe Lady Blackshaw's movements. She did ask Les later on that terrible day how the filly with the gashed leg was and he had looked at her blankly and said there was nothing wrong with any of the fillies. Tending to an animal must have been the first excuse Lady Blackshaw could think of when she gave her account to the police, and who would dare question the word of the Lady of the Park?

All these convictions and suspicions she had confided in no one, not even Sid, in the full expectation of taking them with her to her grave.

It was time to go.

She made her way to the stables as quickly as her old bones would allow her and pushed open the double gates to find Manus and to tell him that Nurse Dixon was about to do harm to Charlotte and would he please come quickly.

Manus thought for a moment his old friend had suddenly flipped into senility, talking about two people who hadn't been near the Park for years. He doubted he would recognise a grown-up Charlotte or a middle-aged Dixon, it was so long since he'd seen them, and he found it difficult to believe first of all that he hadn't heard of their imminent

return – that kind of news would spread like wildfire on the estate –
and secondly, that one would threaten the other, rather than falling
into each other's arms with the joy of reunion.

"You have to trust me," said Lily. "I don't have time to tell you
about the bad blood between them."

She had never said a bad word about Dixon to him.

Manus told her of course he trusted her and to go on ahead. He
would follow as soon as he wrestled into a stall the new wild import
that was intent on inflicting injury on the foals.

He hoped there would be no awkwardness between himself and
Nurse Dixon over their last embarrassing encounter. He would act as
if it had never taken place and he presumed she would do the same.

To this day he could cringe at the thought of it.

83

Charlotte heard footsteps ascending the stairs. The sound from the lowest flight reverberated in the cavernous stairwell. Her eight-year-old heart began to leap around inside her chest, ignoring the directive to be brave.

What had she to be afraid of? she chided herself. Nurse Dixon couldn't be the ten-foot high Amazonian figure that had infested her nightmares for years, but try as she might to talk sense to herself, Charlotte couldn't shrink her former nanny's image to a realistic size.

By the time the footsteps had gained the top floor and the handle of the door turned, Charlotte's heart threatened to somersault into her neck and choke her.

The figure that appeared in the doorway looked old, diminished and ridiculously overdressed for a country visit.

Charlotte repressed an urge to laugh with relief. To think such an insignificant creature had terrorised her childhood.

Elizabeth Dixon's smile faltered when she saw the amused, slim, tall, simply dressed woman standing in front of her.

"It's good to see you again, Charlotte, or should I call you Mrs Carmody?"

Charlotte, noting the hesitancy, answered, "Mrs Carmody would be appropriate."

"You've grown into the striking young woman I knew you would," Dixon continued as smooth as silk, ignoring the snub and recovering her poise. "I'm so glad you were amenable to this meeting."

I've nothing to fear, Charlotte realised. Her heartbeat slowed. I'm glad I came.

As Dixon approached, Charlotte stepped behind the low table to avoid the possibility of any social physical contact, the thought of which made her feel sick. The change of accent was noted, as was the use of the word "amenable". Very different from the grunts and barks that had punctuated Dixon's speech when she reigned over the nursery and Charlotte's early years.

"It's strange seeing the old place again," said Dixon, correctly interpreting Charlotte's movement and staying out of handshake range to make it look as if it were her decision. "Nothing's changed except the addition of dust and cobwebs. We might as well make ourselves comfortable."

You'd think the Park belonged to her family, not mine, the way she's orchestrating this meeting, thought Charlotte.

Dixon used a handkerchief to remove the dust from her old rocking chair and sat on the edge, her back straight, her knees and ankles together and her hands resting on her lap. She took off her gloves, one finger at a time, then reached up to take out the hatpins before removing her hat in a most affected manner.

Quite a performance, thought Charlotte.

"Before I free you from the curse I have two startling pieces of information to give you. Won't you take a seat?" In her impatience to tell her story, hints of her old hectoring tone broke through, making the question sound like an order.

"I'd prefer to stand," said Charlotte.

"Suit yourself." Dixon switched back with an effort to a milder tone. "Though I'm sure you'll change your mind when you hear what I've come to say. But before I get started, I'd like to tell you about my successful life after I had the good fortune to leave the Park. You'll hardly credit that I was manageress of an ho–"

"I'm sure I won't credit it at all so you may as well save your breath. Even if you managed to tell the truth for a change I'm not in the slightest bit interested."

Dixon flushed crimson all over her face and neck and blinked four times before she responded. "If that's your attitude, I might think twice about removing the curse even though I've come twelve thousand miles to oblige you."

"I hope you don't expect me to believe you came back to do me a good turn. I don't believe you would travel one mile, let alone twelve thousand, to give a helping hand to anyone, let alone me, and I couldn't care less about your curse, but if it would make you feel better, don't let me stop you from chanting 'Abracadabra' and dancing around the room waving a stick."

Dixon's face changed to chalk white. "You'll live to regret saying that."

"I have a lot of regrets in my life, but I doubt if saying that will ever be one of them."

"I wouldn't mock if I were you. You'll be smiling on the other side of your face by the time I'm finished with you. I know for a fact my curses work."

"They may do, but not for the reason you think."

Dixon didn't understand the insinuation in the remark, but presumed it was an insult. "Why did you come here, then?"

"To tell you how much I hate you. That's the only reason." And to keep you at a distance from Mary Anne. "I couldn't pass up the opportunity."

"Hate me? What do you have to hate me for? I only ever did what was best for you."

"Who are you trying to fool? You call the way you treated me the best?"

"Most definitely. Life is hard for the likes of me and even for rich folk like you. Look at your poor mother crippled for life. I was doing you a favour, being hard on you to prepare you for it. And all I got for my troubles was ingratitude."

"Now I've heard everything. So that's how you justified yourself? You expect me to be grateful for being a victim of your cruelty and laziness."

"Laziness? On duty twenty-four hours a day and you call that laziness? That's laughable coming from the likes of you who never had to do a hand's turn in your life."

Charlotte clutched her bag containing the doll close to her side and made as if to move off. "I'm sorry that's how you see things but

I for one don't have the time to stay around listening to your self-pity or your mumbo jumbo."

"You haven't heard yet the main reason I came."

It is definitely money she's after, Charlotte thought. She has developed expensive tastes by the look of those clothes she is wearing. How could anyone afford them on an ordinary wage?

"I don't want to hear it, so you can save your breath. I'm going over to Sid's cottage to talk about old times with Miss East now that I've said what I came to say." She walked around the perimeter of the room to stay as far away from Dixon as was possible and made her way to the door. "I'll let you see yourself out."

"Don't you dare turn your back on me when I'm talking to you!" Dixon screeched, standing up and making a forward movement.

Charlotte stopped at the sound of that well-remembered tone and turned around. "I can't believe you said that. You seem to have forgotten you have no authority over me any more. And you have forgotten your place. I'm the daughter of the Lord of the Park, and you are an unwelcome and uninvited presence. Seeing as that's the way you choose to speak to me, I command you to leave the demesne immediately, and forbid you ever to return. I will consider it trespassing and will have you removed by force."

"You won't be talking to me in that superior tone after I've said what I came to say."

"I've already told you I don't want to hear anything that comes out of your mouth. And I haven't said half of what I could say about my hatred of you. All that put-on sweetness in front of my mother and Manus and Teresa Kelly would make anyone's stomach turn. And the way you treated little Victoria was unforgivable. She was only an infant." Charlotte was forced to pause, as she couldn't control the trembling in her voice.

"You told about that, didn't you, and had me thrown out by that old witch?"

"I never said a word to Miss East."

"I don't believe you. You were quick enough to go running to your mother telling tales."

"That was years earlier and they weren't tales. They were the truth. But because of that angelic act you put on in front of her she didn't believe me, and I knew there was no point in telling her anything else, so you won in the end. She never knew you mistreated Victoria. But I knew and I've never forgotten and I've certainly never forgiven you."

"It would make a sick cat laugh to hear you telling me how Victoria was treated. At least I didn't murder her, which is more than can be said for you, you high and mighty hypocrite!"

Charlotte put her hand to her heart as if she'd been stabbed.

"You thought your secret was safe, didn't you? No one would think a child of eight could be guilty of such a crime unless they saw it with their own eyes, and Teresa Kelly did, and she told me personally, and I was the only one who knew as she didn't know herself what she saw. The only one who knew apart from you, of course, and Lily Cooper who only found out twenty minutes ago."

"Miss East?" Charlotte stumbled her way to the low table, feeling behind her like a blind person to guide herself into a sitting position. "You told Miss East?"

"Didn't I say you would need to sit down before I was finished? Yes, Miss East to you and Lily Cooper to me was the first to be told. You won't be surprised to hear she didn't believe me. Oh no. Her angelic little Charlotte wouldn't do a thing like that. It will be interesting to see if the others will believe me." Dixon opened her handbag, took out a letter, and waved it in front of Charlotte's face. "It's all here. All written down in detail. This one's for . . . couldn't remember his name for a minute . . . Dr Lochlann Carmody. Yes, that's it. Dr Lochlann Carmody. I was hoping to get his address from you."

Charlotte reached across and snatched the letter from Dixon's hand.

"Go on, keep it if you want to. I can write a new one without any bother. You already know what's in it, anyway."

Charlotte tore open the envelope and read the first few lines that described her as a child murderer who was a threat to the safety of her own offspring.

"And I've one here for your mother. I'll be delivering it by hand."

Each word on the page activated the blade of the dagger slashing around inside Charlotte's chest. Imagine Lochlann reading those words and turning to ask her if they were true. She thrust the letter into her bag.

Fireworks were combusting inside her head and creating red sparks behind her eyes.

Imagine Mary Anne growing up and hearing of her mother's wicked act.

She turned towards Dixon. "What did you say just then?" Her vision was now pulsing in and out of focus.

"I said I've written a letter to your mother as well. I'll deliver it by hand tomorrow."

Letter to her mother?

Delivering it by hand tomorrow?

If only it had been money she wanted.

"Then there's Manus. It was because of you I didn't marry him and have his children." Dixon's face showed a look of hatred. "It was because of you I ended up with nobody to call my own when I was already an orphan without a family. Here am I now with no husband and no children. I'll really enjoy telling Manus about you. Unless . . ."

"Unless?"

"I'm prepared to make a deal with you. I am prepared to destroy these letters and never tell anyone what happened to Victoria."

"But you've already told Miss East."

"Yes, pity about that. I couldn't resist wiping that smug, superior look off her face. But you don't have to worry about her. She didn't believe me. And even if she did you could trust her never to utter a bad word against you. Your secret is safe with her. As I was saying, I will destroy these letters and keep my mouth shut from now on if you pay me twenty thousand pounds. No one will give me a job at my age and I find myself a little short. After all my hard-earned success I lost my life savings on a bad investment. You have to admit twenty thousand pounds is little to ask to prevent Mary Anne being taken away from you. Cheap at the price if you ask me."

Charlotte let out a primeval howl and launched herself at the unprepared Dixon, pushing her out onto the landing. "How dare you speak her name! How dare you mention her name and money in the same breath? Hand over those letters, you vile woman!"

Dixon twisted her body to keep the bag containing the letters out of Charlotte's reach while trying to shoulder her way back into the nursery.

Charlotte blocked Dixon's movement and shoved harder, slamming her against the banister. It was the eight-year-old inside the raging thirty-four-year-old Charlotte who grabbed Dixon's neck with both hands and squeezed hard and bent her over the banister before

Dixon had time to register what was happening. Dixon tried to struggle but after Charlotte applied more pressure, cutting off her air supply for too many seconds, she remained still, angled so far over the handrail that her head hung upside down. She couldn't lash out with her feet for fear of changing the distribution of her weight and toppling backwards. The hand holding her bag was flailing around in the void, while with the other she tried without success to grasp the rail. Charlotte had no hope of retrieving the bag without removing her hands from Dixon's throat.

"I told you a lie," Dixon whispered. "Teresa Kelly didn't see you push Victoria into the river." Breath. "I made that bit up."

And I gave myself away by my reaction.

Charlotte loosened her grip but kept her hands in position. "What did she see exactly?"

"You carrying Victoria around behind the stables. That's all she saw. As God is my witness, I'm telling the truth. She presumed I was walking in front of you. I swear that's what she thought." She coughed. "I take back what I said. I only said it to get back at you. Let me go. I'll burn the letters and never say a word to anyone. Your daughter is safe with you. You can trust me. Cross my heart and hope to die."

"Then do it."

"What?"

"Cross your heart and hope to die."

Dixon made a feverish cross over her left breast.

Charlotte squeezed tighter. "Now hope to die," she said, ramming her body tightly against Dixon's to prevent her from struggling.

"Don't, Charlotte dear. Don't do it. Let her go."

The voice came from the second-floor stairs straight underneath.

"Miss East, is that you?"

Tears filled Charlotte's eyes and, distracted, she loosened her fingers a little.

Energy surged into Dixon's body. "You heard her. Let me go," she pleaded. "Trust me. I won't say anything to anybody."

"That's one true thing you've said at last."

Charlotte kept Dixon's body balanced over the void. Her fingers, tightening and loosening alternately, stayed on either side of Dixon's windpipe.

The door downstairs banged shut.

"That's Manus, Charlotte dear."

"Thank God," whispered Dixon, relaxing.

"He's coming to help you." Miss East's voice was closer. "Stay still until he gets here."

Charlotte wanted to look down to see her old protector's beloved face, but she couldn't chance taking her eye off Dixon even for a second.

The clatter of ascending footsteps filled the stairwell.

Lily stood on the lower landing. Manus, who had taken the steps four at a time now stood beside the old housekeeper.

"Leave her to me, Miss Charlotte."

It was Manus's soft, beautiful voice.

Dixon smiled.

She thinks I'm going to let her go. That I won't dare do anything to her while Manus is watching.

Charlotte tightened her grip and Dixon's smile switched off.

"Let go of her, there's a good girl," Miss East pleaded. "Let Manus deal with her."

"I'm coming up, Miss Charlotte. Stay steady."

Manus was moving up slowly towards the entangled pair. Miss East stayed where she was, clasping her hands together in an attitude of prayer.

Manus was on the second-last step when Charlotte pushed hard on Dixon's chin with one hand and gave Dixon's shoulder a shove with the other, stepping to one side to allow Dixon's legs to flip over, and her body to fall unhindered into the dark stairwell and crash onto the flagstones three storeys below.

Manus's outstretched arms, ready to grab a hold of Dixon, closed on emptiness. He leaned over the banister and stared down into the stairwell, and then looked back at Charlotte, uncomprehending.

"Are you all right, Charlotte, dear?" Lily asked tenderly.

Manus took off down the stairs, the sound of his boots echoing around the stairwell.

"I'm truly sorry, Miss East, but I can't stay. There's something urgent I have to do." Charlotte darted back into the nursery, and picked up her bag and secured it under her arm. Then, without looking at Lily, she rushed past her to follow Manus down the stairs.

84

Manus was kneeling beside Dixon's motionless body, feeling for a pulse. Charlotte kept her eyes on his hands as she couldn't look him in the face. She felt an urge to kneel down beside him to kiss those sun-browned hands in gratitude for his kindness to her as a child, but she didn't think he would appreciate the gesture from a woman he had just witnessed committing a heinous crime.

"Is she dead?" asked Charlotte.

There was no sign of blood or protruding bones.

"There's no pulse." He crossed himself. "Poor unfortunate woman. God rest her soul."

Charlotte reached down for Dixon's handbag. "There's something in it that belongs to me," she said, ignoring Manus's hand stretched out as if to block her. She opened the bag, removed three letters, dropped the bag and left. She heard Manus calling after her, something about a doctor, but she ignored him.

Halfway between the nursery and the river she slowed down to read the letters addressed to her mother, Manus and Lily Cooper. They all contained the same accusation: that Charlotte had deliberately murdered her pretty little favoured sister and the authorities should be informed so that any child in her care should be removed for its own safety.

It's all true.

All of it. Every poisonous word is true. I have to admit it. Dixon is right. I am not a fit person to rear a child. I should have accepted Benedict's death as the true judgement that it was and left well alone. I didn't deserve a second chance. I didn't deserve a beautiful daughter like Mary Anne. What false reasoning made me think she could replace Victoria and make everything better? Nothing can ever make anything better. I have been fooling myself. And I have been so happy. What right did I have to be happy?

The best I can do now is keep my secret safe. Miss East and I are the only living people who know what happened to Victoria and I would trust Miss East with my life not to tell. It's a consolation to me that Lochlann and Mary Anne will never have to suffer shame because of their association with me now that I know the secret will never be revealed.

When she arrived at the stretch of the river where Victoria had gone in, her legs went from underneath her.

There in front of her was the bank where she had stood helplessly, watching Victoria being carried away by the flood.

She crawled across the gravel onto the grass verge at the edge of the bank. She took the letters from her bag and tore them into tiny pieces. She scattered them into the river and watched them drift away.

She looked down into the river, then turned her head to focus on the spot in the distance where she had last seen Victoria.

I should have followed you in, my pet.

Victoria, it's me. Charlotte. Your big sister.

Is it too late?

Will you come and talk to me?

Manus guided Lily to the rocking chair in the nursery and when she was seated told her that Dixon was dead. He took the red blanket from Victoria's cot and shook the dust out of it. "I'll come straight back and bring you over to the cottage," he said, draping the blanket over his arm. "You look as if you could do with a brandy."

Was that really Charlotte who did that? Manus asked himself as he went back down the stairs. She was such a biddable child and

Dixon was so good to her – it was hard to credit she could have done such a thing.

I can feel your presence, Victoria.

Thank you for coming so quickly. You don't know how much it means to me that you are here. I was afraid you would turn away in disgust when you heard my voice. I'm sorry I sent you on that long cold journey on your own. I wish I'd had the courage to go with you then. It would have saved a lot of people a lot of trouble if I had.

I think I'm suffering from delayed shock. Don't go away, my dear little sister. I need to keep my head down for a bit longer so that I don't pass out. I've been having problems with my nerves lately.

That feels a bit better. I can sit up now. There.

It's nice to feel you beside me. It's a relief to be able to speak openly to you at last. Keeping secrets is such a tiring business.

It makes me sad to think that if Teresa had stopped to speak to us that afternoon how differently our lives would have turned out. Yours, especially. You would have had a chance at least to live yours. I wouldn't have done what I did, and we would have grown up to be close friends as well as sisters. I missed you all my life, even during those years when you hid from me.

I wish with all my heart that I had never pushed you.

I've just killed that horrible Nurse Dixon. You probably already know that seeing as you're on the other side. I had to shut her up. She threatened to tell everyone what I did to you so that my Mary Anne would be taken away from me. She blamed me for her single, childless state. Manus didn't want her and she blamed me.

I deliberately pushed her over the banister outside the nursery. I could say her fall was an accident. I could say that pushing you into the river was an accident as well. Who could contradict me when there were no witnesses? Miss East and Manus would lie about Dixon for me, I know. They would swear that I was nowhere near Dixon when she went over. Would I have the right to ask the two of them to perjure themselves for me? Hardly, when I never came down to see them and I couldn't even look either of them in the eye just now. I hope it's nice where you live, Victoria, and that you have a lot of

401

friends. What do you do all day? Were you allowed to grow into an adult or are you still a young child? Where did your little body end up? You were being swept along with alarming speed last time I saw you. It appears the fishermen were right when they said you were probably washed out to sea and your body would never be found.

I presume you met our brother Harcourt in heaven, even though you didn't know him on earth. It might surprise you to know that you may well have shared the planet with him for a few minutes, even though neither of you was aware of the other's existence for obvious reasons. I didn't work it out until years later. I'll explain that puzzle to you when I see you. We have a lot of catching up to do. The thought of meeting up with Harcourt makes me apprehensive now that our reunion is only hours away. We didn't part on good terms.

How bitter for me to leave Tyringham Park in this way, when I dreamed of living here for the rest of my life, with Lochlann installed as a country doctor, taking up hunting and shooting, and Manus teaching Mary Anne to ride, and Miss East living in luxury, being treated like a queen.

It was a lovely dream, but now it can never be.

Believe it or not, my sweet little Victoria, the prospect of joining you isn't as frightening as I thought it would be. Knowing you and Harcourt and baby Benedict are there ahead of me makes it almost desirable.

If you are too ashamed to introduce me as your sister, I will understand, but please don't abandon me altogether.

Manus made an agreement with Lily that Charlotte would never swing or be imprisoned because of Nurse Dixon. Lily, despite her religious beliefs, was prepared to swear in a court of law that she had pushed Dixon. Manus said no one would believe her because she was so small, and what purpose would it serve taking blame when they could so easily say that Dixon fell accidentally? As the only two witnesses, they could say what they liked, and who was there to contradict them? If Charlotte insisted on confessing, they would tell that decent Inspector Declan Doyle that Charlotte, already disturbed by the death of her brother, was in a nervous state revisiting the scene of Victoria's disappearance after all these years and didn't realise what she was saying. Lily could emphasise that even as a little girl Charlotte used to take the blame for acts she didn't commit, so sensitive was her nature. There could be no case against her.

"You must go and find her and put her mind at rest straight away. And then bring her back to me so I can comfort her," said Lily.

Goodbye, Mary Anne. You gave me such joy that I can only repay you by leaving you. Your Aunt Iseult will care for you beautifully until your daddy comes back, then he will marry Niamh who will be good and kind to you and you won't even remember that I ever existed, while all the time, unbeknown to you, I will be looking after you and keeping you from harm.

Goodbye, Lochlann. Thank you for the happiness you gave me at the expense of your own. I feel almost light-hearted at the prospect of setting you free.

Our mother can do without my good wishes. She never liked me. I didn't blame her for favouring you and Harcourt – she had her reasons which I'll tell you about when we meet – but she didn't have to make it so obvious. She'll be glad I've gone, thinking she'll be able to get her hands on Mary Anne. I'd like to see her face when she reads my will.

"Before I start looking for Charlotte or fetching the doctor, I'll have to check on the stables. Will you be all right staying here and keeping vigil over Nurse Dixon until I get back, Lily? I shouldn't be long. I don't want that new wild colt kicking the door down and trying to cross the river to get home. He could do himself some damage."

"How can you even think of a horse at a time like this, Manus?"

Can you hear me, Victoria? You seem to have left me and gone back to the other side. Is that so you can get ready for me? I hope so.

There's some animal creating a terrible din in the stables. I should go and check but I don't have the time and I might have lost my touch, anyway, and be of no use.

Can you see me from where you are, Victoria? I'm heading towards the Dark Waterhole. It's difficult to be sure exactly where I am. I won't be sure I'm at the Hole until I step off the ledge. I can't feel my feet and the water isn't all that clear. I'm not looking forward to that first inhalation of water. How long before I stop struggling to breathe? Will I sink to the bottom or rise to the surface straight away or later? Will you have a word with God so that I don't end up in that other place with Dixon, where I belong? He'll listen to the request of an innocent child.

It's as well Lily and I have a reputation for being truthful, upright citizens, Manus reflected as he made his way towards the stables to check on the colt. Everyone will believe us when we tell them that the fall was accidental and Charlotte is innocent.

We can't have poor Edwina faced with another tragedy to add to her sorrows. She's already had more than any human being should be expected to bear in two lifetimes.

Soon I'll know exactly what you went through. Keep your eye out for me, Mary Anne. I mean Victoria. How could I make a mistake like that? You look so alike with your pretty faces and your dark curls that it's hard not to confuse you at times, though I couldn't admit that to many people. They would think I wasn't in my right mind.

Your doll is securely tucked under my arm. I'll make sure not to drop it.

Could that be Harcourt? It certainly looks like him.

I don't believe it. What's he doing on the avenue?

I don't have time to pray. Harcourt, you're too early. Go back. You're supposed to wait for me on the other side. It's all arranged. The time has come. Breathe out.

Guide me, Victoria, and when it's all over have your hand out ready to catch me so that I don't fly straight past you. I don't want to end up lost in space, searching for you for all eternity, with no hope of finding you amongst the multitudes.

Are you ready?

IF YOU ENJOYED *TYRINGHAM PARK* PLEASE
DISCUSS WITH YOUR BOOK CLUB.

SOME POINTS FOR
GROUP DISCUSSION

1. Why do fictional stories of 'the big houses' and those that live within them fascinate us so much?

2. Is Charlotte more sinned against than sinning? Does the reader hope she triumphs in life?

3. Is there any hope of Lochlann achieving happiness after what he has done?

4. Isn't Dixon a victim of an abused deprived childhood as much as Charlotte is? Doesn't everything she does spring from her own experience of abuse? Why don't we feel sympathy for her then?

5. Why is Lady Edwina so spiteful without the excuse of an abused childhood? Do the disappointments she has suffered in life excuse or at least explain her spite?

6. Manus is the typical romantic hero. What factors make him so?

7. Charlotte is quite unpleasant and surly a lot of the time and hurts so many people who love her. Yet she is our 'heroine', the focus of our sympathy. How does the author achieve this and make us love her despite all of this?

8. Does the author give us a picture of the entire upper class of the time as being dysfunctional, heartless, selfish and cold? Not even able to love their own children?